The Winter Heir

by

J.A. Nielsen

Fractured Kingdoms, Book 2

The Winter Heir

COPYRIGHT © 2024 by J.A. Nielsen

Cover Art by *The Wild Rose Press, Inc.*

The Wild Rose Press, Inc.
PO Box 708
Adams Basin, NY 14410-0708
Visit us at www.thewildrosepress.com

Publishing History
First Edition, 2024
Trade Paperback ISBN 978-1-5092-5545-0
Digital ISBN 978-1-5092-5546-7

Fractured Kingdoms, Book 2
Published in the United States of America

Dedication

To Molly
For 89 days in Winter and everything before and after.

Chapter 1

Winter had arrived in the kingdom of Telridge, bending all who dwelled there to its capricious whim. And as Spense Ferrous well knew, winter was an unforgiving sovereign.

During the dark season, it was as if King Lumine himself stretched his icy hand from his throne deep in the White Rock Mountains all the way to the human kingdoms, pummeling the leaded windows of The Academy library with insistent sleet. Tap-tapping his impatience. His displeasure.

Spense scowled at the darkening sky, and defiantly returned to his studies in The Academy's oldest tower. He placed his trust in the human-built stone walls that protected the collection of ancient wisdom from the Winter King's sneak-thief wind and angry blizzard. Spense was thankful that Dean Stone had granted him permission to use the library, though he was still too young to become a proper student. He wouldn't waste this opportunity, no matter how tired or numb he became.

So he uncurled his chilled fingers and turned the next page and the next, poring over stacks of moldering books. The one in front of him smelled of overripe orange, as if a doddering scholar had spilled his marmalade on its pages and left it there to infuse the words with wise, pungent knowledge. So far, he'd experienced plenty of the aroma, but none of the wisdom.

He was sure it was there, the knowledge to appease King Lumine, to break his bargain, and free Dewy. She'd once been Lady Dew Drop, Fae royalty of the Summer faeries, not a prisoner of the Winter Court. She could return to her proper place if Spense found the answer to King Lumine's problem, if he found the missing Heir.

But it had been months, and he was no closer than when he started. All the while, Dewy endured amongst the Winter Fae. He knew the creeping chill of that court, the frosty despair that had ensnared his vulnerable human heart in the few days he'd been a guest in The Silver Horn. Would the bloom of Summer submit—as all things must—and shrivel in the face of the cold?

Spense squeezed his eyes shut, but his thoughts were too persistent, and his temples throbbed. He laid his head on the book, closed his eyes and remembered Dewy's sun-kissed face the last time he'd seen her. It was the day he'd been none-too-gently thrown out of the Winter Court. Face first in the snow. The day he'd started on this impossible search.

He groaned, pushed back from the table and slammed the useless book closed. Bits of dust flew off along with something crusty and orange. Three tables down, two Academy students halted their whispered conversation, grabbed their own books, and scurried away.

This was the reaction he was getting around the castle these days. Sidelong glances, and awed, skittish retreats. Once, before he'd met Dewy, he'd been the easily ignored, illegitimate son of King Ferrous and Cait the Head Cook. Now, he was the "young mage who had saved the kingdom."

Only it was a lie. It was Dewy who had done the saving, and she was paying the price.

Footsteps echoed along the lanes of The Academy library. Heavy, precise, military footsteps, followed by a rumbling baritone.

"Little brother? Are you in here?"

Spense sighed. "Here. Back wall."

"There you are!" Dirk planted himself at the end of the row. "Still at it? Sweet Spring! When was the last time you took a break?"

Spense gestured futilely at the text in front of him and the piles beyond it. "I can't."

"Yes, you can." Dirk clamped two strong hands around Spense's arms and removed him from his slumped position. He looked him in the eye. "And you should. You're not going to get anywhere if you're too exhausted to think. All this studying makes a man addled. And I had thought we'd cured you of that. Have you even eaten today?"

Spense shrugged. "It doesn't matter. Think about where Dewy is."

Dirk folded his arms over his broad chest. "She's among the faeries, Spense. Her own kind."

Spense shook his head. "You don't understand…"

"She's a prisoner, Spense. I know she's not lounging on one of the Brecken Isles. But she's not dying."

"You can't know that."

Dirk frowned, wrinkling his chin, the one physical characteristic he and Spense shared. "No, but I can make an educated guess. And I'm guessing that it is in King Lumine's best interests to keep her alive and you working. How else does he get what he wants?"

Spense mashed his lips together.

"See? You've got no argument."

"Maybe I'm just tired and hungry and can't come up with one."

"That is exactly why you need a break. And I happen to have the perfect opportunity to get you out of this drafty library."

Dirk was probably right. Not eating. Not sleeping. Days and nights in the library weren't doing any good. Spense rubbed his dry, overworked eyes. He sighed.

"What is it?"

"There happens to be a little…party."

Spense scowled as he reluctantly rose from the desk and took a step back from his piles of books. "I'll eat, but I'm not really in the mood for a party."

Dirk rotated Spense around and gave him a small shove. "You're going. There's this thing called a Solstice. You may have heard of it."

Spense rolled his eyes. "Yes, and it is not for another night."

"All the more reason to get started now. Solstice Eve, as it were. Must celebrate properly, and all the pomp of tomorrow night is hardly proper." Dirk slung his arm over Spense's shoulders. "This is our opportunity to actually enjoy the holiday, to celebrate with actual friends, for drinking ale, not weak wine."

Spense couldn't imagine enjoying any of the Solstice this year, but he agreed with Dirk about the official royal celebrations. Even on a good year, the ceremonial aspects tended to sour the holiday. But Dirk

4

was Crown Prince and Commander of the Knights. He had responsibilities Spense had never had to worry about. All eyes would be on his brother—many of them eligible young ladies and their ambitious parents. The least he could do was join Dirk on his one night off. And maybe he needed it, too. He could always return tomorrow with fresh eyes.

"So, debauchery?" Spense asked.

Dirk lifted a corner of his mouth. "Wicked Winter, yes." He squeezed Spense's neck tighter. "Maybe even for you!"

"Hmm…" Spense grumbled.

"Come down. Drink with my Knights. By some miracle, you've earned their respect."

"Fine."

Spense had earned the Knights' respect and his brother's friendship. And those weren't things to squander. A year before, it would have been unheard of for Dirk to be seen socializing—in public—with his younger, bookish, skinny half-sibling. But that was before. Before the attacks from Verden and the Winter faeries. Before they'd worked together—as brothers— to defend their kingdom. And before Dewy had sacrificed everything to save him and the people of Telridge, whether they knew the full story or not.

"Give me a few more minutes, just to get these books put away, and I'll be right behind you. Grey Goats Tavern?"

"Where else?" Dirk clapped him on the shoulder. "Hurry up. If you're not there in fifteen minutes, I am sending Lady Xendra up to fetch you, and you know how pissy she gets when you interrupt her drinking."

With a loud clap, Spense closed the book he held,

sending up a puff of dust. He choked and nodded, even as his eyes watered. He had no interest in getting on the Knights' bad side. No one with any sense would. As Dirk left the library, Spense pivoted to the table he'd occupied for the last several hours and stacked his books. It took three trips to deliver all of them to The Academy library's return desk. The clerk had long since left.

A thin green book he didn't remember requesting was on top of the last pile. He lifted the volume and turned the cover to see the title. *Truth Tellers* was lightly embossed on the front. Spense flipped the worn pages. Each section described the four Oracles of the Fae, one for each season. He paused on an illustration of Winter's Oracle.

His heart rate picked up as he scanned the chapter. He had spent hours poring over chronologies and books of human magic, trying to determine a way to find Lumine's Heir and release Dewy. But maybe he'd been going about it all wrong. Why had he never considered omens? The gift of Sight was his father's skill, not his, but he should have thought of it. And wouldn't a Fae Oracle be stronger than even his skilled father? At least for finding a lost Fae?

Spense snapped the book shut and raced out of the library.

Chapter 2

Dirk pulled his plain wool cloak tight as he made his way through the bustling, cobbled streets of Telridge City. His uniform would've been a better protector against the snapping winter wind, but he'd ditched it along with his usual honor guard, donning simple riding trousers and tunic instead. He exited the castle grounds via a servants' entrance. This wasn't a night for custom tailoring, shiny badges of office, or burnished medallions. He'd have to put it all back on for the Royal Solstice Festival tomorrow, but not tonight.

Tonight he was his own man and he wanted to celebrate with his friends—the Knights who stood shoulder to shoulder with him in battle, the squires who served them, even the hands who tended to their horses, and Spense—surprising as that may be. Only months earlier, he wouldn't have invited his half brother. But things had changed between them. And Spense was as much his brother-in-arms as any of the rest.

Dirk ducked his head as he walked, speeding along the crowded pathways. Vendors kept their market stalls open late for the holidays, and the taverns, restaurants, and inns were lively well past the hours when they might otherwise be closed for the night. Dirk wove through purveyors of sweet pies and mulled wine, nearly colliding with revelers making their way through the city. Sometimes he envied Spense for his slight frame and ability to slip through a crowd. Dirk's height and pale skin set him apart from the people of the city just as much as his position. His title—Crown Prince— invited curious looks and gossip wherever he went. But since Spense had become the-young-mage-who'd- saved-the-kingdom, he wasn't exactly anonymous, either.

Dirk turned into a narrow lane and came upon the warm, welcoming lights of the Grey Goats Tavern, shining like beacons against the darkening sky. The flagged street in front of the establishment was swept free of snow. All the shingles and doors were in good working condition. The proprietor kept the place clean and well-ordered. Dirk smiled and pushed his way in.

Barely a step across the threshold and he was immediately bombarded with the savory smells of the tavern kitchen—roasted game and sweet bread—along with raucous shouting from his friends. His real friends. Not the polite acquaintances from the Telridge Court.

"Hail! Commander Ferrous!"

Sir Gervais raised his cup in salute. Foamy ale sloshed over the sides. Echoed sentiments were repeated around the tavern as Dirk made his way in. He shook his head and grinned.

Dirk slapped the Knight's shoulder. "Gerry! I see you've started early!"

"Hardly, sir. You're the last to arrive!"

"Best get caught up then. Point me toward the ale."

Gerry grabbed the nearest young soldier. "Oi, get your commanding officer a mug. Be quick about it."

The stunned soldier turned and blinked. "Yes, sir. Right away."

"Leave him be, Gerry. I'll get my own." Dirk wove his way through the celebratory throngs to the bar keep, a grizzled man who spent more time laughing with his patrons than actually serving. He left that to his charming daughter.

"Lord Ferrous, welcome!" the bar keep said.

Dirk grimaced. "Lord Ferrous is my father. 'Dirk' is fine. What are you serving tonight? Brown ale, I hope."

"Good timing, Commander. Just tapped a barrel. Ainsley! Get the prince a mug!" the tavern keeper yelled over his shoulder.

"Here you are, my lord," Ainsley said, handing Dirk a mug of foaming ale.

"My thanks. What do I owe you?"

"On the house, my lord," Ainsley said with a wink, her standard answer to his standard question. "As always." She nodded to him and then turned back to help her other clamoring customers before he could protest.

Dirk shook his head as he watched her dark curls bounce. He understood that the business his Knights brought in was enough to cover his own fare, but he had no intention of making assumptions. He'd continue this little dance and maybe someday they'd let him actually pay for his beer.

One of the other customers noticed the exchange. "'As always'. That's a nice treat, my lord."

"And wholly unnecessary."

Dirk turned to explain, only to face a young woman, with honey-gold hair and soft brown eyes. She wore the sturdy twill trousers, boots, and vest of her profession. Her roughened hands were wrapped around a mug of ale. He knew those calluses came from honest farm work and tending soldiers' wounds. Some of them his own.

He choked on his ale. "Flora! Good…ah, good to see you."

She cocked her head. "Is it? I haven't seen you around the stables much recently."

Dirk swallowed again. "I know. I've been meaning to come by but… this has been a busy time, and I've been…"

"Busy?"

"Yes." He sighed. "Busy."

He knew she'd stayed on at the castle after the battles with Verden and the Winter faeries. He'd seen her about the grounds and in the stables, tending to the horses, as she'd said, but he hadn't spoken to her much since…everything happened. He'd meant to. Only there was always some duty or responsibility that required his attention these days. Or perhaps—if he was honest—he was avoiding her. How was he supposed to go back to being the Crown Prince after they'd fought side by side? After she'd stayed by him, seen him at his very worst?

It was different with his Knights. They'd always known him as Commander first, expected to fight, bleed, and mourn together. Flora was something else. And he didn't know who to be or how to behave around her.

"Then I suppose it's good that you've gotten away for the evening." Flora raised her mug.

"Indeed." Dirk grimaced. He could keep up polite chatter with any member of the court, flirt with an endless string of debutantes, but faced with Flora, an uncomplicated farm girl turned horse handler, he lost every thought in his head and ended up stupid and babbling. Heat rose along his neck and jaw, and he turned his attention to the mug in his hand.

They both took sips of their ale. Her brown-eyed gaze bored into him over the lip of the mug. As if she knew the thoughts he was too gutless to voice aloud.

"So, uh, how've you—"

He fumbled for simple words. And was saved when his name was shouted across the teeming tavern.

"Dirk!" Spense barreled into him, grasped his forearm, and panted.

"Spense. What—"

"I've found it. I know what to do!" His little brother brandished a thin green book. "Oh, hi, Flora. Good to see you."

She smiled. "Good to see you, too, Master Spense."

Dirk scowled. Of course, it was easy for Spense. She was common. He was…Dirk didn't really know what Spense was, but certainly a lot closer to common than he was. Spense and Flora could be…friends.

"It looks like duty calls." Flora slid off her stool and offered the tiniest of curtsies. Before he could respond with anything more than an open mouth, she'd disappeared into the tavern crowd, leaving the awkward conversation, and the hope of…whatever else he hoped for whenever he saw her, behind.

Dirk turned to his younger brother. "This had better be good."

Chapter 3

As far as prisons went, it really wasn't that bad.

"Lady Dew Drop, your tea." The steward, Siskin, set her tray down. He was spindly, like the evergreen trees surrounding The Silver Horn. His head was crowned with a thick tuft of snow-white hair and like all of King Lumine's servants, he was dressed in dark greens and deep blues. He arranged the creamy ceramic tea service and a selection of herbal sachets with his long fingers.

"Will there be anything else, Lady Dew Drop?"

"No, thank you, Siskin," Dewy murmured.

She hadn't intended to learn their names, any of the army of attendants in Lumine's service. But she supposed it was inevitable. And decent, as they politely and quietly responded to her requests for blankets, books, and endless cups of tea.

They deferred to her as if she were still Lady Dew Drop, future queen of the Summer Court. Her room was in the wing reserved for visiting dignitaries. Most likely on King Lumine's orders. Perhaps the king's idea of a cruel joke. His royal guest.

But she was little more than a political pawn, with a job to do. A prisoner. And worse, it was her fault.

"Very good." Siskin bowed and left.

Dewy shivered. It wasn't the cold. Not really. She could withstand that. Most of her work for the Summer

Court had been performed at night, in the cool pre-dawn hours, after all. She didn't crave the warmth of the sun the way most of the members of Summer so yearned for it.

But the air in the Winter Court was static and empty. It held no water. Outside, it was frozen by the harsh climate deep in the White Rock Mountains. Inside the enclave of The Silver Horn, sparse fires left the air dry and gasping.

In the realm of Summer, the sun gave life. Its radiant warmth was a balm that kissed the skin. In Winter, the paltry heat of the hungry fires was something else. Something consuming and feral. It did little to cut the harsh chill, and Dewy found she was constantly parched.

She missed sweet raindrops and heavy, fat morning clouds. Here, there was only snow and ice. It felt like breathing through a mask. She could survive. But it wasn't easy. It required effort.

Dewy pulled a blanket around her shoulders and settled in the room's single chair. She drew a jagged breath. This was no life for a water faerie.

But she picked up a book from her pile, forcing her thoughts away from that spiraling melancholy. She couldn't go down the path of despair. And there were so many books to pull her away, distract her, to find a deep forgetting place and imagine her own troubles gone. History, chronologies, magic theory, epic tales. Both Fae and Human. Even a little Goblin, though she had trouble with the dialects.

It passed the hours. Especially in those cold moments, when she felt hope draining away, her heart-light going dark, when it seemed that there was no answer to Lumine's puzzle about his lost Winter Heir, and her life would be wasted in Winter.

She often thought of Spense. All she had for these past six months were memories. Little things, like the way his dark brown hair curled around his ears, or his frown that scrunched up his chin like a walnut when he was solving a problem. His skin was warm enough to blend in among the bronze-brown Summer folk. Much more so than her, really. She'd always had to rely on her freckles growing close enough together to give her the hue of Summer. She supposed that was the natural consequence of having a noble, golden father and a common mother whose skin was as white as an alpen-bloom.

In Winter, Dewy had only grown more pale, even less like the Summer royal she was supposed to be. She wondered if Spense's bronze skin had lightened during these cold months and dark days, as well.

She thought of his laugh. It was hard to recall—they'd had so little time for laughter in their short time together. Did he think of her, too? Did he remember her laughter? What she wouldn't give to see his face, hear his voice, and know that he was all right, that her choice had been worth the freedom it had cost her.

A quick, tapping knock pulled her from her brooding. Dewy swiped a hot tear from her cheek, and croaked, "Come in."

She saw Misty's hair first, ice-white, blue-tinted spikes framing her perennially impish face. Perhaps not a typical warden, but like so much else, they did things a little differently in Winter.

"Right where I last saw you." The Fae smirked. She was allegedly noble-born, but Dewy had yet to see anything but irreverence from Lady Mist.

Dewy frowned and raised an eyebrow. "Is there someplace else I should be?"

"Well…" Misty drew out the word as she sidled around the heavy door. "Now that you mention it…you're *not* locked into this little room. You're permitted to go anywhere you like."

"Anywhere in Winter. In the Silver Horn."

Misty rolled her eyes and stomped over to Dewy's unmade bed, plopping herself onto the down and wool blankets with a *humph*. Misty had become her most frequent visitor, imposing herself with no invitation. None of the other Winter Fae took such liberties. This type of common behavior would never have been permitted in Summer.

"Very dignified," Dewy murmured. "Aren't you supposed to be an accomplished ambassador?"

Misty waved her off. "I've never found pompous manners to be all that helpful, actually. You can't tell me you have?"

Dewy shrugged. No, she hadn't. Then again, if she'd followed a few more of her aunt's protocols, she might not have ended up in her present circumstances. Of course, she never would've met Spense. And she couldn't regret that. It had been her folly, and a wondrous and strange coincidence that had led her to Spense. And despite all of the rest, that was as it should be.

"Although," Misty tapped her chin with her first finger. Her lacquered nails were sharp and matched the ice-blue of her hair. "I could use a little help with an ambassadorial matter."

"I know you don't think I could help."

"You did spend a significant amount of time in close proximity to a human, so yes, I think maybe you have insight."

Dewy sat up a little straighter. She set down her tea. "You're going to the human lands?"

Misty nodded. "Telridge, even. Isn't that where your boy is from?"

Dewy lowered her gaze, trying to ignore Misty's taunts. Spense was no boy. And that he was from Telridge wasn't a secret. So, why mention it?

"What is your interest in those lands?"

Misty smirked. "Nice try. You'll need a sharper ice pick to chip away that intel." She sighed and examined her glinting nails. "But I'm sure it would help if you could give us a little idea of what they're like. Human ways are odd, after all. Wouldn't want to offend one of them before we even get started."

"Why should I help you?" Dewy had no interest in playing Winter's spy.

Misty smiled a toothy grin. Dewy drew back into her chair. For all of Misty's irreverence, the threat in her smile was genuine. She had, after all, been one of the Fae who captured Spense all those months ago. "Because I can get a message to your human."

"Spense?" Dewy blurted.

Misty cocked one eyebrow. "Don't you think he'd appreciate hearing from you? You can't think he's forgotten you?" She leaned in, quirking her mouth in a sideways grin. "But what do I know? Humans can be so fickle—not that I'm convinced that your dear Spense is completely human—but close enough."

Dewy tried to flatten her features, to keep the inquisitive, probing Fae from reading her emotions. But it was too late. Her shallow breaths and tantrum-throwing heart gave her away. This was a thing she wanted, and Misty knew it. Dewy's breath caught in her throat, barely giving her space to puzzle over Misty's cryptic assessment.

"Fine." She forced out the breath. She could be cryptic, too, sharing her basic understanding of human culture, without revealing anything of real import, nothing that could be used against Spense's family. "If I write a letter, you'll deliver it to Spense, directly?"

Misty nodded.

"In exchange, I'll tell you what I know about humans?"

"That's the bargain."

Dewy bit her lip. Bargain. An arrangement that hadn't ended well for her the first time. This was the reason she was trapped in Winter—not by physical means, no chains bound her—but by the faerie-made magic of a bargain. And yet, a chance to communicate with Spense through another such agreement. Misty couldn't break the magical laws of the Fae. So, where was the loophole?

"You have to bring me a letter in return. In Spense's own hand."

"Agreed."

Dewy took one more slow breath. "All right. I accept your terms of bargain."

Misty's eyes grew brighter at the formal language.

"What do you want to know?"

"Whatever you know about humans. Culture, customs, history. Particularities." Misty leaned forward, propping her elbows on her knees. She focused her stare, her too-blue eyes centering into Dewy's own. "Tell me everything."

Chapter 4

Dirk rolled his eyes. "That's the last time I ask you to tell me everything."

Spense frowned. Clearly, he wasn't explaining it right. Otherwise, Dirk wouldn't wear that look of doubt on his face. Or show more interest in the dregs of his dark beer than in Spense's discovery.

"Don't you see? I've been going about this all wrong. I've been looking at human records, but that's no way to understand faeries. I have to go to their source of wisdom and knowledge."

"And where does one find their wisdom, dear brother?" Dirk clunked his empty mug onto the worn tavern table. "I don't suppose they have a faerie academy with a nice little library. And even if they did, it's not like they would've kept records of some grandkid Lumine disowned."

Spense hesitated. "Well, I admit, that's the tricky part. But, if I'm understanding this book correctly, I could go to the Oracles." He held up the thin green volume in question.

"Oracles? Which are where, exactly?"

"It says the Winter Oracle is in a place called The Between." He consulted the book, reading aloud. "The space that exists at the nexus of dark and light. It's not exactly located on a map…"

Dirk ran a hand over his face. "And I interrupted

good beer-drinking for this, not to mention…"

Spense blinked. "Not to mention what?"

But Dirk shook his head. "Never mind."

On a different day, Spense might not have let the comment go. He might've pushed to figure out what Dirk was not saying. His older brother's layers were often intriguing. Finding out that he had layers was a marvel in itself. But today, what he'd discovered was too important. Urgency outweighed curiosity.

"I'm sure Father would have an idea, don't you think?" Spense asked.

"And I suppose you want me to go with you to ask him about it?"

"Y-e-e-e-s."

Dirk groaned. "Even if he disagrees, denies you, and thinks you're out of your supposedly brilliant mind? Still, yes?"

Spense pressed his lips into a flat line. Dirk was goading him, but he wouldn't give in. He nodded his head vigorously. If he could make Dirk understand, then surely the two of them together could compel Lord Ferrous to let him pursue this—to go to the Fae lands. But he needed Dirk on his side. Together they might push past his father's prejudices against faeries, which hadn't improved since the conflicts over the summer.

Dirk heaved himself up from the tavern stool. "All right. We'll go talk to him. But when he tells you that you've lost your last bit of sense, don't blame me."

Chapter 5

The letter was written on pearl-white, thick, faerie-made paper. The ink used was glinting with an unnatural sheen, and Lord Ferrous swore he could smell a hint of jasmine. Why did Lumine and his people feel the need to perfume their correspondence? It must be a Fae thing. Ferrous shook his head. Faeries weren't known for making much sense.

Most beguiling were the words on the unnecessarily pretty pages. The Winter King requested that Ferrous meet with a delegation from his court—wise enough not to come himself, of course. One could only guess what they wanted this time.

But before he could over-speculate, there was a sharp rapping on his study door, quickly followed by its opening. Ferrous frowned. Only one person in the kingdom was bold enough to enter his chambers without first being given permission.

Or perhaps two. His sons entered. Both of them.

"I trust this intrusion is important."

Dirk started to say something but his younger brother cut him off. Already this encounter was off to an unusual start.

"I know what to do, my lord. I've found the answer." Spense lurched forward. His eyes were bright, and his face was flushed.

"I assume you're talking about your faerie

21

situation?" Ferrous quirked an eyebrow.

"I was doing some research and came across a book. And there it was. Honestly, I don't know why I've never thought of it before."

Ferrous sighed. Despite his pretense, he knew all about the hours his son spent at The Academy library. He'd hoped the obsession would fade over time, but clearly it had not. "Out with it, then."

"Right. Sorry." Spense took a couple of eager steps closer. "Oracles, my lord."

"Oracles? You'll need to give me more than that."

Spense chuckled nervously.

"It wasn't meant to be a joke."

"No. No, of course not. Just 'give me more than that' is somewhat funny, my lord, because the Oracles are notoriously, you know, cryptic."

Ferrous swiveled his gaze to his other, oddly quiet son. "Has he been into his mother's mead?"

Dirk opened and closed his mouth. The movement brought to mind a large-mouthed fish. Dirk cleared his throat. "Not to my knowledge, my lord. He is, however, very excited."

"Yes, I can see that."

"No mead, my lord, I promise," Spense said. "Well, maybe a little ale with Dirk at the Grey Goats when I was telling him all about it. But that's not important—"

"The Grey Goats…Tavern?" Ferrous stood, pushing away from the desk, meeting Dirk in height and towering over Spense. "Sweet Spring! What on earth were you doing at a common tavern?"

Dirk released an exasperated breath. "What does one usually do at a tavern, my lord?"

Ferrous stalked around his desk. "Do you forget you are the Crown Prince?"

"No, my lord."

"Does your title have no meaning to you?"

"Of course it has meaning to me." Dirk clamped his mouth into a firm line and shifted his stance, chest full, shoulders locked.

"And yet, you conveniently forget your role every time it suits you to go out drinking. I expect you abandoned your honor guard, again?"

Dirk lifted his chin slightly but didn't respond.

"You disappoint me, Dirk."

Spense lunged sideways to stand in front of his brother, as if he were prepared to shield Dirk from an assault, in this case the verbal tirade of his father.

"Yes, my lord, we all know how disappointing Dirk is."

The party in question made a small choking sound.

"But would you mind setting that aside for a moment? This is important. Truly."

Ferrous swiveled his gaze to meet those of his younger son. "Fine. Yes. All right." He waved his hand, circled his desk and lowered himself into his chair—he'd long ago learned the importance of a tactical retreat in a precarious diplomatic situation.

He and Dirk had their conflicts, but they were a private matter, and needed to remain so. The idle disagreement between father and son...perhaps in a normal family, those could be shared with other members, namely a younger brother, but theirs was not normal. They never stopped being King and Crown Prince, even in their quiet moments. There were times when he wished that was not the case, but he couldn't change his destiny nor lose sight of his duty, which necessarily extended to Dirk. Rather than vent his frustration, he welcomed the distraction of Spense's latest quest. "Go ahead, Spense."

"Thank you, my lord." Spense perched himself on the edge of a chair facing the desk, balancing most of his weight on the balls of his feet—as if ready to spring back up at any moment. "You know I've been researching King Lumine's quest to find the Winter Heir—to free Dewy from the bargain—and it occurred to me that I've been going about it all wrong. I need *faerie* answers. Not academic human ones."

Ferrous leaned back. "The last I checked, you placed high value on academic human knowledge."

"I did, my lord, I do. But —"

"And it was no small thing for me to ask a favor of Dean Stone to allow you access to the library early. You weren't meant to begin your studies at The Academy until next year. And she doesn't like to bend rules."

"I know, my lord, and I appreciate that. Really, in a way, it was studying at the library that led me to…well, to where I think I need to go next. Not everything can be learned in a classroom. You know that better than anyone." Spense reached into his cloak and pulled a small green book from his inner pocket.

Ferrous hadn't seen that velvety cover in some time, but he certainly recognized it. "Ah." Ferrous grimaced. "This explains your sudden interest in Oracles. I suppose you went through all of the proper channels to borrow it from The Academy library?"

"Uh, not exactly, my lord."

"No. Of course not. Because that is a rare book that

should never have been removed from the library!" Was it so unreasonable to expect his sons to follow some of the rules?

"You know it, my lord?"

"Yes! I know it. I'm a Seer, remember? It's my business to familiarize myself with all Ways of Knowledge."

Spense leaned forward. "Then you understand—I must go to the faeries. I must find the Winter Oracle."

"The first place you're going is back to the library to return that volume."

Spense glanced at the book in his hands. "Right. Fine. But then, to the Oracles. They could tell me who the Heir is."

"They might. And they might not. And even if they did, there is no reason the answer they give you would grant you anything of true meaning or value." Ferrous frowned. "You're looking for an easy answer, Spense. There is no such thing. Especially not when it comes to Oracles."

"But my lord. I have to try."

Ferrous closed his eyes and breathed deeply. "I know you think that—"

"I do." Spense sprung from the chair, leaving the fragile book on his seat. "I know this is the right path. I can't explain it. But I know, beyond instinct." He beat his fist into his palm.

Ferrous had rarely seen Spense so animated. The only other time had had to do with this same faerie. He'd been more inclined to push boundaries then, too. It had been months since Spense had mistakenly cast a spell over her, but now it was as if he was the one bewitched. Not that he wasn't grateful for all that the young Fae princess had done for his kingdom. But really. His son would never have raised his voice to his father and king before.

"And you also know—beyond instinct—that I will not make a decision about this until I've had time to consider."

"But Father—"

"Enough, Spense. Calm yourself, and perhaps we can speak of this tomorrow. That is my final word for tonight. And for the sake of Grace, return that book."

Spense stood as straight and tall as he was able, the fire of a few moments before tamped down, though his eyes still burned bright, and his jaw was clenched. He'd never looked more like Dirk. "Of course, my lord. We will speak again tomorrow when you've had time to consider. But please also include in your calculations that a faerie's life may depend on this."

He marched from the study and closed the door with a resonant thud.

Chapter 6

"Well, that was dramatic." Ferrous shifted his eyes to his older son.

Dirk kept quiet during Spense's little tirade. He could've told his brother that pleading would never work with their father. By now, Spense should know. But this was how Spense was these days. Reckless. Fanatical with preoccupation.

"You don't know the half of it, my lord."

"I think I've had a fair demonstration. Sit, Dirk, and fill me in on the rest."

Dirk hesitated, but no more than a moment before stepping forward to appropriate the chair Spense had vacated, across from his father's wide desk. He opened his hands, as if kneeling before his father's throne rather than comfortably seated in the stone and wood-paneled study. Or perhaps in supplication to Grace, an unfamiliar gesture for Dirk as he tended to limit his attendance of religious ceremonies to those his father expressly required. "He's obsessed, my lord. Nothing will shake him from this."

"I can see that."

"I've tried to get him out of the library, take him out with the Knights. Nothing's worked."

"Hence the tavern?"

Dirk tilted his head. "Yes. And no. That wasn't just about Spense. I know you don't approve, my lord. You needn't remind me."

"Apparently, I do," Ferrous muttered. His father's disappointment was etched in his drawn expression, causing his chin to wrinkle. Just like his. Just like Spense's.

"But before you become riled and we have another of our famous rows, let me say that I appreciate that you're looking out for your brother."

Dirk bowed his head. That was unexpected. "Thank you, my lord."

"You've changed. I can see that."

"So has Spense."

"Yes." Ferrous reached for the filigreed correspondence on his desk and tapped the heavy paper. "But now, what shall we do with him?"

"Will you let him go? To the faeries—again—to find this Oracle?" He knew it was risky, but if this would help Spense to move on, maybe it was worth it.

"I'm not wholly convinced that it is my choice. This is the path before him."

"You're awfully calm about this."

"No. Not hardly."

Dirk snorted. His father continued toying with the papers on his desk. One of his few tells. When his mind was at work, his fingers were never still.

Ferrous leaned forward, resting his weight on his forearms. "I will always worry about both of my sons. I find I'm overwhelmed almost constantly by the weight you both bear and the things you have already accomplished at your young ages."

Dirk opened his mouth to protest.

Ferrous held up a hand. "I know. You don't believe yourself to be young. You're a wise and experienced military commander."

Dirk scowled. "It's true enough, isn't it?"

"Perhaps you've seen some things. You've learned so much in this last year, particularly," Ferrous conceded. "But you also have much more to learn before you will take my place as king. It's not an easy path. Skill with the blade and battle strategy are not enough. And you'll never have the luxury to forget who you are."

"When did this conversation become about me?"

Ferrous smirked and leaned back in his chair. "You think I don't notice when you're unusually quiet? You've had something on your mind since you stepped into my study."

"I...well, maybe," Dirk said. His gaze shifted to his hands. He folded them in his lap, squeezing tight, holding in the words that were likely to get him in trouble. He had to play this as cool as his father.

"You want me to let him go. And you want to go with him."

Dirk snapped his head up, all pretenses gone. "How...? Did you See that?"

"I don't have to use the Sight to know you, son."

"So...?"

"So." Ferrous threw up his hands. "Have you no understanding of how dangerous the faerie lands can be? They're tricksters by nature. And the Fae lords have powerful elemental magic."

"I'm well aware, Father."

"And yet you think I should permit both of my sons to enter there? To walk into that danger? Lumine is not the only king concerned about his heirs."

Dirk said nothing. He matched Ferrous's gaze and

waited. His father never made so much bluster about matters he'd already decided.

Ferrous released a heavy breath. "And I'm sure I will regret this, but I'm inclined to let you. There's no use fighting fate. You each have a path stretching out before you, and it will find you, with or without my consent."

"Thank you." Dirk nodded.

"Don't thank me too quickly. You'll have to do something for me first, for your kingdom."

"What?"

"Before you go traipsing into the Summer lands, it appears we'll be hosting a delegation from the Winter Court." Ferrous reached across his desk and handed over the creamy envelope he'd been holding. "You, dear son, will be playing diplomat."

Chapter 7

Dewy strolled through the glassed-in garden, followed closely by her frosty-haired inquisitor. "I don't know how any of this will actually help you. Even if you play by all the human rules, they're not inclined to be trusting of our kind."

Misty smirked. "With one obvious exception."

Dewy sighed. "Spense is...different."

"So, I've noticed." Misty twirled her long fingers around a jasmine vine as she ambled along the garden pathways.

It was warm in the glass building, and the ceiling was so high, Dewy could almost imagine she was outdoors on a muggy summer night if it weren't for the fur-clad faeries. Misty currently wore her horrid coat unbuttoned, swinging wide in the balmy air. It—the grotesque evidence of murdered snow hares—pulled Dewy's attention from pestering questions about humans. One human in particular.

Dewy refocused and tried to explain that Spense wasn't considered important in Telridge, but despite her insistence, Misty willfully refused to accept his alleged insignificance. True, he had magic. And he was the son of the king. But he was illegitimate. While he wasn't exactly a commoner, he wasn't nobility, either. Those things mattered to humans.

They mattered to Fae, as well.

None of them would be in their current predicament if Lumine had accepted Princess Snow's choice all those years ago, if he had then blessed their child. Instead, the child grew up in exile, who knew where. And after years and years of separation, Princess Snow eventually chose to accept her passing— prematurely—rather than living on alone. Dewy had only been separated from those she loved for a few months. She couldn't imagine what years of despair would do. The stark, cold beauty of Winter offered little comfort.

Even those born in Winter found ways to push back against it. Dewy wandered to a cluster of citrus trees, barely more than saplings. She curved her palm around a round, firm lime, heavy with life. It was a sort of magic, that this dear fruit grew in the mountains of Winter. Though Misty had explained that it wasn't magic at all, but merely the innovations of the Winter faeries and goblins, who didn't have the luxury of perpetually bountiful harvests like the Summer faeries. This "hot house" was one of several throughout The Silver Horn, most of them devoted to growing fruits and vegetables. It turned out the Winter heathens could not survive on butchered animals alone.

Dewy's stomach turned at the thought. It was one of the reasons she chose to eat in her own room, refusing Lumine's invitations to dine. She couldn't watch faeries consuming the dead flesh of forest creatures. Dewy swallowed, holding back rising bile, and turned her attention back to Misty.

"When do you leave for Telridge?"

"Tomorrow at dawn." Misty turned toward Dewy. "So, I hope you've really told us everything you know."

Dewy spluttered. "I…yes, of course. A promise is a promise." And she'd kept her part of it. If the diplomatic mission failed, it wouldn't be due to her negligence.

Misty lifted the corners of her mouth and winked. Dewy let out a breath. The Fae was teasing her. Again.

"Don't worry, princess. I know you've done what you could. Hopefully, it will be enough. And I have your little love letter securely packed away, to be delivered to your unimportant human at first opportunity."

Dewy bowed her head. "Thank you."

"A promise is a promise." Misty winked.

Dewy nodded again.

"If that's everything, I'm off, better get some rest while I can. Frost always sets a ridiculous pace."

Dewy imagined that Misty had no trouble keeping up, but she was willing to accept the awkward excuse to leave.

"You know your way back to your room?" Misty asked.

"I do."

"All right, then…" She swiveled on a booted foot.

"Misty?"

"Yes?"

Dewy squared her shoulders. "On your journey… may Grace guide you."

Misty ducked her head in a brief, terse nod and jogged down the path.

"That was almost civil."

Dewy jumped as King Lumine stepped out from behind a verdant cluster of jasmine. His indigo and midnight robes were well hidden in the shadowy rows of the garden. He lifted his hands to remove his hood and revealed his pale skin and icy eyes. Dewy always felt chilled under the cool intensity of Lumine's gaze. One reason she avoided him.

And also, she hated him.

Chapter 8

Dewy nodded at the king. "Your Majesty."

Lumine didn't notice, or more likely, chose to overlook her coldness. "I'm pleased to see you out of your chambers and enjoying the warmth of our garden houses."

"Misty thought…" She cleared her throat. "Pardon me. Lady Mist suggested we might conduct our interviews here."

"Quite right. I've told you before, many times. You are welcome to explore The Silver Horn at your leisure. I would prefer that you consider yourself a guest."

Dewy snorted. A guest would be free to leave.

Lumine couldn't have missed the snort but pretended to ignore it. "Of course, one can understand why you might prefer the hot houses. So much green. Must feel a bit like home."

"What brings you here, Your Majesty?"

Was Lumine spying on her? It was his right. She could hardly expect otherwise, in his own realm. Still, it was one thing to know that Misty reported regularly to her king the content of their conversations. It was quite another to stumble upon him herself.

"I, too, often enjoy strolling amongst the greenery." He reached his hand toward a snowy white jasmine bloom. "It reminds me that there are other places, other perspectives, out in the wide world."

Being a person of wide perspective wasn't how Dewy would characterize Lumine. She'd always known him to be singularly focused, especially since the passing of his daughter, the Princess Snow.

"Of course, I was hoping to cross paths with you as well, my dear Lady Dew Drop."

"I'm not your dear," Dewy said. "And you could've found me in my room."

Lumine plucked the blossom from its stem and twirled it slowly between his fingers. "How does the search go?"

"Poorly, Your Majesty. I believe I've exhausted much of the literature you have on the chronologies of faerie-kind."

"You have requested many texts."

"No doubt all you've read or researched before. I don't know what you expected me to find that was different from your own scholars."

"My scholars are very skilled. But they lack a certain insight I believe you to possess." Lumine turned his attention to the garden path.

Her curiosity piqued, Dewy followed, scrambling to match his long strides. "I don't understand what I might do that your skilled people cannot. What does it benefit you to keep me here?"

"That remains to be seen, of course." Lumine waved airily, philosophically.

Dewy didn't believe it. Lumine was up to something.

"But I am certain there are pools of magic you've not yet explored. That combined with our ancient learning could be formidable. You and your human would not have been able to break my lock all those months ago if your magic didn't run deep."

Lumine pursed his lips and elevated his nose, as if he sensed something distasteful. They'd bested him. And he didn't like it.

"How do you know it was me and not Spense?"

"Your human mage?" Lumine scoffed. "I suppose I can't know for certain…but the evidence suggests you. Remember that he'd been a guest for several days before you arrived."

Dewy did remember. She'd tracked Spense to the very doors of Winter, crept into The Silver Horn, only to be stymied by a magical ice lock. And she remembered how broken and distant Spense had been when she arrived, how desperate she'd felt searching for him, fearing the worst, and yet still unable to trust that her feelings were real and not the effect of the Claiming spell he'd accidentally put on her.

But they joined their elemental gifts—of fire and of water—to melt the lock. It both drained and exhilarated her, woke something new inside her, that had nothing to do with the Claiming. The magic of the unintentional spell gave Spense the power to command her actions. It had no control over her heart.

"And what is it you think I can do—other than what I'm already doing—what I've been doing for months?"

"You've barely touched the depths of your magic."

"How could you possibly know that?"

It was Lumine's turn to snort. "Think, girl. What is your gift?"

"Water."

"Yes. Such a simple element, but intrinsic to the natural world." Lumine drifted to a collection of young trees, lightly trailing his fingers along the grey-brown bark. "The life force in the sap of this tree, the juice in its fruit. The very blood in our veins."

"Yes, I suppose…but what difference would that make?"

"You've been studying all the wrong things. Go back to your stacks of books and try again. You might understand better."

Dewy huffed at the slight. As if she wasn't doing enough. Poring over book after book. It wasn't just a distraction from her imprisonment or a temporary escape. It was the only way she might ever leave this place. To suggest she wasn't studying enough or that she was studying wrong… Dewy clamped her jaw. Her hands formed tight fists. Was this Lumine's attempt to keep her forever? Was this a diversion to keep her from something he didn't want her to learn?

Dewy shook her head. "I don't know what you're talking about."

Lumine smiled. "Of course not."

The gesture, his grandfatherly dismissiveness, made her clench her teeth harder. But she couldn't let him see. Couldn't let him know that he got under her skin.

"You know what your precious books haven't explained?"

Lumine raised one eyebrow.

"Why seek Princess Snow's child? Why can't you just name a new Heir? Misty is noble, isn't she? Pick her."

Lumine shuttered his eyes. "If only it were so easy. Don't you think I would have done so already?" His patient demeanor was beginning to fray.

Dewy scowled back at him. "I don't pretend to understand anything you do."

"You should."

"I—"

"You are the Heir of the Summer Court. Your aunt rules in your stead until you come of age."

"What of it?"

"You should know more about the history, about the magic, woven into our kingdoms and our bloodlines. It is what keeps the balance in our lands. When our lines are threatened, the very earth in the faerie world reacts."

This sounded familiar. Like something she was supposed to have paid attention to in her endless hours of tutoring. Only she'd always begged off. Stealing away to dance or gorging herself on fresh berries and new wine with the garden and wood faeries. Anything to avoid the stuffy responsibilities her aunt piled upon her.

That is, up until she met Spense, when everything in her world changed. And her aunt's requirements seemed trifles in comparison to what she'd given up for him. How careless she'd been with her life, with her choices. It all felt very small now.

"Surely, you've noticed the changes in our lands, the fractures, how the edges have become feral and untamed," Lumine said.

Dewy nodded. She had noticed. It was a memory she'd not soon forget, all those months ago, when the forest had turned violent, and she'd watched powerless as Spense nearly bled out on a mountain ridge, pierced by dozens of sharp, evergreen needles. It was a memory that echoed in her nightmares and led her to wake up sweating and screaming in fear that Spense was lost. Then she'd remember that, though he was whole and healthy, he might as well be lost.

"That is why it is so important that we find my Heir. The child my daughter named must be presented before my passing, must accept the mantle of the monarchy."

"So that's it. Your excuse for everything you've done. If Winter is doomed, then why not doom Summer, too? Take us all with you? Or did you forget the little detail that I am the Heir of Summer?"

Lumine stepped toward her, his full height towering over her. "Don't you understand, girl? If Winter crumbles, Summer will die along with it. We're all doomed. Lady Radiant cannot maintain the borders of the faerie lands by herself, nor could you. No singular ruler was meant to."

Dewy swallowed, flinching away from Lumine's intense anger.

He caught himself and stepped back. His eyes softened. "You think me a monster because of what I have done."

Dewy didn't speak, didn't give vent to her own anger and fear. He *was* a monster. Who else would attack a kingdom of innocents to find one person? Who would imprison another Fae?

Lumine turned from her and her unspoken accusations, until he came to a bench formed from a weather-beaten tree. He lowered himself to the curved branch, appearing suddenly as worn down as the old tree, as if the weight of ruling, of protecting the Winter lands had become too much.

The flame of her anger withered as she gazed upon

the king. Had Radiant ever felt the weight of her burden, as Lumine did? What had her aunt done in the name of Summer to protect her people? What might Dewy be expected to do? What compromises would she make when she finally took over her rightful mantle of leadership? She had only to think of Spense to know that fear could cloud her judgment, that she would make any sacrifice for those she loved.

"Perhaps you are right." Lumine turned his tired gaze to her. "My desperation has made me a monster." His eyes filled with cold, mocking fire. "But I regret none of it. I will do anything to save my people, and yours, too, little queen. Including imprisoning you."

Dewy lifted her chin. She returned his deep stare, and this time, did not flinch.

Chapter 9

They arrived with a cabal of attendants, as if they didn't trust humans to take care of their needs and provide respectable hospitality. They were probably right. Telridgians knew little about faerie culture and would likely offend their guests without even trying before the work of actual diplomacy could get underway.

Wagons of faeries and supplies cluttered the city's thoroughfares, as if they wouldn't want to rely on their human hosts. Not a surprise, either. There was quite a lot of iron inside Telridge Castle, and no matter how hearty and strong the Winter faeries were, surrounding themselves with the sickening substance would be hard on them, even debilitating. It likely slowed Dewy's healing those days she dwelled in the castle. Spense's own munitions had caused terrible damage in those summer battles, more than they would have to any human enemy.

So Spense couldn't blame them. Not really.

But it meant that the opening salutations at the castle gates got off to an awkward start.

Lord Ferrous opened his arms, gesturing to the castle and its surrounding out-buildings. "Welcome to Telridge. It is an honor to host you, and your entourage." Ferrous tilted his head in the slightest of bows.

The two official emissaries stepped forward and removed their shimmering, blue hoods. Spense's breath caught when he recognized the icy pale Fae, Lord Frost and his vexing sister, Lady Mist. They'd brought along goblins to attend them along with huddling common faeries, who stayed a good distance back from those iron gates. Spense narrowed his eyes when he spotted Tun conspicuously at ease. King Lumine's smug goblin servant had been the last face Spense had seen when he'd been unceremoniously chucked from the Winter lands all those months ago. When he and Tun locked gazes, the goblin smirked and nodded a silent greeting.

He shook his head, breaking eye contact with Tun, and caught Dirk staring, one eyebrow lifted in question. Spense mouthed "later" to his brother.

"Thank you for your welcome, Lord Ferrous," Frost said.

Spense recognized the clipped words, the cool tone, enough to set his teeth chattering. This was Lumine's ambassador? Frost—just by being Frost— was more likely to *start* another war than prevent one.

"My sister and I prefer our own accommodations. If you could direct us to an open space reasonably distant from your...dwelling, that would suit." The tall Fae lifted his pointed chin as he surveyed the surrounding city and country beyond, the very lands bloodied by a series of unnecessary human-faerie battles only the summer before.

"Of course. If that is your preference."

His father stiffened his shoulders and raised his chin. Spense was sure he felt the snub, even if his gracious words didn't betray his offense. Ferrous waved Spense over.

"I believe you are acquainted with my younger son, Master Spense. He would be happy to provide you with a tour of the grounds."

I would?

Ferrous glowered meaningfully.

"Right. Yes, of course. Happy to, my lord."

"Our Head Cook, Cait, has anticipated that you may require refreshments after your journey. While accommodations are settled, I can escort you to our receiving chambers. I assure you, Cait has been generous in laying out a repast for you, our guests."

Frost's lips flattened in disapproval. But Spense's mother stepped forward and curtsied to the Fae.

"Or…perhaps you and your attendants would prefer to take refreshments in the gardens?"

Both Fae nodded, staring directly at Cait. "Better."

"If you'll follow me, please." Ferrous pretended to ignore Frost's disdain, while directing the Winter guests through the gates and around the stone castle to the far side.

A bevy of servants scurried into the main keep, presumably at Cait's urging, to move the tables of fruit, cheese, fresh bread, and cured meats, along with a selection of juices and wines, to the formal castle gardens. As they often did, Cait's deft maneuvering and gracious words smoothed out an easily bungled diplomatic encounter. But that's how their parents were. Complementary units, who existed in amiable, unspoken collaboration, even if there had never been—and never would be—anything like a real partnership.

"Tun, you'll go with the younger son." Frost waved at Spense. "See if you can locate someplace suitable."

Spense bit his lip as Frost and several faeries followed in the wake of Lord Ferrous and Dirk. He jumped when a cool breeze tickled his ear.

"Don't worry about Frost. You remember what he's like," Lady Mist whispered.

She winked her ice-blue eyes at him, leaving Spense gawking. "Ah, now that's the human creature I remember, complete with the open mouth. Watch out, gents. He might drool," she said, sauntering after her brother.

Spense snapped his mouth shut and scowled down at Tun, while the other goblins and faeries tried—and failed—to contain their mirth.

"Nice to see you, Master Spense." Tun tipped two long, blue-grey fingers in a mock salute. "So, you've got fields, maybe? Open meadows? Sumptin' like that?"

"Yeah, we've got something like that."

Which was how Spense ended up on tent-construction-oversight duty. Tun and his goblins scouted the grounds outside the castle walls, and after several rejected suggestions from Spense, agreed upon a field flanking the orchards, bordered by the river. It was in sight of the castle, a quick ride or slightly longer walk, not too close to the city or any of the nearby farms.

The structures they assembled weren't tents. Not really. In his experience, tents were simple, cloth triangles assembled with two stakes and a line. Maybe an oiled canvas as ground cover. Or the military tents that Dirk's soldiers used. A little more complex, but essentially utilitarian.

The Winter faeries constructed domed palaces in

45

miniature, complete with planked flooring that snapped together like puzzle pieces. And faerie-made brocade sides. Silk canopies rose high to form billowing ceilings. Several of the structures were multi-chambered, offering both private quarters and public spaces to entertain guests. The largest was set up in the center of a half circle with two such sleeping quarters as well as eating and relaxing spaces. In no time, a veritable faerie village arose.

Spense hoped he might join the receiving party back at the gardens, once it was clear he wouldn't be of much use for construction. In part, he was curious how the meeting was going. But mostly, he'd spent his day learning as much as he could about Oracles and had—again—forgotten to eat. One whiff of his mother's fresh bread had his stomach rumbling. It hadn't stopped in all the time he'd been playing tour guide for Tun.

But he was out of luck. As usual. Just as he was making his way back to the castle, the Winter Fae and their close attendants were making their way out. Spense groaned.

He had a feeling this wasn't going to be his first disappointment during the Winter visit.

Chapter 10

Dewy hucked the brassy mug across her small quarters. It hit the edge of the stone fireplace with a satisfying clang and bounced to the floor. She lifted her arm to follow up her first throw with the book she'd spent the last three hours studying, right as Siskin appeared in her doorway, his expression harried as he rushed into the room.

"Are you well, Lady Dew Drop? I heard a crash."

Dewy lowered her throwing arm. "I'm fine, Siskin. Sorry to startle you."

"Is there any way I may be of assistance?" he asked while crossing the room to retrieve the heavy mug.

He glanced between it and the fireplace, examining each for signs of damage, but things were made sturdy in Lumine's house. Neither the mug nor the stone were any worse for the wear.

"No, I don't think so…I just let my temper get the best of me."

He cocked his head like the small finch he was named for. "May I ask what vexes you so?"

Dewy huffed out a breath of frustration. "This book." She lifted the text in question. "Your master. This whole situation."

Siskin opened his mouth, closed it, and opened it again. But no words came out. What was he supposed to say? A servant—even a favored one—knew better than to argue with a visiting dignitary nor could he disparage his king.

"I'm sorry, Siskin. This isn't your problem."

"On the contrary, it is."

She shook her head. "Lumine asks too much of you. You needn't trouble yourself with my ineptitude."

"No, that's not what I meant."

"Oh. Sorry. What did you mean?"

The servant sighed. "I'm not sure where to start."

"Perhaps you should sit down."

"You suggest that I sit in your presence?"

"Of course." She waved to the hearth bench, the only other seating option in her room besides the bed. She'd had this problem in the Summer Court, too. As much time as she'd spent with common faeries, they still deferred to her. Yes, she was royal, *the* royal eventually, but her own mother was common. It never made a difference to her then. It made even less now.

Siskin drew his shoulders in and took a step away. The backs of his knees hit the stone hearth, causing him to bobble the brass mug and lower himself to the seat, likely more abruptly than intended. The servant took a steadying breath, gently placed the mug down, and opened his hands in supplication and explanation.

"This problem you are trying to solve is a problem for all of us. All of faerie, not just those of us who choose to serve in Winter." Siskin ducked his chin, his speech over, and directed his gaze to the floor.

Dewy frowned. "I know."

Her conversation with Lumine weighed on her. The seriousness of the situation almost justified his actions…almost, but not quite. She found herself sympathizing with his cause, if not his methods. She had little hope that the people of Telridge would receive his diplomatic visit with generosity. Maybe if he'd started there. But Ferrous and the Telridgians were right to be angry. He'd attacked their people. She'd tried to prepare Misty as best as she could. But doubts nagged her.

What did she really know of the humans? She had saved them, fought against her own faerie kind, and still they'd looked at her sideways, with suspicion.

And yet, that's where Spense was. These were his people. And if Telridge could produce someone like Spense—decent, kind, and honest—maybe there was hope for the rest of them. If she ever wanted to see him again, to find out if there was something real and true between them, she had to solve the mystery of the Heir. She had to get free. And independent of her bargain with Lumine, she wouldn't really be free unless she knew the realms of faerie were safe.

"You really want to help, Siskin?"

"Of course."

"Well, what do you know about blood magic?"

Siskin frowned. "I'm afraid not much, Lady Dew Drop. Why?"

"It could be a misdirection from your charming king, but for once, I don't think so. He asked me some pointed questions about water. You do know my gifts lie in water?"

"Oh, we're all aware, princess."

"Right. Of course." Dewy smirked. "The lock." She imagined the servants and court were just as gossipy in Winter as they were in Summer. And it was no small magic when she and Spense broke Lumine's ice lock. In fact, it probably caused quite the scandal. Outsiders—prisoners—besting their king.

"Not…the lock. We heard of your abilities well before you defeated King Lumine's ice."

Siskin paused. His gaze rose to hers. Watery and swirling with emotions, none of them deference.

"How you fought for the people of Telridge against our soldiers. Against faeries."

Dewy leaned back. He was right. She'd done that. She'd stopped hundreds of enemy faeries, killed many by drowning them in the River Selden. But to Siskin…they weren't enemies. They were his people. Brave soldiers who defended their lands and followed the orders of their king—no matter how misguided. Her heartbeat quickened.

"Did you know anyone who…?"

Siskin shook his head. "Only distantly."

Dewy released a breath. At least she hadn't caused the death of a cousin. But she could have. It was so easy—in the moment—to see nothing but an attacking force. But every one of those soldiers had a family, friends. They all came from somewhere.

And she'd ended their lives with the stretching of her arms and the extension of her will. Dewy didn't think. She acted. This was the consequence.

"But you may find some in this court who feel…differently."

"Oh."

"Rime lost his mate."

Dewy reflexively lifted a hand to her mouth. She recognized that name. It belonged to a thin, shrewish faerie who attended Frost. "I'm…sorry."

"We were at war."

50

"So, we were…"

It was a wonder that more of Lumine's people didn't hate her. They should. All this time she'd spent despising the king. She was no better than he.

And now she was the instrument of their salvation.

"It seems Grace has a sense of irony."

"The thought had crossed my mind as well, Lady Dew Drop."

"I'm sorry…for the lives lost. I can't be sorry for defending innocent people, but…"

Siskin bowed his head. "I understand. You did what you felt was right, even if it made enemies of friends."

That's what she was now. An enemy. A prisoner.

No. It wasn't that simple.

Dewy made a bargain with a king. She had to honor it. She was magically bound. But she had a choice in how she felt about it. She could choose to act the part of the petulant prisoner. Or she could use this time to make amends.

The lands of Winter were in a precarious state, its people in danger. Their king was an arrogant ass. It didn't mean they should suffer.

"I appreciate your help, Siskin. You've been kind to me when I didn't deserve it. Will you help me save Winter? Protect the faerie lands?"

"Where shall we begin?" Siskin asked. His eyes were clear and open.

Dewy met his gaze, for the first time with understanding and contrition. "Lumine hinted there was a link between my magic and the life water of living things. I just don't know how, or what good it would do. I've requested materials from your libraries, but so

51

far…well, you saw. It's been frustrating."

"Perhaps you're not looking in the right places."

"That thought had occurred to me," Dewy said, deadpan. "If you have any ideas, I'm open."

Siskin tilted his head. A new light entered his eyes. And the smallest of knowing smiles crept onto his face. "Actually, I might."

Chapter 11

Spense was hiding. He spent the morning running errands for his mother, his father, and members of the Winter delegation, including the goblin Tun. His grey-blue tormenter sent him off in search of "toad-tree berries," insisting it was required for treatment of a certain malady that—predictably—didn't have a name humans understood and lacked any specific ailments but was nevertheless essential to his well-being.

When Spense grumbled at the goblin's demand, he was overheard by none other than his mum who spent the next half hour lecturing about the importance of protocol, what with faerie expectations of hospitality, which exceeded even the high standards of Telridge.

"If we want any chance of peace with the courts, we'd best learn to host them, and that means even apprentice mages, so you'd better get your hindquarters moving and figure out what a human would call a blooming toad-tree berry."

Spense held in any further grumbles, even when he discovered that a toad-tree berry was another word for an ordinary gooseberry, the weed shrubs that grew wild along the edge of the orchard where the faeries had set up their tents. They had limited medicinal qualities. He might've slammed the book in The Academy library with a little more gusto than was strictly necessary upon making this discovery.

A couple of snaps of the gardener's shears and he had a basketful for the malevolent goblin. He delivered it as quickly as possible to avoid Tun's smirking and to get away before another tedious request could be made.

Which was why he was hiding. Also, he'd had no chance to learn more about the Oracles since the arrival of the Winter faeries. And he felt, from somewhere deep in his belly, that time was running out. Something was beginning to fray. He couldn't explain it, and Dirk scoffed when he tried to. But Spense knew.

"Hah! There you are!"

Spense jolted, knocking his head against the underside of his hiding space. The alcove was little more than a closet tucked under the stairs. If someone happened to come down to his laboratory and glance into the larger room, they wouldn't see him, though he would hear their steps on the stairs. Or rather he should have.

"Where did *you* come from?" Spense asked.

Lady Mist opened her mouth in a huge grin Spense didn't experience as friendly. The last time he'd laid eyes on her, she'd trussed him up and carried him off to the Silver Horn, where he'd spent several days as King Lumine's prisoner. She'd worn that same smile, then, like kidnapping humans was an amusing game.

"You're not really surprised that I was able to suss you out, are you?"

Spense swallowed. "Uh…I…"

Her eyes brightened. "I think what you mean to say is, 'Of course, I am delighted to see you Lady Mist and am eager to serve you in any way that I can.' Something like that, right? Must remember faerie hospitality."

Spense scrambled to his feet and bowed. "O-of course, yes, Lady Mist."

She laughed and waved him off. "Oh, calm down. We're old friends, you and I. I think you can call me Misty."

"Right." Spense straightened from his bow.

Lady Mist—Misty—turned from him and sauntered through the lab. "Is this yours? The place where you work?"

"It is."

"Where you conjure up spells to compel poor, unsuspecting Summer Fae into your service?" She hopped up onto his workbench.

"That's not exactly what happened. I never meant to—"

"Right." Misty waved a casual hand. "We all know the story. It was an accident. You didn't mean it. It just happened to have worked out rather well for you, though, didn't it?"

"No. That's not what happened." Spense stepped forward. "I freed her. All I ever wanted to do was free her."

"Except that she's not exactly free, now, is she?"

Spense opened and closed his mouth. No, Dewy wasn't free. And it was his fault. The lingering consequences of the Claiming spell. He didn't need an ambassador from the Winter faeries to come and tell him that the reason Dewy was held prisoner was because of him.

"It's not what I wanted for her. I was prepared to pay Lumine's price." Spense couldn't keep the steel from his voice.

But Misty rolled her eyes. "No need to get all

worked up, Master Spense." She hopped off the bench. "I'm only teasing. Dewy never mentioned that you were so touchy."

That got his attention. "Dewy? Do you talk to her? Is she all right?"

"That seems more like it."

Spense didn't know what she meant.

"Your girl is fine. Irritable, but fine."

There were too many things to unpack in those short phrases. His girl? As in *his*, still? And why was she irritable? But he didn't ask about those things. "Define 'fine,'" he said, scowling.

"Wow, you really are the love-sick puppy turned over-protective knight, aren't you? I have to say, I'm not sure I saw that coming."

"Please," he said, running his hands through his hair. "How is she?"

Misty sighed, reached into a small satchel, and pulled from it a folded piece of parchment. "How about she tells you herself?"

Spense locked his gaze on the paper. He stopped breathing as Misty extended her hand. And a letter. He tried to keep his fingers steady as he reached for it. The parchment was smooth. All four corners were folded in, and it was sealed with a dab of ice-blue wax. He wanted to rip open the letter but stopped himself. He gave an experimental tug, but the seal held. The paper wouldn't tear.

"It won't open. How do I know this is really from her?"

Misty shrugged. "She said only you'd be able to open it. Something about shared water."

Spense examined the letter.

"Look, you'll have to figure it out. I promised her I'd deliver the letter, and so I have. Reading it, that's on you."

Spense frowned. "Thanks, I think."

"Oh, you're welcome, but my promise isn't fulfilled unless…well, she asked for a response. In your own hand."

Misty's words sounded almost tender. And he almost forgot she was the fiendish faerie who'd ordered goblins to drag him through the forests of Winter.

"How can I trust that you'll bring it to her…untouched?"

"Listen boy, I promised her, all right? We made a bargain. You know what that means?"

Spense nodded. He knew too well how binding the magic of a bargain could be. "Why?"

Misty bit her lip. Gone was the smug and wickedly playful faerie. "Because." She breathed forcefully in and out her nose. "We need you."

"You need me?"

"Not you-you." She waved both hands in front of her as if she could erase his question. "Humans-you. Telridge."

"Again, why?"

"Because…without the Winter Heir, all the faerie lands are at risk. First, Winter, but eventually, it will affect Summer, too. We know that Telridge has something to do with the Heir, but we don't know what." Misty's words were clipped and strained. All humor had left her voice. Admitting this vulnerability cost her. "Lumine tried pleading with your king, and then tried to enter Telridge's lands by force when Ferrous wouldn't help. We're trying again because we have no choice. And we can't fail a third time."

"Hence the diplomatic visit."

"Hence diplomacy. With humans. And we know little about your kind after years of isolation. Lumine asked me to learn as much as I could. Dewy was a resource. This letter was her price." She gestured at the creamy white letter Spense cradled in his hands. "She made me agree to a bargain, in order to help. Your girl is tenacious."

Spense smiled. It was a good description of Dewy.

"So, figure out how to read the letter. Write one back to her. I will deliver it. And if you still don't trust me, maybe you can seal yours the same way. Does that work for you?"

"All right." He looked at Misty, met her pale blue eyes. "And thank you. This means…it means a lot."

He lifted the letter. It carried a light floral scent when he waved it through the air.

"You're welcome." Misty tilted her frosty head. "If you really want to show your appreciation, maybe a little help at this dinner we're supposed to have tonight? A word or two to smooth the way?"

"I'll do what I can, but I can't make any—"

"Promises," she said. "I understand."

Spense shrugged. He found himself wanting to help her, despite all that happened before. It wasn't like he didn't remember the indignities he'd suffered, but seeing Misty this way and talking to her, helped him understand their perspective. And to be fair, if Dirk or one of his Knights had caught a foreigner skulking about the edge of Telridge's territory, they likely wouldn't have received any better treatment than he had. Possibly worse.

"So, I should get back. And get myself properly fancy for this shindig tonight."

"Do you know your way?" Spense asked.

Misty lifted one silver-white eyebrow. "I'll be fine."

His skin tingled with the thrill of cool magic. The Fae was more than just a fighter. "Maybe I shouldn't ask, but how did you find me anyway?"

"Tracking spell. Worked even with all this iron." Misty waved at the walls around them. "And it's not like you have guards protecting you down here. Your brother and father are just silly with them, but not you. You really should look into that. Your security is seriously lacking."

Chapter 12

The conversation with Lady Mist left Spense feeling a lot of things. The walls of his private laboratory, usually a safe space, were suddenly cloying and chilled, as if the Winter Fae had left behind a coating of hoarfrost that covered every surface and crept into the pages of his books, already softened with age. He shivered, as if he could brush off Misty's unnerving, mischievous, and disruptive questions. He knew it wasn't so simple, but for now, he had a letter. And it was the only thing that really mattered.

But first, he had to figure out how to open it.

Misty said only he could do it, and that it had something to do with shared water.

That was Dewy's element. Water. But Spense didn't have water gifts. He could create potions and cast spells. But his elements were fire and earth. There was nothing shared there.

Unless she meant the Claiming? The spell that had joined them together. When he cast it, they'd both been at the River Selden.

Spense rushed from his laboratory, up the stairs, and through the castle keep. He raced through the city, the market, and past the taverns, the Grey Goats, preparing to open for its evening crowd. He didn't stop running until he'd reached the bridge and collapsed panting in the late afternoon sun, where it all began. At the river.

Spense scuttled down to the water's edge, in the shadow of the bridge, where Dewy once hid from him, the loud and clumsy human. Only she'd placed herself in direct line of his spell. And when he'd reached out for the bridge, he'd lunged too far, and his foolish senses couldn't tell the difference between an old bridge and a lively faerie princess. Spense slipped another step and knelt, reaching into the lapping flow of the river. With his other hand, he clutched the letter. He cupped the water in his hand, let a few drops fall onto the seal.

He waited.

Nothing happened.

He tugged at the seal. It wouldn't budge. The paper wouldn't even tear.

"Master Spense? Is that you?"

Spense looked up. A shadowed form leaned over the edge of the bridge. He couldn't see her face, but he knew her voice.

"Hi, Flora. Yeah, it's me."

"May I ask what you're doing under the bridge?"

Spense laughed. "As if I know," he muttered.

"What did you say?"

"Nothing. I'm coming up."

When he returned topside, Flora smiled broadly. She was leading two horses, one buttery gold, the other a sleek black. It had a white star on its forehead and another on its chest. Spense recognized them both. Her own mare, Buttercup and Dirk's stallion, Lightning Storm. His brother let few people tend to his horse. It was no small thing that Flora had the care of the stallion.

"Sweet Spring, Spense. What was that about?"

He sighed. "Would you believe I was trying to open a letter?"

She tilted her head and squinted her warm brown eyes at him. "Have you heard of a letter opener?"

Spense grimaced. "I wish it were that simple."

"I'm guessing magic is involved?"

He held up the letter, nodding. "It's from Dewy."

Flora's mouth opened, and her eyes softened.

"Only I can't figure out how to get it open."

"Oh."

"Yeah."

"I'm sure she sealed it to protect it. Walk with me? Maybe we can puzzle it out."

Spense took the lead line for Buttercup. "Thanks."

"Sure. So, were you given any clues?"

"Sort of. Misty—Lady Mist, from the Winter Court—said that only I could open it and the key was our 'shared water.'"

Flora snorted.

"What?"

She smirked. "Nothing. Sorry."

"No, what are you thinking?"

"Inappropriate thoughts, of course." She nudged him with her elbow. When he didn't say anything, she rolled her eyes. "Just, you know. There are rumors that you and Dewy shared…a lot more than water."

"What?" A creeping warmth rose in Spense's neck and face. "Oh."

"Yeah." Flora shrugged.

"Will you please disabuse anyone you hear suggesting that?" That was all he needed, for folks to think he was the type of guy who'd take advantage of a girl when she was under his literal spell.

"Sure thing."

They were both quiet after that. The horses' clip-clopping marked the sounds of their walk back to the castle stables.

"So, really? Nothing between you and the faerie?" Flora asked.

It was Spense's turn to roll his eyes. "Not nothing. There was something, but not what people are saying. Not like that. And not while she was under the influence of the Claiming."

She grinned. "All right, fine, you're decent. I get that. But you were exchanging, ahem, fluids."

"Ugh, Flora." He grimaced.

Her grin grew bigger. "I'd say there was plenty of 'shared water,' then, wouldn't you?"

He looked at her. Shared water…

Oh.

Heat rose in his neck as he remembered their one kiss. Something in his middle grew tight and loose at the same time.

He glanced at the letter. Could it be that simple?

Spense licked his lips. He lifted the letter and raised it gently to his mouth.

The ice blue wax began to glow brighter and brighter, and burst like tiny fireworks. River-blue sparkles rained from the letter.

Spense looked up. "Flora, you're a genius." He gave her a quick hug and handed Buttercup's reins back to her.

"Where are you going?"

Spense launched himself into the city's maze of streets, turning back only to yell. "I've got a letter to

63

read!"

****

In the quiet of his chambers—the room he used for sleeping and little else—Spense unfolded the parchment, one corner at a time. He ran his fingers over the looping script. Dewy's writing was light, dusting the paper, but not pressing it in.

Spense paced as he read her words, her simple greeting.

My dear Spense.

He could almost imagine her voice. Straightforward, teasing, sweet. He knew how she whispered when her throat was dry and how she cried out in panic.

The words on this page weren't that. Not panicked.

My dear Spense, the silly boy on the bridge, the deliverer of wondrous bread, and the keeper—though no longer the Claimer—of my heart.

He chuckled. And choked back a hard swallow, somewhere in between a laugh and a sob.

He read on. She assured him she was safe and being treated well, but the sadness crept through. There were words between the words. And some of the words were direct, a spike to the very center of himself.

I miss you. It seems silly, considering how little time we spent together, and how many moons have waxed and waned since we have been separated. I suppose you have made an indelible impression upon my person. I feel your absence, as if a part of me has been harshly cut away.

His chest clenched tight. It was as if she spoke his own words back to him. She was so far away. He couldn't reach her, couldn't wrap her in his arms and share a real kiss, one no less magical than the one needed to open this folded piece of paper.

Every heartbeat and every breath anticipate the day when we are rejoined, and what was broken will be mended. I lean into hope and trust that it will come to pass. Until then, fare well. I leave my heart in your safekeeping.

Dewy

He sighed heavily and kicked the bedpost. Safekeeping. What a poor caretaker he turned out to be. She'd had to resort to a bargain with Fae in order to send this simple missive. And that she would do that. That she would give yet another thing!

Spense brushed away the tears starting to pool. He re-read the simple letter. And put it in the chest at the foot of his bed.

The words were real. They were theirs. He vowed that the next time he heard her voice it would be in person.

For now, he had work to do.

Chapter 13

It was doomed from the start.

It didn't matter that the whole blooming castle had turned out to provide hospitality for the faerie entourage. Or that Dirk and his father had donned their most impractical clothing. It didn't matter that his brother Spense ran his skinny legs ragged throughout the day, back and forth between the Winter faeries' temporary compound and the castle keep, playing emissary to their guests.

Dirk was trained to keep his emotions in check. To calm his thoughts in difficult or tense situations. And he began the evening fully intending to comply with his father's orders, even prepared to offer escort to the Lady Mist.

But Dirk let himself get distracted when he spotted Sir Gervais and Lady Xendra outside the great hall, where they were to feast. Neither of them looked comfortable in their finery. It was always a bit of a shock to see Lady X dressed as a courtier. He was so used to her in fighting gear—leathers, sensible wool, and armor—he often forgot that underneath all that gear, she was a young woman. Her waist-cinching gown and shoulder-baring neckline made it abundantly clear. So maybe he lingered a little too long with his friends, and maybe he missed the cue when the faeries entered, still stunned by the Knights' transformations.

When Xendra nudged him, it was too late. He'd already committed his first insult of the night.

Dirk rushed to offer his greetings, next to his father. He bowed and extended his arm to the female Fae. She lifted her tiny, pointed chin, so that even when he towered over her, she looked down her nose at him. The audacity of the gesture riled him, but he pretended to ignore her snobbery.

"Would you do me the honor of accepting my escort into the great hall, Lady Mist?"

She tilted her head. "You wouldn't care to escort my dear brother, Lord Frost?"

Dirk wasn't sure what he was being asked. Or what the Fae implied. He realized they should've presented an escort to Lord Frost as well as Lady Mist, but...well, there weren't that many courtiers he trusted. He scrambled to offer a solution and caught X's gaze. She widened her eyes. Her arms lifted from her sides, a tiny suggestion.

"Perhaps Lord Frost, you'd like to be escorted by the Lady Xendra?" He gestured to X, knowing that every man—and plenty of the women—in that courtyard would fall all over themselves for that particular honor. If the glinting in Lady Mist's eyes were any indication, he thought she might be one of them, though he couldn't be sure her intent was entirely friendly.

But Frost barely glanced at Lady Xendra before deferring. "I think my sister and I would prefer our own company this evening, Prince Dirk."

"I...ah...of course, if that is your preference." Dirk swallowed the words he would've rather said.

Frost leaned in and whispered to Dirk, "Really, you

didn't expect me to accept the arm of one of your soldiers? Did she even wash it?"

Dirk seethed as Frost sauntered into the room but bit down on his tongue hard enough it was sore. He doubted anyone else heard exactly what was said, but the surrounding courtiers couldn't have missed Frost's intent. Disdain dripped off his icy features.

Xendra caught his elbow. "Whatever it was, let it go."

Dirk shifted his gaze to her. "You don't—"

She squeezed hard. "I don't care what that slush pile thinks of me. Don't make an issue of it."

And Dirk tried not to. He tried to ignore all the little insults and slights. When Frost and his goblins pushed away their dinner of roast lamb and herbed vegetables. When they sniffed at the wine but didn't drink. Lady Mist sampled most of the meal, as did several of her faerie attendants. But Frost couldn't be bothered. Perhaps he didn't know how much effort had gone into the preparations for their benefit.

But Dirk knew. Cait had done her research. While her fare was usually quite good, Spense's mother had outdone herself, and coordinated a truly spectacular meal. He caught a couple of Telridge's courtiers groaning over the honey-drizzled yams, covered in roasted pecans, and the crème custard layered with figs.

When a musical interlude began, performed by Telridge's most accomplished quartet, Frost listened to only a few bars, before turning his head and whispering something to his sister. Dirk wanted to lunge across the long table and wipe the smirk off the Fae's cold face.

But he didn't. He clenched his jaw and turned his attention to the performers.

By the time the real work of the evening began, and Dirk had consumed more than a couple chalices of the flavorful wine, he was primed for a show-down with the arrogant Winter representatives.

"Lord Ferrous, I'm sure you've wondered at the reason for our visit," Lady Mist began. "Other than ensuring the continued mutual respect our two kingdoms enjoy, of course."

Everyone was wondering that. When she finally broached the topic, all other conversation ceased. The moment had come.

"Yes, Lady, we have wondered," Lord Ferrous said. He set down his wine as he continued. "As you know, relations between our courts have been…strained of late." And by late, he meant the past few decades. It wasn't just the brutal attack on Telridge over the summer and the alliance with Verden.

Lady Mist smiled. With a lot of teeth. "Which is why we endeavor now to mend those breaches, to remind you that we are all interdependent. Now, more than ever, we ask for your hand of friendship."

"But not our arm, I guess," Dirk muttered under his breath.

Gerry choked on his wine, and Xendra stomped on his foot.

"Did you have something to add, Prince Dirk?" Frost asked.

"Of course not. Please, carry on. You were saying something about a hand of friendship?"

Frost narrowed his cold blue eyes, as his sister continued.

"We know that you're aware of the Winter Kingdom's current dilemma."

Lord Ferrous nodded. "I have received your correspondence."

"And, of course, my brother Spense filled us in on the rest," Dirk added.

Upon his return, Spense provided a wealth of information about the Winter lands and a harrowing story. He didn't know how his brother could stand to be in the Winter faeries' presence, not after the way they'd treated him. Not to mention the imprisonment of Dewy. That weighed on Spense more than anything. No matter how Spense tried to spin it, tried to take the blame, it wasn't his fault. Not really. King Lumine could've chosen to help Spense and Dewy out of their predicament with the Claiming spell without asking for anything, and definitely not a price so high. But ever the opportunist, Lumine took advantage of their desperation.

"You acknowledge your bastard relation?" Frost asked.

His question was openly curious, as if human ways were primitively fascinating. Dirk gripped the arms of his chair.

"Brother dear," Lady Mist chided. "That word is considered uncouth to humans."

"Ah, right."

Ferrous chose to ignore the interchange. "You were saying, Lady Mist?"

"Yes." She placed her pale hand on her brother's arm as if her touch could still his arrogant tongue. "You know we seek Lumine's grandchild, the Winter Heir. We have reason to believe that the offspring of the late Princess Snow has found their way here, to Telridge. But more than that we do not know."

"And now you ask for our aid?" Ferrous asked.

"If you would be so kind, yes."

Dirk scoffed. "You realize you're looking for your *own* bastard? What if this supposed Heir doesn't want to be found?" He directed his comments to Frost, redirecting his own smug words back at him.

"Why wouldn't they?" Frost asked, clearly incredulous at the notion, as if he believed the faerie world so superior to that of humans it was inevitable the Heir would want to return to their frozen kingdom.

Dirk raised his brows. "You've never considered that this Heir remains in hiding from *you*? Maybe doesn't *want* to be found? Maybe doesn't care to redeem your sorry legacy?"

"How dare you suggest—"

"I do suggest. And I also suggest that if this person—whoever they may be—has taken refuge in the kingdom of Telridge after your king exiled them, that if they are now a citizen of this land, then it is our duty and honor to protect them."

"*Dirk.*"

He heard his father's tone and ignored it. "I'm sorry, Father, but if King Lumine really wanted our help, he shouldn't have attacked our people."

Frost lifted his chin. "The use of force before was…regrettable, but let's not forget the stance Telridge took to precipitate that."

Dirk rose. "I know you're not going to put this on us."

Frost bristled. "Perhaps not you, personally. From what I've seen of your skill set, it is unlikely that diplomatic correspondence has ever been part of your responsibilities. If you can even read."

Dirk drew back. "Are you kidding me?"

He caught a glimpse of his brother, standing near the back wall. His eyes were wide, imploring. He shook his head back and forth. As if he knew what Dirk was thinking, what he wanted to say, how he wanted to act. Proving—as Frost believed—that he was little more than a thug and brute.

Maybe he was. He didn't care.

Spense didn't have to deal with this type of horseshit every day. All the wearying pretense. The fake flattery. The not-so-subtle insults. But Dirk put up with the games of Telridge's human court. He knew that when it mattered, despite all the internal day-to-day bickering, Telridgians would always come together as a people. They would unite when facing a common enemy.

But these faeries, they *were* the enemy. And he didn't have to put up with them.

"I'm done with this." Dirk threw his linen on the table and turned to go. Let his father deal with the fallout.

But that arrogant Fae, Frost, had to get in one more word. He whispered to his sister loudly enough for all to hear, "I suppose we can't expect better behavior. We've already seen what this family is like from the younger son."

Dirk turned back slowly. Gerry and X read his stance and were immediately on their feet. To her credit, Lady Mist sat back in her chair and became still. Spense was his brother—maybe illegitimate—but family. And what he endured in Winter and on the journey there, most men, neither human nor faerie, could've withstood that experience and not come out the other side broken.

But not Spense. He came home. And he got to work. Had been working to help Lumine, to help these puffed-up faeries all these many months, because he was decent. To suggest otherwise…

Dirk saw red and, for once, leaned into it. Training discarded.

No one stopped him, not even his father. Likely he felt the same way.

"How dare you come to our kingdom, the home you and your snow-covered, little minions attacked without reason, and speak to us like this—"

"We had plenty of reason." Frost bolted from his place at the table. "And you well know it."

"What I know is that you and your king are nothing but cowards!" He stalked toward the faerie lordling.

The Winter delegation rose as one, a wall of ice to protect their lord.

"Oh, fine." Dirk held up his hands, smirking. "Hide behind your goblins. We know they do your dirty work. My family remembers well."

He waved to Spense, who stood glacier-still while Dirk railed. He'd seen the still-healing cuts and bruises on Spense from when those goblins had dragged his brother through the dirt and snow of Winter. It was one insult he'd never forget and never forgive.

Frost sneered. "Your weak family is pathetic, a pretense of nobility. It disgusts me that we demean ourselves to meet with you." His eyes were bitter with cold.

Dirk didn't know what he said after that. There was more swearing, and possibly some allusions to the Fae's mother. Frost took offense and hurled his own share of high-volume insults.

So much for diplomacy.

By the time they both finished yelling, the noble Fae and all their companions declared they'd be leaving at dawn.

In a cool corner of his mind, Dirk knew it all was bad. This dinner. His opening his foolish mouth. The failure of military discipline. And he let that faerie condescension get under his skin. It was in Telridge's interest, and therefore his, to remain at peace with the faerie kingdoms. He didn't care about that, though.

As far as Dirk was concerned, sunrise couldn't come soon enough.

Chapter 14

Spense remained along the far wall of the great hall. His arms had grown slack at his sides. What his brother had said and done—if it weren't so disastrous, he'd be touched.

Lord Ferrous kept his seat at the head of the long table. His expression was closed, but not angry. He made no move to correct Dirk's outburst nor to placate the Winter faeries.

Which meant…the faeries were leaving.

The letter!

Spense blinked. His fingers twitched as his eyes followed the retreating faeries. He had to get the letter to Misty—if she'd still deliver it—before they were gone.

Spense read and re-read Dewy's words. He spent the last hours before the dinner—when he should've been getting cleaned and dressed—stewing over his response.

There wasn't anything poetic in his missive. He wrote that he missed her. He wouldn't give up until she was free. That sort of thing. He spent several long minutes fretting over how to sign it. Everything seemed too formal, too titled. It wasn't how they were together. In end, he went with honesty and wrote "with love," followed by his name.

He found the spell to seal it in an old book. It was

relatively simple. But powerful enough that no one but Dewy could open it.

But how was he going to get it to her if the Winter faeries all left in a rush? Dirk had picked a really inconvenient time to become brotherly.

Spense held a frantic breath as the Winter faeries filed out, and the hush of the Telridge court gave way to frantic whispers. It didn't take long. As soon as Dirk and his closest Knights, Sir Gervais and Lady Xendra, made their brisk departure, wide-eyed courtiers started their gossiping. He didn't think any of them had ever seen Dirk lose his cool demeanor. That he'd done so in defense of Spense—this display would provide juicy material for weeks.

But before the many courtiers could turn their attention to him, Spense slipped out a side entrance. He followed behind the Winter faeries, as they made haste back to their encampment.

He didn't know why he assumed he could walk right in after what happened at dinner—maybe because he'd been running back and forth all day with no interference—but this time he was stopped. Abruptly.

His legs went out from under him and before he could find his feet, the cool blade of Tun's hawthorn dagger pushed against his throat with enough pressure he dared not swallow. It didn't draw blood, provided that Spense remain very still.

"Oh. It's you," the goblin said.

Spense's eyes grew wide, as he attempted to acknowledge Tun's words, without using the usual signs of agreement, like nodding or speaking.

"Trying to break into our camp? Thought you could pull off one more insult against my Fae lords?"

Spense twitched his head in the smallest possible side-to-side motion, more a shiver than a shake of the head.

Tun sniffed. "Humans." He pulled his blade back a finger's width. "Explain yourself."

Spense took a deep breath, making sure he maintained eye contact with Tun. "I came to see Misty—"

The goblin's eyes narrowed.

"I mean, Lady Mist. I have a letter for her." Spense reached inside his coat, and Tun was again on top of him, straddling his chest, and pinning his arm to the ground with his knee. "It's in my pocket," Spense all but squealed.

"How do I know you're not going for a weapon? Or something magical? I remember the battles from last summer. You humans are full of tricks."

"No weapon. Or any tricks, I swear. Just a letter." Spense raised his free hand, palm open.

"A letter?"

"I swear." Spense grunted. Tun's knee had cut off circulation to his pocket hand.

"Let me see it."

"All right. Sure."

Tun leaned closer. His bulbous nose was only a hands-breadth away from Spense's. "Slowly," Tun whispered, his breath full of oil and garlic. He released the pressure on his wrist.

Spense's hand throbbed as blood rushed back in. He felt for the letter in his pocket and ever-so-slowly withdrew it. "See? Just a letter."

Tun tilted his head and scowled.

"Leave him alone, Tun, he's not a threat."

Spense glanced to his side at the blessed sound of a new voice. Misty emerged from the shadows and towered over where he and Tun lay sprawled in the orchards.

"No?" Tun asked.

"No."

"Sure?"

Misty rolled her eyes. "Will you get off him, please?"

"Fine, fine."

Spense pushed himself into a seated position as the goblin rolled away. Tun tucked his dagger into his belt and folded his arms over his chest.

"That's enough, Tun. Run along. I can handle this."

Tun frowned and muttered. But he gave in to his lady's command and stalked off toward the collection of faerie-made structures.

"For all of your people's familial bravado, their attention to your security is truly abysmal." Misty nodded to the letter Spense held before him. "That what I think it is?"

"Yes, Lady Mist. If you'll still take it." He ignored her other assessment. It wasn't worth explaining.

Misty reached out a hand and yanked Spense to his feet. "It's not like I have a choice, remember? Bargain?"

"Thank you," he said brushing off his trousers. "No, of course, you wouldn't break a bargain. I just wasn't sure, after what happened…"

Misty snorted. "Oh, don't worry. I'm plenty pissed about what went down." She jerked her head back toward the castle. "But it's not your fault."

"Again, thank you, lady."

She took a step toward him and poked his chest. "Your beloved brother is a right prat, though."

Spense didn't have a response. He'd witnessed Dirk's more colorful nature. And now the whole of Telridge—as well as the Winter ambassadors—had, too.

She sighed. "But it's not like Frost was any better. He can be...prickly. I don't blame your brother for taking offense. And Frost did provoke him. Honestly, it's impressive that Prince Dirk didn't snap sooner."

Spense bit back a laugh. "I'm sorry that it went so badly."

Misty rolled her eyes. "Maybe it was bound to. Maybe we're not ready—our people—to see each other as anything more than 'other,' you know?"

"I hope that's not true—at least not forever."

"You're sweet, Spense. No wonder Dewy likes you."

Relief flooded through Spense's limbs, the aftereffects of his tussle with Tun, perhaps. Or something else. Something about Misty. He knew she was dangerous. He'd seen it firsthand. And yet, his heart told him she had layers. There was an honesty and genuine intention beneath the silver-smooth persona.

"By sweet, you mean naïve, right? Too idealistic?"

She shrugged. "Maybe."

"You're not the first to say that." Over the past few months, it had been suggested to him by nearly every member of his family that he was obsessing over a lost cause, that humans and faeries weren't supposed to mix. There were good reasons that they'd lived separately for so long.

But that didn't make sense to him. It felt like the distance was causing more problems. It left too many holes in their understanding of one another. If this visit was any indication, he was right.

And letting Dewy go because she was supposedly with her own people, that wasn't something he could do. She wasn't with her people. Being a faerie didn't make them the same. The spell he'd cast upon Dewy was gone, but the claim on his heart wasn't something that would go away. Their differences didn't matter, not really, not for them. And if they got past them, it felt like their people should be able to as well.

Also, Misty was right. The things she said before it all fell apart. The threats to the Winter lands would affect everyone. How could they not? Maybe the dinner had gone badly. Things were said. And shouted. But the problem remained. The Heir was still missing, and the Winter lands were growing unstable. They needed help.

"But I won't give up, even if I'm being idealistic. I want to help you find the Heir."

Misty narrowed her ice-blue eyes and cocked her head. "Why?"

"Because it's like you said, this affects us all. If your people and your lands suffer, so will ours."

"I'm afraid I wasn't able to make that case tonight."

"Maybe not to all, but I heard you."

"Thank you." Misty smiled. It seemed genuine. "You know, if people like you and Dewy were in charge, our world might be a different place."

Spense ducked his head in a nod. What a thought.

"So, you've got a letter for me, Master Spense?"

"Yes, that, I do." He handed Misty his letter for

Dewy. "Keep it safe."

"I promise."

Spense met Misty's clear, blue gaze. His once-abductor had shown she wasn't what he'd first thought her to be. Like him, like Dirk, she wanted peace for her people and she was willing to fight for it. In any way she had to. Patrolling her own lands and capturing trespassers or traveling into human territory knowing her kind wouldn't be received well, these were all part of the responsibilities she embraced to serve her people.

And when she made a promise, Spense believed her.

Chapter 15

"So, that went well."

Dirk folded his arms over his chest and frowned. "Sarcasm doesn't become you, Father."

They both peered out the window of his father's study as the Winter ambassadors made their way from their kingdom. Before the sun crested the White Rock Mountains, the faeries had struck camp and loaded their wagons. The first rays of dawn shone down on the group as they kicked Telridge's dust from their feet.

Ferrous quirked an eyebrow. "You're allowed to lose all sense of decorum, but I'm not allowed one witty comment?"

"It wasn't that witty," Dirk grumbled.

"No, I suppose not."

"And, again, I'm sorry." Dirk tucked his head close to his chest. He knew the shameful consequences of this debacle would linger.

"And I will say, again, you are forgiven. Not that there is much to forgive. That Fae emissary earned every insult."

Dirk raised his gaze. "But aren't we supposed to be above that? Haven't you trained me not to be provoked? You had no problem holding your tongue."

Ferrous clapped him on the shoulder. "I've had more practice." His father retreated from the window as the train of faeries snaked beyond easy visibility.

Dirk remained at his post. He wanted to be sure every last Fae lord, goblin, and common faerie were out of his country.

"Believe me, son, I was thinking every word you said."

Dirk closed his eyes and swallowed. He appreciated the understanding, but it didn't feel right. "I think Spense might be disappointed."

"Perhaps. Your brother has developed a unique perspective in regard to faerie-kind."

Dirk finally turned from the window. "That's my point exactly."

"How so?"

"If any of us has cause to despise faeries, it's Spense. He's received the worst treatment. But he defends them—both Summer and Winter—despite all that they've done."

Ferrous grunted a nonresponse.

Dirk crossed the room and collapsed into one of his father's leather chairs. He let his arms drape over the sides, dangling. His legs sprawled out. Sweet Spring, he was tired. He'd had little sleep overnight, and rose early, well before dawn, to meet his father.

As if their brooding had conjured him, Spense tapped the open office door and peeked his head around the frame.

"Oh, good. You're both here," Spense said.

"And there's my other progeny," Ferrous said, waving Spense in. "Coming to lecture us, boy? Dirk thinks you may not approve of our behavior."

"I, uh, no. Not exactly, my lord."

His father lifted one side of his mouth in a smile. He looked at Dirk. "Do you notice how he adds on the 'my lord' at the end, there?"

Dirk shook his head. He didn't know what to do with his father's nonchalance. It was a little too easy. Or perhaps, despite his words to the contrary, it was his father's way of coping with his extreme frustration. He should be furious. Dirk deserved anger. What was supposed to be a step toward lasting peace ended with greater tension.

Dirk turned his head to Spense. "Our esteemed father is punishing me through mockery. Would you mind, dear brother, yelling at me and putting me out of my misery? It would be the merciful thing to do."

"Uh…"

"Oh, yes, Spense, let's have it," Ferrous said.

Spense fidgeted. "I was going to tell you of my encounter with Lady Mist, but if you'd rather not hear it…"

Dirk sat up straighter.

"Pardon?" Ferrous asked.

"I followed her—them—after the dinner."

"Why would you do that?" Dirk asked. "Those faeries have magic, and more than a few of them are trained warriors, and in case you hadn't noticed they were well and truly pissed when they left the great hall."

"I know that, Dirk. Tun—the goblin—actually pulled a knife on me—"

"He what?"

Spense waved him off. "It was a misunderstanding. He was only protecting his lords. And anyway, Misty showed up and it was all fine."

"Misty?" Ferrous asked.

"Oh, sorry. Lady Mist."

"How is it fine that a goblin held you at knifepoint?" Dirk asked. He knew his voice had risen, but it wasn't Spense who deserved his anger. No member of his family should suffer these indignities. The Winter ambassadors should know that there could be repercussions, but they treated Spense as if he didn't matter, as if he was…illegitimate.

"He didn't hurt me, Dirk."

"You were saying something about Lady Mist?" Ferrous cut in before Dirk could object again.

"Yes. Right. So, she brought me a letter from Dewy and asked me to write one in return."

"When was this?"

"Yesterday. Afternoon, I guess. Before the dinner."

"She came to you?" Dirk asked.

Spense shrugged. "She found me in my laboratory."

"She was inside the keep?" If there was a magically gifted Fae casually wandering around the castle grounds, he would need to have a serious talk with his guards. It would involve loud cursing. And a particularly demeaning punishment.

"Yes, but you're missing the point."

"Please go on with your story, son. You said Lady Mist brought you a missive? Were you able to be sure it was from the Summer princess?" Ferrous said.

"Thank you, my lord. Yes. There was a spell to seal it. Only I could open it." Spense said. His cheeks and neck turned pink and blotchy.

Dirk wondered what in the letter caused Spense to react like that.

"Dewy made a bargain with Misty to get her to deliver the letter and get one from me in return."

"Another bargain? You'd think the girl would learn," Dirk muttered.

Ferrous shot him a sharp glare.

"I'd planned to give the letter to her during the dinner last night, only…"

"Only it was a diplomatic catastrophe, and everyone left early," Ferrous said.

"Well, yes."

Dirk rolled his eyes. This night would be talked of for years to come. Dirk's terrible blunder. How he, the oafish prince, chased off foreign dignitaries.

"But it wasn't. Not completely," Spense said.

"What do you mean, son?"

"I was able to talk to Misty. She wasn't too pleased by the outcome, either. I think she genuinely wants—needs—our help."

"Did she say as much?"

Spense nodded. He told them of their post-knifepoint chat in the orchards. It sounded as if Lady Mist was mortified by Frost's behavior, especially since it thwarted their cause.

"I don't think we should dismiss them so quickly, no matter how Frost acted."

"It was almost like he didn't want our help. Not really," Ferrous said. His brows dipped and his chin wrinkled into the familiar Ferrous Frown.

"You think?" Dirk asked, layering on the ire.

"I imagine it's hard for them to ask humans for help with anything," Spense said, ignoring Dirk's quip. "I mean, remember what happened before? When you wouldn't give aid to Lumine?"

"We remember," Dirk growled.

He'd lost soldiers. There were many who lived,

despite their injuries, but would never be soldiers again. Parts of the castle still needed repair, as well as the city and farms beyond the walls. All because his father had stubbornly refused King Lumine assistance, and Lumine had responded with violence.

"But I think Misty is different," Spense insisted. "And she understands how important this is, not just to Winter, but to all of us."

"So she said." Ferrous sat back in his deep, high-backed desk chair. His fingers formed a steeple under his chin. "And as much as I hate to admit it, she'd be right. If Winter falls—be it now or decades in the future—it would create a power vacuum that I imagine certain leaders might try to fill."

"Like Verden. Greedy bastards," Dirk said.

They were as much to blame for the wrongs committed against Telridge as their faerie collaborators.

"Perhaps them. Or others. And when such a thing occurs, there tends to be collateral damage, often in the form of human lives." Ferrous looked at Spense, scrutinizing. "You're right, Spense. We can't let that happen."

"No, my lord."

Ferrous sighed deeply. "You think you have a connection with Lady Mist, an in?"

"I think so, yes."

"Well, then, this whole thing may not have been the disaster we thought it was. It looks like your little brother salvaged something here and saved our collective backsides, Dirk."

Dirk shuttered his eyes. "You'd think I might start getting used to it."

Ferrous chortled. "Oh, you really would think that,

wouldn't you?"

Spense looked back and forth between his father and brother. "So, I'm going to the Oracles? To find the Winter Heir? You'll support me in it?"

Dirk couldn't interpret his father's expression, but the Ferrous Frown was well and truly present. At last, Ferrous spoke.

"I suppose we must."

Chapter 16

As soon as Dewy arrived in the kitchens, Cook greeted her with wide, open arms.

"Ah, there's the dear girl. Lady Dew Drop. We wondered when we'd get a glimpse of the Summer royal out and about. Haven't seen you much since you first arrived."

Dewy tried to smile. It was true. She'd kept her distance. Not because of Cook, herself. The woman's red-cheeked warmth and girth filled the space of the busy kitchen and drew in everyone within her reach.

But she couldn't stomach the food preparations. It'd been bad enough in the company of humans when they'd once served venison in her presence. She'd run from the Telridge Commander's table, gagging, and hid in the camp stables until Spense found her. After that, he was careful to only partake of fare she also ate.

But when Dewy arrived in Winter, she realized her preferences weren't a trait of the faeries, as she always assumed, but a cultural particularity of the Summer folk. The one time she'd stumbled into Cook's domain—the kitchens of the Silver Horn—it had been on a Hunt Day. Piles of dead, dripping animal flesh lay upon the counters as a team of faeries chopped, carved, and pounded.

She'd become dizzy and light-headed at the grotesque sight. A quick catch from one of Cook's assistants kept her from crashing to the floor as she swayed. Cook had fretted and fussed over her until she'd been delivered back to her room with a mug full of hot, mulled wine.

Dewy hadn't been back to the kitchens since. After that, the servants attending her had noted her gastronomic preferences, even if they'd done so with a *tsk* or a frown.

"Come down for a bite, didja? Lord knows you'll waste away if all you eat are fruits, nuts, and tea. Sit down and I'll get you something proper."

"No, no, thank you." Dewy waved away Cook's offer, swallowing down bile and the memory of her last encounter. She didn't have the heart to tell the kind woman how much her carefully crafted meals repulsed her. "I'm just here to meet Siskin."

"Are you sure I can't get you something while you wait? Maybe a bowl of hearty stew to stick to those skinny ribs of yours?"

Dewy shook her head.

The cook frowned. "Well, if you're sure. You can sit on that stool by the ovens while you wait. You must be freezing your little Summer…ahem. You must be cold, here in Winter."

Dewy pressed her lips to avoid smiling at the faerie's quick correction. She had a feeling Cook didn't hold back around other visitors.

The woman returned to a large wood worktable, where she scooped a round ball of raw dough from a bowl. She sprinkled the table with a generous dusting of ground-up wheat heads—something she inexplicably called "flower"—and threw the dough on top.

Bread. Cook was making bread.

It was the one human invention she acknowledged as an improvement upon the gifts of nature. The sweet, rich smell of baking bread reminded her so much of Spense and his mother. It was the smell of safety. And she rested, warm by the fire while Cook beat and rolled and worked the dough.

"Lady Dew Drop. You're here. Forgive my delay." Siskin rushed into the kitchens from the back door, stamping his snow-covered boots in the alcove.

Dewy waved away his apologies. "No need. Cook has been keeping me company."

"And I'm happy to do so, lass," Cook said as she continued to pummel the dough. "You're always welcome in my kitchens."

Dewy nodded her thanks.

"Shall we, Lady Dew Drop?" Siskin asked.

"Where are you taking the young princess, Siskin?" Cook asked.

Siskin hesitated.

Cook narrowed her eyes. "I hope it's nowhere the king wouldn't approve. I know he gave the girl leave to wander the grounds, but he also told us to watch out for her. I intend to keep my word. I hope you do, too. Out with it. Where're you off to?"

Siskin sighed. "Calm yourself, dear Cook. I'm taking the lady to see Cinna."

"Well, why didn't you say so right off? There's nothing sly 'bout that. You had me worried there for a minute, you did."

Dewy glanced between Siskin and Cook, sure she was missing something in their exchange.

"Better make sure she's dressed for it. And here, let's get you a tumbler of something hot for the journey.

It'll just take a minute." Cook abandoned her bread-making to search for a tall mug. She ladled a scoop of hot cider from a kettle simmering on the great brick stove. "Here you are, dear."

The clay mug immediately warmed Dewy's perpetually chilled fingers.

"Are we going far?" she asked.

"No, not too far. And I've made it shorter for you. Come see."

She followed Siskin through the alcove, past the back door, and into the snow. It banked in piles around the kitchen yard. She hadn't set foot outdoors since she'd arrived. "Are you sure I'm allowed to…leave?"

"Oh, we're not going off-grounds, but it's a bit of a trek, so I made some arrangements."

He gestured to a covered sleigh. Hitched to it were two pale grey stags, almost silver in the soft white light. They both had majestic antlers, and diamond-white crowns upon their heads.

Siskin offered Dewy a hand and helped her settle into the sleigh, with the added benefit of a thick, fleecy blanket. That, combined with the steaming cider, served to keep the chill at bay. Mostly. She worried about the creatures who'd sacrificed their coat for her comfort, and sent a silent thanks to them, hoping they were not presently shivering in a barn.

Siskin settled himself beside her and picked up the reins, though he hardly needed to. A quick whisper to the stags and they were off, circling the Silver Horn. She hadn't appreciated the great structure of the Horn when she'd arrived all those months ago, focusing more on how to break into it, than its architectural artistry. Like so many faerie constructs, it grew naturally out of the cliff side, bending and blending with the mountaintop forest surrounding it. Siskin soon led them away into the spiny trees, along a well-maintained track. They wove up and up and up.

Tall evergreens bowed over them as they climbed, growing thinner, with more space in between. It felt as if the light was slowly growing brighter with every surge forward. The wind whispered small gusts through the branches, and errant snowflakes landed on Dewy's cheeks and nose. She greeted each tiny frozen drop, drawing them in, and then releasing them back into the world, to the winter-starved pines and fir trees surrounding her. It'd been so long since she'd used her water gifts. But returning to them felt like a homecoming, small and familiar.

As they approached the tree line, the stags pulled the sleigh to a gentle halt in front of a timbered cabin. The runners shushed softly as they dragged across the snow. As quiet as their arrival was, it alerted the occupant of the cabin, and a rounded, wood door cracked open. By the time Dewy and Siskin stepped down from the sleigh, a petite woman had emerged.

She was wrapped in wool and fleece, and she wore thick boots. Her skin was weathered and wrinkled like a pecan. Snowy white hair crowned her head, not unlike the stags' antlers. Given faeries' long lifespans, to appear old, this faerie must be ancient, indeed.

"Siskin, I see you've brought a guest from our neighbor court," the woman said. Her voice was warm and rough. She delivered her words slow and easy.

"Yes, Grandmum. Shall I introduce her, or should I just assume you already know who she is?"

There was a lightness in Siskin's speech Dewy

hadn't heard before. A teasing.

"Grandmum?" Dewy asked.

"Well, it's easier than trying to count all the greats." Cinna stepped toward them, and rolled her hand to Siskin, beckoning him. "Might as well get through the formalities." She looked at Dewy and winked. "Mustn't deprive him of this part."

Siskin cleared his throat. "Cinna, let me present Lady Dew Drop of the Summer Court, Crown Princess and Heir, and…current guest of King Lumine." He turned to Dewy. "Lady Dew Drop, this is the Wise Woman of the Winter Court, the wizard, Cinnamon."

"And don't we just sound so exalted when he puts it like that?" Cinna whispered to Dewy. "Come in, dear. You must be chilled to the bone."

"Thank you, Lady Cinnamon," Dewy said.

"Cinna is fine. Not a lady, and the other titles are just pretension on the part of that boy king down the road." Cinna ushered Dewy past the threshold. "Come in, come in. Warm yourself. And, Siskin, take our noble friends around to the barn. You'll find some oats for them there."

Dewy stepped into the round cottage and experienced a momentary flash of memory. The interior of the cabin was so familiar: the steps down into the room, the stone kitchen that bubbled off the main part of the house, and the way that the wood furniture was all molded and shaped. Nothing had been sawn or hammered together.

"What is it, dear? You look as if a winter freeze has come upon you."

Dewy blinked. "Your cabin…it feels as if I've been here before." She shook her head. "Of course, that's impossible."

Cinna squinted at her as she seated herself in a well-loved chair by the open fire. She gestured for Dewy to take the opposite seat.

"Siskin called you a 'wizard.' I thought only humans used that term."

Cinna sighed. "Ah, youth. Never learn your history."

"I'm sorry?"

"Wizard comes from two words, 'wise' and 'art.' I think the humans actually prefer the term 'seer' these days. I suppose that's their prerogative. It is mostly they who practice the Sight. But faerie-kind would do well to remember that it wasn't always the case."

"What do you mean?"

"You probably think that elemental magic belongs to the faeries and Sight to the humans, except for the few mages who dabble in spell work."

Dewy nodded, though she knew one obvious exception to that. Spense was a human who had strengths in two elements, after all.

"In my youth—back when I was still called Cinnamon, if you can believe that an old lady like me could have ever been called such a sweet and silly name—there was no such distinction. Humans and faeries learned from each other. Both practicing elemental magic and seeing. Blending them together, even."

Dewy frowned as she tried to imagine it and couldn't. How would a thing be done? And to what purpose?

"But that was before the wars," Cinna continued. "Before everything was divided up. Winter, Summer.

Light, Dark. Human and faerie. Now, we like everything in its nice, neat boxes."

If Cinna was old enough to remember the wars... ancient was an understatement.

"Take my darling boy Siskin, for example," she said. "His mother had a touch of the Sight, but chose to lean into her element, air. Which is all well and good. We need storms to bring rains and wind to release the cones, so that our forests can regenerate, but she could've been more, if she chose it. And Siskin is the same way."

Dewy smiled. "How so?"

Cinna scoffed. "He chose academic magic and service to the Crown, when he might've stayed out here in the forest with me and learned the ways of the wild."

"And I consider that service an honor, Grandmum," Siskin said as he came through the door, knocking snow from his feet.

"Och," she said.

Dewy laughed. She wondered what it would be like to grow up with teasing grandparents. Her own grandmother was gone years before she'd been born and her grandfather, the king of Summer, chose passing shortly after the tragic deaths of her parents. He'd lived only long enough to bless Dewy as his Heir and her aunt as Regent until Dewy came of age. When she was small, she'd had an abundance of family: both parents, a kindly grandfather, and her mischievous and affectionate Aunt Ollie—Lady Olive Branch to most. But when her parents died, followed by her grandfather, and Ollie became Lady Radiant, she'd morphed into someone else, someone unrecognizable from the fun-loving aunt she'd been before.

Dewy's initial laugh turned into something wistful as Siskin placed a reverent kiss on his great-many-grandmother's forehead.

"So, shall we get to it? Your reason for this visit? In truth, I'm surprised Lumine allowed you to bring her up. Considering that I'm such a bad influence."

Siskin hedged. "He doesn't technically know."

"Wicked Winter, boy. Aren't you the rebel!" Cinna chortled.

Siskin shrugged. "It seemed like…you might have more answers for her than what she's finding in the library."

Cinna's eyes twinkled. "Oh, the boy admits that academic learning has limits! This gets better and better."

"I've always valued your gifts, Grandmum."

"Or you're desperate."

"Do you know about the task Lumine has required of me?" Dewy asked.

The old faerie's eyes sparked. "Of you?" she asked pointedly.

Dewy wobbled her head. "Of…a friend."

"But which you took on."

"Yes." Dewy raised her chin and held the woman's all-seeing gaze.

There were many who would judge her actions harshly. To defend a human. To take on his burden. For many, it would be unthinkable. For her, there wasn't a choice.

She could help.

She could save him.

So she did.

"Put your hackles down, dear. I know all about

your story, and I don't judge you for it. Quite the opposite." Cinna reached out a wrinkled hand and laid it on top of Dewy's. Her fingers were warm, the skin softer than Dewy would've expected. "To sacrifice for the sake of another is a beautiful thing. You call your human a friend. I think we can all see he is more than that."

Dewy tucked her chin to her chest. She knew many who would judge her for that, too.

"So, let's talk about how we can get you two back in the same place, shall we?"

"Thank you," Dewy murmured.

"No thanks needed. If we can help you find the Heir, you'll save us all."

"Do you have any thoughts where I should be looking, or how?"

"I might."

"Do you think my magic could be useful? Lumine said something about my water magic having more depth…but it didn't make much sense to me."

"Lumine remembers the old ways." She nodded. "It's nice to know. Just when I thought the whole world had moved past."

"What do you think he meant?" Dewy leaned forward, squeezing Cinna's hand, eager to hear her take on Lumine's cryptic assessment.

The old woman squeezed back. "I think…that your hands are freezing." She turned to Siskin. "I've got some soup simmering on the stove. Get a bowl for Dewy, won't you dear?"

Dewy tried to protest and withdraw her hands, but Cinna held tight.

"Don't worry. It's a vegetable stew, mostly roots.

Nothing to offend your delicate Summer sensibilities.

Dewy relaxed.

"There's something in your magic. Lumine can sense it. Something he doesn't have. But hear me, now." Cinna leaned forward, her eyes imploring, searching, as if she could see into Dewy's core with her fierce gaze. "If your body isn't strong enough, you won't be able to reach the root of that magic, and you won't be able to find the Heir."

Cinna released Dewy's hands as Siskin returned with a bowl and spoon.

"Eat up, girl. We've got a lot to do. And you'll need to find that strength."

Dewy eyed the old woman warily, but she did as commanded and took a bite.

Chapter 17

Dirk spent the rest of his morning in the stables, brushing Lightning Storm's mane and tail, picking out his hooves, and even cleaning his stall. Storm was patient with his ministrations, as if he knew the mood his owner was in and didn't want to be another source of frustration.

Because Dirk was frustrated. He hated how he'd behaved. He hated that it was up to Spense—again—to find a solution. He hated this whole thing. How had it become the responsibility of the blooming world to rescue King Lumine from his own folly? He tossed the brush into a nearby pail. It made a satisfying clanging.

"Sounds like your day is going well, my lord."

Dirk looked up. Flora led two mares into the stables. Her cheeks were flushed and honey-brown hair windswept. Both horses had a light glisten to their coats.

"Did you have a nice ride?" he asked.

She breathed deeply. "Yes, I did. Thank you. And so did my girls." She patted each of the horses' necks as she walked them to their individual stalls. "Thought I'd get them out for a bit while the weather was clear. Too much time locked up in the stables. They tend to get a little antsy."

He smirked. "I know how they feel."

"Hmmm…"

Dirk rolled his eyes. "Don't tell me you heard about my theatrics with the Winter faeries?"

"Actually…" Flora cringed. "I was there."

Dirk frowned. "You were? I didn't see you."

"Well, I wasn't there as a courtier." Her laughter was clear and warm. "Cait asked for help with the preparations. Any of us who could be spared. I volunteered."

Of course, she volunteered. That's who she was. When Telridge had been at war, she'd jumped in then, too. She wasn't a soldier or a Knight, but there'd been no hesitation. Her whole family was the same, offering their farm as a rendezvous point in the forest. And it had cost them. At least one barn was destroyed completely, and a number of the livestock were never recovered.

For him personally, her actions had saved his life. By fighting beside him, providing cover fire, and tending to his wounds afterward.

And these many months since, he'd barely spoken to her. Dirk winced. "So, you saw?"

"I saw." Flora nodded.

Somehow it was worse. He really didn't care that a roomful of gossiping nobility had seen him lose it, though there'd be a price to pay there. But he cared what Flora thought of him. Those weeks when they'd lived and planned and fought together, she'd seen something in him, something more than his reputation as a military commander. When he was near her, he wanted to be that person, too. More.

But when they'd returned to the castle and peace had been declared, tenuous though it may be, life had slid back to normal. Or whatever normal they could find after the bloodshed and loss.

Only he'd been different. Restless. As if he were trying to squeeze a new version of himself into an old box, and he didn't fit anymore. Maybe he'd been avoiding her because she reminded him of that difference. And the more he was reminded, the smaller that box became.

She reached over into Storm's stall and retrieved the brush. "So, what's all the kerfuffle about, anyway?" Flora asked as she rubbed down one of the mares.

"Kerfuffle?" he asked.

She grinned. Her smile was wide and bright. "Yeah, you know. Hullaballoo. Uproar. Why is everyone so worked up? The way I saw it, that Fae, Lord Frost, found every single chink in your armor, and then he went after Master Spense!" Flora paused in the rubdown and pointed the brush at him.

"That he did."

"Why were the faeries here, anyway? They wanted our help? Interesting way to ask for it."

He laughed. It was dry. Humorless. "You're not wrong. But…you don't know the tale?"

She shrugged. "Something about the Winter Heir. I know Spense has been working on it for months. But it doesn't seem to be going well."

It rankled that she'd had enough contact with Spense to keep up with his progress. Even with how busy and preoccupied Spense had been, he'd still found time to visit with Flora. It made his own absence all the more obvious.

"And if all of this is going to get us involved in another war, then I'd rather be prepared."

"We're trying to avoid that," Dirk said.

"Right. Avoidance of war. That's exactly what I saw last night."

He leaned over the stall. "You want to hear this or not?"

"Apologies, my lord. Please continue."

Dirk looked at her sideways. Why was it that whenever Flora invoked his title or addressed him as the royalty he was, he felt like she was teasing him? He smiled. He didn't actually mind.

"So the way I understand it, Lumine made a big mistake years and years ago when he decided that his daughter's chosen love wasn't good enough for the Winter Court."

"Lumine's daughter fell in love with a common faerie?"

"Not just common. Part human."

Flora's eyes grew wide. "Lumine didn't like it."

"Not at all. When he realized what'd been going on, he went into a rage. The results were catastrophic for everyone. The mixed-blood faerie was kicked out, along with the newborn grandchild."

"He exiled his own grandchild?"

"You saw how snooty those Winter faeries were around us? Imagine finding out that your own royal line had been combined with human blood?"

Flora bit her lips, full and pink from the cold.

Dirk cleared his throat and continued. "So, the daughter, Princess Snow, was so heartbroken that she refused all other suitors. She was the Heir, so she was stuck in Winter while her lost love and child were elsewhere. Eventually, she chose passing instead of living in a world without them. From what Spense has told me, the part-human lover died in exile not too long ago, and when the princess got word, she shocked everyone—including Lumine—and ended it."

"What? That's horrible. So sad."

"Well, not as bad as you think. It's a faerie thing, I guess. They live these really, really long lives, and when they decide that their time has come, they pass on to the next life. Only Princess Snow chose to go without naming an Heir. It was her last chance to stick it to her old man, I guess. Because he had chosen her, only she could name the next Heir or—and here's the fun loophole—someone in her direct line."

"Her child."

"Yep."

"Lumine didn't see that coming?"

"Like I said, faeries can live really long lives."

"And hold extra-long grudges?"

"Exactly."

"And that's what started all of this?" Flora sniffed. "The Winter Court's family drama, and we end up with the consequences? We had to go to war? I don't get it."

"Old Lumine seems to think that Telridge is harboring his Heir."

"The grandchild he tossed out?"

"Yeah."

She blew a raspberry-like sound. It was unladylike. None of the women at court would do such a thing. Almost horsey. It was perfect.

"Seems to me, he got what he deserved."

"You're not the only one to see it that way."

"But…" She lifted an eyebrow.

"But, if the Winter King cannot identify the Heir through Princess Snow's bloodline, his lands will fail. Become feral and wild. From what Spense has reported, it's started already."

"That doesn't sound good."

"Not good at all."

She sighed. "So, I guess we have to help them."

"We?"

She blushed. It was charming and distracting. "I mean…you, royal leader-types." She waved at him with both hands.

Dirk smiled ruefully. "You saw how well I did that yesterday."

"That was one day. It's not like you make a habit of yelling at people."

"Don't I? That's kind of my job."

She conceded. "Your job is to command Telridge's army, and be Telridge's Crown Prince, a warrior of honor we all look up to, someone we can be proud of."

Sweet Spring. It almost sounded noble when she said it. The role. The responsibility. Something he should want to aspire to and be honored to have that privilege. There was a weight to her words, her expectations. But also an empathy, like she knew exactly what Telridge asked of him, what she, herself, asked of him.

"Sometimes, I tire of being thought of as the warrior brute." He remembered the conversations they'd had, how she'd seen him, all of him.

Flora met his gaze. He could feel her silent offer to bear that weight, too, if he asked it of her. He let the silence stretch. When the quiet had gone on too long, grown too heavy, she took a breath and broke it. He didn't know if he was disappointed or relieved.

"Perhaps you shouldn't yell at Fae ambassadors, then."

Flora's delivery was deadpan, but there was a warmth in her eyes, a spark. He waited for another moment, just looking.

And then he burst out laughing. Her mouth started to twitch. And she lost whatever control she had. Soon he was shaking. Tears escaped from his eyes. And Flora laughed along with him. Egging him on.

"Did you see how Frost tilted his nose so high? I thought he was trying to smell the ceiling!"

"Remember how all the courtiers were staring with their mouths wide open!"

"I know. I thought someone might fall in!"

"Probably one of those blue goblins."

"We'd have to send someone in to fish him out!"

They continued with more incredulous and ridiculous observations. Lamented over Spense and all the errands he'd had to run. They mocked the wide-eyed courtiers. Until their laughter started to fade, and their cheeks ached.

It was exactly what he needed. Dirk had to get over himself and this situation and get back to work. But he couldn't do that with his head and emotions all tied up in knots. Brooding and guilty. Maybe Flora knew that. Or maybe that's just who she was.

"Flora?

"Yeah?"

"Thank you."

"For what?" She tilted her head.

"For talking to me and for…being you."

"Anytime, my lord."

He knew she meant it.

Chapter 18

"You're in a hurry."

It wasn't a question. Or an accusation. A statement of fact, like so many of his mother's observations, in which Spense was often found wanting. He wasn't the only one. Many a kitchen hand withered under her commands and critiques.

It wasn't that she wasn't generous or kind. She was. There was never a moment when he hadn't felt the love of his mother. But he regularly felt her push to do better, be better, become more.

Because that's how Cait lived her own life, always striving for the next, greatest accomplishment. As if she had something to prove to the world. It was why the daughter of a nobody orchardist had risen to the rank of Head Cook.

Her creations were exquisite. Dignitaries from The Peaks to the Brecken Isles had marveled at the food presented to them. Which was why the rebuff from the Winter ambassadors stung. It had put her in a mood, the likes of which Spense had never seen before. Cait may be driven, but she was always calm, cool, moved with ease.

That calm had been disrupted by the Winter faeries.

It made Spense extra cautious and was why he hesitated before answering. "Ye-e-s-s."

"Off to see your father?" she asked.

He noted she didn't use Lord Ferrous's title.

"I am. And Dirk."

She nodded but didn't look up from her task. Shelling peas. A simple, tedious job any of the kitchen staff could've done.

"You've met with them both quite a lot recently."

"I have," Spense said.

He waited for something further. One of those observations. An assessment. But she pursed her lips and said nothing.

"I should get going…unless you need me here?"

"No."

"All right, then, so I'll be off…"

"Be well." She didn't meet his gaze. Kept focused on the great ceramic bowl of shiny green legumes.

Spense leaned in and kissed her cheek. "Take care, Mum."

"And you," she said.

Spense turned to glance back at her on his way out of the kitchen. *What was that?* He shook his head. He didn't have time to puzzle it out, as he was already rushing to his father's urgent summons. He could almost hear the words she wasn't saying. Disapproval, but why?

"Spense!" Dirk jogged along the corridor, catching him at the entrance to their father's study. His brother's cheeks were flushed, his breathing heavy.

"Where've you been? Why are you breathing so hard?"

Dirk planted his hands on his knees. "The stables." He panted. "There when I got the message. Ran. The whole way."

Spense squinted at his brother. He knew Dirk liked to care for his own horse, but from what Spense had heard and seen, he'd let others take over that responsibility lately, spending more time with his Knights on the training grounds…and in the tavern.

"Need a minute?"

Dirk waved him off, straightening up. "I'm good."

"All right." He knocked three times on the door.

"Enter," his father said.

Spense and Dirk exchanged a look. It was the Lord Ferrous voice. Gruff and commanding. He took a deep, steadying breath and opened the door.

This felt familiar. And strange. It was becoming habit for the two of them to enter this study together, discuss issues of national importance with Lord Ferrous. Planning and plotting for the future of the kingdom. It made sense for Dirk, but when had it become normal for Spense to be included, as if he weren't just the younger, barely acknowledged son, but almost as if…

Spense shook his head. He'd never be seen as a prince like Dirk. He was a useful instrument. A common tool. Nothing more.

"My lord." Spense hinged at the waist in a deep bow.

Dirk muttered the same and ducked his head.

"Come in, and be seated," Ferrous said.

"You've a plan, then?" Dirk asked.

"I've considered all we discussed."

"And?" Spense asked.

"There are things about this I don't like. Things you should be aware of."

He waited. This wasn't new information. But

Ferrous wouldn't have called them back in so soon, only to restate old news.

"But," Ferrous began again. "Allow me a father's prerogative to warn you. It may be a potential solution. It might not. The Oracles are not the easy path you're hoping for. They will test you. And you may still walk away with nothing."

Spense nodded. Also, not new information.

"But you're still letting Spense go?"

Ferrous pushed up from his desk with both hands. "Yes. Because it appears that I don't have a choice." He paced to the window and peered out, as if he could see the whole of Telridge. "Because the Winter faeries have gotten themselves into a bit of a mess, and us, right along with them, whether we like it or not. We can't pretend it will go away, that they'll solve their own problems. Not anymore." Ferrous turned to face them. "I should have seen that this problem was bigger than you wanting to save your faerie princess."

"How soon can I leave?"

Spense dared not breathe or move too quickly. His father had already given permission. This posturing and advice-giving was the last step. It was happening.

Ferrous sighed. "As soon as we assemble a team to accompany you."

A whole team? Spense opened his mouth to speak, but Ferrous held up a hand.

"Don't protest. I'm not letting you off on another adventure without an official guard. You almost didn't make it back the last time."

Spense closed his mouth.

"Have you any thoughts who you might want to bring with you? I would suggest at least one Knight,

110

preferably two."

"I'll go," Dirk spoke up, before Spense could say a word, before he could even consider his options.

"You?" Ferrous asked.

"Who else? I'm a skilled warrior. I know the countryside, and I can speak on behalf of the Crown."

Dirk's words were frank, simple, and pragmatic. But Spense found himself swallowing against a rise of emotion.

Ferrous nodded and turned to Spense. "Is that agreeable to you, Spense?"

"Of course, my lord."

"I'll talk to Sir Gervais and Lady Xendra. As you said, my lord, it would be good to have a Knight or two."

"Thank you," Spense said. "How soon can we go?"

"We can be ready to leave by dawn tomorrow." He turned to face Spense. "Does that suit you?"

Spense released a breath and nodded. "That would be…acceptable."

The Winter Oracle. A path and a purpose. It felt right. Maybe that wasn't much to go on, but it was enough.

Chapter 19

The door to the study shut with a firm click. His brother's light steps hurtled down the corridor, away from their father's study.

"You can wipe the smirk off your face," Ferrous said.

"I'm sorry, my lord?"

"Don't pretend this isn't exactly what you wanted."

"I'm sure I don't know what you mean." Dirk strained to remove as much inflection as possible.

"Please. You've been twitchy for months, since our renewed peace with Verden and the faerie folk."

Dirk scowled.

"You need this. I've been forcing you to attend balls and dine with courtiers and it's stifling you. If going off and saving the world will help you deal with whatever is eating at you, then, go. Do it. Telridge will be here when you get back."

"That's generous of you."

"Not hardly. I need you here. In command, and focused. If this is what it takes, then so be it."

"Have I failed in my duties to you, my lord?"

Dirk prepared for the rebuke. If he had areas where he needed correction, he'd hear them, even if he didn't like them. That's how it'd always been. Dirk braced his arms on his knees, directed his gaze to the intricately patterned rug covering the floor of the study, and waited for the lecture.

"No," his father said.

Dirk glanced up.

Instead of settling back into his deep chair behind his great desk—what Dirk had come to know as lecture position—Ferrous rose and walked to the far side of the study. "Apart from tavern-hopping, you've been all I could expect—all anyone could hope for—in Commander and Crown Prince. You serve Telridge well." Ferrous sighed heavily. "But I think it's killing you. You need this. And I think you and Spense need this."

"How so?"

Ferrous opened the doors of a cabinet and withdrew a wrapped object. "Not sure if you noticed, but you just scared the wits out of your younger brother."

Dirk laughed. "What?"

His father made his way back across the study, and settled into his chair, causing the old wood to creak. He laid the parcel on the desk. It was the length of his forearm and narrow. "I've watched you two for a long time. For years, you barely acknowledged him. Then, you tried to recruit him for soldier training—the sole purpose of which seemed to be so that you'd have the excuse to pound him into the ground on a regular basis. But in the past year, something has changed between you."

His father pulled the silk ties, folded back the rich fabric.

"Spense never broke. He didn't fear you when you ignored him, or when you broke his nose. Yes, I know about that. Respected you but didn't fear you. But what you just did, that terrified him."

"What did I do?"

"You treated him as an equal."

"I—" Dirk frowned.

It was true. Been coming on for a while. Maybe even before Spense cast that spell on the faerie. But he'd shown his true feelings when Frost had suggested Spense was lesser because he was bastard-born. It was horseshit, meant to provoke him, and it had worked. Dirk knew he was a lot of things. Whatever he said to the contrary, he disappointed his father with consistency. But he was also loyal to his family. That absolutely included Spense.

"I'd protect him with my life."

"I know," Ferrous said. "And if needed, you'll use this to do it."

Approval glinted in his father's eyes. A deep-seated understanding. As if, like Flora, he saw more than the trained warrior. He saw a man who knew when and how to brandish a blade and when not to—in the case of this blade, when to flash the seal engraved in the handle and when to use the pointy end.

Chapter 20

Dirk crossed the castle courtyard, hurrying to the gates. To the city and the Grey Goats Tavern, where else. Gerry and Xendra agreed to meet him, either to commiserate his failed attempt to sway his father, or to enlist them for his team. He picked up his pace, emboldened that it was the latter. He heard the boots of his honor guard clunking behind him as they quickened their steps.

His father had called the pair of soldiers to his study and ordered them not to let Dirk out of their sight, as if he could read his son's intentions. Dirk gave the guards a reprieve, slowing as he approached the stables.

A thought struck him. A wild, reckless thought.

"Just a moment, gentlemen. I need to check something."

The soldiers glanced at each other. The slightly senior of the two spoke up.

"I'm sorry, Lord Dirk. We were instructed not to let you enter any building unaccompanied."

"We're not even off castle grounds."

"I'm sorry, sir."

Dirk tapped the side of his leg. "Fine," he grumbled. It was only for this last night. In the morning, he'd be free of his off-grounds shadows. As he turned to the entrance, he said, "Just be discreet, all right?"

"Of course, my lord."

Dirk pushed his way in. He scanned the stalls. All the castle horses were housed for the evening. No late day rides. A couple of stable hands moved between stalls, checking equipment and cleaning. He was looking for one, in particular.

There. At the end. Gently whispering to a golden mare while she brushed her down. It wasn't a castle mount in that last stall, but Flora's own horse, Buttercup, whom she'd brought with her from her family's farm.

He stalked down the lane. His shadows, wisely, kept their distance.

"Careful, or you'll spoil that horse."

She turned. "Not possible, my lord. Only the very best for my girl."

He smiled. Flora's braid had loosened during the day so that soft hairs framed her face. She had a flush to her cheeks, a glisten of sweat along her brow, and bits of straw stuck to her hair and clothes.

"Was there something you needed, Lord Dirk?" Flora asked.

Dirk huffed a small laugh, realizing he hadn't responded to her first comment. "Yeah. Uh…"

She raised her brows.

He swallowed and nodded to the golden horse. "Any chance your girl could bear to part with you for a week or so?"

Flora's brows drew together. "Why? Has something happened?"

"Yes. No. Sort of."

She laughed. It was unforced. Easy.

"You'll have to explain that."

116

"I'm going away."

Flora frowned.

"With Spense," he quickly added. "It should be a short mission. I'll be asking a couple of people I trust to come along with us." Dirk paused. Here it was, his foolish idea. He didn't even know why he was asking, but he pushed on. "Would you come?"

"Me? Why?"

"Like I said, I need people I trust." Dirk shrugged. "I trust you."

It really was that simple. If he had other motives, they weren't something he wanted to take out and pick apart. But this made sense. Especially to any listening shadows who might be inclined to report to his father.

"I-I am honored that you'd think of me."

"And?

Her hands stilled on Buttercup. "When do you leave?"

"Tomorrow morning. Dawn."

Flora blinked. "Not much time to decide."

"I'm sorry, no."

She blew out a breath of air and looked at him sideways. "This is big. Important."

"The mission? Yes. And if you're asking if it's important that you come…" Dirk took a step forward, closing the gap between them. "I think my answer to that would be yes, also. I can't explain it, so don't ask me to."

Flora lifted her chin and met his gaze. "All right, then."

"Yes?"

"Yes."

Dirk grinned. "Care to meet the other recruits?"

"When?"

"I'm headed there now."

She shook her head, baffled and amused, but it wasn't a refusal. "Sure…why not?"

****

When Dirk arrived at the Grey Goats, followed by the two foot-soldiers and Flora walking at his side, Gerry and Xendra tried to cover their surprise. Tried, but failed. They were both well into their ale, lounging on tall stools by the long oak counter that served as the bar.

"How did it go, my lord?" Xendra asked.

Gerry nudged him. "Are we off on a grand adventure or stuck here mopping up your royal tears?"

"I'm afraid you'll have to sober up, my friend." Dirk clapped Gerry's shoulder. "We leave at dawn."

Gerry gulped. "Doesn't leave much time to pack, now does it?"

Xendra rolled her eyes. "Ignore him. He's been packed for days, just in case."

Gerry started to protest, but relented and took another swallow of his ale instead. "I might've," he grumbled.

"And Flora, good to see you. Am I to assume you've been drafted into this insanity?" Xendra asked.

Flora laughed, nodding. "It seems I have."

"Grace help you, girl," Gerry said.

Xendra smiled broadly. "Yes, well, I'm already thanking Grace we'll have someone sensible on the team."

Dirk shared their levity and smiled along with them. It was why he trusted Gerry and X implicitly. They got him. Knew his moods. They understood that he'd be celebrating tonight, so that he could focus come the morning.

For all the laughter and smiles, the days ahead would be long and tiring, and vitally important they succeed, especially after the Winter fiasco. It may have been Spense's crazy notion that got them started.

But Dirk tapped the dagger he now wore on his belt and committed himself to seeing it through.

Chapter 21

Dewy had declined every invitation to dine with Lumine since her imprisonment. She had no interest in his pretense that she was a guest, but mostly, she feared spending time with him. The encounter in the glassed-in gardens had left her chilled, as if his presence had tainted her with frost. It had also left her with questions she preferred not to examine too closely.

When she declared she would join the king and his court, it raised more than a few eyebrows, from Siskin, in particular.

"You accept the king's invitation?" he asked.

Dewy rolled her eyes. It was his second clarification. "Is there something unclear about my intentions?"

"Uh…no, Lady Dew Drop."

"Good. Can you please communicate that to your lord?"

"Of course, only…"

"Yes?" If it weren't so frustrating to repeat herself, it might've been amusing, making Siskin fidget.

"You've never accepted before. May I ask why you choose to do so now?"

Dewy sighed. A few months back, when she could scarcely distinguish one servant from the next, when they'd been an invisible and anonymous force, they'd also been quiet. But things had shifted between her and

Siskin since their visit to Cinna. She could no longer pretend he was a nameless, thoughtless minion, a piece of scenery in her prison she'd had no desire to know any more than the timbers that held up the walls. But they were people, full of feeling and heart.

Inevitably, she'd learned the names of other servants, as well. Marten, apparently a cousin, could have been Siskin's twin in looks and manner. He was usually the one to bring her books from the library. And the spritely Holly—also a relative—kept her in clean linens. There was a cabal of Cinna's distant relations working in the Silver Horn, though Siskin confessed that many more of the family chose a life in the forest or deep in the mountains.

The consequence of noticing her attendants was that Dewy also noticed subtle changes in their behavior. And today they were bustling. She had a good idea why.

"Because...Misty and Frost have returned from Telridge."

Siskin raised his eyebrows. "How did you know?"

Dewy quirked her own brow and smiled with one corner of her mouth. "You just told me."

Siskin's eyes shuttered. "So, I did. I'll let the king know of your intentions immediately. And Cook."

She thanked Siskin, and he promised to return to escort her to dinner.

****

When she entered the dining chamber, Dewy found a place had been set for her, marked with a crisp, white card, near to King Lumine at the head of the table. She'd sit across from Misty and Frost. Their names were written in a deep blue, filigreed script. It must've been Siskin's work. Surely the lord and lady knew their places at Lumine's table.

But the wayward ambassadors had not arrived yet. Nor had the king.

While she strolled the hall, awaiting her dining companions, a servant offered her a glass of ice wine. It was clear and sweet, and relieved her dry mouth. She reminded herself not to drink it too quickly. She intended to remain clear-eyed and focused during this dinner. Whenever it might actually begin.

Dewy circumnavigated the dining hall twice and was re-examining a tapestry woven with iridescent silver thread when voices rose from outside the doors. They were the shouted whispers of people who were trying to keep their voices down, but not succeeding. Dewy slid a couple of near-silent steps closer to the door.

"I don't want your excuses, Frost," Lumine hissed. "You had one simple requirement, and you have failed."

"Can we save the bickering until after we eat, Uncle? I'm starving."

A moment later, Misty strode through the open doorway and into the dining hall. She caught sight of Dewy. "Oh. You're here, huh?"

The urgent whispers halted immediately. Lumine glided through the door, followed by Frost. His steps were confident and sure, but there was something about him that felt subdued, less haughty than usual. His regular attendant, Rime, shadowed him as usual. The faerie blanched when he caught sight of her, but quickly recovered. Dewy's chest tightened as she remembered the servant had lost his mate in the battle at Telridge

Castle.

"Lady Dew Drop." Lumine spoke in cool, practiced tones. "It is lovely to have you as our guest this evening."

"Thank you." She nodded to the sibling pair. "I suppose I should welcome you home, Lady Mist. Lord Frost."

Frost scowled and ignored her, turning to find his seat. Rime drifted to the shadows. But Misty indulged a small smile.

"It's nice to see you, Dewy. At least someone is happy we've returned."

Lumine's mouth flattened into a thin line. He said nothing to acknowledge his niece's words.

"Please be seated, Lady Dew Drop." Lumine gestured to the place setting with her name scrolled on it. "I apologize if we're not in the most hospitable of dispositions."

Dewy walked slowly to the table. "Is something amiss?"

Lumine smiled politely, but his eyes remained cold, guarded. "Nothing to trouble you with, of course. Truly. Nothing has changed that would have any effect upon you."

Dewy frowned. She was not as skilled at the language of court. Lumine alluded to something, but she had no idea what. She guessed that the barbs hidden in his words were directed to someone else in the room. Most likely, Frost, who sat mute and brooding before his empty plate.

"I understand you ventured outside of these walls recently," Lumine said.

"Really? You finally left the Horn?" Misty asked.

"I didn't leave the grounds," Dewy said.

"There are a LOT of grounds. I'd be impressed if you did." Misty lifted her eyebrows. "Where'd you go?"

"The lady went to visit our Wise Woman, Cinnamon," Lumine offered before Dewy could reply.

"Cinna!" Misty raised her eyebrows. She leaned across the table. "And how did you find our benevolent witch?"

Dewy balked. "I thought she called herself a wizard."

"Witch, wizard, seer. It's all the same." Misty waved her hand.

Frost scoffed.

"Something to add, my dear brother?" Misty cocked her head.

"Nothing you don't already know, sister." Frost hissed at his sibling and then shifted his gaze to Dewy. "You should consider what Cinna says carefully. She's lived a long time—many would say too long—and it's not clear that she's completely sane."

"She seemed very coherent to me," Dewy replied.

Cinna had also been kind. Frost's words and bearing dripped with disdain.

"Please. Do you know she chooses to live out in the woods like that? She's been offered generous quarters here at the Silver Horn, and instead stays in that squatty cabin, like a forest-dwelling hermit."

"In the Summer lands, it is considered a privilege to dwell amongst living things," she said.

"Well, you're in Winter now, Lady Dew Drop. Best get used to some differences."

Frost turned his attention to the plate placed before

him. It was piled with red meat, still oozing its juices.

Dewy kept the bile down that rose in her throat as she turned her gaze to the meal presented to her. A bowl filled with a sweet, herbed celery broth and cut root vegetables. No sign of any dead creatures. She breathed a sigh of relief as she spooned her first bite.

The rest of the dinner continued in stilted silence. No word of Telridge. And from the scowl on Lumine's face, no room for questions. Dewy was more than thankful when she finished her soup and was able to excuse herself before the tension grew any thicker.

She'd hoped for a few brief words. Any news. But it seemed she would learn nothing this night. She'd forced herself through a dinner with Lumine and the perpetually frustrating combination of Frost and Misty. And for what? The royal trio offered terse silence, and very little more.

But she'd try again—corner Misty if she had to—and find what she was looking for.

Chapter 22

"So that was a surprise," Misty muttered, as the great oak door closed behind Dewy. The Summer Fae's quick footsteps pattered lightly as she retreated.

"The part where she spoke with us or where she actually ate something in our presence?" Frost asked. Her brother raised his eyebrows.

"That she was here at all." Misty picked up her wine and swirled it slowly. "I wonder why she came. She's never accepted your invitation before, Uncle."

Lumine released a heavy sigh. He'd been doing that a lot lately. "Because she wanted information."

"Information?" Frost asked.

"About your disastrous journey, of course. She wants to hear about her beloved human boy in Telridge. And I'm afraid we've been rather disappointing."

Frost frowned. "How much do you think she heard from the hall?"

"Nothing of import." Lumine smirked. "Perhaps my displeasure with you. Does that concern you? Do you seek the Summer princess's approval?"

"Hardly." Frost tilted his goblet and swallowed a mouthful.

"Perhaps you should," Lumine said.

"What do you mean?" Frost eyed Lumine warily.

"It is always better to create allies than enemies. You seem to have forgotten that recently."

"Forgive me, my lord, but can you really describe your own methods as those of an ally? Or her response? I lost an entire fighting unit to that witch-girl." Frost leaned forward. His eyes hardened as he trained them on his uncle.

Misty glanced to the shadowy corners of the hall, where Frost's attendant, Rime, stood stiffly in the corner, his hands clutched tightly around a pitcher of ice wine.

Lumine breathed in and out. He matched Frost's cold stare. "You're quite correct. My own attempts at diplomacy have been no more successful than yours. And I think we can all agree that aggression was the wrong choice, as well. I suppose that means we'll have to rely on magic."

"I thought you'd already tried..." Misty turned toward her uncle.

This was why they pursued Telridge so relentlessly. Lumine declared the blood of the Heir was in the kingdom. He said he'd known for months, but without being able to walk those grounds himself, there was little he could do to pinpoint the location. And it wasn't as if Misty's not-so-discreet movements throughout Telridge's castle keep and grounds had revealed anything either. No Lumine doppelgangers were conveniently walking around the city.

"I have tried," Lumine said. "My gifts are...limited."

Misty scowled, sure her uncle was holding something back. She wasn't so bold as to push further into the king's secrets, though.

The moment passed and his face cleared, tucking away whatever private thoughts he wasn't ready to share. "That is why we must look to someone whose magic is as yet untested."

"You can't mean that Summer princess?" Frost asked. He could take the simplest statement and turn it into an insult.

"Lady Dew Drop, yes," Lumine answered testily. "You've seen the workings of her power already, and she is nowhere near her full strength."

Misty considered this. Dewy had shown remarkable abilities. On the battlefield and in the Silver Horn, Lumine's own stronghold. And if her uncle thought she was still developing...Dewy would be a force if she ever were to channel the depths of her magic.

But there were costs. Deep magic required deep strength. Both physically and in the mind. Diving too deep had the potential to harm a faerie's very soul. Which is why most practitioners of magic—human or faerie—learned their limits and stayed within them.

"What if she refuses to develop her magic in that way?" Misty asked.

"That is why, Lady Mist, my darling niece, it is so important that we cultivate a friendly relationship with the girl. In fact, you already seem to be well on your way. I fully expect you to exploit that."

Misty frowned. She'd reached out to Dewy because she seemed to be in need of a friend, not because she was trying to manipulate her. Unlike many in Winter—including her brother—she held no ill will toward the princess for her part in the Telridge battle. There'd been losses on all sides. But she should've known that there could never be anything as simple as friendship between Fae.

"Haven't you already struck a bargain with her…something about a letter?"

"Wicked Winter, yes. I can't believe I forgot. May I take my leave, my lord?"

Lumine's eyes sparked. "I think you'd better."

Misty swallowed the last of her wine, tossed her linen onto the table, and lunged for the door.

She hurtled down the long corridor. Her fitted leather boots thudded unbecomingly on the flagstones. She reached Dewy just outside the girl's quarters.

"You're quick," Misty said.

Dewy's eyes were wide. "No more than most faeries, I think."

Misty shrugged while she caught her breath. "Well, aren't you going to invite me into your room, offer me some tea, maybe a 'welcome home' or something? It's common courtesy."

Dewy blanched. "You've never required an invitation before."

"No, I suppose that's true. So how about it?"

Dewy sighed. "Why not?"

In the short time Misty had been in the human lands, little had changed about the princess's quarters. Piles of books. Extra blankets. One of the Silver Horn's many stewards stoked the fire, adding another log to it. Apart from the hot houses, it was likely the warmest room in all of the Silver Horn. She immediately removed her overcoat.

"Siskin, would you mind bringing some tea? It seems I have a guest," Dewy said to the attendant.

"Of course, Lady Dew Drop. Right away." The servant—Siskin—bowed and left.

"You're learning our names, now? What we're

called, at least."

Dewy floated to her one chair and lowered herself into it. "Some of them."

She folded her hands in her lap, the picture of royal poise. It was so different from the reckless creature Dewy had been when she'd first arrived. But over the months, the princess retreated more and more into herself. More quiet. More still. More…like the Summer royals she was used to dealing with.

It was annoying.

And it was a big reason Misty spent so much time pestering the girl. Not because of any mercenary interests of her uncle, the king. She just liked her. And she wanted to see that spark again. But if it was still there, it was long buried under the façade of this increasingly pale girl.

Misty smirked. She had one trick up her sleeve to draw her out. Literally. She stalked to the neatly made bed, and flopped onto it, then kicked off her boots, and tucked her feet up underneath her. Dewy frowned but said nothing.

"You're not wondering why I'm here?" Misty asked.

Dewy waited.

"Wasn't there something you asked me to do…"

Dewy took a deep breath and let it slowly out of her nose. "Yes, but…"

"You doubted I would hold up my end of the bargain? That's disappointing. You do know how bargains work, right?"

Dewy tilted her head to the side and narrowed her eyes. "And did you…?"

"Fulfill my promise? As a matter of fact, I have."

Misty scrambled to her overcoat and reached into the hidden interior pocket of the wide sleeves. She withdrew the carefully folded letter and handed it over.

Dewy's hand shook slightly as the small weight of the parchment settled on her open palm. She puffed out a wobbly breath. A little color returned to her cheeks. *There it is. There's life in there after all.*

"You going to open it?"

"Now?" Dewy asked.

"Don't you want to confirm that it's from whom I say it is?"

Dewy frowned. "Is it sealed?"

"Oh, yes. He said that he sealed it the same way you had…so whatever you did, he figured it out. Smart boy, that Spense."

"I…" Dewy rolled her lips into a puckering line.

"Oh, I get it. You don't trust me. Fine. Fine." Misty held up her hands in mock surrender.

"I'm sorry."

"Why? I can't imagine I'd feel differently in your position." She tried to see what it might be like to be the prisoner-guest of the Summer Court, of Lady Radiant. Most likely, hot. "Don't worry about it."

Dewy nodded. Serenely. It was enough to drive a faerie mad.

"Want to hear some delightful gossip? I promise it's juicy." She wiggled her eyebrows.

"What? You would tell me…what exactly?"

"I would tell you what you were fishing for when you came to dinner." Misty leaned back on her hands, appreciating the comfort of the small bed.

At least Lumine treated Winter's guests well.

"And why would you do that?"

131

"Because one of these days, I would like us to be friends."

Dewy raised one eyebrow.

"Or at least better…allies." Misty amended. "Is that fair?"

"Yes, that's fair." The eyebrow settled.

"See? And isn't it nice to know that something in this wicked world is?"

Dewy nodded. "I suppose so."

"Good. I'm glad you see it that way. So let me tell you all about how my dear brother completely bungled his role as envoy, royally pissed off Crown Prince Dirk, and got us thrown out of a state dinner in our honor. And if you're extra nice, I will tell you about Spense and how he was…"

"Yes?"

"Actually, he's not a bad sort at all."

Dewy smiled. "I already knew that."

"I mean, not my taste. I'd go for one of the Knights. Lady Xendra is quite lovely. But to each their own." She shrugged.

"You were going to tell me about your visit."

"Fine, fine. Such impatience."

Misty grinned. And she told Dewy everything. Every ridiculous, awkward, cringe-worthy detail. If she wasn't mistaken that smile turned into a laugh. It was a good sound.

It was the sound of hope.

Chapter 23

The fire in the hearth burned down to coals. Misty retreated to her own quarters, leaving Dewy with her "tales of Telridge." No matter how much she coated the re-telling in mirth, Dewy read Misty's disappointment, the dip of her chin at the end of each story, the laugh that was cut off too soon. They'd been sent on a mission of alliance, of increased understanding, and failed spectacularly. And perhaps Frost had played a large part in that, but it wasn't all on him. Faeries and humans had chosen to live separately, had chosen to set themselves up for misunderstanding and offense.

But not all was lost. Dewy held the one success—the promise kept—in her hands. She'd clutched the letter all through "tea-time" with Misty, tucked in her lap, one hand resting upon it, reminding herself of its presence, reassuring her it was still there.

Her hands trembled as she raised the parchment to her lips, releasing the spell on the green wax seal. The folds opened like blossoms. In fact, tiny purple petals fell from the letter. Dewy seized a flower between her thumb and forefinger. She stared at it for a long moment and wiped a tear from her eye.

A pea-lily.

One of several. Spense had filled the letter with them.

It was inconsequential, a tiny thing, when she'd

plucked a wild pea-lily from the forest and tucked it in his overcoat. She didn't know he'd kept it or put any special importance upon it. But he did. And he wanted her to know.

It was so easy to start to forget, for the person of Spense to become an abstract memory.

But these pale purple flowers were a reminder that he was real. That they were real. There were memories they shared that had nothing to do with spells or bargains, or her heritage or his, but were just about them.

Dewy opened the letter and began to read.

****

She slid the parchment under her pillow in the morning. She'd read and re-read as if she'd conjure Spense from his words. She almost could. She remembered the youthful timbre in his voice, knew how he'd chuckle, and what words he'd emphasize.

Dewy, dearest princess of light and beauty, mischievous creature, and keeper of my heart...

With a renewed sense of purpose, Dewy headed out to meet with Lumine. The existence of the letter buoyed her. It was a tangible reminder that someone outside of these cold walls remembered her as something other than a tool to be wielded, an informant to be drawn out. She strolled confidently through the corridors, warmed by Spense's words, her shoulders back and head held high. Like the royal she was.

Know that you are not alone. I'm working to free you...

When she got to the receiving hall, and Lumine's steward requested she wait outside the wide double doors, it occurred to her the king might not be as keen to meet with her. Not that it mattered. She was determined upon this new course, and she'd wait as long as needed. It renewed her to know she was not alone in her efforts. She and Spense were unified in purpose, joined in affection. He'd finished his letter simply, with love. That love glowed bright, with uncomplicated hope.

Lumine appeared a few moments later. "It is good to see you out again, Lady Dew Drop."

Dewy dipped her chin in a polite nod.

"I wonder if you'd care to accompany me to the garden houses? There are some rare floral species that require extra attention, and I'd like to see how they're getting on."

"Of course," Dewy said.

It was hard to imagine the stern Winter king taking an interest in…flowers. But what did she know? A lot she'd assumed about the world had since turned out to surprise her.

Humans, for instance, had been very different from what she'd expected. And not just Spense. Both of his parents, in their own ways, had treated her with unanticipated dignity and respect. Cait cared for her after the attack on Telridge when she'd thrown around enough magic it caused her to collapse. She'd never tried to command so much water at once, and nothing with the force of the River Selden. But it had heeded her, as if she were its general. And when she'd fallen exhausted by its banks, the humans scooped her up and found her a safe place to heal.

Spense's father, the King of Telridge, acted as if Dewy was the royal personage of her birth, not a recent exile from the land of Summer. She'd always thought humans were boorish, loud oafs. She thought they cared nothing for the lives of faeries. But Lord Ferrous had been generous, his manner as dignified as her own aunt. Dewy had marveled.

True, there'd been some misunderstandings regarding the eating of meat and the use of bows, but that had been overcome and apologies were offered and received. By the time Dewy parted ways with Spense's older brother, Dirk, she'd come to realize even he had a thoughtful side. She'd been raised to believe human soldiers did not possess that quality, that they fought and hunted and killed. Nothing more. But it wasn't true. There was so much more to them.

And perhaps there was more to Lumine, too. It was easy to believe that he sat upon his throne, scheming and plotting. She wanted to think him cold, unforgiving. But how could a Fae with only ice in his veins have the capacity to appreciate the growing, green things of the world, enough so that he checked in on these delicate flowers?

Dewy eyed him sideways as they strolled through the glassed-in hot house. His gait was slow, deliberate. No sign of his usual arrogant glide. They wandered the lanes until he found the specimens he was looking for.

Of course, it would be orchids.

"Do you know these grow wild in the Brecken Isles?" Lumine asked as he leaned over to inhale the light fragrance from a bloom.

"I did, actually."

The island nation hardly needed the attention of faeries to maintain their verdant flora. The air was steeped with heavy, hanging water, misting from barely visible clouds, and wafting from the sea spray.

Everything was green and lush. Even the Summer lands were not as beautifully wild as the Brecken Isles. There was a special magic at work there.

"I've gathered samples over the years from everywhere. Sometimes I need to remember that there are places in the world not covered with ice and snow, that there are ways of living differently."

Was this a confession? An admission of something? Dewy narrowed her eyes as the king continued.

"When you walk outside these doors, you will find things growing, but only the hardiest, darkest conifers. Nothing so fragile as this rare flower. Not ever."

She examined the waxy petals of the orchid, striped with deep purple, fading to white near the center. He was right, of course. The spiny trees surrounding the Silver Horn were a dark grey-green. They produced spiked cones, not delicate stamens. Even the noble trees' children were hardened to a harsh world.

It was a reality Dewy had never known, before Spense, before the Claiming, before she found herself in the wilderness, first the brittle iron of the human world and then the cold of the Winter faeries. How could two faerie peoples be so dissimilar? Did that make the Winter folk any less faerie? Perhaps there were human people groups—those who lived in balmy island nations—who were more like the faeries of Summer than their human brethren who lived behind stone walls.

"In what ways have you come to live differently, King Lumine?"

Lumine's eyes sparked. "That is a much longer conversation than I think you intended when you sought me out today."

Dewy inclined her head. Perhaps.

"And why did you seek me out?" he asked.

Dewy considered how to phrase her request. She'd been considering all morning. Everything sounded stilted and awkward in her head.

"You know I went to see Cinna…"

"Yes?"

She took a step along the path, moving from one fragile flower to the next. The blooms were protected in the hot house, provided with perfect conditions for humidity and warming sunlight. She couldn't help but compare herself to the flowers. Had she been protected in the warm lands of Summer? Was she protected still, even in Winter's capital? Perhaps the Winter faeries viewed her as Lumine saw his rare orchids, a prize specimen to be cultivated, to be kept within her limited parameters.

"Cinna posed some questions…I'm afraid I don't have answers for."

"Is that right? Would it comfort you to know that most feel the same when they cross Wizard Cinnamon's threshold?"

Dewy wasn't surprised. "No. But she challenged me."

"Also, not an uncommon occurrence."

She was stalling. Lumine's leading comments made that clear.

"You've spoken of my magic. My water magic. You think there might be some depths I haven't explored…that could help in finding your Heir?"

"That is true."

"Cinna thinks so, too. Only…only she doesn't feel

I can reach those depths."

"Doesn't she?"

Dewy hesitated. It wasn't exactly true. Cinna said she had physical limitations, that she wouldn't be able to reach the depths of her water magic unless she were stronger. In body and mind.

"She thinks…I'm not enough. Physically."

"And she would be right, of course. Cinna usually is."

"She had some ideas about how I was to go about becoming so."

"Oh, I'm sure she had ideas."

"You must understand that some of her suggestions…" Dewy swallowed, choking down the bitterness that rose in her throat.

"Are repugnant to you?"

Dewy nodded. "She wanted me to eat as you eat…said I was too pale, and too weak."

She resisted the idea that consuming murdered beings would give her strength. In Summer, strength was gained from discipline, from existing as one with the natural world, and providing order to all things under the sun.

"I can appreciate your reluctance."

"Can you?"

She lifted her gaze to him, searching. Where was the mercy and understanding behind that silver-smooth countenance?

"Of course. There are many things I find perplexing or confusing about the way that you Summer faeries live—or humans—but as with these flowers, I've come to appreciate some of those differences. I will admit it hasn't been easy or come naturally to me. But it's amazing how a shift in perspective can change an outlook. Don't you agree?"

"I suppose so…"

"So, the question is, will you challenge your own perspective in order to achieve something great, possibly greater than you thought you could?"

"I wonder if it will be worth it," Dewy confessed.

"That is something you must answer for yourself."

"Then help me. Give me more information. What is it you think I'll be able to do if I'm stronger?"

Lumine grinned. "And now we come to it."

She waited.

"Cinnamon already led you along this path, I'm sure, probably told you some tales of the old ways, how faeries used to combine their elemental gifts with Sight."

"Ye-e-s…"

"That is all I am suggesting. You have the gift of water. And it is strong in you, already." Lumine turned from his tending of the flowers to face her directly. "And what is blood made of but water? It is our life-water, is it not?"

Dewy drew her brows together. "You think I could have power over…blood?"

It was a substance more potent, and far less malleable than water. It flowed through the pumping of a heart, not the gravity of a mountain. And a person's life blood—be they faerie or human or goblin or any other species—carried so much more. It carried their spirit, and the spirits of their ancestors.

"Yes," Lumine answered. "I think you may possess the power to manipulate blood, like you do with water, but also to See blood. You feel the spirit of the waters

140

you work, do you not? It's not so different."

Dewy's mouth dropped open. How could anyone have such a power, and if they did, what could they do with it?

"But, Lady Dew Drop, we will only know if you begin to train and allow your body to strengthen. And, let me assure you, there is no better place to do that than in the lands of Winter."

It was a challenge, a push, a dare.

Lumine had placated her these many months with books, allowing her to exhaust herself in research, knowing she'd eventually reach this point. He'd been patient. He'd let her get there on her own.

And now, she must decide. Could she build strength as a Winter faerie would? Could she swallow her reservations, among other things, and accept that a different way of living, was not inherently wrong, that it was simply different?

The orchids had found a way to live in Winter, but they were coddled. Lumine asked her to be an orchid no longer, to push through the snow and become one of the first blooms of Spring, not waiting until the air grew warmer to thrive.

It was time for Dewy to become a crocus.

Chapter 24

"Do you have everything you need?"

"Since the last time you asked four minutes ago? Or the time before that, maybe…seven minutes ago?" Spense paused in his packing, turned to his mother, and put his arms around her. He squeezed tight. "Where's the fussing coming from, Mum? You didn't act this way the last time I left Telridge."

"The last time was with Dewy."

"Right. One faerie. I mean, one fierce, magic-wielding Fae princess, but still. This time, I'll have a whole team, including Dirk and two Knights. Plus, Flora's coming along. I'm way better off, don't you think?"

"You got hurt last time."

Spense rolled his eyes and returned to his packing. "And I'll probably get hurt this time."

"You're not making me feel better."

"I doubt I'll be attacked by feral trees again. But seriously," Spense braced his mother, cupping her narrow shoulders, and looked into her eyes, "there could be some blisters."

"Your humor is not as cute as you think it is."

"Fine. I'm sorry, but you're not usually like this."

Cait placed her palm over her heart and lowered herself to the edge of Spense's bed. "I just…have a feeling."

142

"Now, you're a Seer, too?"

She scoffed. His mother's gifts were subtle, but elemental. Flame and Earth, technically. Used in service to her hearth, her cooking. Most of the time, she denied she had them.

"No. Call it mother's intuition."

"All right, then."

"But...it's more than that."

Spense sighed. Whatever was causing this uncharacteristic fretting, he had a feeling he was going to have to hear her out before he'd be able to go. "Care to explain?"

His mother nodded, clasping her hands together in a tight ball.

"But, Mum? It's going to have to be quick. I'm supposed to meet Dirk by the stables at dawn and you know how he is. That military timeliness thing is...well, it's a thing with him."

She took a deep breath, steadying herself, as if she were about to do something unpleasant. And the thing was not saying farewell to her nearly grown son for a brief trip. More like facing a hungry mountain lion or walking into a burning building.

"Mum?"

She glanced up at him. Her eyes had gone cold, icy. "You're going to the faerie Oracles."

"Ye-e-s."

That was the whole point of the trip. There was nothing revelatory there. Or anything she need fear.

"I think...you may find some things out about yourself."

"Mum, I know all the warnings. The Oracles will try to get me off my guard, will distract me, so that I miss whatever message I was trying to glean. I do know how it works."

"But the thing they will catch you with, you don't know that."

"Well, no, but how shocking could it be?"

"Pretty shocking, I think." Her voice had grown strange, thin.

Spense stilled his hands, just as he was about to stuff in his notebooks. "Back to that motherly intuition?"

"It's not intuition. Not in this case."

"What are you talking about?"

"Better sit down. It's time I told you something, or better yet, showed you."

Spense frowned, but he did as she requested.

Cait stood before him. She clenched and unclenched her usually steady hands before raising them to the wrap that always covered her head. A requirement for a cook, she insisted, to keep her hair contained and out of her face. He'd never questioned that rationale. Until now. Until she carefully unwove the delicate scarf and removed it.

Her dark hair hung in long lengths, wispy on top from the scarf. She tucked her hair behind one ear. And then another.

"Look closely," she said.

Both ears were scarred at the top, as if a jagged knife had cut the round tops right off. Only, why would anyone do that? Unless…

"What are you trying to tell me?" Spense asked.

"I think you know."

Spense swallowed. "Something happened to your ears."

"Yes."

"Why?"

She blinked at him. Impatient. But he couldn't say it. She had to.

"Because they were pointed, Spense."

He knew what she was saying, but how could it be true? How was it possible that he never knew? "You're…faerie?"

"In part."

"Why have you never told me?"

"I wanted to keep you safe. I wanted you to feel like you belonged here, in the human world."

But Spense had never fit in. Not completely. And it had nothing to do with his blood…unless maybe it did.

"Grandfather Clove?" he guessed.

She nodded. "He was at least half. I know nothing of my mother. She was never spoken of."

"So, you could be mostly faerie?"

"I don't know what I am, in that way." She grasped his hands, her grip steel-strong. "But I do know that I am your mother, and I want the best for you, and always have. And, you may feel I have slighted you all these years…but I didn't want you to go to the Oracles not knowing."

"I suppose I should thank you." Spense pulled his hands away. His words came out stiff. His jaw was tight.

"That is up to you."

Spense didn't know what else to say. He didn't have time to decide if it mattered. But the not knowing, the keeping it from him. That definitely mattered. He knew it did. But it wasn't something he could deal with now. Maybe when he got back.

"Be well, Mother." Spense kissed her temple, as usual.

"Grace go with you."

"And with you," he muttered as he slung his pack over his shoulder and walked out the door, trying to ignore the heat and tightness in his chest and stomach.

He'd made it to the courtyard when his other parent cornered him. Ferrous pulled Spense to the side.

"My lord," Spense said, ducking his head in a bow.

"Son…"

"Yes?"

"I wanted to wish you well on your journey."

"Thank you."

"And…" His father wore the same worried expression his mother had.

Spense waited.

"I know not what the Oracles will say to you, but I feel I must say that I sense something…momentous."

"Oh no, not you, too."

"Sorry?"

"Nothing. Something Mum said."

"Your mother is a wise soul."

"Wise, maybe. Definitely secretive." Spense scowled.

"Ah. So, she's told you."

Spense started. "You knew?"

"That she was part faerie? I've known for quite a long time."

"And you never said…"

"It was not my secret to share. But it seems she has finally deemed it time. I'm glad she told you. I was worried I'd betray something if it had been me."

Spense shook his head in disbelief. How many

other secrets had his parents kept? Separately or in collusion? His mother's concerns about the Oracles became more worrisome. Assuming that this—admittedly big—thing was what they felt he must know, what else had they decided to keep to themselves, with the pretended concern for his well-being?

"I'm sorry, my lord. I really must be going. Dirk is expecting me."

"So, he is. May I walk with you? I'd like to say farewell to my other son, as well."

"Of course."

It's not like Spense could stop him. He was the king. He could walk wherever he wanted to, whenever he wanted to. But truth be told, Spense wasn't feeling a whole lot of warmth toward either parent.

"Will you tell Dirk?" Ferrous asked.

Spense knew what he meant.

"Will it make a difference?"

Ferrous took a deep inhale and let it out in a gust. "I don't know. I think that is up to Dirk. But it is up to you if you'd like to keep this to yourself for a time. It would be understandable."

And that decided him. It would be soon. He didn't want Dirk to experience this bewildering anger and betrayal. He wouldn't be a part of that.

He huffed. It's not like this would really change anything. Spense had always known he was different, that he didn't quite fit. He would always be not just the younger brother, but to many, the lesser. It was ridiculous and bigoted, but also his permanent reality. Finding out that he had faerie blood was just more of the same, another reason for the sidelong glances, the wary distrust.

Spense had been eager to set out on this mission. He had an important purpose after all.

But now leaving Telridge and this blooming castle felt more necessary than ever.

Chapter 25

Dewy dined with Lumine and the two lordlings the next three evenings. She drank their wine. She didn't share in their meal. Each night a bowl of vegetable stew was prepared for her in substitution of the regular menu. Cook also supplied a little dish of toasted hazelnuts. Dewy savored their salty, rich texture, knowing the oil and substance of the nut would help her gain back some of the weight she'd lost the past few months.

She swallowed every bite. And then some. Even sneaking down to the kitchen later for extra portions of Cook's dark, chewy bread. It was nothing like Cait's milky, soft bread from the Telridge court. But it was dense and sweet and filled her belly.

Dewy needed all of it. She'd asked Misty to train with her, to help her strengthen her physical body. She should've known from that first glinting smile and Misty's words—*it would be my pleasure*—that she was in for pain. It was more than likely Misty pushed her hard the first morning as a challenge, to see if she'd actually return the next day.

But return she did. She bundled herself in fleece-lined pants and tucked them into boots, donning leather for the first time in her life. The smooth, flexible boot hugged her feet and calves. And she thanked whatever creature had given itself for her comfort and warmth as she ventured into the unforgiving Winter landscape. She ran where Misty told her to run, inhaling frigid air in sharp, icy puffs, climbed where Misty directed, and carried logs and boulders from point to point for no apparent purpose, other than Misty's own amusement.

And when she was panting and covered in sweat, her tormenter changed tactics and ordered her to work on strengthening what she called her core muscles. The first exercise required her to hover above the ground, stiff and straight like a recently fallen tree. Only her forearms and toes touched the cold earth. If she dropped a knee or let her body droop, she'd find herself drenched in a cold, slushy puddle. Dewy gritted her teeth and held, preferring the ache of her muscles to the ice bath.

And when they'd finished that first session, Dewy slogged back to the Silver Horn and melted before the fire in her room, until Siskin arrived and pressed a mug of near-scalding tea into her stiff fingers. He enlisted Holly to help her with her boots and prepare her for the evening's meal.

She arrived at dinner with her head held high, no matter how much it pained her, and met Misty the next morning.

As she approached the dining hall this night, the Fae fell in step beside her.

"Back again? You must love punishment."

"What I must do is grow stronger. You're helping with that," Dewy said, biting her words.

"Oh, you're welcome, Lady Dew Drop." Misty folded into a deep curtsy.

Dewy rolled her eyes. "Thank you."

Misty grinned. With a lot of teeth. "Let's see how

long you keep thanking me," she said as she pushed open the doors of the hall.

"Welcome again, Lady Dew Drop," Lumine said. "Please join us."

Frost, as usual, scowled at her arrival.

Misty scampered to the seat beside her brother and plucked his full wine glass from his hand. Frost's frown deepened, but he didn't raise his voice to rebuke her. Instead, he waved to his skulking attendant, Rime, and gestured at the empty glass at his sister's place setting.

"How was the session with Lady Mist?" Lumine asked.

"She certainly knows how to test a faerie." Dewy forced her voice into a lightness she did not feel. She took on a relaxed countenance, even as her aching muscles screamed for a long rest in front of a warm fire.

"Is that so? I believe I'm happy to hear it, as she oversees my army's training."

"Then I believe you have nothing to worry about, King Lumine. Your soldiers are sure to be in peak physical condition."

Or peak physical pain.

Dewy had seen those warriors in action. They were certainly not weak. She reached for her wine goblet and managed to move with a relative degree of fluidity, even if she gritted her teeth to do it.

"So, you have heeded Cinna's encouragement to develop your bodily strength."

"I have."

"And are there other ways we can assist you in your growth?"

Dewy marshaled her thoughts as the attendants approached with the meal, questioning the words, the request, she was about to make. She waited until the servants had retreated and everyone had taken their first bites to respond. Straightening her spine, imagining she was an evergreen sapling facing a harsh life in a snow-choked mountain, she said, "I believe there are ways you can assist me, King Lumine."

"Oh? And what might that be?"

His pretended nonchalance was unconvincing. Marten had provided as many books as she asked for, and even helped her pore through text after text, looking for more links between water and blood magic. Everything she found was theoretical. She needed a practitioner to help her understand how the magic worked, how it felt. Dewy was sure that Lumine knew this, but like before, had allowed her to exhaust all other resources first.

"I'm hoping to gain greater understanding of my own water magic. But…I may need a tutor."

It sounded like a simple request, as if she were enquiring after an additional servant, a teacher to come and work with her for a couple of hours a day. It was anything but. She needed someone whose skill and power matched and even exceeded her own. There was only one person in the whole of Winter who qualified.

She knew what she was asking. And whom she was asking. Briefly she worried what Spense would think of her making this request, reaching out for aid to the person who'd imprisoned the both of them, who wielded bargains like weapons. But surely deep down, Spense would understand; he'd see the need for sacrificing this one small thing. It was hardly noteworthy, considering all they'd each given so far.

"You would learn from me, scheming political

monster that I am?"

Dewy breathed slowly in and out her nose, cooling the churning thoughts and acerbic words straining to break forth, to lash and bite at her preening jailer, the king. "I would hope to learn from you, skilled as you are in elemental magic, King Lumine." A careful, neutral answer.

The king nodded. Dewy caught the wide-eyed gaze of Misty, who held her wine glass up, but moved no further to take a drink. Frost scowled.

"I would be happy to undertake instructing you as you expand your understanding of magic."

Lumine's eyes sparked. With what emotion, she could not say. Eagerness, certainly. A sharp desire. The corner of his mouth lifted, in satisfaction it had finally come to this, and Dewy asked more of him than his hospitality.

"But just the magic, King Lumine. You can keep the monstrous politics to yourself."

Frost made a noise. It might have been a laugh. Misty choked on her wine.

"Oh," Lumine crooned. "You are Heir to Summer. You might find scheming useful someday."

"For now, just magic, thank you."

"As you wish. Shall we begin tomorrow?"

"If you are able. Would the afternoon suit you? I would hate to postpone my training with Lady Mist."

Misty held up her hands. "Don't bring me into this. I serve at your pleasure, as always, Uncle."

"No, no. Afternoon is fine. Frost and I can reschedule our daily briefing with my commanders." He turned to his nephew, one brow raised. "Can't we?"

"Of course, my lord."

"Then it is settled. We will begin tomorrow."

They resumed their meal, everyone except Misty.

Lumine noticed. "What is it, dear niece?"

"Are you...I mean to say...should I..." Misty fumbled her words. It may have been the first time ever.

"Yes?"

"Should I go easier on her if you are training with her later?"

"No!" Dewy said, before anyone else could respond for her. "If the whole point is for me to get stronger, then I can't let up, not anywhere."

"Well, all right then, if you're sure."

Dewy smirked. "I'll see you tomorrow morning."

Chapter 26

Merciless winter winds finally gave way, and the morning sparkled, bright and gleaming. Sun on clean snow. Bluebird skies. If their task wasn't so important, it would almost make for a pleasant journey. An adventurous excursion through the forests of Telridge. A holiday. And Sweet Spring, Dirk could use one.

But not everyone in their party was as cheered by the warming sun and bright snow. Dirk knew Spense took the mission seriously, but he thought that by the time they set forth, his brother might demonstrate a little more…energy. Instead, he looked as if his favorite pet tortoise had died. Dirk didn't know if Spense actually had any pets. He'd certainly never been gifted a horse. And he was a brewer of potions. Probably best not to give him anything that could find its blood or toes essential to a spell.

He leaned over. "Do I want to know what that face is about?"

"Interesting question," Spense said. "I've been pondering it myself."

"Pardon me?"

Spense met Dirk's eyes. "I have some news."

"News?"

He released a dry chuckle. "Well, not new news. Just new to me, I guess."

"I have no idea what you're talking about."

"No, you wouldn't."

"Well, this is fun and cryptic." Dirk was used to mysterious comments from his father, but Lord Ferrous was the king and a Seer. Of course, he spoke in riddles and his words were laden with secrets. And of course, Dirk wasn't supposed to question him. But Spense was his little brother, and from him, it was annoying. "Care to fill me in?"

"I actually want to," Spense said. "But I think now's not the time." He glanced meaningfully at their travel companions.

"I can't imagine you could find a more trustworthy group."

Gerry and Xendra had been his closest friends since they began training, and Flora...well, she was Flora.

"It's not that I don't trust them. It's more...that it's personal. And until I know how I feel about it, I don't know that I want it bandied around." His eyes were wide, face open and earnest, like a bright full moon on a cloudless night. Truth be told, Spense's face was always earnest. "Can you understand that?"

Dirk sighed. "I can, actually."

Spense quirked an eyebrow. "That's generous of you."

Dirk elbowed him. "Just so long as you aren't keeping state secrets."

"No, this information affects no one but me. I can assure you."

"All right, then." He might be curious, but he could also leave Spense to his thoughts, however troubling. Dirk appreciated the luxury of private thoughts, and hoarded his own with miserly attention.

Maybe the peace of the road would help Spense gain perspective. It always helped Dirk's own outlook.

But he'd already had plenty of the peace of nature today. His legs could use a rest and his stomach growled.

"Oi, Gerry!"

"Yes, my lord?" Gerry answered with exaggerated subservience.

Dirk knew that wouldn't last long. He wondered whose benefit it was for.

"Did I put you on navigation for this venture? Any idea where we are? And more importantly, how soon until we break for lunch?"

"I'm game whenever you are, my lord," Gerry called back from the head of their team. He was immediately smacked in the back of the head by Xendra.

"No, you did *not* put him on navigation. You put me on that detail. Because Gerry couldn't find the side of a mountain if we were standing at its base."

Dirk chuckled. "Of course. Apologies."

"As for your second question, we'll be crossing a stream in another quarter of an hour or so. Wouldn't be a bad place to stop."

"My thanks, good lady. I don't know where we'd be without you."

"Lost!" she yelled back, which drew more chuckles.

Even Spense cracked a smile, and Dirk caught Flora biting her lip. He breathed deep, allowing a smile to creep over his face as well. He was with his brother and his closest friends, far from the overbearing court of Telridge. Yes, they were setting out on a venture of importance. It would impact the human and faerie lands. But neither the weighty significance of the mission nor Spense's brooding could hold him down. He craved this feeling of optimism and freedom, and he drew in every breath of it, just as he sucked down the clean, sharp air.

He should've known better.

"You hear something?" Spense asked.

"Uh...no..."

Dirk had been lost in his thoughts, leaving it to the Knights to be on guard. It was bad form. Behavior of a spoiled prince who expected others to watch out for him. He cocked his ear to listen better. And caught the rustle of leaves a stone's throw to their right.

"Probably a bird or squirrel. They make more noise than you'd think possible for something so small."

Spense frowned. "I don't think it's a squirrel. Something doesn't feel right about this forest. Can you sense it?"

Dirk lifted an eyebrow and laughed. "No. I don't have any of Father's Sight or your elemental magic, remember? Have to rely on good old human senses."

Just then a small rabbit darted across the roadway, startling the horses and their caretaker. As it scurried away, Flora laughed. A nervous, silly laugh. And Dirk couldn't help but chuckle alongside her. Her cheeks flushed pink, as she calmed the restless beasts, avoiding eye contact with him.

"You see? Nothing but a woodland hare." Dirk patted Spense brusquely on the back.

But still his young brother frowned. "It wasn't the rabbit—"

A loud crash cut off whatever else Spense was

going to say, followed by the thumping beats of sprinting deer.

"Out of the way!" Gerry lunged in front of Xendra as half a dozen deer stampeded past—right in front of their party.

The deer's eyes were rolling and wild. Their heads swayed as they thundered into the foliage.

Not a moment later, Dirk spotted what caused the panic. A couple of mangy foxes tore out of the woods behind their quarry, an angry, orangey blur. The pair snapped and growled, mouths foaming, and fur spiked.

Dirk launched himself at his pack on Lightning Storm, furiously pulling at the ties to his scabbard, while the stallion stamped and snorted. Before he could get his blade free, he heard the whistle of one…two…arrows, drawn and released.

Thunk. Thunk.

One of the scrawny beasts went down. It snapped and pawed piteously, grotesquely at the air, as blood seeped from its scraggly, matted body.

The other threw itself at the archer—Flora—clamping on to her tough riding leathers. It was enough to knock her off her feet. Dirk was there in an instant, but his now free sword was nearly useless at the writhing, scrambling melee that was fox and young woman. She kicked and pulled. It dove, under, over, never getting purchase, but also not fleeing. What was wrong with this creature?

Dirk made short, brisk stabs, but he was too slow, the feral animal too slippery. He did no more than nick the fox and make it even angrier.

"Get back!" Spense yelled. He held out his hands before him, cupped as if he were holding a bowl. He whispered a few words—incantations—and blew. A swirl of flames burst forth, leapt from Spense's hands as he opened them like a blossom. The fiery gust struck the fox. It shrieked loud and piercing, before a well-placed boot hit its snout dead on and the thing went flying. The creature thudded across the forest road, skidding on dirt and gravel and half-frozen slush. A heartbeat later, Gerry thrust his dagger into its throat.

Dirk rushed to Flora, sliding on his knees in the dirt. She leaned back on her hands and breathed heavily, her chest rising and falling in short, quick succession. He grasped her shoulder with one hand and braced her body with his other. She fell back against him, as her breathing eased.

"Are you all right?" He scanned the scuffs on her pants, scratches on her boots.

Flora nodded. "It couldn't get through the leather."

"Thank Grace and all that is free and good in this land." Dirk's breath whooshed out of him.

Xendra sauntered over to each of the dead foxes— impaled, burnt, and now slowly cooling in the dirty snow. She yanked Flora's arrows from one. "Gerry, get your blade, before this thing's diseased blood corrodes it." She gestured with an arrow, spraying blood and clotted fur on to the ground.

Dirk helped Flora to her feet. Spense breathed quietly, his eyes half-closed, as he moved toward the horses. He rested one hand on Flora's mount, Buttercup. Dirk wasn't sure who was comforting whom.

"Wicked Winter, what was that?" Gerry whistled through his teeth, while he cleaned his dagger on the slushy grass near the side of the road.

"Foxes," Xendra said, deadpan.

"Those weren't ordinary foxes," Gerry said.

"No shit," Dirk muttered.

"They weren't right." Spense's voice was low and labored.

"Like I said."

Spense turned to him. "No, I mean, they weren't just diseased. They feel...off." He shuddered. "I can't explain it. They are—were—out of balance with the natural world. Disease is a natural occurrence. Sometimes tragic, but natural. These are something else."

"You're right." Flora stepped toward Spense and her horse. "I've seen this before—months ago. Sometimes we had problems with the foxes near my family's farm."

Dirk wondered who'd taken up that responsibility now that Flora was working at the castle. It never occurred to him it might cost her aunt and uncle to let her go. He just appreciated seeing her in the stables and about the grounds. He shook his head. He was such an ass, avoiding her these many months.

"Nice shooting, by the way."

She shrugged. "I've had practice."

"Well, whatever's wrong with them, I'm glad they're dead." Xendra toed the fried corpse of the nearest fox.

"I think the forest would agree with you." Spense turned his face up, as if to catch the breezy whispers of the swaying trees.

Maybe Spense could hear the trees talking. Why not? There wasn't much about his little brother that could surprise him at this point.

161

Xendra returned Flora's cast-aside bow and freshly cleaned arrows. "There's a village up ahead with an inn, just a little beyond the stream we were going to stop at anyway. I don't know about the rest of you, but I, for one, could use one tonight. You, mighty slayer of feral creatures, might want to get yourself cleaned up."

Flora glanced down. She brushed her hands off on her trousers, and ineffectually flicked a few stray hairs away from her dirt-smeared face. "If you really insist."

****

Flora and Spense emerged from the inn, bleak expressions and a good coating of road debris still on their faces.

"What? No rooms?"

"No…there are rooms, my lord," Flora said.

"Just not very many," Spense explained. "We told them that our lords had coin, but…" Spense held his hands out, palms up, and shrugged.

"They can't make something from nothing," Flora added. "We got the last two."

Dirk rubbed his chin. "Is this still from Solstice? That was days ago."

"Yes, my lord, and people travel to see their families or come to the city for the festivities. Then, they have to travel back." Flora raised her eyebrows as if explaining to a very dull child.

Dirk frowned. "I get it."

He caught a snicker coming from behind him and whirled around. Both Gerry and Xendra wore mischievous grins on their faces.

"What?" he snapped.

"Nothing, my lord." Gerry tucked his head, breaking eye contact.

Xendra rolled her eyes and stalked over to him. "It appears you may have to share with some of this lot tonight. And I'm sorry, my lord, we know you're not used to that sort of thing, but it looks like you'll have to sacrifice just this once for the sake of the cause."

Dirk's scowl deepened. "You know I could've chosen anyone for this trip. I have plenty of loyal, trustworthy, respectful Knights."

"Yes, but none of them will kick you in the ass when you need it and knock you off your pretentious high horse." Xendra walked past him and linked her arm with Flora. "Care to show us these rooms?"

"Of course," Flora said, a faint smile on her lips.

"Looks like we girls will finally get a moment's peace tonight."

"Sarcasm hardly becomes a lady of the court."

Xendra turned her head back toward him to offer one last jibe. "Good thing your dad made me a Knight, then, isn't it?"

Chapter 27

Flora cracked her eyes as the first light of dawn crept through the inn's shutters. She slid further into the smooth sheets, nestling in the clean linens. She'd indulged in a hot bath when they'd arrived at the inn, as their room boasted its own private bathing chambers.

Lady Xendra claimed the considerably more luxurious of the two chambers. It had a pair of large down-filled beds and an antechamber for receiving guests. Dirk, Spense, and Gerry were left with a basic bunk set-up. They shared a bath with four other similarly arranged rooms. It was hard to picture the prince making do in that circumstance, but after a few colorfully descriptive comments, spoken mostly in jest, they'd said their goodnights, and she'd had to assume that it was agreeable, if not ideal.

The irony wasn't lost on her. She normally slept in the grooms' barracks in the stables. She had her own curtained-off corner and a battered cabinet to keep her possessions, but privacy wasn't a priority amongst the grooms. The dorms at The Academy hadn't offered much more, but in her brief time as a student, there'd at least been the air of respectability. But nothing like what the prince was used to. Dirk had chambers in the castle. *Chambers*. Plural. For sleeping, study, and apparently, sitting. She smiled at the role reversal, and the easy manner in which he'd handled the situation.

The prince could've insisted that he occupy the more comfortable room, as was befitting his station, and forced the rest of the party into the small bunk room.

But...he didn't.

Dirk knew who he was, and what his responsibilities were. He wasn't like other leaders, who sought the glory of exalted position with none of the work. She'd seen plenty of that sort, selling wool in her family's market stall or tending to the horses of visiting courtiers. Dirk sought out the work, but often shirked away from the attention. They may not have had many conversations over the past few months, but it wasn't as if she didn't see him. Everyone saw him.

But maybe not everyone saw how he tended to his own mount, or how he pulled at his tunic collar during formal events, how he smiled through those events, but never with his eyes. His laughter was reserved for those who judged him only for his work ethic and courage, who were more concerned that he kept his blade sharp and oiled, not how shiny his dress armor was.

When Dirk asked her to come along, there'd been no hesitation. Maybe there should've been. She had work to do, a life she was making for herself, and a stable master who was less than pleased with her sudden request for time off. Not that he'd grumbled to anyone but her. Dirk was still the Crown Prince. And a keeper of horses didn't say no to royalty.

Flora squeezed her eyes tighter and slithered further into the welcoming bed. She could think on these things later. Or not at all. For now, she was happy to indulge in the upside-down world where the Prince of Telridge slept in a bunk bed, and she luxuriated in a private room, shared only with a Lady of the Court. For one night, why not revel in the good-natured teasing between friends?

Not that she expected it to last. Not really.

Too soon, thudding knocks on the outer door signaled her journey into dreamland was over and it was time to go back to tending the horses and managing the supplies. Flora groaned, threw off the fluffy blankets and stalked to the door.

She wrenched it open. "Yes?"

"And good morning to you." Prince Dirk stood before her, looking clean and energized and ready to march forward through any type of terrain for days, just so he could relish the forest adventure.

"Umm…yes, my lord. Morning." She wobbled a half-curtsy.

"We're…uh…gathering downstairs for a hot morning meal. Just as soon as you're ready." Dirk's gaze was pointedly not directed to her. More in the direction of the floor, the wall next to the door, roaming around her person like the hands of a timepiece.

Flora looked down and belatedly noticed the state of her bedclothes and hair. Heat rose in her cheeks. Her thin linen night shirt hung loosely, to mid-thigh, leaving a less-than-courtly amount of bare leg showing.

"Of course. Right away, my lord."

Dirk cleared his throat. "Very good." He started to turn away. "Oh—"

"Yes?"

"Can you please let Lady Xendra know as well?"

A muffled grumbling came from the other bed.

"Did you catch that?" he whispered.

The party in question flipped the covers back and glared at the royal intruder in the doorway. "I heard.

We'll be there."

Dirk leaned toward Flora. She caught the faint scent of cedar-infused soap. "Cranky, isn't she?"

A whizzing sounded in Flora's ear followed by a thud as Xendra's black-handled knife lodged into the door frame near the prince's head.

"Quit flirting with Flora and shut the door so we can get dressed."

Flora covered her mouth with her hand, concealing the laugh that bubbled up.

Dirk rolled his eyes. "Of course, you keep your family dagger under your pillow while you sleep."

"You might be a little more appreciative of that habit, your royal prince-li-ness." Lady Xendra lifted an cycbrow.

"Humble apologies, ladies." Dirk held up both hands and took a step back.

Flora wrenched the blade out and softly closed the door behind her. She flipped the knife once and tossed it onto Xendra's bed.

The morning was off to an interesting start.

Chapter 28

Spense sensed the murmurs of the forest, the chattering breeze between tree limbs, and the muted symphony of creatures, winged and furred. After three days, the forest was calm. Rested. He wasn't the only one who noticed.

"Looks like our feral friends took the day off," Gerry mused.

"That's the magic of Summer, Sir Knight." Spense breathed deep, as the charmed air filled him to his toes. A wave of warm energy washed over him. "You're right. The land is healthier here, more at ease."

"The mangy foxes are gone, sure, but I'd hardly call this lot domesticated." Lady Xendra waved casually in the direction of Gerry and Dirk. "No amount of faerie magic could fix that."

Flora chortled and covered her mouth with her free hand. Dirk and Gerry pretended offense.

It was warming to observe Flora taking part in the gentle mockery. First with Lady Xendra and Sir Gervais, but with Dirk, too. Even if she hid her expression and looked away.

He knew it was hard for commoners to throw off their sense of awe, of that royal mystique. Sometimes Spense got caught up in the whole thing himself. The Solstice festivities had ceremonial aspects, and the pageantry was impressive, even for someone like him who'd seen it all before and was often tasked with some inane responsibility to make part of it happen. Flora had seen that, too, working in the castle these days and learning what was behind the proverbial curtain of majestic glory.

He didn't think that was what held her back, though. Perhaps it was as simple as respect. From what he understood, she'd fought right alongside Dirk and his soldiers. For that, along with many other reasons, he was thankful to have her on this team.

But she often kept herself apart from Dirk especially. Like she wouldn't permit herself to become too friendly with him. Spense knew a little something about that, so when he caught Flora elbow Dirk for one of his more obnoxious comments, it put a smile on his lips.

That camaraderie was good. For each of them. And for the team. And it would make it easier as they traveled this wilderness where there were no more inns, polite excuses, or closed doors. In Spense's days trekking through the wilds with Dewy, the journey itself became a part of their story. She fought alongside him. They defended each other, and she came to his rescue—repeatedly.

He had to hope that by the time he arrived to pay the debt, it wasn't too late.

But for now, this team was with him, on this journey. Sometimes teasing, sometimes terse. They all attended to their tasks. Water and brush down the horses. Collect firewood. Prepare meals. Set up camp. Everyone knew their role and did it with routine efficiency. They'd established basic responsibilities before setting out, but there was no one who didn't pitch in to help another, who couldn't take over and shift roles, if needed.

They'd had several nights of making camp in the wintry forests of Telridge. The country's huge cedars protected them from snarling winds as they bivouacked in the centers of groves of ancient trees. But there was nothing that could be done about the snow and ice or the chilling night-time temperatures. They'd all been as brisk as they could in tending to their needs and huddling in tents each night. But now, in the Summer territory, Spense gave thanks for the first whisper of warmer air.

They all shed layers and moved with ease, lingering around the fire after the meal to share stories, mostly at Dirk's expense. Spense kept most of his thoughts to himself, as had become his new habit, but the rest poked and jested as old friends, well-worn and comfortable with each other. Gerry and Xendra treated Flora as if she'd always been there. But with Dirk, the comments were more gentle, not aloof, exactly, but different. He grinned like a bear at Gerry's often bawdy stories. He snarked at Xendra as if they were siblings in perpetual competition. But with Flora, there was a reserve, a deference.

Spense wondered—not for the first time—why his brother had asked her to come along, and why she'd agreed. The Knights were obvious choices, but Flora? Dirk could've chosen any number of stable hands. They danced around each other, always polite, often friendly but there was something else. Something familiar.

As their first night in Summer lengthened, and Spense regarded his friends across the sparking fire, it came to him. It was how his father behaved around his mother. And just like the older pair, whatever glint of feeling was there, it was overwhelmed by their relative social positions. Like his father, Dirk was royal, the Crown Prince, and Flora was as common as they came, a near-orphan farm girl who'd lived with her aunt and uncle until she'd taken the job at the castle. The thing he saw as reserve was sadness.

Wicked Winter. Dirk liked her.

But he couldn't be with her—not the way he might want to—and whatever his faults, Dirk was an honorable guy, and wouldn't want her any other way.

In the midst of the jokes and stories, Spense discovered a new sinking sensation in his chest and belly to accompany the one he'd carried for months. He'd never pitied Dirk for anything—not ever.

But this…

The sharp pain was too familiar and too much to bear. Spense quietly excused himself from the revelry, claiming fatigue.

It was close enough to the truth.

Chapter 29

They were down to shirtsleeves and trousers by the second night in the Summer lands. The air was balmy and sweet—warm sun on pine—as they wove through the woods of Summer. Though they climbed in elevation, the air had not grown colder. Dirk used a cloth to discreetly wipe sweat from his brow.

"How much farther to The Vail?" Gerry asked.

Dirk lifted the corner of his mouth in a knowing smile. Gerry may be a Knight, well-trained, adept in all manner of military skill, disciplined to a fault, but in private, he was as impatient as any child on a long journey.

He turned to his brother. "Spense, you're the only one of us who's actually been here—at least recently—can you satisfy our whining toddler's request for information?"

Spense shook his head. "No. Sadly, I wasn't quite conscious for the last bit of the journey."

Dirk started. He knew of Spense's injuries, but he hadn't realized they were that serious. Spense said he'd been cut by a group of feral trees who wouldn't respond to Dewy's faerie magic. Dirk had imagined the type of lashings he often came home with when he took Storm out for a race through the woods. Minor abrasions that quickly healed. Nothing that would cause a loss of consciousness. Dirk wondered how many slices Spense had gotten. How many drops of his brother's blood watered this forest floor?

"I-I didn't realize—" Dirk began.

But Spense waved him off. "It was months ago. I got better. But as to where we are, I can only say that we've passed through anything I recognize, so I don't think that it will be too much farther, but who knows? Faeries can move pretty fast when they want to."

"So, you're saying you have no idea."

"Pretty much."

Dirk sighed. All he had was an outdated map. And his memory was hazy. He'd been to The Vail as a small child, before his mother had gotten sick. His parents had been on an ambassadorial tour of the kingdoms neighboring Telridge. What little he remembered of the Summer land was that it was green. So green, it made his young eyes widen in amazement. Everything was growing. Everything. The furniture wasn't made from sawn logs, but from living trees and bushes, shaped and formed to provide places to sit or set a book.

He'd asked if he could have growing things in his bedroom and was succinctly told that trees were not grown inside of stone castles. He'd kept his mouth shut after that but had been mesmerized just the same. Back then, he'd been a small boy, with few expectations or responsibilities. Now, he couldn't afford to become distracted by the magic of the land or of its people.

"Perhaps we should prepare to make camp soon," Dirk said. He knew disappointment edged his words.

"I'm sure we could push on a little more, my lord," Flora said.

They may be half a day's ride away from the capital, or possibly less. It would be tempting to continue, to reach their destination sooner. But who knew how late that would be? "Better to start fresh in the morning, even if we only have a short distance to go."

Flora nodded. He appreciated her suggestion. It was likely what they all thought, but she helped him reason it out, so everyone understood his conclusion. The assist was the type of thing that a second would do, a partner.

Dirk led his horse off the main path and followed a stream to a small meadow, surrounded by whispering aspens, under the watchful gaze of the forest. He was used to whispering, to having eyes upon him. In court. Throughout the city. Sometimes, it felt as if the whisperers knew his thoughts. He knew he hadn't yet mastered his father's ability to veil his emotions. If those trees knew his thoughts now, they kept it amongst themselves. And he was grateful.

He couldn't have thoughts of…appreciation for Flora. She couldn't be a person he depended upon for anything except the care of his horse. Anything else was unthinkable and put them both in a precarious position. He wasn't the type to engage in a frivolous dalliance.

He had no training or schooling for this, only his father's anemic example. Dirk was meant to form a strategic, diplomatically beneficial attachment, dictated by Telridgian law and tradition to someday choose a partner. There'd been no hint that anything like feeling should be involved. That something so foreign to his plans, and those of his father should interfere…

It was a complication and obstacle, for which he had no tactical plan.

Chapter 30

Spense set to his task—gathering firewood—with mechanical proficiency. He was careful to take only fallen timbers and branches. He knew better than to bring an axe to the forests of Summer.

Cheerful voices carried as he collected an armful. The light laughter and easy conversation continued as it had for days. The Telridgians might've been on holiday, for all the banter, and Spense felt the pull of invitation.

But his purpose was neither light nor easy. His thoughts were in a different place. Many leagues away in the high mountains of Winter, where the warming sun he now appreciated was but an idea.

He filled his arms and began his first few steps back toward camp when he heard a sharp rustle and crack of trod-upon branches. Spense paused.

"I'm going to go ahead and assume you wanted me to hear that," he said.

"Of course." A shadow slid from behind a cluster of aspens and emerged as the person of Thorn, Lady Radiant's personal steward and spy. He was clad in dusky greens and greys, blending in with the surrounding forest. "Had I not wanted to garner your attention, I would not have."

"I believe you."

Thorn had been Spense's unasked-for companion

during his trudge back to Telridge, so many months ago. In that time, he'd witnessed the spy's skills. Seemingly disappearing when they approached human villages and homesteads where he deemed his presence might not be welcome, and then reappearing as if he'd been strolling alongside Spense the whole time. But the Fae male's quiet and unassuming demeanor had also been a balm. He'd listened to Spense's frustrations and ranting grief without judgment, and he'd helped Spense set a new course.

Spense's lips lifted in a small smile. "It's good to see you, friend. I take it the queen got our message."

Thorn raised his dark eyebrows. "She did. You've piqued her curiosity. And mine, too, truth be told."

"Please. You've already developed a handful of speculations, weighed them, and have accurately predicted why we've come."

"Perhaps."

"Would you like to meet my friends properly? I'm sure you've already scouted their whereabouts and identities."

Thorn's warm, brown face stretched into a grin. His mirth took a malicious bent. "It would be my pleasure. Lead the way."

Spense rolled his eyes. As if Thorn didn't know exactly where the group was noisily setting up camp.

As he set off again, Spense said, "I don't suppose your companions would like to join us."

Thorn blinked once.

"Gentlemen," he said. "If you please."

Two more faeries emerged from the forest, out of the shadows. They were dressed as Thorn, in mottled green and grey.

"So, this is him?" The taller of the two nodded in Spense's direction.

"Indeed. Allow me to introduce you to Master Spense of the kingdom of Telridge. Practitioner of elemental magic, *friend* to our dear Lady Dew Drop, and, apparently, collector of firewood." Thorn waved. The gesture was both gallant and casually dismissive.

The faerie who'd spoken smirked. "I'm called Cedar. This is Leaf." He nodded to his silent companion, who leaned against an aspen.

The male's arms were crossed, and his eyes held a far-away gaze. It was a deception often employed by Telridgian guards, appearing as if they were looking at nothing while taking in everything.

"Glad to make your acquaintance," Spense said, ducking his head in a small bow. "Would you care to join me and my companions?"

"Please," Thorn said.

Spense knew a wiser man wouldn't let the faerie sentinels out of his sight, wouldn't let them fall behind as he and Thorn strolled back to the camp, but he needed to demonstrate trust, to at least pretend the friendliness that Thorn implied.

He whistled a short two-note trill as they approached. It was enough to catch Dirk's attention, and that of the Knights. Whatever joke his friends shared ended abruptly. As he stepped into the camp-site glen accompanied by three faeries, Dirk, Gerry, and Lady Xendra rose, their hands drifting to their weapons belts. Dirk took a half step forward, subtly positioning himself in between Flora and the new arrivals.

"What's this?" Dirk asked.

"It seems we will have an escort for our remaining

travels, my lord." Spense layered on as much cheer as he could. He knew he sounded stupidly naïve, but better that than suspicious or threatening.

"Is that so? How accommodating."

"Isn't it, though?" Spense dropped his bundle of wood. "You remember Thorn?"

"Of course," Dirk nodded. "Good to see you, again, sir."

"And you, Prince Dirk." Thorn dipped his head.

Spense noted the quick glance between the faerie sentinels, who'd taken position on either side of their leader. Maybe they hadn't been briefed that this was a royal visit.

Thorn stepped forward and grasped hands with Dirk. Quick introductions were made for the rest of both parties, and Spense learned that the two males he'd taken as mere sentinels were noble Fae, part of Lady Radiant's court.

He prepared tea and shared it with his fellow Telridgians as well as the Summer arrivals. While there remained an undercurrent of heightened awareness— the careful words, restrained gestures—Telridge and the Summer Court were true allies, and not merely at a present détente. At least, there were no goblins holding a knife to his throat.

As he settled back, reclining on a downed timber, Spense breathed easier, relaxing, as he hadn't since…since he and Thorn had parted ways, all those months ago.

Then, it had been as if the last connection he'd had to Dewy was torn away. With a shared cup of verbena-infused tea, Spense took a step toward Dewy, and got back a little piece of her, that feeling of home he found with her.

He hoped that in the next few days, he didn't screw it up.

Chapter 31

There were faeries leading their party.
Faeries.
One at the front, chatting amiably with Spense, and two others who drifted in and out of view, trailing behind. Escorts, guides, jailers, Flora wasn't sure.

With the exception of her cousin's half-faerie child, Petal, she hadn't spent much time in the company of the fair folk. Her acquaintance with Dewy had been brief, and the visit from the Winter ambassadors hadn't done much to impress. She hoped the Summer faeries didn't run quite so cold.

If their encounter—so far—provided any clues, it was that this group was very different from their chilly Winter counterparts. The Summer Fae agreed to make camp and share a meal with the Telridgians—with humans. Surely that meant something.

Overnight, Dirk and each of the Knights took turns keeping watch, along with one of the Fae sentinels. Not that they would've needed to, Spense and Thorn stayed up half the night talking by the fire, behaving as old friends, now reunited, sharing news and updates, and in predictable Spense-fashion, launching into academic speculation. Spense's research, by fate and coincidence, led them on this journey to seek the Oracles, after all.

It felt above Flora's reckoning or responsibility. She was no longer an academic, just the caretaker of the horses. What was her role in all of this? Her questions didn't prevent her from listening to the waxing conversation as she tried to settle in, though. And anyway, sleep was elusive with three well-armed Fae inhabiting their camp.

But the morning broke, bright and warming, as only a morning in the lands of Summer could, she supposed. There was a thin layer of mist that cleared early, by the time they shared another small meal and packed up the horses. And soon they found their way again, following the pattern the group had so quickly established after that awkward first night at the inn. The track Thorn led them on was well traveled, wide enough to walk side by side. With Spense and Thorn out front, Flora found herself paired with Dirk, who took the lead of one of the horses like a common groom. If only the pampered ladies and gentlemen of the Telridgian Court could see him now.

"Dare I ask what that chuckle means?" Dirk leaned over to ask her. She caught the forest-infused scent of him. The ends of his hair were still damp from his quick wash at a stream and curled slightly at the nape of his neck. His face was pinked by the stream-side shave. He'd let stubble grow for the past several days, but she supposed that wouldn't do if he was to be presented to Lady Radiant, the Summer Queen. Flora didn't mind the less-polished version of him, but it wasn't as if she had the right to form an opinion.

She loosed a breath. "Just wondering what the fawning courtiers would think of their future king who sleeps under the stars, shaves by the river, and tends to his own horse."

Dirk snorted. "If they'd any sense, they'd get over

themselves and learn to do these things, too."

"You'll be such a disappointment to your peers," she teased.

"As if I care what a bunch of dandies think of me."

"You should, though."

"Sorry?"

"Someday, you'll lead them, and not in battle, well, at least not with swords and spears. I can't pretend to understand the politics of court, but it seems like it's just as important to the good governing of Telridge. Keeping all of those courtiers content."

"You sound like my father." He released a heavy sigh. "And just when I thought we were going to have a nice morning chat in the forest."

"Apologies, my lord."

"No. Don't be sorry. Folks seem to think he's wise."

"Isn't he?"

Dirk laughed. The sound was dry and hard. "Of course. He's the king."

"I…umm…" Flora mashed her bottom lip in between her teeth.

"Ignore me." Dirk shook his head. "These are things I should hear. Though I find I'm much more receptive to your counsel than his."

Flora turned her eyes back to the wide trail. Heat crept up her neck that had little to do with the morning sun. She let the silence between them linger until it became a comfortable thing again, when her ears settled upon the jangle of the horses' leads, the thudding of their hooves, the murmured voices up ahead of them, and the quiet space between them turned into a place of rest, where it was a reasonable thing that she should give advice to Dirk, the young man who was her friend first and all of his other titles later. As if it could ever be that easy.

****

As the morning light transformed into broad day, and their pace became regular and mechanical, Flora took in the changing forest around her. She couldn't say what was different from the trees surrounding Telridge. They were a similar species, but there'd been a growing darkness in the woods near her aunt and uncle's farm, as if the forest had become untamed, dangerous, like those foxes. None of that was present amongst the Summer trees, where light tickled the verdant boughs, and the very air sparkled. It had a wildness to it, as well, but in this case, it felt like freedom, not decay.

And she swore that the birds' calls morphed into trills of laughter. When forest creatures darted across their path, or ran alongside them in the trees—squirrels, rabbits, deer, and healthy foxes—she had the sense that they were aware and communicating with the Fae in their party.

Her suspicions were proven correct when Thorn turned to Dirk. "I hope you don't mind, but your welcoming entourage has grown." He circled his hand above him, indicating the clusters of tittering jays. "Some of our people, it seemed, couldn't resist the curiosity that a visiting human noble presented."

Dirk raised an eyebrow and glanced above him.

"Perhaps you'd like to meet the prince, ladies?" Thorn called up. "If that is amenable to you, of course, Lord Dirk?"

"Of course. By all means."

Two of the jays swooped from their perches

overhead, their green-blue wings lengthening and transforming into gauzy gowns as the young women reached the forest floor.

"May I present Lady Thistle and Lady Shamrock, both members of Queen Radiant's council."

The Fae—one with dark blue-black hair, and the other deep green—ducked their heads in a bow in unison, a bit of practiced choreography. As they began to speak, Flora suspected it was something else, as the two were uncannily attuned to each other.

"Prince Dirk…

"So delighted to make your acquaintance."

"We've been so curious…"

"After our Lady Radiant received your correspondence."

"And of course…"

"After the visit from your dear brother."

"Half brother, Shamrock."

"Of course, Thistle. Half brother."

Dirk's gaze darted between the two as they fired off their twittering remarks. "Pleased to meet you both," he managed to comment.

"And you, Prince Dirk."

"And all of your people, of course." The green-haired faerie—Lady Shamrock—nodded her petite head at the other Telridgians, Flora included. She'd never been acknowledged in such a way, even as an aside.

"My thanks, ladies."

The blue-haired Lady Thistle drifted to Dirk's side and extended her hand. Her dusky skin glistened, along willowy limbs, as if infused with starlight. Dirk towered above her, but she maintained the picture of serene elegance and poise. Her sister offered an arm to Spense.

"Shall we, Lord Dirk?"

"Master Spense?"

Dirk allowed a tight smile. "Of course. It would be an honor."

He lifted the faerie's small hand with his own. The contrast couldn't be more plain. His hand was battle-scarred, a calligraphy of nicks and scratches earned from his life as a soldier. The faerie's was fine and delicate. Flora examined her own calluses and blunted fingernails.

Dirk, Spense, and their faerie companions stepped to the head of the party—a royal and semi-royal parade. Flora remained back with the horses. Where she belonged. Her quick moment of inclusion was over. Gerry stepped to Dirk's place next to her and took a lead line. He winked as they proceeded into the heart of the Summer lands, trailing behind their prince.

The air was warm. The sun sparkled through the towering trees. And the welcome had been gracious.

Then why did Flora feel a sudden chill?

Chapter 32

Dewy fell to her knees, bracing herself with one hand and sucking in sharp, fragmented breaths. She swiped at her running nose. Her fingers came away red.

"What is…?"

"Here, let me help." Misty knelt on the ground beside her, but her voice sounded distant and echoing.

Dewy felt hands and arms supporting her, shifting her to a seated position on the pebbled floor of the glassed-in garden. Misty pulled a cloth from a pile of rags and held it to Dewy's bleeding nose.

"Hold that there for a moment."

Her breathing calmed. She leaned against the pot of a lemon tree. Its leafy branches curved over her, weighed down with fruit.

"Hmm…" Lumine tutted from the other side of the garden walkway. His midnight robes slowly came in to focus. "We may have pushed too hard."

"You think?" Misty said.

Dewy closed her eyes. The trickle from her nose had stopped, but fatigue oozed through her. She could happily tip over and sleep right here in the garden. The idea had merit.

"Oh no you don't." The hands and arms had returned.

She leaned against a person now. Misty.

The Fae was warm. Her arms were strong, body

solid. From her lithe frame and cool skin, it would be easy to think that Misty was cold and fragile, like a snowflake.

But no. That's me.

Dewy's legs splayed out on the gravel. Perspiration beaded up under her hairline, icy and chilled. The garden quivered, shook.

Wait. Me again.

"Uncle…" Misty said.

A moment later, another set of arms circled around her, under her knees and supporting her back. Dewy flew up to the height of the lemon tree—its new leaves tickled her limp arm. She rested her head against something solid that smelled of jasmine and new frost.

Chapter 33

"She's exhausted. That's all."

"You're sure?"

The wise woman, Cinnamon, eyed Lumine. You'd never know he was king by the way that Cinna spoke to him. Just another young and wayward Fae, with a disappointing understanding of the magical world. It's how everyone felt in Cinna's presence. It was definitely how Misty felt.

She was pretty sure that showing up with a passed-out Summer Fae didn't do much to improve Cinna's estimation of either her or her uncle's abilities—certainly not their wisdom.

"What did you two do to the poor girl?" Cinna asked, tucking blankets around the slumbering form of Lady Dew Drop.

The princess had lost much of her Summer coloring and was nearly as pale as many Winter folk. The bloody nose and abrupt loss of consciousness didn't help.

Lumine flattened his mouth into a thin line. He raised one eyebrow.

Cinna waggled her gnarled finger at the king. "No, you don't get to play that game with me. I'm not impressed by your royal mystique."

Misty bit her lip. She'd never address King Lumine with so much irreverence. She'd barely think it. But then, he was her uncle. He'd always occupied a place of authority in her life. Cinna had been old when Lumine was still an uncontrollable toddler, leaving miniature ice sculptures and slippery, frozen corridors in his wake.

"Can you help her?"

Cinna narrowed her gaze. "Of course, I can help her. It's why you brought her to me, isn't it?"

"If you would be so kind..." Lumine gestured to Dewy's still form.

Cinna wobbled her way over to the hearth and tossed in another log. As if it weren't already sweltering in her small, woodland cottage.

"You see, that's the problem. You pretended to be kind, but you, young man, don't understand the word. Instead, you were indulgent. You gave her tea and books and let her fester, all alone in your cold palace."

Lumine lifted his chin, the only indication that he'd heard Cinna's rebuke.

"I know what you're after. You want her to use her magic for your special project, and she can't do that on rabbit food."

Misty snorted.

Both Fae turned to her.

"Sorry." Misty shifted her gaze to the well-worn rug on Cinna's cottage floor.

Lumine rumbled a low growl.

"What? It's a rabbit that got us here."

Cinna frowned. "Excuse me?"

"She was working on sensing a rabbit—its blood—in one of the garden houses," Lumine said. "When she collapsed."

"Blood magic? You had her sensing blood?" Cinna

shook her head. "Sweet Spring."

"Her gifts are strong. I've never met an elemental with as much raw energy before."

Lumine strolled the small cottage. If he was trying to justify his actions, Cinna was having none of it.

"It doesn't mean she's ready for blood magic." She looked at the prone girl. Considered. Sighed. "Yes, her water abilities are...impressive. And in time, she may be able to accomplish what you need."

Lumine stared intently at the old woman.

"You realize what you're asking me?"

"I do. But you understand the urgency."

Cinna grabbed another quilt from a basket near the bed. She laid it gently over Dewy. "Fine, but I'm going to do it my way. I'm going to show her actual kindness, and I don't want any of your interference."

Lumine bowed low, hinging at the waist. "Thank you, dear lady. I am in your debt."

"Humph. Don't you forget it."

Chapter 34

Towering cedars and aspens ushered guests into the heart of Summer's capital. The transition from the forest to the palace was seamless. No distinction between outdoors and in. Spense smiled. He remembered Dewy's rants against the human tendency to tuck themselves behind walls and under ceilings. But constrained to the lands of Winter, Dewy must've learned the custom did not belong to humans, alone.

He glanced behind him. Flora and the two Knights were as wide-eyed and open-mouthed as he'd been his first time in The Vail. How many humans had been to this serene palace, where the air was balmy, and the sun shone through the green canopy above in sky-lit rays? Dirk kept his expression neutral, but there was something soft in his eyes, perhaps the return to a memory nearly forgotten. Spense knew it wasn't his half brother's first time in faerie lands, either.

They moved further into the palace. Trunks and branches bent and stretched, creating archways, corridors, and secluded rooms, and their greeters grew in number. By the time the Telridgians reached the slender aspens framing the entrance to the queen's royal chambers, a throng of faerie-kind surrounded them, peering out between leaves, hovering overhead. Whispers and giggles bounced between the trees until Lady Radiant arrived and the crowd settled into a reverent silence.

The golden queen regent glided through the archway and down the stone stairs, on the arm of a bark-colored faerie. Her smile was kind, but her eyes were searching. Spense ducked his head in a bow. Cloth and leather rustled as the other Telridgians repeated the gesture.

"Young Master Spense," she said. "It does my heart good to see you."

Spense lifted his head, meeting Radiant's knowing gaze. He recognized the shared sadness, the deep pang that came from missing Dewy. But did she see her niece's green eyes when she caught her own reflection in a looking glass? Or remember Dewy preferred to dress in the same style as common faeries? These little things, these reminders, made her absence all the more conspicuous.

"Thank you, Lady Radiant. It is an honor to be here."

"Would you care to introduce your companions?"

"Of course. May I present, first, the Lord Commander and Crown Prince of Telridge, Dirk Ferrous." Spense gestured to his half brother, who stepped forward and bowed deeply.

"Such an exalted string of titles." Lady Radiant eyed Dirk carefully. "Might you also mention you are kin?"

Dirk smiled. "You are quick to catch my brother's oversight, Lady Radiant."

Spense's face heated. It wasn't so much that he'd been caught in an error of omission, but that Dirk had not qualified their relationship. He'd said brother. Not half brother.

"And your other friends?" Radiant asked.

"If you'll allow me." Dirk turned. "This is the Lady Xendra, and Sir Gervais, both Telridge Knights, and...Lady Flora, a close friend of the Crown."

Flora blinked rapidly. Her mouth opened and closed, before Lady Xendra grabbed her by the elbow, and the three stepped forward.

"You've had a long journey. I imagine you'd like some time to rest and refresh yourselves. My ladies, Thistle and Shamrock, can escort you to chambers. We will dine together this evening."

The travel-worn group of Telridgians ducked, curtsied and bowed, murmuring words of thanks.

"And Spense?" Lady Radiant said.

"Yes, my lady?"

"I look forward to talking with you further about the progress you've made these past months."

"Of course, my lady." Spense gulped.

Radiant's gracious words didn't veil the reminder that it had been months, and still her beloved niece was kept from her. As it was Spense's fault, it was also his responsibility to get her back. The queen might hold some vicarious affection for Spense, but she was also a powerful Fae.

Her patience may soon run out.

Chapter 35

Lady Xendra leaned over to whisper in Flora's ear. "You're fidgeting."

Flora stilled her hands, pressing them flat against the smooth fabric of the borrowed gown. "Sorry. It's weird."

"You are familiar with the concept of dresses?"

Flora glared pointedly at the knighted lady, "Yes, I have skirts. But they're wool or linen. I don't even know what this is."

"It's called silk, dear."

Flora pressed her lips together. Whatever its name, the gown was shimmery and light. The faerie-made dress cinched in just below her breasts and flowed out in a wide skirt. When she walked, she felt like a dandelion seed drifting on unseen air currents. As she and Lady Xendra were escorted into the Summer palace's large hall by the two sentinels, Cedar and Leaf, Flora felt exposed, on display.

Her place in the kingdom of Telridge was one of invisibility. For a time, she'd been one of a throng of anonymous students. More recently, whether she was mucking out stalls, tending to her family's chickens and sheep, or providing support to the castle attendants during a feast, her goal was to make it appear as if the work of the kingdom just happened, unseen, as if by magic. But here, in a land of actual magic, she was insignificant Flora, and she had no job to do, to hide behind.

"Ladies."

An untethered voice broke into Flora's anxious thoughts. She looked up as Dirk approached, accompanied by Sir Gervais. She'd seen the prince in the trappings of court before. He'd never seemed quite comfortable. But like the rest of their party, he'd accepted the faerie's offerings and wore the silk garments of the Summer Fae. He was no less refined than at Telridge's court, but he seemed more at ease, his movements less restricted. The evidence was in his smooth stride and relaxed smile.

"We'll take over from here. But thank you, gents, for helping our ladies find their way." Dirk nodded to the two sentinels, who scowled, but nevertheless slipped away.

"Shall we?" Dirk asked, holding out his arm.

Flora snapped her mouth shut and fumbled her arm into the proper position. Her hand slid to the natural hinge in Dirk's arm, where her fingers splayed to grasp the curve of his bicep, and she steadied, as if she were leeching strength from him.

Our ladies.

She knew it was court speech. It didn't mean anything. It was probably easier than to explain. But those two small words of implied belonging opened up a wanting Flora had tried to ignore.

Dirk led Flora to the throne—made of woven camellia branches—where Lady Radiant presided. Spense was already in deep conversation with the queen.

"Lady Radiant." Dirk and Flora bent into deep

bows. Gerry and Lady Xendra mimicked them.

"Welcome, Prince Dirk. And honored Telridgians."

"Thank you. I see my brother has already garnered your attention."

Radiant smiled and placed a hand on Spense's arm. "That he has. We've much in common, as you know. He was telling me of his adventures with my dear niece. And I confess it comforts me to hear stories of her."

"Of course. Though I hope I might distract you and join you for a dance this evening?" Dirk asked.

"No, no. I never dance." The queen lifted her golden hand in a small wave. "But this evening's festivities are for your rest and enjoyment. I insist that you proceed. We will talk of more serious matters in the morning."

Dirk bowed again. "Thank you, Lady Radiant."

"Go. Dance with your own lady."

Flora's cheeks warmed. It worsened as Dirk turned to her. "Well, how about it? Will you favor me with a dance? The queen insists."

Flora glanced at the faeries, weaving and twirling to the sounds of lilting music. A cluster of faerie musicians played pipes and horns—more delicate and rustic than any instruments in the human lands. "I'm not sure I'm familiar with these dances, my lord."

Dirk followed her gaze. "I don't think that matters."

She could see no pattern, no consistent or repeated steps. Unlike the strict choreographies of the Telridgian court, the faerie movements were loose, leaving each dancer, pairing, or group to interpret their own combinations. To twirl each other with merry abandon or simply sway to the piped melody.

"Shall we?" Dirk rotated his arm and lifted his hand.

An offering. An invitation. If she were brave enough to accept it. Flora raised her gaze to his. She followed with her hand and placed it in Dirk's.

Without another word, they entered the flow of dancing faeries. She spotted the blue-haired Thistle and her sister, Shamrock, who winked at her before spinning away. Smiling faces with high cheek bones and pointed ears whirled past her, lost in the delights of the music. Flora scanned their faces. Who in the crowd might be a relative of her cousin's daughter? Was Petal's mother among the dancers? When the babe had arrived at their farmhouse door, there was nothing more than a note identifying her. And her cousin Rook had never again seen the faerie he'd met in the forest— presumably at a dance similar to this.

She'd always wondered how Rook had been swept away by that faerie girl, to the point their dalliance had resulted in Petal. But perhaps it was easier to see now. The heady scent of flowers tickled her nose, while the strains of the sweet melody captured her. She leaned into the feeling as much as she relied on Dirk's hands, one firmly holding hers, another around her waist, following the slight squeeze of his fingers or the nudge of his hip. Learning to listen, instead of fighting, his cues, moving past the inevitable stumbles and missteps, the strained laughter.

Their dance became an interplay of silent communication, a partnership, a small turn away from other dancers to avoid collision, a drawing in and a releasing. Her floating skirts swirled, and her apprehensions drained away. For this moment at least, they were just Flora and Dirk. No titles. No responsibilities.

And Flora drank it in. Dirk's own free laughter. The easy light in his eyes, as he trained them on her.

For one night, she could dance with the prince and pretend she was someone else.

Chapter 36

His brother twirled Flora among the throngs of faerie dancers. Joy lit up their faces, and their eyes were bright. Spense wasn't sure he'd ever seen Dirk so unguarded. Certainly never at any official Telridgian balls. *Of all places to lose himself.*

"They make a lovely pairing," Radiant observed.

"They do," he agreed.

"So, why the frown?"

"Because it's not that simple." Spense glanced at the queen. "You know the difficulties of nobility, of who they can and cannot care for."

The queen let her gaze settle onto her hands, folded demurely in her lap. Her head held high and erect. She was the picture of serene and regal grace. If anyone understood, it would be her.

"Of course. But…sometimes the heart has ideas of its own. Is your brother's affection for his stable girl any more unusual than my own brother's and his commoner wife? Or for you and my dear niece—the Princess and Heir of Summer?"

The queen's comments provoked a number of questions. He went with the simplest "How did you know of Flora's…profession?"

Radiant shrugged. "Thorn."

Spense should've known. "Of course."

"I like to be informed—know who my guests are—

it doesn't mean that I'm biased against them, or willing to let someone's status at birth color my impression of them."

"She used to study at The Academy."

"Interesting. Do you know why she left?" Radiant tilted her head and narrowed her gaze.

Spense shook his head. "I've never learned the reason. I imagine it has something to do with her parents' deaths."

"So, you see, there is a story there, I'm sure. And it proves my point. We all have layers, if one chooses to look."

He let her words rest for a moment, considering the stories she shared, and what they revealed. Such a simple, easy notion. That love could conquer all. It was a tempting thought. He wanted it to be true.

But he knew better.

He would pursue the Oracles and find the Heir, all to free Dewy—because he cared for her. Anything he hoped to happen after would be her decision. He wasn't so naïve to think that it would be her free choice.

As if to drive home the point, a member of the queen's council approached the camellia throne. He'd been introduced as Oak, a tall and lean Fae, dressed in spring greens, and wearing a crown of leaves. Several Fae and common faeries alike paid court to the queen during Spense's conversation with her. And while they showed him the respect that a guest of faerie was due, he knew there was no love for humans. And of him, personally, a fair amount of skepticism and derision. He was, after all, the mage who'd gotten their princess into this predicament in the first place. Oak was no different. Nor were his apparent sidekicks, the sentinels,

Leaf and Cedar.

"My queen." Oak bowed over her hand. "And Master Spense, of course. Of Telridge."

Spense ducked a brief nod.

"Will you partake of the dance tonight, Oak? What of you, Leaf? Cedar?" Lady Radiant asked.

"We will stay to escort our human guests back to their quarters as you've requested, my lady," Cedar said.

Oak took a sip of his wine and scanned the revelers. "I might stay for a bit. It is quite something how charmingly the humans clean up, though they could never match the fineness of the Fae."

"Careful, Oak. These are our friends and allies. Though their ways may be foreign to us, it does not make them lesser," the queen cautioned.

"Of course not, my lady. Forgive the implication." Oak bowed and departed, without another glance to Spense, the allegedly charming human in question.

Spense's chest tightened. He wondered what they'd think if they knew of his mixed heritage. He appeared human, and so human he must be, at least in their eyes.

"Pay him no heed, Master Spense," Thorn whispered at his side.

Spense jolted. When had Thorn arrived? The steward was disturbingly adept at his less-public arts.

"Pardon?"

"The lad is jealous of you. This is how he shows it."

Thorn nodded in the direction of Oak, who was now wending his way amongst the dancing faeries. Some of whom draped their arms around him or whispered in his pointed ear before flitting off to dance elsewhere. It did not appear that Oak was short of attention.

"What could he possibly be jealous of?"

"It is well known that you captured the heart of Lady Dew Drop," Radiant said.

"You mean The Claiming." Spense frowned. Would he never live down the shame of that? "But she is free now."

"She may be free of the spell. She fell in love with you."

Spense opened his mouth to protest. He looked back and forth between Radiant and her spy. How could they know that?

Thorn held up his hand. "Don't deny it—you love her, too—It's why you're here. And that love is a powerful thing. Much more so than any spell. That is what Oak is jealous of."

Oak danced and swayed in a close grouping with Leaf and Cedar, as well as two more faeries with deep violet and rose-pink hair, their skin glistening as they moved.

"He doesn't appear to want for companions."

"Oh no—that is not his challenge. You might have even seen Dew Drop out there with him once upon a time. They're friends, have been since childhood. She was a particular devotee of the nightly dance," Lady Radiant added wistfully.

Spense could see it. There was so much about the Summer lands that felt restrained, but not here. This was a place of freedom and release. It was having that effect on the Telridgians, as well.

Dewy would've loved it.

The joy of the revelry. If not for him, she'd be

dancing now.

"Truth be told…they were more than friends," Thorn said.

Spense looked sharply at Thorn.

"Don't make it more than it was, Thorn," Lady Radiant said. "But, yes, Oak would have been one of several Fae suitors in contention for a marriage alliance with Lady Dew Drop. You see how important the matter of heirs is to the lands of faerie. She will have to pick someone, eventually."

Heirs. The royal line of Summer. Was there nothing he hadn't cost her or her people? Oak was right to be angry with him. They all were. If not for him, their princess would be among them, safe and free to dance away her nights in joyful abandon with her prospective Fae suitors. Not an apprentice mage. His belly roiled, and the sharp taste of bile rose in his throat. Was this the cost of love?

"I think I'd like to return to my guest chambers, now," Spense said, turning away from the sensual frivolity of the dance, the reminder of all that Dewy had given up…because of him.

Chapter 37

Dewy woke, warm and heavy. Woolly, knitted blankets piled on her body. Her head rested on a down-filled cushion.

"Well done, Lumine. You didn't kill her off."

She opened sleep-crusted eyelids to a dim room, lit with firelight and golden candles. It smelled of baking things, sweet and spicy.

"Where...?" The word grated along her throat, coming out croaking and broken.

"Hush, child."

Dewy knew that voice. "Cinna?"

The old faerie hobbled to the bed. Her welcoming smile re-aligned the wrinkles on her face and the glow of candlelight gave her a halo.

"How long...?"

"You slept through the evening meal and moonrise."

Dewy nodded. Her head felt as if it were stuffed with thistle down, but the hazy bits cleared as she took in the details of Cinna's cottage, and the persons inhabiting it. There were three faeries. Their heart beats ticked in quiet rhythm.

Siskin took form and shape next to his great-great-grandmother. "Are you well, Lady Dew Drop?"

"Not sure how to answer that. Were you keeping vigil?"

This wasn't the first time reaching into her magic had drained her. But when she wielded the waters of the River Selden, so many months ago, it had taken her more than a day to recover. She supposed this reaction was an improvement. Dewy pushed herself up onto her elbows.

"Allow me, my lady." Siskin helped her to a seated position and placed another cushion behind her. "Is there anything I may get you?"

"Water?"

"Of course."

The faerie darted across the cottage to the nook of the little house that made up the kitchen. From the vials and herbs ordered on shelves and hanging from beams, Dewy guessed it was also a still, not so different from Spense's laboratory in Telridge or her aunt's private offices in the Summer lands.

Cinna touched Dewy's forehead, frowning as she assessed her patient's present condition.

"Will I live?" Dewy joked.

No one laughed.

Her gaze drifted across the cottage. How bad had it been? Lumine leaned against a cupboard, his arms folded across his chest, his mouth set in a firm line, and his brows drawn together. His heart beat slightly faster than Siskin's, its rushing shallow. With anger? Frustration? It's not like she ever expected Lumine to have a sense of humor, anyway.

Siskin returned with a cup and held it for her to drink. The blessedly cool water wetted her lips and slid down her throat. While Siskin had provided for her needs over the past several months with consistency and competency—as he would for any guest of the

Winter court—he'd never given her quite so much attention. He'd never fussed.

Cinna stepped back. "You'll live. But your body needs to strengthen."

"I thought that's what we'd been doing."

"No. What you've been doing is testing your endurance, finding its breaking point."

"Oh."

Dewy looked down at her body, mounded with blankets. She was warm. The chills had long since abated. But she still felt drained.

The magic they practiced was not complicated, but it required more of her. Finding water had never been a challenge. She could call up rivers and creeks, draw moisture from the air. But this small task—tracking a winter hare through the garden house via its blood—required a different type of focus. And so much more energy of will.

She'd pushed herself past the point when Lumine suggested they stop, that she rest. She sensed the pumping blood in that little rabbit's heart, the swirl of it through the animal's body. But it was faint, like she was listening for the tiniest spring, fathoms below the surface of the earth. And she strained to follow it, to find its pattering spirit. Until her body took over. And the tiny sound disappeared.

"Blood is different than water, girl."

"I'm well aware."

"From what Lumine has reported, you've got the gift." Cinna cast a glance in the direction of the brooding king. "If you're strong enough, you'll experience depths of magic you've not known before."

Dewy closed her eyes.

She wanted this.

But she dreaded it.

What would it take? What would she have to do? Her belly tightened. She knew what Cinna was going to say, but she didn't want to hear it.

"You've got to eat food with real sustenance to build your body and replenish it."

Dewy swallowed down the bitter saliva pooling in her mouth. "From animals. I've heard this before."

"Maybe. But you haven't listened."

"I know. There is a force, in blood and flesh, that provides strength, energy, and heat to the body." Dewy recited the lines she'd heard repeatedly over the last week.

"It is how we Winter faeries live here in the cold. You need that. Your magic needs that." Cinna lifted her weathered hand to Dewy's hair, running her palm over the top of her head. "Good thing for you we know something about how to help you get there."

Chapter 38

Dewy poked at the broth in front of her with a spoon. She made small whirlpools, causing tiny ripples in the soup bowl. She did not lift the spoon to her mouth. Steamy and savory aromas wafted under her nose. The familiar combination of herbs, sage and rosemary were the strongest. She recognized the scent of new onions, fresh roots, and something else, rich, and tangy. Of the earth and its minerals.

Cinna *tsked*. "You won't get anything from it by staring at it. No more stalling. I cleared out those Fae busybodies, so you could eat and rest in peace. It's just you and me and a bowl of soup, now." Cinna folded her arms over her chest. It was clear who'd win in a battle of wills. "Go on. Take a bite."

In texture, the soup appeared the same as the vegetable broths Cook had been preparing for her these past months. Dewy worked her throat several times and braced herself. She'd sat across from the Winter king and his court as they ate animal meat. She understood the care the Winter folk took in honoring and utilizing the whole creature, even thanking it for its life gifts. She had taken to wearing leather boots with gratitude, justifying the need as she and Misty ran through the ice and snow.

But this last step. Consuming. Taking a creature into herself. It was one more step away from the

Summer faerie she'd always known herself to be.

That faerie was too weak. Her viewpoint too narrow. Life in Winter had shown her that.

Dewy took one small spoonful. She let the liquid swish in her mouth a moment before swallowing. She tasted salt and fat, but unlike any of the oils pressed from olives or churned from cream. This was heartier.

It was not unpleasant.

As she took another bite and another, she recognized the tiny, chopped onions, a hint of root vegetable—possibly carrot—shredded into the broth. And that underlying element brought out the flavors in the vegetables, making them both sweeter and more savory. Before she knew it, she had emptied the small bowl and leaned back from the table.

"There, now. You see? It's not too terrible."

It wasn't. Not at all. Dewy's chest and belly were comfortably warm from the hot broth. A little of her energy returned, buoyed by the nourishment of the small meal.

She dared not ask what, exactly, was in the thin soup. She didn't want to know what creature had given its lifeblood for her.

For now, she would rest in ignorance, and let the hearty substance do its work.

Chapter 39

She swirled, twirled, floated.

That couldn't be right.

Flora was not a floaty type of girl. Nor was she the type to dance the night away with a prince on her arm, under the forest canopy of a faerie palace. But…

She blinked rapidly until her vision cleared. Sunlight flickered overhead, streaming through the aspen boughs. She nestled in the linen embrace of a faerie-made bed—or cloud. Hard to tell. And across the giant pillowy cloud-bed, wound up in a pile of blankets on the floor, another person rolled over, groaning in his sleep.

His sleep. He. Him. Brown hair, a familiar tunic…

Sweet Spring.

Dirk.

Crown Prince Dirk, Lord Commander Ferrous. In her room.

"What…is happening?" Flora whispered.

"Oh, good. You're awake."

She bolted upright, whipping her head around until she located the origin of the comment. Not a great idea. How many of those honeyed faerie wine drinks had she had last night?

"Good morning."

When she got her eyesight to align with her hearing, she found Spense, grinning. He leaned against a treed archway separating the sleeping area from the shared common space of their guest quarters.

"Morning…" Flora said. It was as much a question as a greeting.

"So glad you're up. I'm meeting with Thorn this morning, and I wanted to make sure someone knew where I'd gone."

"Right. Sure. I can…relay that information."

"Excellent. Appreciate it." Spense unfolded his arms and took a step back through the arch. He paused and turned back to her. "Oh, and Flora, if my brother snores, just nudge him until he rolls over."

Flora's mouth fell open. The heat of a blush rose in her cheeks.

"I don't snore…" Dirk's voice came out muffled and scratchy.

Spense laughed. "Right. Well. I'll be off then. See you later, Flora. Dirk."

"Uh, all right," Flora said.

Dirk groaned. Again.

Flora pulled the linen coverings up to her chest, as Dirk twisted toward her. His eyes slowly opened. She stared as his face transformed from groggy with sleep to a confused frown. His brow pulled in tight as he squinted up at her in the bright morning sunlight.

"H-hi," he said.

"Hi."

"Uh…how…?" He scanned the room from his lowly position.

Flora grimaced. "I seem to recall that other beds were…occupied when we got to our quarters last night."

Dirk winced. "Gerry and X…?"

She nodded.

"They were…"

"Occupied," she confirmed. "Very."

Flora squeezed her eyes shut, trying to block out the hazy images of the two Knights tangled in each other. It didn't help—no more so than the linen curtain Dirk had drawn over the archway. She and the prince had stumbled, snickering, across the guest quarters to a chamber as far as they could get from the affectionate pair.

"Right. Why am I on the floor of your room?"

"I don't know." She recalled something of an inebriated declaration regarding a Knight's imperative to defend his lady.

"But we…?"

"No!"

"No. Definitely not," he said shaking his head.

Well, of course not. Because he was…him. And she was just Flora.

"No, I think we're safe, there, my lord."

Dirk pushed himself to a seated position. He ran his hands through his sleep-tousled hair. He glanced over at her, and then looked down at himself. He needn't have checked. She already had. They were both fully clothed. Truly, nothing happened that would cause regret. At least, not on her part. Dirk may reconsider his sleeping arrangements once he'd worked out his surely stiff shoulders and paradoxical choices. Whatever would the servants think of a future king who slept on his stable maid's floor?

"I think…last night, we were just…"

"Tired," he said.

Flora nodded eagerly. "That faerie wine has quite a

kick, huh?"

"Right. Yeah. Exactly." Dirk lifted his lips into a crooked grin.

And she remembered every charming glance from the night before. The dancing. The laughter and the sweet wine. Her neck and face grew impossibly warmer. Whatever happened, whatever boundaries fell away, she felt the stinging urge to replace them, as quickly as possible. To return to a safe space where she was a person who tended to a prince's horse, but she did not...

She scrambled to her feet, pulling the linens tightly around her. She gestured to the bathing chambers. "I'm just going to..."

"All right. Yes. Of course."

Flora had a life. A job. Independence. All things she had no interest in risking. Not for a fantastical night filled with Dirk's tempting smiles. There was nothing but heartbreak for her in a prince's smiles.

Chapter 40

"Your thoughts lean to the Lady Dew Drop?"

Spense jumped and discovered Thorn standing next to him. "How did you know that?"

He'd been gazing at the crystalline glass, hanging like windows in the grand treed ballroom where Thorn had asked to meet with him. The sun cut through the morning mist, and he couldn't help but think of Dewy. Like any other lovelorn fool. Especially after the dream-like dancing from the previous night. It appeared his companions had been enthralled by the faerie magic as well and consequently, with each other. But for Spense, there was no one—faerie or human—who could take Dewy's place. If he were to dance, it would only be with her.

Thorn smirked. "It would be natural."

Natural. There was nothing natural about this whole situation. Spense gripped the slender trunk of an alder. His fingers dug into its leathery bark. Dewy should be here. She was a Summer Fae, The Summer Fae, but she was stuck in Winter, where the cloud cover and morning mist were rarely pierced by warming rays of golden sun. "It's hard to picture her there in Winter. I worry."

"Of course. You're not alone in that."

"No. I know."

Dewy had faeries who cared for her, more than

214

Spense had realized. Her aunt, the queen—that was to be expected. But so many members of the court, as well as common faeries. They asked after her. They judged him for the separation.

"Which is why I sent you that message this morning. I'm glad you got it."

"Oh?"

"It wasn't actually I who summoned you, Master Spense. The queen would like a private conference."

Spense frowned. That wasn't ominous at all.

"Nothing too alarming, I assure you," Thorn said.

"Why don't I believe you?"

Thorn chuckled. "Follow me, please."

He led Spense down the corridors of The Vail until they'd reached Lady Radiant's private study. The last time he'd been there, he'd also felt the sharp-eyed scrutiny of the queen. And then, like now, he was sure he'd be found wanting.

"Welcome, Spense."

Spense bowed in the fashion of the Telridgian court. He could at least pretend to fulfill his responsibilities as an emissary and bring some honor to his homeland. "Thank you, Lady Radiant."

"Come in, dear." She gestured to the pair of woven chairs in front of her large desk. Unlike his father's, Lady Radiant's was not polished to a mirrored sheen. Instead, the wood was left to its natural state, worn smooth with time. A long table and shelves stretched behind her, lined with vials and pots.

Spense knew from his time with Dewy that Lady Radiant possessed powerful earth magic and dabbled in potions and spells. There was something comforting in that, seeing her workspace. And though it was larger and had much better light, it wasn't so different from his own laboratory in the cellar of Telridge Castle.

Spense straightened and stepped forward.

"You also, Thorn. None of your skulking. What I have to discuss concerns you as well."

Thorn nodded a quick bow and took his place next to Spense. If the green and grey-clad Fae was concerned or confused by this invitation, he didn't show it. Always blending in, to dark corners, to the forests cocooning the Summer lands. Thorn was an exemplary shadow.

"I want to discuss your plans, Spense, without a court-full of onlookers and gossipers and without all of the formality."

Spense preferred it that way, too. But, if they were discussing plans, his brother should be present. He almost voiced this suggestion when Lady Radiant held up one slim, golden hand.

"Before you protest the importance of diplomacy and political precedence—as I'm sure you're going to—let me remind you of the importance of your mission."

Spense narrowed his eyes. He didn't need reminding.

The queen continued. "We simply don't have time for all the play-acting, the niceties, the back-and-forth. Wouldn't you agree?"

"I would."

"You're here because you want to enter The Between. You want to speak with the Oracles."

Spense twitched and pulled back into his chair. They hadn't so much as hinted at their intention. "How could you know that?" He was beginning to wonder how many of the Summer Fae had a touch of the Sight. Their queen was awfully canny.

Thorn chuckled. "As I said before, it's only natural." He glanced at Lady Radiant before proceeding. "And we've come to the same conclusion."

Radiant leaned forward. "There may be magical means of locating this lost Heir. I'm sure Lumine has looked into it. But I'm equally sure that if he hasn't succeeded yet, then we need to explore other options. It appears you've realized this, too." She rose from behind her workspace and circled around to Spense's side of the large table. "I'm honestly surprised we didn't hear from you sooner."

Spense worried his lips.

"I want my niece back, Master Spense and I know you do, too."

He lowered his eyes, from the queen's all-seeing, all-knowing observation, to his hands clenched tight together on his lap. "I do."

"And we want to help you. All of the Summer Court, in any way we can."

Spense lifted his gaze. "With respect, not all of them."

The queen tilted her head.

Thorn smirked.

"Lord Oak...didn't seem pleased by my presence."

Radiant's expression cleared. "Ah. No, I suppose not. But you'll just have to prove yourself worthy. I have no doubt you will. Bring Lady Dew Drop home and the court will come around."

Spense lowered his eyes again, but the queen was having none of it. She reached for his chin and tilted his face up.

"We have work to do—and I can't have you dejected—I need you focused."

"Of course, my lady."

"Good." She released his chin and strode back around to her side of the table. "You seek The Between, the Oracles."

Spense nodded.

"And you understand how tricksome they can be?"

"I've been told. Yes."

"Then we understand one another. And you'll fully appreciate why I won't let you go in alone."

"I did bring a team with me."

"Oh, your Telridgian Knights are brave, but that's not what I mean."

Thorn scowled. "What are you suggesting, my lady?"

Radiant lifted her lips into a soft smile as she turned her head to her loyal steward. "You, dear Thorn, are going with them."

Spense had never seen Thorn caught off guard. The Fae covered it quickly, dipping his head in a small bow, the picture of subservience. But for a moment, it was there, the flash of surprise, the slight widening of his eyes and raising of his brows.

"As you wish, my lady. As always." Their eyes met.

Spense could swear there was a flicker of something there, something other than the honored respect between a queen and her steward.

"When would you like us to depart?" Thorn asked.

Radiant turned her face to Spense, away from Thorn and away from whatever had been communicated—through whatever empathic means the

Fae queen possessed. "I believe we are all in accord—
the sooner, the better."

"Thank you, my lady. I will inform my brother.
Uh, I mean, Prince Dirk," Spense said, rising from his
seat.

"Of course. But please take your time. You may
want to go easy on your friends this morning. Our
faerie wine tends to leave the uninitiated a little worse
for wear."

Spense stifled a laugh. That was an understatement.
He would heed the queen's words, though. He needed
every one of his companions at their best and, if they
were entering the mystical lands of The Between, on
their guard.

Chapter 41

After a day of respite, Dewy hit her training with a new determination. She'd had rest, and more of Cinna's warming soup at each of her meals. That, in addition to the vegetables and nuts she'd already been eating. She'd never required so much food before.

In the Summer lands, life was easier, dances and frivolities were abundant, and most meals were partaken merely for the sweet satisfaction of the fruits or drinks. But here, in Winter, the focus was on survival, before anything else. She was beginning to understand. After so many years—decades and decades—living in parallel but separate worlds, the Winter faeries and Summer faeries had lost the thread of what made them one people. They weren't anymore. They were as different as…well, sunlight and moonlight. One, bright and radiant. The other, luminous, but cool. Like their monarchs.

But they balanced each other, needed each other. As did the natural world they served.

Dewy took in the towering evergreens and snow-covered boulders in a blur as she and Misty began their morning with a brisk run. Their breaths puffed out in clouds of white vapor, quickly blowing past as they picked up speed. Dewy pushed her legs, lengthening each stride, breathed deep into her chest and all the way to her belly, until her body found a rhythm and the pumping of her limbs kept time with the flow of blood in her body, with the flutter of wings overhead as the winter sparrows joined their sprint.

She'd never imagined such exertion in a cold and unforgiving place could also bring with it a thrill, so different from the warm, easy air of Summer. Every point of her skin prickled with life. Too soon, she and Misty had rounded their loop, and the shining dome of the Silver Horn came back into view.

"What's next?" Dewy asked.

The look Misty gave her—smiling, mischievous, a touch wicked—should've alarmed her. Instead, Dewy grinned back, eager to see what the Fae would throw at her. She wouldn't merely endure the challenge.

She'd best it.

Chapter 42

"You spoke with the queen without me?" Dirk bristled.

Spense threw his arms up. "What part of 'they summoned me' wasn't clear? We can have the official conversation, where you get to be princely and she's fancified and regal. But to get things going, this was more efficient."

Little brother was getting awfully comfortable. Long gone was the skinny kid who bowed in Dirk's presence.

"It's not like we don't use back channels in the Telridge court all the time," Xendra said.

He was pretty sure X had never bothered to bow, and that was a big reason why they were friends.

She plucked a small citrusy fruit from the bowl on the table and methodically removed its peel. Dirk had already had two, along with a large mug of steaming tea, to counteract the wine that still left his head spinning. Discovering that his little brother had been off colluding with their hosts was not helping his headache.

"Don't they have any real food?" Gerry moaned, as he made his way through the fruit. There was a pile of peels in front of him.

"We've got plenty of provisions for the trip," Flora said. "I was planning to check on the horses this morning, anyway. I can bring you some biscuits and dried pork."

"You are a gift from Grace." Gerry grinned and clasped his hands together in adoration.

Dappled sunlight filtered in through the trees of their private guest chambers overhead, crowning the Knight in a brilliant halo. Dirk snorted. Gerry was possibly the least devout person he knew. He would've smacked him upside the head and knocked his sunlit crown right off, but Xendra beat him to it.

"Hey!" Gerry yelped.

"Can we focus on something other than your stomach, please?" Dirk asked. He knew he was grousing and petulant. He didn't care. "And Flora, first, thank you for attending to our mounts. But don't bother being nice to him. Those provisions are for the road."

Gerry scowled. Xendra smirked and poked Gerry in the shoulder. Sweet Spring, this wasn't going to be a thing, now, was it? Dirk knew that his closest friends had been more than friendly, but it'd been the type of situation where everyone pretended that they didn't know what they all obviously knew. And it didn't affect how they worked together. Dirk liked it that way. But this, the teasing, was starting to look like a relationship, like courting. It was weird. What was in that wine?

Dirk took another swig of the tea in front of him. "So when are we scheduled to have the official meeting?"

"I think Lady Radiant was hoping for a discussion during a private dinner," Spense said.

"And by private, you mean..."

"The queen, us, and her entire council. I believe there are eight of them at present."

Dirk cringed.

"Plus any companions the council members choose to bring."

His cringe deepened. "We might as well be in Telridge, dealing with the court."

Xendra piped up. "If it makes you feel any better, I doubt we could embarrass ourselves any more than we did last night."

Dirk shot a glare over to his second. "It doesn't. And I would prefer if we just don't—ever—talk about what happened last night at that faerie shindig."

Spense choked on his tea. Gerry and Xendra shared a look.

"I think I'll go see about the horses, now." Flora snagged a couple of figs from the large glass bowl. "Master Spense, do you think you could help me find my way?"

He scrambled to his feet, pushing away from the long, curving wood table. "Of course, happy to. I can at least find you some official faerie escorts."

Dirk laid his head on the table's velvety smooth surface and clasped both hands to the back of his head. He hadn't meant to make Flora feel uncomfortable. More uncomfortable. He didn't want her to think that he didn't value her, or that if the situation was different, he wouldn't be overjoyed to wake up near her smiling, tousled head.

But the situation wasn't different. It was…what it was. He was a blooming prince. And more than that, honor and decency mattered to him.

"So…we'll just go now?" Spense asked.

Dirk waved one hand vaguely in the direction of their voices. "Sure. Yeah. Do whatever."

Could this day get any worse?

A pair of voices floated in through the open archway.

"Lord Dirk?"

"Are you in?"

"Have you broken your fast?"

"Recovered from the night's festivities?" This last comment was followed by twittering giggles.

Dirk lifted his head, exchanged pained glances with Gerry and Xendra, and cleared his throat. "We're here. Please come in."

The two faeries—blue-haired and green—drifted through the slender aspens. Thistle and Shamrock. Their arms were linked, and their heads tilted inward toward each other.

"We've come to you…"

"At Lady Radiant's request."

"Quite right, sister. Lady Radiant has instructed us…"

"To see to your needs."

"As your personal attendants."

Dirk closed his eyes and bit out his next words, digging deep, especially given the throbbing state of his head. "Please express my gratitude to your queen."

Why did I ask?

This day could absolutely get worse.

Chapter 43

Dewy closed her eyes and reached out with her senses.

The rabbit's blood pumped through its small heart. *Shush-shush-shush.*

It's just a different form of water.

Water is life.

The blood pulsed through the rabbit's small body, channeling in tiny rivers and streams, arterials of life-giving fluid, distributing breath and clean air to every corner of the creature's frail, quivering body. The heart worked with rapid, mechanical precision, cleansing and processing as the blood circulated. She saw the shape and workings of the creature in her mind.

Dewy tilted her head as she focused, expanding her awareness to the elements outside of the rabbit. There were lush plants drinking in water that had been distributed through snaking pipes and tubing throughout the glassed-in building. The water told her the shape of each shrub and flower.

"On the far side of the rose bush, the budding one."

"Well done, my dear."

"I am not your dear." Dewy slit her lids open and sent a dark gaze in Lumine's direction.

He chuckled. "Of course not." His laugh was dry and lacked humor. "Your skills are growing."

She nodded. It was true. She could perceive more,

as if a filter had been lifted from the world, and the flowing waters of all things were hers to read at will. She'd always sensed water, running water especially, like springs and rivers, but what was once muted began to trill for her, humming with life. Each droplet told a story, describing and defining its world, so that Dewy could visualize a space as the water understood it. The knowledge fed her, energized her, as the waters in her own body resonated in quiet harmony with water everywhere.

"Shall we try again?"

Lumine pressed his lips together. "I think I will take Cinna's advice. And give you your rest."

"I can keep going."

"Oh, I believe you. Nevertheless, I am content with our progress today. Let us take the victory and enjoy it."

Dewy released an exasperated breath. She didn't try to hide her annoyance. But fine. Whatever. She could keep practicing with or without Lumine's guidance in the comfort of her room.

And what he didn't know...well, he wouldn't know.

Chapter 44

Another dinner. Another round of playing nice. Dignified and official. Without the benefit of faerie libations. Dirk steered clear of that.

The conversation recapped everything Spense had reported earlier in the day. But, officially, with the whole Fae court in attendance. Watching him. Judging him. As if he hadn't given them enough of a show last night.

He just wanted to sleep and to get on with their actual mission. His little brother had other plans.

"Dirk, wait up!"

Spense jogged along the tree-lined hallway. His breathing was easy, cheeks lightly flushed. He'd been going at a pretty good clip, but he wasn't at all winded. Maybe the faerie atmosphere and faerie food agreed with him better than the rest of them. Personally, Dirk would do anything for a steak…or nice cut of venison…or bacon. His mouth watered and stomach grumbled. Fruits and nuts were not going to quell his hunger.

"Hi, are you all right?" Spense asked.

He grimaced. "I'm just hungry. How are you not starving?"

Spense shrugged. "I got pretty used to Summer fare on the road with Dewy but there's something I need to talk to you about."

"Something else? I thought we were all set for tomorrow."

"We are, but...yeah, something else."

"This is that personal thing you've been brooding over since we set out?" It wasn't a difficult conclusion to draw. Whatever was bothering Spense, it clearly hadn't gone away.

"You noticed?"

"That you've been broodier than usual? And staring alternately at the clouds or your own navel? Yes. I noticed."

Spense flattened his mouth. "Yeah. That."

"So..." Dirk gestured with one hand.

He glanced back down the tree-lined corridor. "Not here."

"All right."

Dirk took a step toward their quarters, but Spense stopped him, placing a hand on his shoulder.

"Maybe not the common area, either. This is..."

"Personal. You've said." Dirk rolled his eyes. Spense was making quite the show out of this. It was a bit dramatic, even for his brother. But he got an idea. "I know someplace relatively private. You can talk. And I can eat real food. Follow me."

They confirmed directions a couple of times as they wove through the labyrinth-like passageways of The Vail. Dirk held no delusion they were unescorted. Attentive birds flew overhead. Probably more of the faerie shape-shifters. Not at all creepy. He imagined what he could do with a couple of these folk on Telridge's payroll. So many possibilities for clandestine work. Scouts who could fly? Very convenient. Then again, how many of these faerie types might he have missed before? In his own kingdom? The thought chilled him, even in the balmy air of Summer.

When they arrived in the stables, Dirk was unsurprised to find Flora tending the mounts.

"Tell me you didn't sneak food from the court of the Summer Fae to give to our horses," Dirk said, approaching Lightning Storm, and patting the stallion's strong neck.

His horse was too busy munching an apple to pay him much attention.

Flora glanced up. Ducked her head in the smallest of bows. "All right then, my lord. I won't tell you."

Spense chuckled. "Evening, Flora."

"Master Spense." She swept down Buttercup's flank with smooth, swift strokes. Flora had insisted they bring the farm horse, and Dirk was pleased he'd listened to her judgement. Buttercup was a tireless pack horse and worked well in a team with Lightning Storm. "What can I help you with?" Flora asked.

"We were just checking on the horses, but I see you have that well in hand." Dirk ran his hand along Storm's flank.

Flora clicked at her mare. "Can't leave these two all alone."

"We were also hoping…" Dirk cleared his throat. "To uh, see about some of the provisions."

She laughed. "One step ahead of you. I was already planning to bring some salt pork back to our quarters." She leaned in and whispered, "I've got some in my pack, if you'd like an early start."

Dirk darted to the canvas satchel, propped on a faerie-made stool. Inside were several pouches of the flavorful dried meat.

"You are all things good and right in this Grace-forsaken world."

Spense coughed.

Flora blushed and turned back to the horses.

"Right. I mean, this is good. It's great," Dirk said, in between bites. "Thank you."

Spense plucked one of the pouches from her bag as well. "You know what, Flora? Why don't you head back? I imagine Sir Gervais and Lady Xendra would be appreciative. We can finish up here."

Her eyes narrowed. "Oh. Are you sure?"

"Of course." Dirk grinned, catching on to Spense's hint. "You do enough. And we're heading into The Between tomorrow. You should get your rest."

Flora's brows drew together even tighter. She glanced between the brothers. "All right...I'll see you both later."

She scooped up her satchel and threw the strap crosswise over her body. She still wore the overlapping silk gown from dinner, but now bits of straw and horsehair freckled the draping sleeves. She handed the brush off to Dirk, plunking it into his hands. A small charge shot through his fingertips as they grazed hers.

"Good night, my lord. Master Spense." She offered a small curtsy and quickly left the stable area.

Dirk watched her retreating figure, the swish of her honey-brown hair. She wore it free from its usual braid for the evening, and it cascaded down her back in rippling waves, catching the last of the waning light trickling in through tall trees.

Spense coughed. Again.

"Straw getting to you, little brother?"

"Yes. That's it. Must be."

Dirk dove under Storm's neck and popped up on the other side. He took the brush in hand and swept it down the horse's neck and side. "So what's so important you couldn't even tell Flora?"

He didn't mean to sound bitter. It was just that...it was Flora. She was trustworthy. And kind. Whatever special secret Spense had, it was something she could handle, and she'd likely say just the right words in response.

Spense drifted across the stall and dropped onto a stool.

"My mum...and our father...wanted to make sure that I knew something, about myself, before going in to see the Oracles."

"Oh, yeah? What's that?" Dirk brushed and patted Storm while he waited for his brother to continue. He waited a while.

Spense drew a deep breath and slowly let it out. "They wanted me to know...I'm part faerie."

He raised his gaze to meet Dirk's. His eyes were wide and questioning.

"Huh." Dirk kept brushing, moving down to Storm's tail. He really thought it was going to be something bigger.

"That's it? All you have to say? Don't you have questions?"

"Well, not really. I mean, are we surprised?"

Spense bolted from his stool. "Yeah. I was."

Dirk shrugged. "Spense, you have magic—strong, elemental magic—that's a faerie thing, right?"

He frowned the Ferrous Frown. Maybe Spense was a little faerie, but he was also, very obviously, a Ferrous. He was his brother. Before he was anything

232

else.

"I guess so. But there are plenty of human mages who practice elemental magic."

"Not like you, though." He turned to his open-mouthed brother. "Does your mum have magic? She's never let on."

Spense nodded. "Why do you think her cooking is so good?"

"Huh."

"That's really all you've got? You're not shocked or repulsed, even a little?"

"No. Why would I be?" Dirk switched to Storm's other side. "I don't know what the big deal is. Do you know how many people have faerie in their blood? Kind of makes you wonder how many faeries are a little bit human. Even Flora. Did you know her cousin had a tryst with a faerie, and he has a half-faerie kid?"

Spense shook his head. "No, I didn't. She told you that?"

"When we were at her family's farm, we talked about a lot of things. I mean, I was semi-conscious for a bit there. I think she was trying to keep me awake. Anyway, yeah. Little girl. Her name is Petal. Cute, right?"

"Uh, yes. Sure. Cute." Spense choked on a papery laugh. "Just when I think I understand you…"

Dirk sauntered over to Spense. He clapped him on the shoulder. "Do keep up, little brother. If you want to shock me, you'll have to try a lot harder."

Chapter 45

"So, this is it?"

"This is it."

"I thought it would be bigger."

Gerry snorted. Xendra promptly cuffed him on the head.

"Do you have to behave this way in front of guests?" Dirk shook his head and cringed.

"It's Thorn. He's practically one of us." Gerry rubbed his head where Xendra hit him.

Spense laughed lightly. He felt he shared a camaraderie with Thorn. It was encouraging that his fully human companions felt the same. The steward and spymaster was no doubt cagey, but Spense knew his essential goodness. He turned to Thorn. "Thank you, again, for accompanying us. Apologies for this lot."

Thorn grinned, wide and with a lot of teeth. "You're quite welcome—not that I had a choice. But I enjoy you Telridgians."

"At least we're good for a laugh."

There were more chuckles, nervous and light. Everyone stared at the small, unimposing gate. It was made of bent branches, artfully woven together, creating the only break in a vine-covered wall. None of it seemed out of place in the Summer court's royal gardens. The only indication that this closed-off section was any different was the presence of two faerie sentinels. And despite the levity of the gaping crowd, the guards wore steely, serious expressions.

"Only two guards? Isn't this place supposed to be important?" Gerry spoke in an undertone to Dirk and Xendra, but just loudly enough for all to hear.

Thorn ignored the Knight's commentary, maintaining an even smile as he approached. "Hail, keepers of the gate to The Beyond, Betwixt, and Between."

One of the faeries, a bronze-skinned female, slid her gaze to Thorn and nodded. Spense had never heard the full name before—like so many things in faerie lands, names were prized and carefully guarded secrets.

"I trust you've been notified of our mission."

"We have, Lord Thorn. There are six in your party?"

"Correct. Thank you for confirming."

The sentinel lifted one eyebrow. "We endeavor to be thorough in all matters." She shifted her gaze to Gerry.

He lifted his hands in surrender. "Hey, I didn't mean to question."

The sentinel tilted her head to the side, scrutinizing. "I believe you did, Sir Gervais." Her partner remained stony and expressionless. "Would you care for a demonstration?"

"Sorry, of what?"

She nodded to the other faerie, a male with skin like hickory, reminding Spense of his grandfather Clove. That was where the resemblance ended. In the next moment, a blur of motion, followed by a thudding stillness, indicated that the faerie sentinel had moved. And Gerry—a highly trained Knight of Telridge—was on the ground, a coil of vine around his feet and wrists. The faerie returned to his post.

"Wicked Winter!"

The golden female sentinel blinked once slowly in response to Gerry's exclamation. "I assure you we take the security of this gate and the land it protects quite seriously. Are you satisfied now?"

"Quite," Gerry gurgled. "A-apologies."

"Well, then. Now that that's out of the way, shall we proceed?" Thorn asked of the wide-mouthed, gawking Telridgians.

Mouths closed. Heads nodded. No one spoke.

The male shifted toward the gate and waved a carved wooden talisman over the latch. A braid of twisting vines unwound themselves, as if they were growing in reverse. At the same time, the vines hobbling Gerry released, falling from his wrists and ankles. The simple gate swung inward on its hinges. The sentinel stepped back. He gestured to the opening.

The move was superfluous. Spense felt the invitation. Whatever was on the other side of the wall called to him. The Between. His nerves vibrated and blood hummed with each heartbeat.

"After you," Thorn said, his words gentle in the hush of the gardens.

Spense glanced to his brother, his companions, and met Thorn's gaze.

As if a gear had been turned in a machine, the group all stepped forward, one mechanical, interdependent unit. They fell into line, finding their relative positions in the procession. First, Spense, then Thorn a half-step behind him, acting as steward, but this time for him and not the queen. Dirk and Flora followed behind, shoulder-to-shoulder. Gerry brushed himself off and the Knights took rear guard.

In pairs, they crossed over from the sweet gardens of the Summer Court into a land where little was known, and rarely recorded. Spense had combed through every archaic text in The Academy library with a mention of the Oracles and the place they resided. There wasn't much.

With each step, the chirping birds faded away. The songs of insects and rustling of wind through green and growing things all became silence. Still and calm. The sunlight became a memory, as if a candle had been snuffed out and only the dimmest spark of the wick remained. Just enough light to push through a sudden, milky fog.

Spense put one foot in front of another, slow and measured. Feeling the ground beneath his soft boots, spreading his toes, and sensing the living dirt, connecting his whole foot with every step. He grounded himself in the element of earth. And pushed forward.

He noted the sharp inhales of his companions, acknowledged them, and then let them drift to the back of his awareness. His focus shifted from a place of tension to a place of rest.

Every step was another invitation, a beckoning. Slowly, the hard swallows, the shallow breaths of his companions eased off. He felt the cadence of their footsteps changing from disoriented and unsure, to steady but aware, as they each, in turn followed…him.

In the space of a few moments, they'd redefined the acknowledged leader of their party, another slide of a gear, a clockwork motion, easy and expected.

Spense lifted his chin and honed his gaze. He drew

a full breath into his chest. And he walked into the Oracles' home, a land of mists and mysteries, into the tricky, shifting Between, as if he were strolling a familiar forest path on a crisp, clear morning.

Chapter 46

It was just a rabbit. A little, hoppity, bunny. By now she should have no problem locating such a small, insignificant creature. Dewy had done so several times in the confines of the glassed-in hot houses, with less physical effects. During the last test, she'd found the furry, quivering bunny crouched among the raspberry vines in a few moments. No dizziness. No nosebleeds.

Which was why they'd moved outdoors. Dewy needed a new challenge.

And it was indeed, proving to be a challenge.

She snorted a frustrated breath. Perhaps she'd been relying on her expectations too much in the hot house. There were only so many places a rabbit could hop to in a cultivated garden, with neat rows and groomed pathways.

In the forested grounds outside of The Silver Horn, the rabbit's movements were annoyingly non-linear.

Dewy closed her eyes, steadied her breathing. She reached out to the cold, icy water all around. Extended her senses to the underground spring many layers beneath her feet, said a quick hello, and raised her awareness up, up, up to the hard surface of the forest floor. She tilted her ear, listening for the shushing of the creature's lifeblood as it coursed through its tiny body. Quieted the eager, excited greetings of the forest's many water sources.

The animal's tiny heart rapped a staccato drum that echoed through the flowing blood. As if it were tapping a glass pitcher full of water. On the outside, a tap was nothing, a meaningless, almost soundless gesture, but to the water within, it resounded and thrummed.

There'd been many Summer Court dinners Dewy departed from abruptly when someone—usually Oak—got fidgety and started flicking a full glass or vase or pitcher. The sound made her teeth vibrate, as she experienced each warbled *thrum*. Oak was pleasant to look at, an enjoyable dance partner, and could be a delightful evening companion, but he'd never been a serious candidate for suitor. That fidgeting was insufferable.

But her aunt had pushed her in Oak's confident, charming direction repeatedly. From the outside, it made sense. He was Fae, from the wood faeries. Relatively strong earth magic. A reasonable complement to her and to her gifts.

Who would have expected the one to capture her heart would be a humble mage from the human lands? So different from an ennobled Fae like Oak.

But Spense, he didn't fidget. His gaze was quiet and serious. His hands were calm, whether he was casting a spell, pouring tea, or gently comforting a forlorn faerie princess in the stillness of a forest cave.

Dewy sensed her own life waters—tears—leaking from her eyes. She brushed them away with a small smile, and refocused.

Where was that bunny?

Shush. Shush. Shush.

Dewy crept through the forest, gently placing her feet, and keeping careful attention to the sound of that small pump, that heart propelling blood through the rabbit's body. It scampered beneath a prickly thorn bush, made its way through the nettles and brambles, that both threatened and protected it from predators.

Dewy waited. Listened. Ready to lunge. Ready to pounce. She'd become the predator.

Hop. Hop. Quiver. Dash.

Through the underbrush, camouflaged between drifts of snow and shadows. The bunny hid from the watchful gaze of the hawk or owl.

It could not hide from her.

She heard a new trill, a fresh coursing of blood, singing in harmony with her target. But what is this?

Another rabbit. Rabbits. Family.

Tucked behind those sharp thorns, nestled into a curving, cozy burrow. The little bunny had found its friends. It's home.

The rabbit's blood was the melody. Theirs—her brothers and sisters—was the echoing harmony, the refrain. The same and not the same.

Dewy reached for the bit of liquid water present in the cold Winter air. She drew it in and released it, giving nourishment to that crotchety, old, thorn bush. In thanks, it heeded her request and separated slightly, pulling away from the opening of the burrow.

Slowly, gently, Dewy crouched down and reached for her quarry.

No. Wrong again.

Not her quarry. Her friend. Her teacher. She withdrew the greens she'd been keeping in her pocket and offered them to the small animal. To its many, many siblings. She scooped up the scampering bunnies, letting them wriggle in the crisscross of her folded legs as she sat in the snow. She rubbed the rabbit's long, soft ears and smiled, losing herself to the chorus of their heartbeats and swishing blood.

The arrival of a slim shadow broke her reverie, pulling her attention away from the cottontail orchestra.

"Good, you found it." Misty stood over her, hands on her hips. "Can we eat, now?"

Dewy smirked. She released the bunnies back into their burrow, coaxed the thorn's branches to replace its protective gate. She picked herself up from the cold ground and brushed off the snow. Her new boots kept her feet dry, along with the wool trousers. The thick pants were freckled with snow and beads of cool water, which rolled off as she stood, returning gently to the earth.

"Fine," she said. "Let's go."

They maneuvered their way back through the forest on partially overgrown deer tracks. Dewy hadn't realized how far she'd traveled. That rabbit could get going when it was properly motivated. She glanced back into the warrens of trees and shrubs in the direction of her rabbit friends, content they'd found each other, found home and family, in the most treacherous of environments.

As she traipsed behind Misty, eager to return to the warmth of The Silver Horn, Dewy's mind drifted again to Spense—to the person where she'd found home—in the most unexpected of places.

Chapter 47

The mists thinned. Spense detected shapes and forms. Tall, tall hedges rose in the distance. Spires from an ethereal castle-like structure from unfamiliar architecture. Not human. Not faerie. Something else. Something other.

"Welcome to The Beyond, Betwixt, and Between, travelers from afar."

Spense startled. His human companions along with him. Thorn chuckled.

"Good to see you, old friend," Thorn said, and tipped his head in deference to...*was that a rabbit?*

"Ah...hello." Spense was the first to recover his speech. "Wh-who are you?"

"Might as well start off with the big questions, I guess." The rabbit chortled. "Nice and existential. Who am I? Who are any of us...really?"

Spense blinked slowly. His forehead creased.

"Oh, but maybe you meant that as a more practical, informational type of query." The rabbit rose onto its haunches, making itself the tiniest bit taller. "I'm the guide, the tracker, the keeper of the Oracles, and marshal of these lands. Technically, I'm Hosioi, but that's a bit of a mouthful. You can call me Hoss."

"I...what... 'Hoss?'" Spense spluttered. The rest of his party was notably quiet, except for Thorn who laughed quietly. Spense shot a glare in the steward's

243

direction.

The rabbit nodded its head vigorously.

"Umm…well, all right."

"Didn't fit your expectations?"

"Not exactly."

"Don't worry. You'll get used to it."

"My mum said I'd see some strange things…" Spense muttered, shaking his head.

"It's always best to listen to your mother." The rabbit—Hoss—pointed his front foot at Spense.

He'd never been scolded by a bunny before. "Right."

"How about a little orientation? Would that help? I'm guessing this trickster didn't tell you much." Hoss nodded his furry, long-eared head in the direction of Thorn.

"I thought it best they experience The Between for themselves," Thorn said.

"Too right. Too right."

"What is happening?" Dirk finally found his voice. And a scowl to match.

The bunny nodded sagely to Dirk. "You, Prince Dirk Ferrous, have entered the land of the Oracles, The Beyond, Be—"

"We know that." Dirk's words were clipped. "But who or what are you?"

Hoss frowned. "I just explained that." He turned to Thorn and said as an aside, "Not the brightest bunch to enter our realm."

"They mean well." Thorn grinned.

"Well, at least there's that."

"You said something about an orientation?" Spense asked, before the conversation could get more off course.

"That I did." Hoss swept into an elegant bow. "At your service."

"Are you seeing what I'm seeing?" Gerry whispered to Xendra.

The rabbit perked up. "Oh! Not likely, Sir Knight."

Gerry blushed red. "Sorry?"

"That's the first bit of orientation. 'You will see what you see.' It's different for everyone. The land, the Oracles, even me. It all has to do with desires and expectations, but I must admit that it's a bit mystical and mysterious. I'm here to get you started and fish you out if you come to any trouble."

Flora held up a hand. "Are you saying—Hoss—that you look different to each one of us?"

"Sure, sure. It's always amusing to see what species or gender folks assign to me. Sometimes, I'm not even a something, just an amorphous cloud. For instance, you, dear girl, are talking to a really, quite attractive owl, excellent choice. Love the golden feathers. Our Knights are each perceiving a glowing Fae female with what we'll call priestess robes and...an old, withered crone, respectively." Hoss gestured to Gerry and Xendra in turn. "Our prince is seeing a court jester—think I might actually find that one offensive—and young Master Spense thinks I'm a rabbit!" Hoss thumped his back foot with glee. "Have fun unpacking the meaning behind that...oh, wait. Actually, I get it. Nice."

Spense coughed. He had no idea what the bunny was talking about, or why he now nodded in approval.

"Looks like this one is focused. I like it. Good to know what you want."

Hoss spoke too quickly and in too many riddles for Spense to sort it all. His head began to grow hot, vision swirling.

"Uh-oh, maybe less focused than I thought. Thorn? Want to help here?"

Thorn gripped Spense's shoulders as he swayed.

"Easy there, Spense. I know it's a lot. Don't let it overwhelm you."

As if that were possible.

"Why don't you all gather round? Take a seat." Hoss hopped to a grouping of log rounds, tipped on end to form stools. The rabbit had grown significantly in height in the space of a few seconds, and its features blurred with that of a faerie. Two sets of ears, one gently pointed and on the side of the creature's head, the other set furry and perched on top of the male's dark, curly hair.

With Thorn's help, Spense stumbled to the closest log round, and collapsed onto it. He put his head in his hands as the verbose bunny-faerie chattered on.

"Now, what you see behind me will look different for each of you—as I explained—but you're all seeing a maze or labyrinth of a sort, correct?"

Spense lifted his gaze. Lady Xendra arched a brow, Sir Gervais shrugged, and Flora nodded cautiously. Beyond the rabbit, Spense saw more trimmed hedges, a little taller than the height of a man. The mists continued to swirl over and through the rows of an ornate garden maze.

Dirk frowned. "I don't see a maze…"

"Oh, no, you're a strange one, prince." The bunny swiveled on its hind legs. "Looks like a human village. Lots of twisty alleys and roads. It's maze-like, enough,

246

I guess."

Dirk sported the Ferrous Frown in all its wrinkled glory.

"Do we have to pay some sort of tribute to enter, answer a riddle or something?" Flora asked.

"There you go with the expectations, again. But no. If you passed through the gate, you were deemed worthy. Your pursuit of wisdom and truth is honorable."

Spense looked back at Hoss. Again, fully rabbit.

"What do we do, then?"

"Why, I thought that was obvious. You enter the maze. You seek an Oracle. You ask questions. Fairly basic stuff."

"And then what?" Flora asked.

"When you're ready to leave, just call out. I'll be right around the corner."

Spense braced his hands on his thighs, drew in deep calming breaths and slowly released them.

Sure. It sounded simple.

Enter. Seek. Ask.

Why did he have the feeling it wouldn't be so easy?

Chapter 48

"We just walk in?" Dirk asked.

Hoss the jester shrugged. The creature had grown ears and whiskers that shot out on either side of his belled floppy hat. "Yes."

"Should we stick together?" That was Flora. She glanced around the group, eyes wide and churning.

"That's up to you, of course."

They decided to go in pairs to further their chances of finding the Winter Oracle sooner. They'd circle back to the entrance after three rotations of the clock—if time could be measured in this realm. Thorn agreed to send up a signal when the sun dipped toward the tops of the trees.

It sounded good in theory, but Dirk clamped his jaw tight as his friends broke up and set off in different directions. He and Flora took the path to the right—to him a cobbled street filled with shops—Spense headed straight in, and Gerry and Xendra took the left path. They'd linked arms and leaned in toward each other. Dirk released the breath he'd been holding and chuckled at the two Knights and their newly demonstrative display. Maybe it had something to do with the faeries. By being in their lands, it was easy to relax the rigid rules of Telridgian protocol.

Dirk felt that pull himself, dancing with Flora, waking up on the floor of her room, and now entering the maze. It hadn't even been a question. There was no discussion. They all just lined up in what felt like natural pairs, the same way they'd entered The Between. It was the most reasonable thing in the world, Flora by his side, and he by hers.

She headed into the twisty lane with her head held high, confident and alert—or faking it brilliantly.

Dirk nudged her with his elbow. "What do you see?"

"Sorry?" She turned her wide-eyed face to him.

"Hoss—the guide—said we all saw this world differently." He gestured to the village road, stretching before him. "What do you see?"

"Oh…" Flora's gaze fanned the path before them. She raised her eyes, and she smiled. "I see a forest—with criss-crossing trails—more like deer tracks than a road. There are birds and squirrels in the trees, almost like they're pointing the way. And everything is filled with new blossoms, bright, green apical buds."

Dirk laughed. "I don't see any of that."

She shrugged. "Maybe I'm just tired of winter. I want it to be spring already and Hoss said our desires affect this place."

It wasn't winter in Dirk's village, either. Sun glinted off clean windowpanes. Signs for shops, bakeries, and public houses rocked in the gentlest of warm breezes, bearing comforting names. The Blooming Rose. It looked like an ale house, similar to the Grey Goats back in Telridge. Beech's Sundries. General store. The Golden Owl Bookshop. All places of invitation and welcome.

Dirk wondered if Flora felt the same. But she said she saw a forest. Did she feel that sense of welcome?

What did it say that they perceived such totally unrelated things? Not a surprise. Not really. Just a reminder how different they were, from such separate experiences and backgrounds.

"Are you all right?"

Dirk looked down. Flora rested her hand on his arm, grazing the fabric of his tunic.

"Of course. Why do you ask?"

She stopped walking and peered up into his eyes, searching. "You got quiet and...frowny."

"Letting my mind wander, I guess."

"Not sure that's the safest choice here."

"No, you're probably right." He took hold of her hand, the one she'd placed on his arm, and gave it a squeeze. There was something solid and sure in having her hand in his. Grounding.

"Oh...wow," Flora breathed.

"What?"

"I see...shops, now. A bakery. Bookshop. Where did those come from?"

"Huh."

Dirked laughed. He looked around. The village had changed. There were small trees in between the buildings and surrounding the edges of the town.

"I think our visions merged."

Flora laughed along with him. Her smile was open, her eyes glittering in amazement. She gave his hand an extra squeeze. He held on tight.

Such a small shift, an outstretched hand.

And it made all the difference.

Chapter 49

"I have a confession."

Xendra swiveled her gaze to Gerry. And waited.

"I have no idea what I'm doing here."

She laughed. "That is no confession. It's a statement of fact."

He tugged her in closer. "True. At least, we're lost and clueless together."

"Speak for yourself on that clueless bit. I'm wandering a lovely walk in the woods with my dearest friend. There's nowhere else I'd rather be."

"Really? Not out slaying enemies? Landing an arrow in a shot no one else could make, just to make idiot men drool all over themselves?"

"No, not even that." She grinned. It was easy.

"You really mean that, don't you?" Gerry sounded skeptical.

"You don't believe me?" Xendra asked.

It hurt that he still had doubts. That he didn't trust her. Them.

"Well look at us, who would've thought?"

Xendra looked. At the pair of them, casually sauntering through a golden wood, like any other couple. They'd never been so public before. Maybe that was her fault. She'd spent so much time in shadows, she found it comfortable there.

He kept quiet and discreet when he needed to,

played the part of the taciturn and ennobled Sir Gervais, but it wasn't his nature. He wore his affection and friendship openly. It was one of the things that drew her to him. Even when they were still squires, only aspiring to be Knights. That first time she put him in the dirt when no one else had, and he came up laughing, even raised her arm high, acknowledging that she'd bested him.

He showed up the next day and started training with her. He didn't care that she was a high-born, or that she was a girl. She was the only person who'd beat him, and he wanted to learn how. They'd been near inseparable ever since. Took their Knights' oaths together.

And included a scrappy prince into their trio. Prince Dirk was all arrows and no aim, full of grief and determination, and as much a misfit as either of them. Through training together, competing, and getting into trouble, they'd become allies, then friends.

Flora was one of them, too, a wild horse who couldn't be contained by a small pasture. She fit with them. Xendra could see it. That same fierce drive. She wondered how long it would take Dirk to get that. She loved him like a brother, but sometimes his head was well and truly stuck up his ass.

Not that she and Gerry had been any better. Maybe it took them both forever to figure it out because they let stupid things—like family status—get in the way. Gerry was the embodiment of her parents' fears when she started training as a squire. That she'd get her elbows dirty when she rubbed them with common folk. But Xendra wasn't like her sisters. She wasn't going to be content to play politics and/or elegant music. Sure, as a girl she attended to her studies with interest. She wore the dresses and participated in the dances, but in the afternoons, when she was through with her language lessons or history or dance or whatever else her dear mother came up with, she put her leathers back on and went hunting.

And Gerry, he was her hunting partner. Xendra leaned into him as they continued their walk through the golden wood.

"That is a rather nice meadow up ahead..." He narrowed his eyes in speculation.

"It is." She quirked her eyebrow.

"Shame to waste such a beautiful spot."

"Might as well make the most of the time we have."

"It's what I always say." A small voice squeaked from a nearby tree. It belonged to a red-brown squirrel who popped out from between the branches.

Xendra started.

"Talking squirrel?" Gerry whispered in her ear.

"Yeah..." She eyed the furry forest animal suspiciously. And appreciatively. It was rare for anyone to catch her off-guard.

"Just checking."

"I'm not just any talking squirrel, thank you very much." The creature in question scampered from the tree and puffed himself up near their feet. "I am *the* talking squirrel. I am Autumn."

Xendra pinched her lips together and peered closer at the creature.

"You are the Autumn Oracle. A squirrel?"

The squirrel shrugged. "Today, I felt like being a squirrel. I like change. I'm whimsical." He put his fingered paws on his hips with as much indignation as a squirrel could have.

"All right, then…"

She wasn't going to challenge an Oracle. If it wanted to be a squirrel, then a squirrel it would be.

"Like you said, we should make the most of the time we have." The furry creature scampered into the trees, calling back to them from high in an old oak, "Enjoy your time in Autumn. It really is a lovely meadow."

Xendra was left blinking furiously. Her hands fell loose at her sides.

Gerry turned to her, a mischievous smile on his lips and a familiar flash in his eyes. "You heard the squirrel. We should make the most of our time and this lovely meadow."

She shifted her gaze to Gerry and lifted one corner of her mouth. "The Oracle has spoken…"

Chapter 50

His friends disappeared into the maze on his right and left. Spense barely nodded to Thorn, before heading straight in. His steps were deliberate, his mind focused. Nothing would deter him from this task. The sooner he found the Winter Oracle, the sooner he'd find answers. Protocols and permissions and elegant long-winded speeches had done nothing but add delays. But now, he would finally get what he needed. Months of fruitless study could come to an end.

"It's not a race." Thorn kept pace with him easily.

Spense shot a glance at his companion. "It kind of is."

Thorn tutted. "We're in the Be—"

"Beyond, Betwixt and Between. Right. I know."

"I don't think you do. Time functions differently here. Rushing through this maze—" Thorn waved at the high hedges surrounding them. "—will have no outcome on finding your answers sooner."

Spense halted his clipped steps and threw his hands out to the sides. "It makes me feel better, all right?"

"Ah." Thorn nodded sagely. "That is something else, altogether. Very well, then. Proceed."

"No more commentary?"

"None, whatsoever." Thorn gestured with one hand, urging Spense to continue.

He resumed his quick pace through the column of

hedge, scarcely noting the floral greenery or the gravel walkway beneath his feet. The path was clear and straight before him.

Until it wasn't. Spense came to his first inevitable intersection. Continue straight, turn left, or turn right. He kept his heading, plunging forward. Thorn remained quiet.

The path started to veer ever so slightly to the right, and then somewhat later, corrected itself and looped back to the left. They carried on with no other forks or intersections. Spense felt time slipping past, whatever Thorn said about the nature of the land. Where was that blooming Oracle? He picked up his pace.

And finally, finally came upon another intersection. Something new, at least.

Thorn exhaled a regretful sigh.

Spense whipped his head to him. "What?"

Thorn pointed to a cluster of white flowers growing at the base of the hedgerow.

"Alpen-bloom, I think," Spense said. "What about them?"

Thorn grimaced. Waited. And then, "We've seen them before."

Spense looked closer at the flowers, frowning. "We have?"

The steward closed his eyes. "This is the same junction."

"We've looped around? But we went right…and then left…"

"And apparently left quite a lot more."

"Gah!"

Spense kicked at the ground and the bushes. Bits of leaf and dust flew about, coating his shoes and trousers with a thin layer of botanical grime.

"Master Spense."

Spense continued his spastic, child-like tantrum. "What?"

"Stop. Think. We know which way to proceed now."

Spense stopped. He looked at Thorn. He looked at the sparkly, white alpen-bloom flowers, taunting him with their sprightly petals. He frowned. Stupid flowers. Stupid mountain flowers. What were they doing in this balmy garden hedge? They grew on the side of mountains, in...cold, alpine climates.

"Wicked Winter!"

"My thoughts exactly."

Spense hung his head.

"All right, let's go." Spense stepped forward. He proceeded along the path at a more measured pace, making sure to note the presence of the alpen-bloom every few minutes, like bright signposts along the way. They came across a few more intersections and forks, and each time Spense sought out the small white flowers.

"Do you think this was a test?"

Thorn shrugged. "I honestly don't know."

"Do you hear that?" Spense asked.

There was a soft thumping, growing steadily louder until...

"Oh, hello there, travelers." The Hosioi—or rather, Hoss, the rabbit guide—approached, hopping on all fours.

"Have you come to check on us?"

Hoss raised himself to his fuzzy back feet and shrugged his tiny bunny shoulders. "Something like that. How is your journey?"

"Frustrating," Spense admitted.

"Looks like you're finding your way."

"The maze seems bent on forcing me to slow down and pay attention."

The bunny tilted his whiskered head. "Always good advice, don't you think?"

Spense smirked. "I suppose so."

Thorn kept silent, but his eyebrows rose, and mouth thinned into what Spense was beginning to recognize as Thorn's "smug face."

"Mind if I join you for a bit?"

"Please. Always good to have companions along the way."

"Also, sound advice." Hoss nodded enthusiastically while scampering near their feet. He was alarmingly quick, but then he wasn't actually a bunny.

The path curled and curved in a lazy meander of round, green leaves and white flowers. The air grew chilly, heavier, as a damp mist swirled about them. The hedge branches and leaves were first dusted, then encased, in hoarfrost the further they traveled. Spense drew his cloak tighter.

They reached what seemed to be a dead end, a small enclosure, formed from intertwining cedars, flocked with powder light snow. A small figure rested in a bower of evergreens. Her body, face, and hair were clouded by an opaque swirling mist.

But her ice-blue eyes were as crystalline as a glacier-fed lake. They lit up at the trio's approach.

"Ah, Hosioi, who have you brought? Lord Thorn, I believe. And young Master Spense." The Winter Oracle—who else could she be?—spoke with a clear, pure voice. She focused her bright eyes on Spense. "You are welcome here. Do not be afraid. Come in. Look inside."

Chapter 51

Dirk followed Flora into one shop and then the next, darting in between the shelves, and marveling at the goods on display, laughing and playing like puppies or small children. There were pastries at the bakery, dripping with honey and speckled with crushed almonds. And brown ale served by an eager raccoon at the tavern. It was rich with nutty flavor. A hatter—an overlarge jay and, why not—provided for every manner of creature. Helmets, caps, veils, and crowns of all sizes. Dirk plucked a gilded tiara, encrusted with dew-drop jewels, from a shelf and waved Flora over. He placed it on her head, smoothing out her wind-blown hair.

She pretended to preen. "How do I look?"

"Perfect," Dirk whispered. He knew she asked in jest, but at the sight of her in a crown, his throat closed, and he found himself short of breath.

Flora laughed. "I don't think so."

She pulled the tiara from her hair. A few loose strands got tangled and Dirk reached over to help.

"Here, let me."

"Ouch."

"Sorry."

"No, it's fine. Did you get it?" Flora peered up at him from an awkward, stooped angle, giving him better access to free the tenacious crown.

Her long, honey-brown hair slipped through his fingers as he unwound it from the tines.

"Almost there."

One more untwisting, and she was free. Dirk held the tiara in one hand, his other still laced in Flora's silk curls. She straightened, and their faces nearly touched. Her gaze rose to his. Locked onto him. As securely as the tiara had woven itself onto her head. He couldn't tear away.

But Flora chuckled. "I guess we can say for certain I wasn't meant to wear a crown." She stepped back.

Out of his reach.

"I thought it suited you." Dirk let his hand drop from where it had held those golden-brown tresses.

She took another step back. And turned from him. He placed the tiara on its shelf. A couple of strands were still tangled in the crown. Dirk pulled them free and wound them into a tiny coil. He pocketed the lock before Flora noticed.

But she'd already skipped ahead to the next shop over, through the adjoining walls that made one long, interior marketplace, shop after shop, connecting through open archways.

He stumbled backward. "I'm going back to the tavern. I can, uh…climb to the roof, see if I can make sense of this maze, maybe look for our friends."

"Sounds good." Flora waved at him over her shoulder. "I'm curious about this flower shop. There's something here, I think."

He wanted to follow her.

He wanted to flee.

They'd let themselves get distracted. They were here to find an Oracle, not play about in shops, pretending that…

Dirk clamped his jaw hard. This was no time for pretend.

If he couldn't find an Oracle, maybe he could find his brother or Gerry and Xendra. Someone else was surely making more progress.

Dirk surveyed the tavern. It was set up like any village inn. Stairs led to a second floor. Dirk took them two at a time, craving the burning in his thighs as he launched from step to step. A quick check and he found another set of stairs, narrow and doubling back upon itself as it reached for the attics. He pushed through to the wide, low-ceilinged top floor under the peaked roof. Across the dust-filled space was a door leading outside. Dirk braced himself against the balmy winds, stronger up on the rooftop. He stepped out onto the flat decking that encircled the building.

He was halfway around before he took a full, unencumbered breath. Inhaling his usual calm, his soldier-trained focus, exhaling his racing thoughts, the temptations of impossibilities. Dirk opened his eyes and scanned the twisting village lanes, the encroaching forest. He heard bird song, the twittering and chirping of so many forest creatures, the inhabitants of this maze world.

"Unless that's just my imagination, too," Dirk muttered.

A large blue jay hopped near him, taking perch on the deck railing. It tilted its shiny head. "Does it matter, prince?"

Dirk started, then chuckled. He recognized the outsized bird from the hat shop. "Does what matter?"

"What you see in your imagination, is it any less

real?"

He frowned. "That's charmingly cryptic."

The bird spread its glossy blue wings wide and bowed. "I am an Oracle. It's really what we do."

"Y-you're an Oracle?"

"I am." The bird straightened up.

"Sweet Spring." Dirk shook his head in bewildered wonder.

"Well, no. She's down below. Loves the flowers. Obviously. I'm Summer."

"Of course, you are."

"Not what you expected?"

"Nothing in this place is. I thought that the faeries' Summer lands were disorienting, but this…" He whistled through his teeth.

"Well, perhaps, Sir Prince, you could do to let a few of those expectations go." With that, the jay spread his wings and launched into the skies, circling the forests and swooping into the trees, the late sun gilding his wings like verdigris.

Dirk tracked the bird's progress, until his attention was pulled by a flare of shooting green sparks, off in the distance, on the very farthest side of the maze.

That was Thorn's signal.

The trees surrounding the area were covered in white and a mist hung low.

Spense had found the Winter Oracle.

Chapter 52

Flora drifted into the garden shop. Funny that it stayed a shop, even after she'd let go of Dirk's hand. The vision—their shared vision—remained. It opened into lanes and lanes of growing things, carefully cultivated by a caring hand. Slender timber beams supported a glass ceiling. Vines and small trees stretched for the sparkling sun overhead. Flora suppressed a small giggle burbling up. The very air and wonder of this place was infectious.

"Laughter is welcome here, as are you, Lady Flora." A blue jay soared overhead and landed neatly on a great flowering bush. It ruffled its blue feathers, as it settled on a branch.

"Thank you," Flora said. "Didn't I just see you in the hat shop?"

"Oh, you mistake me for my mate."

"My apologies." Flora looked closer and, indeed the creature before her was slightly smaller, its feathers a softer blue. "Your mate?"

The crowned bird opened its wings. "It's the closest approximation, for whatever we are. I suppose we're technically a foursome, but Summer and I…its always felt like a closer partnership."

"Summer? But that means…are you the Spring Oracle?"

"Well, yes. Weren't you looking for me?"

Flora laughed. "I don't know."

"Of course, you were. And how appropriate, that a young lady named Flora, should find me."

She hadn't realized she was searching for anything, not for herself. She was just a lesser member of the team. Her role was to support Spense and Dirk in their mission. She didn't have one of her own. Maybe she'd indulged in the play-acting, the dancing, and gleefully sharing in the wonder of both this place and the Summer Lands. But that was all temporary, a momentary distraction, before she returned to Telridge, and once again, took up her place in the background.

"Think, child. Or perhaps, in your case, stop thinking so much." The bird hopped to a closer branch. "You are here for a reason. What do you seek?"

She shook her head. "Me? I'm not sure. Happiness. Contentment. Isn't that what we all seek?"

The peace of the small, quiet life that was hers, all she would ever have, and so it was all she ever considered. Even in her days as a student, she loved the quiet and peace of the library, learning about the world and its history, but only as an observer.

"Contentment...hmm. Perhaps, but how we define that...that is the true mystery, isn't it?" The Spring Oracle tilted its head. Its dark eyes sparkled. "For every being that is a different thing."

"I suppose."

"Then you must determine how you define it, and then you will see how to achieve it."

Flora scoffed. "Sounds simple."

"Oh, it's anything but."

She rolled her eyes. Apparently, Oracles didn't understand sarcasm.

"All right. How do I determine what it is that makes me happy?"

She was afraid to ask, afraid to hear the answer. Once it was out there, if it was unattainable, wouldn't that be more of a disappointment? Better to remain safe, leave off without too close of an examination of her capricious heart.

The Oracle leaned in. "Why do you think you came to me? The Oracle of Spring?"

Flora frowned. Why had she walked into this glassed-in garden shop? "It seemed right. Flowers, trees, all these new growing things. New possibilities, I guess."

"Hmm…and what is it that you hope to be possible?"

Flora bit down on her lip. She shook her head as hot tears formed. No. She couldn't think about that…about him.

"Flora? Flora! There you are! I've been looking for you." Dirk jogged down the lane of flowers, coming to a stop in front of her and the bright, blue bird.

The Spring Oracle flapped its wings and launched into the high, open space of the garden. It brushed her cheek with a feather as it flew by, a comforting caress. As if it had seen her. It knew. Of course, it did. It was an Oracle.

Flora turned to Dirk. "You've been…what?" She brushed furiously at her stinging eyes.

"Who was that?" Dirk traced the bird's flight with his eyes.

"The Spring Oracle, who else?" She waved her hand, casually, as if encounters with probing, mystical birds was an ordinary occurrence.

"Oh. *Oh*."

"Yeah."

"Funny. I just met Summer."

"Really?"

"Yes, but it's not important, not right now." Dirk's words were too clipped. Too dismissive. "I saw where Spense is, too. I think he found the Winter Oracle. Thorn sent up a signal."

She stared at him, wide-eyed. "Do you know how to get there?"

He nodded. "Pretty sure." He gestured to the forest, his arm swung wide, gallant. "Shall we?"

Dirk offered his hand, openly and without guile.

"Yes…" Flora grasped his outstretched hand.

He gave hers a quick squeeze before leading her back along the glassed-in garden path.

Such a simple gesture. An easy fit, her hand in his. On any other day, and in another place, such a thing would've seemed impossible.

Chapter 53

"Ah, here they are." Hoss sat back on his furry haunches, a self-satisfied smile on his whiskered face.

Spense strained to hear, closed his eyes, and let his senses reach into the earth. Thumping steps, echoing on the graveled paths. From his right and left. Two linked pairs arrived at almost the same moment. Two sets of flushed faces.

He released a relieved breath. While he hadn't been consciously fretting, he must've held on to a niggling concern. And seeing his brother, Flora, and the two Knights safe and whole...he let go of that small tension. One less thing to worry over.

"We saw your signal. What's going on? What did you find?" Dirk asked, barely out of breath from his jog.

Flora kept pace with him, her face similarly expectant.

He gestured to the enclosure, where the Winter Oracle lounged on her bower. Her smile was inviting, disarming, too easy, and that set off all Spense's warning bells. So, he waited. He hadn't entered the space, not without everyone present.

"I've found the Winter Oracle."

"And did you ask...her?" Flora narrowed her eyes, peering at the woman surrounded by a cool, swirling mist.

The Oracle's eyes glowed brighter, sharper. She winked at Flora. "Young Master Spense is remarkably patient when he chooses to be."

Spense recognized the barb—the accusation—in the Oracle's clarion-clear voice. He was anything but patient as he blundered through the maze, only slowing down when Thorn pointed out the alpen-bloom. Nor was he patient as he paced near the entrance of the Oracle's domain waiting for his friends to find him. But he was also not foolish or reckless enough to continue his blundering ways, not when the stakes were so high.

"I've noticed something about this place. Or at least, I think I have. And I'm wondering if you're experiencing the same phenomenon."

"If you mean that it's weird, and twisty, and these Oracles are on the strange side, then sure, we've all noticed," Gerry said. He gave Lady Xendra a pointed look.

"You've seen another Oracle?" Spense hadn't expected that.

"Autumn," Xendra confirmed. "It was a squirrel."

"Summer was a blue jay," Dirk said.

"So was Spring," Flora added.

Between the six of them, they'd found and spoken with all four Oracles. Did that mean something or was it a coincidence? Spense shook his head. He could do without another puzzle.

"And what do you see now?"

Spense gestured to the Oracle. She tilted her head. Her smile lifted a little, patiently enduring Spense and his experiment charade.

"A snowy owl," Dirk and Flora answered in unison.

"A grey wolf," Xendra said.

"With big teeth." Gerry followed up.

The Oracle's grin stretched wider. Spense could almost see the wolf. He reached out his hands.

"As I thought. Can you all take my hands? I want to try something. You, too Thorn."

The group linked together and formed a chain, facing the Oracle. Her presence shimmered and shifted. The swirls of clouds morphed into feathers—milky-white wings with a dusting of speckles. The lady's feral smile grew wider, her teeth longer. And her floating, gauzy gown became furred.

"Oh."

"Wow."

"Exactly," Spense said. "When Thorn grabbed my shoulders earlier, Hoss, here, changed form. Thorn's perception and mine merged for a moment."

The guide stretched herself to her full height. Hoss appeared as a "her" now. A faerie-like female in a golden gown, bearing coppery wings and silky rabbit ears. "Told you." Hoss shrugged.

"That's wild," Gerry said.

"Well, yes, Sir Knight. Obviously." The faerie-owl-rabbit creature rolled its eyes. "Kind of the point. The Beyond, Betwixt, and Between is the last of the truly wild places. Magic runs free here."

"This is why I wanted you all here before I spoke with this Oracle. I think if we're anchored to each other, we'll be—the magic will be—grounded."

"Magically speaking?" Gerry asked.

"That actually makes sense." Dirk frowned, catching Flora's gaze for a moment. "We noticed something similar when we…joined hands."

Xendra shrugged. "It's worth a try."

Spense turned to the Oracle. "Lady Winter, we have come seeking—"

"You seek many things."

"Perhaps. But we only ask one thing of you in this moment."

The Oracle waited. Her chin lifted.

Spense took a deep, calming breath and slowly released it, letting his vapors form clouds of condensation before drifting in the cool, winter wind. "Can you tell us how to find the Winter Heir?"

"No. I don't think so."

"I'm sorry?"

"Best if I show you. Telling you won't work. You won't want to understand."

Spense's heart clenched, beating hard.

"Look inside." The Oracle waved her feathered arms, and the mists around her coalesced into an opaque surface, nearly solid.

Spense glanced to his right and left, receiving nods from his friends before they stepped forward and entered the evergreen cave. The cloud drew them in, and they huddled, shoulder to shoulder together in front of its whirling mass.

The Oracle stood, waving over the cloud. Colors formed in its surface, crystallizing into images.

"You seek the one with the blood of iron. The one who will rule. This is where you will find it."

The picture on the cloud began as a map. And shifted, like a bird was flying over the land, the forests...

Was that The Vail?

That flittering, zooming bird ducked through the

trees forming the canopy ceiling of the Summer palace, darting through corridors until it reached a familiar study and workspace. Lady Radiant's shelves were filled with vials and jars, herbs and shining liquids. And on that top shelf, carefully marked and preserved in a code known and understood by no one other than the queen herself, rows upon rows of vials, filled with shimmering liquid from dark crimson to pinkish red. A dainty copper snowflake marked the stopper of one such vial. Their view changed so that the tiny glass container filled the picture on the cloud, glowing brighter and brighter.

And then winked out. The cloud dispersed. And the Winter Oracle returned to her bower.

"What, in all of the kingdoms, was that?" Dirk barked.

Chapter 54

"What is that?" Dewy eyed Lumine sideways, her suspicion growing.

"This is a show of faith, of trust." Lumine brandished a small glass jar. "From one royal to another."

"It looks like…"

"Blood? That's because it is."

Dewy withdrew the hand she'd begun to stretch toward the king. "May I ask whose?"

"Mine, of course."

She frowned. "You would offer me your blood."

"That was the goal all along, was it not?"

Locating the rabbits in the garden was no challenge at all anymore. And she'd repeatedly detected their brethren outside in the grounds of The Silver Horn. Recently, she'd moved on to other creatures, utilizing smaller and smaller samples. But she'd not yet tried with the blood of a faerie. Or even a goblin.

"You think I'm ready?"

"I do. And I think time is not on our side." Lumine's face settled into a sad smile. The king's eyes were soft, the skin around them filigreed with fine, crepe-like lines. Was Lumine aging?

He shook the tiny vial. "Shall we try? Perhaps a game of seeking?"

Dewy extended a hand and accepted the proffered

item from Lumine's long, thin fingers. The red liquid swirled, clinging like wine to the inside of the glass before dripping into the shimmery bulb. This was so much more than a sampling of his body. He was giving her the truth of himself, his secrets.

"You want to play a child's game? With your lifeblood?"

Lumine grinned. His ice-chip eyes grew flinty in the dim light of the gardens.

"Well, I…" Before she could mutter an objection, the king disappeared in a swish of indigo robes and was out of sight.

"I guess that means we've started."

She removed the waxy stopper and inhaled the coppery tang of the blood. His life force was powerful, electric, and charged like a lightning storm. Dewy closed her eyes and let the sense of it become a part of her, tasting, breathing the essence that was Lumine. She opened her eyes and smiled.

"I see you, Lord Winter."

****

It took longer than chasing down a rabbit. Of course, her quarry didn't remain still or in one place. The rabbits always went to ground, seeking a safe spot in which to hide from the freckled faerie huntress.

But Lumine was not a fearful, quivering bunny. And if he was going to play this game, he'd make it a challenge, leading her throughout the grounds and corridors of The Silver Horn. Dewy grimaced as she returned for the second time to the tower entrance. The sneak thief had led her in circles.

She'd followed the trail to this tower early in the search, only to be stymied and frustrated when he was no longer there. Then it led outdoors, well into the forested grounds, and she tracked the king through slushy snow. She might've cheated a bit and used the water all around as an aid as her feet grew chilled and her stomach growled.

And now the blasted, icy monarch had looped back inside.

I suppose I should appreciate the small comforts. Dewy groused as she shook off the crusted snow from her woolen cloak and slogged—again—up the stone tower stairs. Deliberately and quietly, so as not to spook her prey, but slogging all the same.

At the top, she gently pushed the tower door open, reaching out to the wood to keep it from creaking. She needn't have bothered. Lumine, Misty, and Frost lounged under a canopy, in front of a toasty fire, and sipped tea, all facing her direction, as if they were waiting for a comedic play to begin.

"Wicked Winter." Dewy muttered a few more colorful expressions under her breath as she stomped toward the trio of Winter Fae.

Lumine's eyes brightened, like sunlight dancing on ice. Misty chortled. And even Frost's cool demeanor cracked, as he lifted one corner of his mouth.

"Well done, princess." Misty launched from the cushions, grabbing a knitted blanket. She threw it around Dewy's shoulders and gave her an affectionate squeeze.

"Please join us," Lumine said. He raised his cup of tea.

Dewy sighed. Nothing in the world sounded better. She collapsed onto a furred cushion, as near to the kindled fire as she could bear, drawing the blanket tighter with one hand and accepting a mug of hot tea with the other. From that first sip, the elixir of the drink warmed her lips, washed the frost from her tongue and teeth, and slid deliciously down her throat.

"Hungry?"

The mere thought of food set her belly aching. How long had it been? How many breaths and heartbeats had passed? The muted sun was low in the sky, but Dewy was so intent on her task, she'd hardly noticed. Until now.

"Yes. Please."

Misty, acting as host, removed a cloth from a basket, unearthing a neat stack of rolls. Dewy tore into the warm, dark bread, savoring the dense wheat and rye. Another platter held a mixture of cheeses, pickled vegetables and...cold, sliced chicken. From the breast of the bird.

"Care to make a meal of it? We opted to sup casually this evening."

Dewy hungered for a soup or stew from the kitchens. But she swallowed down the soft bread. The simple feast in front of her would do just as well.

Cook had been sneaking larger and larger bits of meat into her meals, from all manner of creatures. At first, she mistook the small chunks of seared flesh for forest fare, smooth and chewy like the most flavorful mushroom, but richer, tangy with fat.

"It's just chicken."

Dewy nodded. They'd discussed this. Though living creatures they might be, and certainly worthy of her respect and care, chickens were possibly the dumbest birds in all the kingdoms. Not that that excused raising them as food, ending their simple, stupid lives with a quick slice of an ax, but it helped assuage her conscience.

She reached for another roll and gouged it open with her fingers. She took some cheese along with a tender slice of the chicken and mashed them into the pocket of the roll. Dewy thanked the dim creature for its sacrifice and wished it well wherever it may be. And took a bite. The cheese was sharp, the chicken coated in herbs, and it all complemented the hearty bread in a satisfying mouthful. She rounded it out with the pickled vegetables, bitter and sugary cucumbers, beets, and carrots she ate unabashedly with her fingers.

"You've done well." Lumine reclined in his own cushioned chair, continuing to sip on his tea. "And you're growing stronger." He nodded toward her and the meal she devoured without the slightest bit of Fae decorum.

Dewy chomped through another bite. He was right. She was stronger. The dizziness and nose bleeds were a thing of the past.

"Thank you."

"It's no compliment. It's a statement of fact." Lumine narrowed his eyes, assessing, speculating. "I wonder what you'll do next."

Frost rolled his eyes. "That is the whole point of this exercise, is it not?"

"Indeed."

Dewy rinsed her mouth with the warming tea, taking time to appreciate the subtle root flavors.

"Shall we try again tomorrow?" Misty added a mischievous wink to her query.

Dewy waited for Lumine's response.

"I think a day of rest may be in order. It is taxing,

the use of so much magic. Best build your strength incrementally."

She met his eyes, challenging his care and kindness. She didn't need his protective concern. It would be too easy to fall into the trap of this strange Winter family and become someone more than an obligatory guest under Lumine's roof.

"Of course, you are free to do as you wish," he said.

"Perhaps we should return to training in the forest…" Misty said.

Dewy recognized her taunting spark. It had become familiar and the thing that drove her up the next trail or over the next boulder.

"What did you have in mind?"

Misty glanced over the crenellated half walls of the tower's rooftop where they lounged, to the rising hills and stony peaks, well past Cinna's woodsy cabin. "I might have some ideas."

Frost rose from his seat and turned to Dewy. "I'd be careful of her ideas, if I were you."

"You don't want to join us, then?" Misty asked, her face plastered unconvincingly with a mask of innocence.

"Certainly not. And if you don't mind, I'll take my leave of you all."

"I'll accompany you, nephew," Lumine said.

As the pair dispersed, Dewy settled back into the blankets, sipping her tea. The warmth of the fire, the hearty food, and the tea were doing good work. Misty tucked her feet up underneath her, partaking of her own cup.

They grew quiet, watching the embers burn down,

a contrast to the darkening sky and the first pinpricks of starlight. It was easier with Misty. Comfortable. How could that have happened? The Summer princess and a Winter noble, nestled like any pair of young girls, more than allies, as friends.

Dewy slid further into her blankets, as her thoughts wandered. She wanted to resist the camaraderie, but it lulled her, beckoning, that ease of friendship. She longed for home, for Summer lands, and also for the home that was Spense's smile, his comforting embrace.

And yet, there was a home here, too, for the people of Winter, common faerie, goblin, and Fae. Again, that pang of guilt rose up. These were people she'd battled and had once made her enemy. They were not. They lived differently—their priorities nearly the opposite of the Summer faeries—but it didn't make them wrong. It was just a different way of being.

She reached a hand into her trouser pocket, to that glass bulb, filled with Lumine's own blood. She rolled it between her fingers. In her overtired, thought-muddled state, her senses took over. Returning to the place of seeking where her heart and mind had been all day. She tracked Lumine with no more than half a thought. He'd returned to his chambers, his study to be exact.

And as she stretched her legs out on the rooftop lounge, her senses stretched, too. Beyond the curving walls of The Silver Horn, into the forests and grounds, and beyond. Through the rocky passes, crossing into the border of Summer...still reaching, seeking that small hint of Lumine's life blood.

It flickered. A small flame, a tiny light. No images came to her, nothing clear or definite. But this was her land. She understood it, would recognize its essence as she would no other.

Dewy bolted up, nearly spilling her tea.

"What is it?" Misty asked.

"Lumine's blood...or the Heir's..." Dewy whispered. "It's in Summer."

Chapter 55

They emerged into the Summer gardens. Dirk stayed close by Flora's side, as Spense and Thorn crossed through the gates, and Gerry and Xendra followed behind. The same two faerie guards stood watch and wore the same stony expressions, as well they might. They matched their own, his little brother, especially. Thorn nodded to the faeries, as their party made their way back through the unassuming gardens, and into the balmy, sweetly floral landscaping.

"All right...I'm just going to say it," Gerry started. "That was disappointing as—*oof!*"

Xendra withdrew her hand.

Gerry grabbed the back of his head. "What was that for?"

She rolled her eyes. Dirk grimaced. He didn't think Spense even noticed.

"But come on. Did the Oracle—Oracles—actually tell us anything? Don't hit me again." Gerry danced out of sharp elbow range.

Flora came to his rescue. Of course, she did. "No...you're right. A lot of what we heard, I've heard the same type of thing in Telridge City by cheap fortune tellers."

"That would've been an easier journey," Gerry muttered, still rubbing the back of his head.

Spense plowed ahead, as if he didn't hear, through

the cultivated, winding greenery, back toward the palace. Dirk recognized his brother's determined face. The Ferrous Frown was on full display.

"But, what about the vision? We all saw that, right? When we joined our hands together?" Flora asked.

Dirk had no idea what it meant. A bunch of vials in Lady Radiant's workroom. At least he thought it was hers. It was a lot cleaner than Spense's and definitely in The Vail.

"Thorn? Any thoughts?"

"Many," Thorn said.

"Care to share?"

Thorn slid his gaze sideways. "I feel I must consult with my queen before I reveal anything—"

Spense whirled around and pressed the Fae steward up against a nearby cedar. That previous look of frustrated determination turned darker. "What are you keeping back? Tell me. *Now*."

Spense pressed one hand into Thorn's chest. The other he held out to his side, a small flame hovered, flickering above, as if Spense were clutching a ball-shaped candle, only there was no candle.

"Spense, calm down," Dirk barked.

He lunged towards his brother and grabbed his shoulders. Gerry and Xendra joined him, and together they pulled him away.

Dirk stepped in between Spense and Thorn, making sure his brother's gaze was on him and him alone. Dirk had dealt with plenty of rage-filled soldiers, and like them, there was a wildness swirling in Spense's eyes, like the flames he held in his hand came from within. When had little brother learned *that* trick?

"Spense, look at me."

Spense blanched. The flames winked out, and he dropped his hand.

"What gives, Spense? I know you're frustrated. We expected more, but—"

"But what? 'Calm down.' 'Don't lose your temper.' 'Be reasonable.' 'Take time off.' I've been calm and reasonable for months. And just when I thought I might get some answers, real answers—this!" He threw up his hands, and turned away, stomping a couple of steps down the pebbled garden path. Just as quickly, he turned back around, and pointed at Gerry. "Gerry's right. Except for that vision—and no, I have no idea what it means, either—we didn't learn a blooming thing!" Spense looked from face to face, meeting their gazes.

"But the vision, if that's all we have to go on, then it must mean something." Flora stepped forward, stretching out a hand to Spense. She approached as if he were a spooked horse, a wild creature.

Maybe he was.

"What? What does it mean?" Spense's face was pleading and desperate. His voice cracked as he asked Flora, as he asked all of them, the towery, lacy trees in the garden, the refined land itself, so different from the wildness of The Between.

"I don't know, Spense. But remember all the things you've figured out. You'll figure this out, too. And you have all of us to help you." Flora gestured to the group, all standing still, careful not to break the soothing calm of her voice.

Or maybe Dirk was a coward, and for the first time, feared his little brother. Not just what his magic could do, but where his emotions might take him. He couldn't think that way, not about Spense.

He stepped forward, joining Flora. "She's right. You'll use that brain, and together we'll work this out. We know one more thing. It's not a lot, and it's confusing, but we only need to take the next step. We don't need to know the whole journey."

Spense crumpled on the garden path, sinking to his knees. He buried his face in his hands. "I just...I thought..."

Dirk knelt down. He put one hand on his brother's shoulder. "I know, brother. I know."

Chapter 56

Spense swiped at his traitorous eyes. What started out as frustration with the Oracles devolved into something else, not as simple as anger, more desperate, crazed. His father warned him that the Oracles might test him.

But his friends didn't judge, just clustered around him. First Flora and Dirk, then the Knights. He was making a spectacle of himself. They deserved better than this.

Thorn cleared his throat. He fidgeted on the periphery of their circle. "Perhaps...perhaps there is something I can share that might shed light on this situation."

Spense looked at the steward. He'd never seen him show the least sign of discomfort, but he was practically squirming now.

"Anything would help," Spense whispered. He knew he couldn't push, even if he desperately wanted to. He rose to his feet and grasped Dirk's steady arm but kept his gaze trained on Thorn.

"You should know that..." Thorn seethed in air. His body stiffened as if he were about to face a severe judgment. "Lady Radiant collects samples of guests who visit The Vail."

"Samples? What are we talking about here?" Dirk asked.

"Often blood. Hair. Eyelashes."

"There's quite a lot of magic that can be performed with that type of thing." Spense narrowed his eyes, careful not to accuse.

"Yes. That's true," Thorn said.

"Does she have samples of *us*?" Dirk asked.

Gerry looked positively green.

"She usually gains consent." He dropped his gaze to the ground near his feet. "Sometimes a situation presents itself, though."

Spense frowned. "Like when a certain Telridgian mage arrives bleeding and passed out?"

"Just so," Thorn said. His eyes shuttered.

Dirk winced. Clearly, he'd made the connection as quickly as Spense had. Lady Radiant must've taken a sample of his blood when it seeped out of him all those months ago. It would've been easy.

I think…" Thorn shook his head. "I know that's what we all saw in the Oracle's vision." He drifted from the group, found a bench formed from smooth branches, similar to Radiant's throne in The Vail's receiving chambers, and sank to the seat. "Please do not judge her too harshly for this. Lady Radiant is generous in hosting wayward travelers—refugees, injured humans, and the like. But yes, she does ask for something from them before they leave. It's the only explanation I can think of."

Spense paced the manicured path in front of Thorn. His thoughts churned, leaning dangerously toward something that looked like hope. "Is it possible? We know that the child and the child's father—Snow's chosen lover—were banished from the Winter lands."

"Could they have made their way here, to

Summer?" Flora asked.

Thorn held out his hands. "I suppose. Anything is possible."

"And if Lady Radiant took a sample from them..." Spense said, putting the pieces together.

"Not quite." Thorn frowned. "This would've been well before Radiant's reign, before her time, even. But the practice...it isn't new or unique to her."

That took Spense aback. And he knew it was costing Thorn, revealing this type of information about the secret practices of the Summer court.

"Just how long ago was this? I thought we were looking for a kid," Dirk said.

"No, not hardly. Many, many years have passed. The Heir would be into their own middle age at least, by human standards. Could even have children of their own."

"So, I don't get it. If Lumine knew this was going to be a problem, why did he just start looking for the kid, now?" Gerry asked.

Thorn scoffed. "Two things. When his daughter Snow chose passing, she left him no choice. And I— we—believe the king may be fading, himself. He's quite advanced in age—not that you'd know it—we faeries don't show our age the way that humans do. But his own magic, as deep and powerful as it is, may be weakening. He knows his time is approaching."

"How do you know all this?" Dirk asked.

"My dear prince, it is my business to know." Thorn lifted an eyebrow, a subtle reminder that he was more than a steward to the Summer queen.

He was her spy.

J.A. Nielsen

A thought—reckless and foolish—was forming. Spense looked closely at Thorn. He just might need that spy version of him.

Chapter 57

Spense trailed behind Thorn through the winding passages of The Vail, until they reached Lady Radiant's study door. The Fae steward tapped lightly before unlocking and entering. A moment later, Thorn turned back, frowned, and gestured to Spense to follow him. Spense unlocked his stiff limbs and tripped behind, into the study and workroom he'd viewed so clearly from the Oracles.

But now the queen presided over her worktable, full of notebooks and ephemera. The space was alive, a working, breathing space, so different from the flat crystalline image he'd seen. Dust motes danced in slanting sun rays, and his nose filled with the heady scent of lavender.

Spense bowed. And as he lifted his gaze, he couldn't help but scan the shelves behind Lady Radiant, filled with rows and rows of dried herbs, shimmering liquids, and at the very top, small, stoppered bottles.

"Was your trip to The Between productive?" Radiant lowered a weathered parchment and placed it neatly on her expansive desk.

"I suppose it's still hard to tell," Thorn said.

"That sounds about right." She pursed her lips. "Please, be seated. Tell me more. I'd like to know."

Thorn glanced quickly in Spense's direction. "My lady, the Oracle revealed something about our court you may have preferred to be kept secret."

"I see."

"About…your collection," Thorn clarified.

Radiant elevated her chin. Her lips pressed into a hard line.

"They know, Ollie," Thorn whispered.

Radiant shifted her gaze to Spense. "Is that so?"

He cleared his throat and matched her level look. "We saw a vision. The Winter Oracle showed us a vial from your study. We believe it to be the blood of the Heir."

The queen tilted her head, frowning.

Thorn stepped forward. His movements were slow and measured as he offered an explanation. "It was likely your father who collected it. It would've been before your time."

"Ah." She leaned back in her chair and pressed her hands flat before her on her desk. "And you are now asking me to gift it to you?"

Spense sucked in a deep breath. It shouldn't have surprised him that she came so quickly to the point. He nodded.

Her eyes narrowed. "You know I cannot possibly do that."

He opened his mouth to speak, closed it again. Thorn's face remained stoic and calm, revealing nothing. No surprise. Not even a blink. Spense's stomach tightened as he realized Thorn must've expected this outcome, even when he revealed the Summer Court's secret practice of acquiring—with or without permission—samples of their guests.

"Y-you cannot?" He wondered if he'd heard her correctly. "Why?"

Radiant leaned forward. "Think, young Master Spense."

He tried. His mind was blank except for the desperate recurring thought that he had nothing else, but this one small clue, no other hope but this, a tiny shred of a possibility that might, just maybe, sway Lumine into releasing Dewy. And the queen was saying no. His chest hollowed and his breaths became shallow.

"You are asking for the blood of the Heir of Winter, while the Heir of Summer whiles away her days in exile." Radiant rose from her seat. Her face filled with color as she spoke. "You have shown the depth and strength of your magic, enough that you were able to cast a spell of Claiming on my niece. And it's also because of you that she is so far from me now. I may choose to believe you to be of good character, that none of this was your intention. I'm not so naïve as to relinquish that kind of power, the power inherent in blood magic. Not to you. Not to anyone."

While she spoke, Spense shrunk into his chair. The churning swirl of shame and hopelessness tightened his bowels and caused bile to rise in his throat.

"I understand," he whispered.

Her brown eyes filled with the heat of a late summer sun. "I hope that you do."

****

Spense replayed Lady Radiant's words again and again as he drifted back to the guest quarters she'd so graciously provided. He couldn't see a way around her position. It was reasonable. Whatever affection or respect she might hold for him, how could he possibly ask her to give away something so volatile, so powerful, and to the son of a rival kingdom?

Quick steps sounded behind him. He glanced up as Thorn rushed to catch him.

"Master Spense, a moment before you return to your chambers."

"Of course." He halted and waited for Thorn to begin, likely his own version of Radiant's rebuke.

"We need to discuss this matter of the Heir's blood."

"What is there to discuss? Radiant made her position clear." Spense shrugged. "One can hardly blame her. How could I have even asked it of her?"

Thorn reached out and laid his hand gently on Spense's shoulder. "You had to ask. She had to say no."

"I know. I understand."

"No. You're not hearing me."

Spense looked up and squinted at Thorn. "I don't follow."

"There was no way she could hand over that item. It's too powerful. It would cause a revolt if any of her council knew."

"I see that now." The weight of his failure pressed on his chest and belly, dull, solid, and leaden.

"But we don't have a choice. You *must* get that vial."

Spense frowned. "You're talking in circles, Thorn. Again."

The steward smirked. "Maybe. I'm known for it, I suppose."

He folded his arms over his chest and gazed sharply at Thorn. "If she won't give it to me. But we must have it…"

Thorn's eyes glinted. "Then we have to steal it."

Chapter 58

"I'm sorry. You want to do what?"

Dirk collapsed on one of the lounges in the common area of their guest quarters. The Summer environs were no less ethereal than The Between, but they were at least grounded in reality. Real trees. Real birds. Mostly. Sometimes the faeries in the corridors morphed from one thing to the next, but at least he knew they were all seeing the same things.

The Telridgians had escaped the clustering Fae nobility who wanted to hear all about their venture into the land of the Oracles. Gossipy lot. Not that they'd gotten anything out of them. And Thorn had agreed to keep their secrets. For now.

Just as they were finally settling in for the night, Spense burst through the entry and launched into his latest wild scheme. Dirk groaned, letting his head fall back on the lounge. He closed his eyes.

"I've already asked. Radiant won't just hand it over. We have to steal it," Spense said. Little brother's explanation didn't make it sound any better the second time.

"We can't just steal from the Summer faeries...can we?" Gerry asked.

"No. We can't." That was Flora.

Thank you, voice of sanity.

"Plus, you've already alerted her. She'll know it

was us."

Spense paced. He was getting nice and worked up. "We shouldn't. Of course. I know it's a terrible idea. We want to maintain good relationships. But we have no choice."

Dirk squinted his eyes, zeroed in on his—once again—semi-crazed brother. "What you said about this being a terrible idea, let's focus on that, shall we?"

"We need that vial, that blood." Spense marched back and forth, smacking the back of one hand into the other, as if he were arguing a point before a tribunal. "We may not have the Heir, but if we have the Heir's blood, it would get Lumine one step closer. It might be enough for the bargain. Maybe he'd let Dewy go."

"That's a lot of ifs and maybes. And you want to risk angering Lady Radiant—royally—for this small chance?"

The consequences were too big. As much as Dirk dreaded the drudgery of politics, he knew the value of alliances. And he didn't want to make the Summer queen his adversary.

"If it works, she'd get her niece back. I think she'd forgive us."

"Sounds like another 'if.' A big one."

"We've got Thorn. He'll know how to pull this off."

"There is no way Thorn would go along with this. Would *you*? Steal from your king? Spense, you're asking him to do something akin to treason."

"He understands how vital this is."

"What is it I understand?" Thorn slipped into their chambers.

Dirk cringed. What had he overheard?

"I'm so glad you're here." Spense rushed over to the steward.

"Lady Radiant bid me to check you had all you required, and she would like to extend an invitation to dine with her this evening."

"Please give her our thanks."

"Of course. Now, I believe I walked in on something. How may I be of service?"

"How do you feel about theft, deceit, and possible treason?" Dirk asked.

Thorn chuckled. "Tell me more, young prince."

Chapter 59

They proceeded into the receiving chambers as planned, once again decked out in finery. It was jarring, but not unwelcome, to see Flora and the Knights in their faerie gowns and fine tunics. Spense was used to seeing Dirk dandied up. But still, not one of them seemed fully comfortable. Spense admired the pairings—Flora and Dirk as well as Sir Gervais and Lady Xendra—like matched sets. Maybe it was the atmosphere. The need to lean into one another.

The pressure of their intended crime.

Spense approached Lady Radiant and bowed deeply.

"Rise, Master Spense, and come join me."

He did as he was bidden, taking the open camellia branch seat beside the queen.

"I hear you are preparing to leave our fair domain."

"Unfortunately, that is the case, Lady Radiant. We have completed our task, as best we can. It's time."

Nearly, anyway.

"Though you didn't get what you came for." Lady Radiant lifted her chin and narrowed her eyes.

"Regrettably, no. I would've preferred something a little more direct from the Oracles, but I've come to understand that isn't their way." Spense lifted his hands as he shrugged. Casual. Easy. *Nothing to see here.*

"I'm sorry for you."

"I'm sorry for all of us."

"True." The queen's gaze was clear and piercing.

Dewy had said her aunt was an astute empath. He hoped she couldn't read the shadow of deception behind his words. Though nothing he'd said so far was technically a lie, it wasn't quite the whole truth, either.

"I hope that sharing the vision we saw will be enough, something to at least get closer to finding Lumine's Heir."

Along with a small vial I'm going to steal from you. Spense tried to school his thoughts, and pressed his damp palms along his thighs.

"We can only hope." Radiant turned to the small crowd forming. The private dinner with the queen again included most of her council. "It appears your brother and his lady have made quite the impression upon our court."

"Oh. Flora's not—"

"We've been over this, dear Spense. And, besides, it does not do to correct a queen in her own home."

"Of course." He turned his attention to Dirk and Flora, as they made their way through the small grouping of faeries, speaking cordially to each. And serving his purpose by providing a distraction. One of their planned sleights of hands.

The other was in the form of the Knights, who were to appear to partake of too much honeyed faerie wine and become so enamored with each other that they were asked to excuse themselves. It wasn't much of a stretch—their play-acting. In fact, it's pretty much what they did a couple nights before. Spense just hoped they didn't actually drink the wine. He needed them on alert, while he stole through the corridors.

Their third misdirection of the evening arrived promptly. Thorn bowed to his lady, exchanged pleasantries, and was just as quickly given leave to make the rounds. His role—for Spense's purposes—was to ensure that the attendees and the queen in particular, were paying attention to the other Telridgian guests.

It wasn't hard. Once again, Flora and Dirk drew everyone's eyes. He'd never known his brother to be charming, but with Flora on his arm, he could see it. Her own bright laughter seemed to shine a ray onto Dirk. Thorn led them from one Fae to the next, all bent on hearing about their visit to the Oracles. Dirk chuckled as he admitted that all he'd seen in the maze village was Flora. She was the only thing he was ever technically seeking. The captivating smile she gave him glowed, enough that all of the faerie dinner guests were drawn in, wanting to hear more of their story and soak up their light-filled presence.

Which meant it was Spense's time to go.

He caught Thorn's gaze across the long table and tipped his chin, a micro-movement. Barely a nod. As the faerie servants danced between the guests, removing plates and refilling wine goblets, Spense slipped away.

Thorn met him in a small alcove near the entryway.

"You sure you're all right with this?" Spense asked.

"I've made my peace with what must be done."

"It should be soon."

Thorn scanned the room. "Indeed."

Gerry and Xendra were well into their cups, or at least, they appeared so. Dirk discreetly asked them to return to quarters, but not so discreet that everyone in the dinner hadn't heard the exchange. As they stumbled out, Dirk made his apologies to the queen. Lady Xendra winked at Spense on her way through the entry.

He heard her laughter trailing down the corridors. Waited a moment, and then followed quietly behind them, ducking into the shadows of aspens as he crept through the winding pathways of The Vail.

"It's thissh way."

"No, you lout, it's this way." Lady Xendra tugged Gerry's elbow demonstratively as two faeries skittered by, their eyes wide and mouths pinched.

As soon as the faeries passed them, the Knights dropped their pretense and continued their way through the corridors. Their intentionally loud guffaws turned to quiet whispers as they double-checked the map Xendra had secreted up her wide sleeve.

They were deep in consultation when Spense caught the beat of footsteps through the earthen floor. Sensing them, but not hearing them. Which meant his human companions would not hear them at all and wouldn't know to resume their ruse.

Spense cursed silently.

The steps grew closer. Two pairs. Whisper-light.

There was nothing for it. He skated through the shadows, faster than he would've liked. He swiped a collection of tiny pebbles from cracks in between the stone pavers, cupped them in his hands, and whispered to them. It was a ridiculous spell, meant for entertaining small children in the castle keep at Telridge. He sent the pebbles dancing, swirling about Lady Xendra's head and pinging off the trunks of the tall trees.

"Wicked Winter, what's that?" Gerry asked as the tiny stones danced a halo around Lady Xendra.

She whipped her head around, peering down the corridors. A heartbeat later, she giggled loudly, throwing herself into Gerry. Exaggerating a stumble.

"Wha—" Gerry frowned.

Spense released the spell. The playful stones fell.

In the next heartbeat, two members of Lady Radiant's court—Thistle and Shamrock—floated around the corner. They were in Fae form, but they nearly flew, as if their transformation wasn't quite complete and they could take to the trees as twittering, all-seeing birds at any moment. Their gowns were embellished with blue and green iridescent feathers, sewn into the bodices and along the edges of their sleeves and trains.

"Oh my."

"What do we have here?"

"Seems our guests are lost."

"You know, sister, the effects of honey wine."

A short giggle. "Indeed."

"Of course, sometimes it's good to get lost."

Gerry's gaze zipped back and forth between the two, trying to follow the conversation. Xendra smiled sleepily. At least someone remembered their role. But Gerry stood gob-smacked as the two faeries ran their hands along his arms, back, and chest. Teasing, tantalizing. Engrossed by the bumbling human male in front of them.

It was as much distraction as Spense would get. He hoped it was enough as he slid through dark and light, through the arching trees, and wove his way to the entrance of Lady Radiant's study, one of the few locked doors in the whole of The Vail.

If Thorn had done his job, the lock would be no

barrier at all. Spense pressed one hand to the oak door, squeezed the handle, expecting the latch to slide free. He was met with solid resistance.

He jostled the handle, but the door didn't give. He sucked in air through his teeth.

Where was that steward?

Chapter 60

Voices carried along the corridor. Xendra and Gerry's faked slurs. Thistle and Shamrock's lilting murmurs. And they were moving this way.

Spense ducked back into the shadows. He waited. The blue and green feathered faeries drifted near, chuckling over the stumbling humans.

"I do enjoy these Telridgians."

"Yes, sister. I noticed. Which do you prefer?"

"Hmm...Both are quite charming. I suppose you fancied the lady."

One of the twins chortled.

"She is lovely. And so fierce." A sigh.

Their light faerie feet danced on by. Spense inhaled the floral scent that wafted around so many of the Summer faeries. Cloyingly sweet, honeyed. He released his breath in a slow exhale once he was sure the Court Fae were well past.

There was a soft click coming from the door. Sweet Spring. Finally.

After checking once more that the corridors were clear, Spense entered Radiant's study, and closed the door quietly behind him. The silhouetted shape of Thorn ushered him in, guiding him around obstacles he might otherwise stumble over in the darkened space. Spense gestured silently—but angrily—at Thorn who glowered back. He could just make out Thorn's frustrated brow line.

"What happened?" Spense mouthed.

"I was delayed. It couldn't be helped." Thorn hissed.

"Fine. All right. Let's just find that vial."

But the interior of the study was too dark. Night had crept in, and the forest canopy that made the roof of the study blocked out the moonlight. Spense lifted his hand. With barely a thought, he created a tiny orb of firelight. It worked as a small lantern, enough to search the shelves.

"Here." Thorn waved Spense over.

High on the top shelf were rows upon rows of glass globes and vials, each filled with dark liquid. Spense had been in this workspace twice before and hadn't noticed the racks. He scanned the shelf. The image from the vision was clear in his memory. He held his lantern arm high and moved it along the rows, casting a flickering glow over each vial and jar.

There. The tiny golden stamp of a snowflake. Exactly like the one in the Oracle's projection. Spense lifted the vial from its place in the rack.

He frowned. It left an obvious vacancy.

Thorn noticed, too, and reached for another vial, from a back row, to replace it and fill the gap. They nodded at each other. It was done.

Spense pocketed the snowflake-printed glass tube and lowered his torch-bearing hand. Light flew across the jars and bottles. A small beam flickered across a vial with green lettering…what was that writing?

SF—Tlrdg Em

Spense halted.

Thorn was already near the door. In another breath,

he'd be there. Spense needed to go. Now. But...

That vial. Could it be...Spense Ferrous. Telridge. Emissary?

Spense swiped the vial, secured it in his pocket next to the Heir's blood before Thorn glanced back in his direction. He pressed his hand against his overcoat to keep the glass from tinkling as he moved.

The steward opened the door a crack and peered out. Without looking behind him, Thorn waved Spense along, reached for his tunic, and in one motion thrust him through the barely open doorway.

The door closed with a quiet thud.

And Spense was alone—with not one, but two stolen items from the queen of the Summer faeries.

He shuttered his eyes and felt the tiny presence of the vials in his pocket, heavy with accusation.

This was what it was like to be a criminal.

Chapter 61

Another night. Another dinner. Crown Prince Dirk of Telridge on her arm.

Again.

It was getting to be routine.

Except that it wasn't. And could never be.

Best to smile and enjoy the moment, create the distraction Spense needed for his new venture into criminal activity. The wine, the gown, the charming Fae, her more-than-charming companion. It would all be over soon.

Flora greeted and chatted with faeries as if she represented Telridge, as if she was Dirk's real partner. Perhaps it was good for the faeries to meet some common folk, but did they realize she was common? She shook her head. How could they not?

"Shall I ask about that smile? You look as if you're keeping a joke to yourself. Care to share?" Dirk leaned in as he asked. His eyebrows lifted, along with the corners of his mouth.

"I…it's nothing."Flora's cheeks heated.

It was as he said. A joke. Play-acting. Nothing more.

If Dirk wanted to question her further, he lost the opportunity. A dark-haired faerie in a sunset-pink gown approached. The diminutive lady bowed her head and reached for Flora's hands. Her own were small and smooth, but she had a firm grip, and she squeezed as she spoke.

"I've been meaning to speak with you, but I'm afraid it took me until now to work up the courage."

"Please," Dirk said. "We're happy to make your acquaintance, Lady…?"

The faerie blushed and withdrew her hands. "Rosehip, Lord Ferrous. I'm the presiding secretary for the Summer Council and often assist Lady Radiant in her responsibilities."

"An important role in this court, I'm sure," he said.

Flora pressed her lips together. Dirk could pile on the magnanimity when he wanted. But she knew what he was like covered in dust and sweat, and she also knew he preferred it.

"Yes. Thank you. It is a privilege. One I do not take lightly. But of course, there are…sacrifices to serving in such a role." Rosehip bit her plump, raspberry-colored lips.

"Life in service to the crown can be a burden. I understand," Dirk said.

Flora wondered if he did, really. Even if he preferred the dirt, he always had the option to shake it off. Not everyone had that privilege.

"How can we be of help, Lady Rosehip?" Flora asked.

"Well, you see, even with such responsibilities, we faeries do enjoy a lively dance or frolic in the forest."

Flora wondered where this was going.

"Usually, my duties interfere with such frivolities, but every now and then…" Rosehip slid her gaze to the side and lifted her thin arms.

"Sometimes you need to shrug off your

responsibilities? Enjoy life with your friends?"

"Yes, that's it exactly. I knew you'd understand. I had that sense about you."

More than you know.

"What is it you're asking of us?" Dirk leaned in. He had to stoop—quite a lot—to get close to the faerie.

Rosehip folded her hands together in a tight clasp. She took a deep breath and slowly let it out.

Flora laid one hand on Rosehip's shoulder. "Go ahead. It's all right, whatever it is you need to say."

She lifted her gaze to meet Flora's. Silver pools lined the faerie's eyes. "Several years ago, I met a young man—a human—in the forest. He was clever and kind and we so enjoyed each other's company. We only had a few nights together. I was given a respite from my duties while my lady was traveling and I believe he was on some sort of adventure, a hunt perhaps, with his friends. It was as if our days were happening outside of normal time."

"It sounds like a dream."

Flora knew more than a little about that. These past days—in the lands of faerie and The Between—certainly existed outside of normal.

"It was. But of course, it couldn't last for either of us. We had to return to our lives."

"And…are you wondering if we might locate this young man for you?" Dirk asked.

"Oh no. I know exactly where he is. His family tends a lovely farm at the edge of the forest in Telridge."

"Then, what is it you seek from us?"

"Well, you see, there were consequences to our actions. Neither of us thought to take a daily tea. I know it was irresponsible, but…"

Flora's spine stiffened. She pulled away from the faerie. Looked at her features closer. Her round, dark eyes. Her delicately pointed ears.

"What are you saying? You had a child?"

"A little girl. But I couldn't care for her. Not with my duties, here, so I…" Rosehip hiccupped her words. The tears pooling in her eyes overflowed.

"You brought her to the girl's father, left him a note? Said the child's name was Petal?" Her conjecture tumbled out flat, landing like heavy stones.

"Yes," the faerie whispered. "But, how could you know that?"

Flora brushed away her own tears. Heated prickles had risen in her neck. Her heart thumped erratically in her chest. Almost to the point of pain. She couldn't speak. She could hardly breathe.

"Petal is Lady Flora's niece," Dirk said. He glanced at her. "Sort of niece. Rook—Petal's father— he's her cousin."

"Could it be true?"

Flora nodded. Rosehip lunged forward and embraced her. Flora returned the gesture. And in moments, they were both a babbling, crying pair of overflowing emotions.

"How is she? How is Rook? I never meant. I'm so sorry. Do you think…?"

Flora held on, hoping to calm and reassure them both, saying whatever came into her head. She never thought Petal's mother would be anything like Rosehip. She'd worked up so many false ideas and images in her head about a reckless and thoughtless faerie. She realized now they were unfair. She should've guessed there was more to the story. A few nights of frivolous play-acting sometimes had real-world consequences. A lesson she'd best remember. "It's all right," she said to the faerie. "They're both well. She's...Petal's the most amazing child—"

"Is everything all right, here?" Spense broke in.

"Yes, brother. A bit of a surprise. This is Rosehip. She's...well, I guess she's Petal's mother."

"Who?"

"Flora's niece. I thought you knew her family?"

"Oh. Right. Sorry."

Spense had an uncanny gift for remembering details. It warmed her that it was Dirk who had remembered this time. Her family was so far beneath his notice. And she'd never revealed that there were faeries in her family. How was he to react to that?

"Everything all right with *you*, Spense?" Dirk asked.

Spense turned to his brother. "Yes, everything is very much all right. Got our wayward Knights settled in, back in quarters. They have everything they need." He spoke a little too loudly, gaining the attention of faeries nearby, and the queen.

"My apologies, my Telridgian friends." Lady Radiant drifted toward them. "The frivolities of our court can be quite the experience."

Dirk chuckled. "You'd think they'd learn after the other night."

Flora bit the inside of her cheek. He was a little too jovial. It was a good thing neither of the Ferrous brothers were pursuing a career in the theater. Flora had nearly forgotten—with the shock of meeting Rosehip— what their actual goal was for the evening, thieving that vial of the Winter Heir's blood in the small hope it would be enough to release Dewy. If Dirk and Spense weren't more careful, they'd arouse suspicion.

"To speak plainly, I think your Knights might have the right notion. I find myself ready to return to chambers myself." Lady Radiant's smile was—as always—warm and generous. "Rosehip, might you care to escort me this evening?"

Rosehip wiped the last crystal tears from her face and turned her attention to her queen.

"I shall take my leave of you all, then. Will I see you in the morning?"

"I'm sorry, Lady Radiant. We'd hoped to have an early start," Dirk said.

"In that case, rest well. I pray a good journey for you all, especially considering you are borrowing my steward for the trip north. I hope to see you again soon, hopefully with better news."

Spense bowed deeply. Dirk ducked his head. Flora curtsied.

If the queen thought their behavior was forced or strange, she didn't let on. Perhaps it was her own skill at political subterfuge on display or perhaps she really was as generous as she seemed.

But Flora was happy to put away those thoughts. Such musings and observations weren't for the likes of her. What did it matter what a stable hand thought of the Summer queen?

No. She'd done her part, and now her play-acting was over. As soon as they were on their way in the morning, Flora would cheerfully return to her place amongst the horses.

She'd gained so much from this adventure that

she'd never expected. The quizzical Oracles and Dirk's vexing behavior, she'd be happy to leave behind. But meeting Rosehip. The joy. The tears. They were all too real.

And it was good to be reminded of the things in this world that were.

Chapter 62

Lady Radiant strolled into her private workspace. It was her place of reprieve, of quiet and study. She craved visits at the end of long days such as this, after the pressures of hosting foreign dignitaries, and resolving diplomatic matters. Breathing in the spicy, pungent air, the simple aromas of dried herbs, it was cleansing, easing to her thoughts.

She found Thorn leaning against the bench where she conducted her experiments and created potions. It wasn't queenly work, but it focused her mind, gave her hands something to do.

Her steward's arms were folded over his chest, feet crossed at the ankles.

"It is done, then?"

"It is," Thorn said.

"I can't help but wonder if this was truly the only option." Radiant moved closer to Thorn, but turned her face to the shelves, searching out the empty place. The young mage had been careful—or perhaps Thorn had—substituting another vial for the one he'd stolen. The casual inspection would reveal nothing amiss.

Her servant, spy, and friend chuckled drily. "It was, after all, your idea."

Radiant rolled her eyes as she made her way to Thorn's side, settling against the long work counter as casually as he. "And young Master Spense's."

"Do try to remember that it was you who convinced me, my lady." Thorn lifted the corner of his mouth in a conciliatory smile. "You couldn't make a public gift of this item, not unless you wanted Summer's practice to keep such things to become widely known. This way, we ensure the discretion of the Telridgians, as they, likewise, wouldn't want it known that their prince, official emissary, and two of their Knights were party to a theft. By keeping their own secrets, they keep yours as well."

Radiant patted Thorn's cheek. "Such lovely logic. It's rather neat, isn't it?"

"A bit manipulative, perhaps." He lifted one eyebrow.

"It's what I do."

He covered her hand with his own. "And I try to serve you as best I can."

"I know. And I am grateful. Sometimes I wish..."

But her reverie was cut short as her gaze continued to take inventory of her shelves and workspace. There was another vial gone. Taken in haste. No attempt had been made to hide the fact.

"Ollie?"

Radiant checked her expression. Made sure it remained pleasant, serene, even with the familiarity the use of her given name implied. Few faeries addressed her as anything but Radiant anymore. She withdrew her hand, sliding it from Thorn's handsome face and warm, brown hand. "Best we leave wishes to themselves, I think. You have a journey before you."

She wondered if he knew of the second theft. Had Spense been subtle enough to get something past her spy? The idea amused her. It was charming, in a way, that Thorn might have a blind spot when it came to Spense, and another reason to remember her own role. Radiant was queen regent. She liked the young mage, but it didn't mean she had room for sentiment.

"Of course, my lady." Thorn stepped back, ducking his head in a bow, as if he could read her thoughts, or more likely, the stiffening of her shoulders.

For his part, Thorn was the picture of obeisance, the loyal servant to the rigid queen. The thought sent a sharp pang into her heart. Her usually comforting study became chilly.

She'd have to find her quietude in faith and in the trust she'd placed in the most unlikely of places—a peculiar but determined group of human thieves.

Chapter 63

"You're sure of this?"

Dewy glared.

Lumine held up his hands in surrender. "I believe you. It's only…" He smiled and shook his head.

Dewy didn't know if she'd ever get used to Lumine smiling without wondering about his ulterior motives. "What?"

"Your powers, abilities, they're growing. Impressively. I'm encouraged. But please forgive me if I find it humbling. You've gone beyond me."

"That is what you wanted."

Dewy deepened her scowl. Lumine had pushed, manipulated, and attempted to charm her for weeks now. It wasn't subtle. That's how obviously desperate he was. He'd just have to deal with the consequences he didn't like right alongside those he needed.

"It is," Lumine conceded.

"The Heir's blood—a part of your blood—is in Summer. I'm sure of it. But there's more."

"More?"

The trill of the blood had grown stronger overnight. It gave her the confidence to share her news with assurance.

By the morning, something had shifted. Not her awareness of it. That continued to be strong. Once she'd homed in on it, she felt its steady signal. But there was something else.

"The blood—what I sense of it—is moving."

"Moving? Really?"

She widened her eyes. "We are assuming this blood is inside a person, right? They tend to move around."

Lumine waved her off. "Obviously. Where are they headed?"

She closed her eyes and retraced the path of the blood. It was purposeful and directed, on a clear trajectory through familiar forested trails, a driving rhythm of song.

"Here." She met Lumine's icy, probing gaze. "They're coming here."

Chapter 64

They left before dawn. Even in the land of Summer, the pre-morning air was chilled. It grew colder the further they traveled from The Vail. And as usual, Dirk's little brother had a pensive look about him.

"Fix your face."

"Sorry?" Spense scowled and looked over at him.

Over, not up. When did that happen? Spense was still scrawny. Long and lean. Like a faerie, he supposed. And still overly academic and way too much in his head. At least, some things never changed.

"You look guilty. Stop it."

Spense whispered, "We are guilty."

"We did what we had to. You seem to be forgetting it was your idea."

"No, I didn't forget. I just feel bad."

"Well, get used to it. We don't always get easy choices. Sometimes it's a matter of choosing the least terrible thing."

"I know that, but I don't want to get used to it. I mean, it seems like you and Father have to make these kinds of decisions all the time. In case you hadn't noticed, I lead a simpler life than you."

"You really think that's true anymore?"

"I…" Spense stopped walking. Without fixing his face. If anything, it was worse. The Ferrous Frown was

317

super wrinkly.

"Everything all right, here?" Flora asked.

Dirk gestured at his brother. "The usual. Spense is overthinking things and reaching all sorts of outlandish, terrible conclusions."

Flora snickered.

"He's worked up that we may have betrayed Lady Radiant," Dirk said.

"We did do that," Spense protested.

"Did we, though?" Flora asked.

"I don't know what you mean." Spense cast his gaze to the trail in front of him. At the same time Dirk said, "Wait, what's that?"

"Well, I'm certainly no expert on thievery, but it seemed to go awfully smooth for first-timers."

Dirk stood open-mouthed before her. Morning sun slanted onto her face, making her eyes appear extra bright, as if the light shone from within.

"Wouldn't you have expected some sort of enchanted seal on her door in addition to a regular lock?"

"I thought you said Thorn opened the lock..."

Dirk glanced ahead, to where Thorn was leading their group. Having a friendly chat with Gerry and Xendra. Remarkably at ease, despite recent circumstances.

Spense cleared his throat. His gaze wandered all over the place.

"You were part of this? With the queen?"

"Uh, excuse me." Spense jogged ahead to join the advance party.

Dirk scoffed. "Can't believe I didn't see it."

"You can't be expected to notice everything."

Dirk raised an eyebrow.

"Oh, I guess we do sort of expect that, don't we?"

Dirk shrugged. "Welcome to the life of Telridge's Commander."

She nudged his arm with her shoulder. "Don't forget 'prince.'"

"I never do. I don't have that luxury." He smirked.

"You really don't, do you? Not you. Not your father or these faerie rulers. Or even Spense. It's sad, really."

"Are you pitying your monarchy?"

"Forgive me. It's just that we never see it from your point of view. It seems lonely, that's all."

Dirk pinched the bridge of his nose. This road seemed extra dusty. Making it hard to breathe, hard to scc.

Who was he kidding? It was hard to be seen.

"You're not wrong." He could admit that much.

They walked on in silence. Dirk's thoughts roiled through him. He was probably sporting the Ferrous Frown every bit as much as his brother.

"Do you know the story…why King Lumine and my father are so much at odds?"

"Everyone knows." Flora shrugged and brushed a honey-brown curl off her face. "Your father asked for King Lumine's aid when your mother was sick. He came to help. Only it didn't help. She died."

"That's the public version. It was a little more complicated than that."

"It usually is."

"My father never forgave him. Blamed him, actually."

"A lot of people did. People loved your mother. I

was really little, no older than Petal, but even I remember. And you know they still talk about her, right?"

Dirk brushed debris from his eyes. More of that road dust. It seemed to dance in the air, circling around him, like firelit gnats.

"You know why he reached out to Lumine?"

Flora shrugged. "His magic, I'd guess."

"It wasn't just that. He knew Lumine had lost his wife years and years before and his daughter, Snow, wasn't speaking to him. I think my father thought that he'd understand. And he did. Too well. As soon as he arrived, he could tell my mum was almost gone. There wasn't anything anyone could do except maybe make it a little easier on her. Even I knew that, and I was just a kid.

"But my father wouldn't hear it. And he took his grief out on King Lumine. I mean, he was an easy target, right?"

"I think…I think we all say and do things when we're grieving, things we don't really mean."

"That's all well and good, but for most people it doesn't have international consequences."

"True. But…"

"But what?"

"I'm not sure it's my place to say." Flora ducked her head, turned away from him.

"Please. I'd like to hear your thoughts."

He meant it. He trusted her observations. She saw things others didn't, like Thorn's suspiciously comfortable demeanor this morning and Spense's guilt. She had a way of speaking to him so that he saw the world a little differently, with a wider perspective.

She looked up. Her gaze was warm and soft. "Everyone grieves. It's what you do with it that matters. And you have an opportunity here, to make different choices. To mend what's been broken."

Dirk sucked in cool air between his teeth. "That's asking a lot. Remember our visit from the Winter faeries?"

"I remember. But I also know you, or at least, I think I do. And I don't think you're the type to hold a grudge for decades like your father."

"You sure about that?" Dirk grinned. He was pretty sure Lord Frost would be happy to keep the grudge fest going.

"I have faith in you, my lord."

Dirk worked a lump in his throat. He gripped the lead of Storm a little tighter. Flora's opinion was quickly becoming the one that mattered to him the most. But this little adventure would come to a close soon enough and they'd go back to their lives and proper roles in Telridge society once again. And he'd have to give up these chats, this time, just talking to Flora. He'd miss them. He'd been missing them. And he wanted to tell her that. But what good would that do?

Instead, he said, "Thank you."

Best to leave it at that.

Chapter 65

Dewy approached the great hall for dinner. She
wondered when the Winter faeries stopped feeling like
her captors and more like…people? Like a strange
diplomatic partnership between the Summer and Winter
Fae, working on a special assignment. Was this how it
used to be? Before ancient treaties divided faerie-kind?

Faint trills of music floated down the corridor as
she approached the hall. String instruments playing
something jaunty. Before she knew what was
happening, the great oak doors burst open, and Misty
emerged with a flagon in her hand.

"Ah! There you are!" She lunged forward, grabbed
Dewy's arm, and pulled her in.

"What's all this?"

The usually somber dining hall was festooned with
cedar garlands. A cluster of musicians played pipes and
fiddles in the corner. And it seemed as if Lumine's
whole court had come to partake in the evident
merriment.

"We're celebrating!"

"I can see that. But why?"

"You, silly!"

"Me?"

"Of course. You've come so far and you were able
to locate the Heir's living blood, from so far away. It's
astonishing—like a miracle—and we could use one

around here." Misty looped her arm through Dewy's, escorting her through the crowd.

She wondered how much cider the faerie had already consumed as she skipped and winked her way across the hall.

"This…is unexpected."

"That's only because you don't know us, not really. You've had it in your head for too long that we're some sort of warmongering, meat-eating, dark version of faerie kind."

It was true. Dewy'd thought every one of those things. And she hadn't looked for evidence to counter her thoughts. But it was there. How much these people loved their forested, mountainous lands, every bit as much as the Summer faeries loved theirs. The warm smiles on faerie and goblin faces, that was joy.

And how hard must it be for them to share such merriment with her? How many of them had friends and family injured or killed in the attack on Telridge? It must be a strange irony indeed, that she was now the instrument of hope, of salvation for the Winter lands. That this court would embrace her—in the case of Misty, literally—after all that had happened. She'd felt the shift herself. That she was no longer just a prisoner. She was something else. Captor and captive working together. No longer adversaries.

If this were possible, could that cooperative relationship grow? Could it encompass the human lands, as well? It seemed too frail a hope to even suggest.

Misty dragged Dewy to the head table, where Lumine and Frost were deep in conversation, or at least Frost was. Lumine lounged in his chair. He held a

323

flagon of his own in his hand. One glance at Lord Frost, and Dewy immediately retracted her hopeful thoughts. It was hard to imagine him ever extending grace to anyone outside of the Winter realm, to anyone anywhere, really.

Lumine ignored whatever entreaty Frost was pressing, as Dewy and Misty approached. "Ah! There you are. What do you think of our impromptu fete?"

"I…ah…it's lovely. Of course."

"Perhaps not quite the galas I understand the Summer people frequently enjoy. We are a bit out of practice. Surely, you've noticed."

"I am honored to join you this evening." Dewy chose careful, noncommittal words. Those of a diplomat. Those of her aunt.

The way Lumine's eyes sparked, she was sure he caught the hesitancy.

"I understand your surprise. It has been quite a long time since we had much to celebrate in these Winter lands. Your growing abilities give us all hope. Forgive me if I felt like indulging my court."

"Not at all."

Lumine glanced at Lord Frost, who sat stiffly and silently at Lumine's side. His hand clutched a goblet, but Dewy hadn't seen him drink. He hadn't participated in the greetings, either. Frost was one member of the Winter court who had no qualms about revealing his feelings toward her and her presence. For him, it wasn't complicated. He—apparently—loathed her. Nearly as much as he hated the humans who were her friends.

Lumine clapped Frost on the shoulder. "My young nephew shares your reserve, Lady Dew Drop. Perhaps the two of you can find your way to some sense of cordiality together?"

Dewy blurted, "Excuse me?"

At the same time, Frost said, "Sorry?"

And Misty—eyes bright—said, "Oh, yes. That is a delightful notion."

"What is?" Dewy glanced between Lumine and Misty.

Frost rose slowly to his feet. He rolled his eyes, heaved a sigh, and extended his hand. "Would you do me the honor of a dance, Lady Dew Drop?"

Dewy's mouth opened. No words came out. But it was Lumine's suggestion. The king's insistence meant it was Frost's command. And since he'd done his part, no matter how begrudgingly, faerie protocol dictated that she accept.

Sweet Spring. Dewy attempted something of a smile. She doubted it was convincing. But it hardly mattered. Frost wasn't actually looking at her.

"I…uh…gladly. Of course."

He came around to her side of the large, heavily laden table, and reached for her hand. "Shall we?"

"All right." She surveyed the handful of dancers, swirling and bouncing to the light jig. It brought to mind snow flurries caught in the wind. But the movements were familiar, not so dissimilar to many of the courtly dances in Summer.

She and Frost strolled to the edge of the dancing. He faced her and clasped her hand in his own. His fingers were cool and strong, like stones in a riverbed. He might have been preparing for a military exercise, if the look on his face was any indication. Perhaps he felt he was.

As they began the steps, weaving around one

another, joining, and then changing hands, Dewy couldn't hold back. The temptation to tease, to push the icy Fae was too strong.

"Are you enjoying yourself, Lord Frost?"

He eyed her coldly.

"This is a dance of celebration. It's not meant for the terse. Or is this behavior reserved solely for me? Might there be someone for whom you relax that clenched jaw?"

"I am terse, as you say, around everyone. You are not exempted."

"But you can't even join in the celebrating? Certainly, we've made good progress. One might think you don't want me to succeed. Not really."

"Perhaps…I don't."

They turned away and briefly joined with another pair of dancers before returning to each other, where they grasped both hands and faced each other for the next series.

"But why not?"

"Because…"

Frost seemed to be concentrating on the choreography, but she guessed—like her—that this was one of many dances he'd been required to learn from childhood. He could perform these steps as easily as breathing or shooting an arrow.

He leaned in, keeping his voice low. "How would you feel if you learned that there was human blood in your royal line?"

"My mother was common. There very well might be."

"Never has such pollution sullied the line of Winter. But we know who Princess Snow debased herself with. And now there will always be that taint. Snow chose to poison the Winter lineage to spite her father, but she also threw that spite to the rest of us. All of Winter will forever suffer this indignity if we are to find the Heir." He'd never sounded colder. And for Frost, that was saying something.

Could his hatred truly run so deep?

"But if we don't find the Heir, then Winter will collapse. Surely you can't want that?"

"Sometimes…I think I would prefer it."

The dance ended. Frost performed a stiff bow. And swiftly retreated from the dance floor. He didn't return to his seat by the king, but gestured to his shadowy servant, Rime, and abandoned the hall completely.

Dewy was left with a chill that had very little to do with the cool Winter atmosphere.

Chapter 66

Misty saw her brother depart in what was becoming his tediously characteristic cold huff. She didn't get it. Everyone was worried for the Winter lands, but Frost seemed to have taken the crisis as a personal affront and had been growing edgier for months now. And just as they began to have real hope, big brother went and grew more icicles. She was about to follow him when a pair of scouts rushed through the entry, headed directly to Lumine.

"You have news?" Lumine asked of the scouts.

They bowed. "Yes, King Lumine."

"A party on the southern border. Well-armed."

Lumine raised his brows and glanced toward Misty.

"Sounds like playtime." She grinned.

"Carry on." Lumine waved her off, his version of an avuncular blessing.

Misty ducked a quick bow and pivoted, taking long strides toward the exit. She'd need Tun and his team, and she'd have to track down her surly brother, no matter what mood he was in.

Before she was through the threshold, Dewy darted in front of her.

"What's happening?"

"Intruders. Southern border. Going to check it out."

Dewy's brows drew together. "Be careful."

"Aww, how sweet. You care." Misty laughed. "Don't worry about me."

"I'm actually more concerned about whoever you'll encounter." Dewy leaned in. "I told Lumine—maybe you don't know—the Heir or the blood of the Heir is moving and headed this way. Just…you wouldn't want to injure your future monarch."

Misty blinked several times. That was an interesting detail Lumine had conveniently forgotten to mention. And could've ended awkwardly. She was still hearing about how she'd handled Spense, back before she knew he was Telridge's emissary and the Summer princess's lovesick human.

"Thanks for letting me know."

"Be careful."

"Always am."

Chapter 67

Cait caught him using the looking glass, that is, after he'd found it. Consequently, Ferrous's office was a shambles of objects and ephemera pulled from the large cabinet in the corner.

"Hello? Lord Ferrous?" Cait said.

"Back here."

He'd been squatting like a child on the floor once he'd dragged the heavy glass out. The picture in the mirror immediately darkened, and the glass returned to its blank, shiny state as soon as he lost focus.

"I was just coming by to get your approval for the week's menu. Whatever are you doing?" She gestured wide-eyed at the items strewn about.

"As usual, seeking insight. No more."

Bird-like, Cait cocked her head to the side. "I didn't know you practiced scrying, my lord."

"I usually don't. Forgive me if I seem a little desperate."

"You're a father. And both of your sons are far from home. Desperation is a given."

"Of course, you are right." Ferrous scrambled to his feet. He'd been down just long enough for things to be a little creaky about the knees.

"Glad you realize that."

"Aren't you worried?" He peered at her quizzically.

"Shall I confess something to you?"

"By all means."

"I may have done a little dabbling with a scrying glass myself."

"I didn't think you had any Seer magic."

"Not much. The gifts Grace has granted me are mostly in earth magic. And likely muted because of my life here. But sometimes...well, according to old faerie lore, we can bend the elemental magics to serve in a similar way as what you experience with the Sight."

"Interesting theory."

She nudged him. "That's a diplomatic way of saying it's all faerie rubbish."

"I'd never suggest such a thing."

Cait smirked.

"Were you successful?" Ferrous was curious. He might be biased by his background as an academic and a human, but he hoped he'd learned a little wisdom along the way as well. And he knew that the knowledge succinctly codified by Academy scholars wasn't the complete picture.

"Honestly, I'm not sure. It all seems fuzzy and vague. How do I tell if I'm Seeing something or if I just want something, so that's what I interpret?"

"I think you've neatly summed up the difficulties of all Seers." Ferrous took a step closer to Cait. He took her hand. "Would it help if I told you the vague, fuzzy things I have Seen?"

"Perhaps."

She did not let go. It had been a long time since he'd held her hand. But his fingers remembered the smoothness of her calluses, the strength in her grasp.

"Very well. I believe the team is hale and whole. In

fact, they seem to have added a member."

"A summer faerie?"

"I think so…it seems likely. Of course, that's more conjecture."

She nodded, as if in confirmation. "And did you see them surrounded by snow, on their way to the Winter lands?"

"I did."

Cait leaned away. She folded her arms across her chest. "Does it mean something if we both saw the same vague images?"

"Perhaps."

Cait rolled her eyes. "You are the worst."

Ferrous grinned. "I know, but that's why you love me."

Cait was one of the few people he felt he could jest with. It was starting to happen with Dirk, that shifting of relationship. And Ferrous appreciated that feeling of ease in the company of another soul. It was all too rare in his life.

"Of course, my lord."

It wasn't quite the affirmation he was hoping for. Her closed response told him he'd overstepped. He tucked both arms behind his back. Perhaps he'd been hoping to see something there that wasn't, not so different from his attempts at scrying.

"I wish there was more. I don't quite know what to do with myself, all this wondering and worry," she admitted.

"We know a little. That will have to do."

"I suppose."

"And I think we can be relatively sure they're on their way."

"That doesn't mean they've arrived safely or accomplished what they needed to. There are many, many dangers in the forests of the world."

Ferrous stepped toward her, gently cupped her shoulders, and waited until she met his gaze. "Then we pray that Grace is with them for whatever lies ahead."

Chapter 68

As usual, Spense's thoughts were in a swirl. His approach to problems had always been methodical, academic. If he couldn't find his answers in a book, he figured they weren't worth knowing. But that was all before Dewy. When he realized how important emotions and intention were to his magic.

And he'd changed.

His magic became more instinctive. He didn't rely on the recipe-like spells of past practitioners nearly as much. He was learning to listen, to lean into his senses.

And those senses told him that something was up with Thorn, along with Flora's intuition. He'd betrayed his queen and employed a pretty thin argument to do it.

Flora was right. The theft had been too easy.

Spense sidled up to the steward as they made their way through a narrow road in the mountain passes separating the Summer lands from Winter. He felt the moment they crossed the boundary. The air grew brisk. The cold wind picked up. His magic practically sang with the icy energy of the Winter forest.

"You all right?" Spense asked.

"Of course. Why wouldn't I be?" Thorn raised his brows.

Spense counted off on his gloved fingers. "We stole from your queen, and you participated. We've scampered away with those goods. And now we've entered foreign territory. You'd think that you might be…on edge. But, like you said, you're just fine."

Thorn narrowed his eyes. "What are you getting at, Master Spense?"

"She knows, doesn't she?"

"I don't know what you mean." Thorn's face was blank and clear.

He made a mental note to never, ever engage in games of chance with Thorn. "All right. We'll play it like that. Fine."

"Fine."

"And you have a letter of passage?"

"I'm a diplomat for the Summer Court. I always carry such a document."

"Riiiight…"

"Where has your imagination taken you, Master Spense?"

"I need to know I can trust you. It helps if I have all of the information. But you're keeping things from me."

Thorn shook his head, chuckling. He muttered something largely unintelligible, "pesky" and "upstart" mixed in with a few choice expletives. The self-titled diplomat clapped Spense on the back. "You might amount to something, yet. See if you notice a little quicker next time?"

He frowned. Thorn hadn't technically confirmed or denied anything. He really was good at his job. Jobs. However many he had. The endless roles he easily slipped into at the beckoning of his queen.

"And…" Spense prompted.

"And you know I'll say nothing more. You'll have to let your conjectures rest."

Spense bit down the words he was tempted to utter. Frustration with Thorn and his perennially cagey behavior. And with himself. Some criminal mastermind he turned out to be.

"Pushing me won't help," Thorn continued. "Don't deny you're tempted. But whatever I say, it won't answer the question you're asking." The Fae glanced his way. "I understand you need to know if I'm someone you can trust."

"Are you?"

"Where you place your trust, that's up to you. I hope my actions over these many months speak for me."

Spense pondered Thorn's response—his non-response, really—but before he could formulate one of his own, a sharp whistling sounded, followed by a thump. And a burst of blue-grey powder.

Spense coughed as smoke blew around their party.

Xendra cursed. "Not again."

"Cover your nose and mouth!" That was Dirk, his commanding voice muffled by the cloth he'd pulled over his face.

Spense scrambled for the edge of his tunic, pulling it high.

"Flora!" Xendra again.

"On it." Flora ran stooped over. She thrust an unlit torch in front of Spense. "I need you to light it. Can you do that?"

In between spasms, Spense nodded. He didn't know why she wanted the torch. Their visibility was only mildly impaired by the smoke. But she was insistent. He cupped his hands around it and uttered the simple Flame spell.

The torch caught, and Flora waved it through the smoky air. It sizzled and zapped tiny particulates.

Oh.

Through watering eyes, hacking coughs, and growing dizziness, Spense fought to hold his focus on another spell. He leaned into his emotions, spoke the words and threw his hands in the air, releasing hundreds of sparking, snapping fire-lights.

It was a trick he'd learned for some of the Solstice festivities, mostly to entertain children whose parents were busy with preparations in the castle and city. In those moments where he'd been exhausted from his time in the library, and figured if he wasn't making much progress himself, he could at least put a smile on someone else's face.

His trick worked here for a different purpose: showering the air with cleansing fire.

But it was a few moments too late.

Chapter 69

They regained visibility just in time to see a small horde of short, blue-grey soldiers emerge from the clearing smoke. Weapons raised. Voices shrieking and feral. Cursed goblins.

"Form up!"

Gerry and Xendra drew their weapons and flanked their commander in response to Dirk's charge. Thorn and Flora were right behind. She wielded the flaming torch. Spense was a half-beat later. He scuttled toward the group, backing up to the party's small circle.

He'd begun the thoughts to make more fire when he was hit from the side. A goblin ducked under Dirk's blade and barreled into Spense, knocking him on his side.

A crack followed. Spense felt something cool and liquid along his rib-line. He thrashed and kicked and had just enough presence of mind to summon flames. He sent a small streak of fire toward the screaming goblin as if he were playing a game of lances. The goblin ducked and came at him again. His blue skin stretched wide over sharp teeth, a familiar, mischievous glint in his eye.

Wait.

"Tun! Stop! It's me!"

But Tun didn't stop. As if he didn't hear. Or chose not to.

All around him, the handful of other goblins were just as intent. Attacking again and again, no matter how many kicks or strikes they received from Dirk, the Knights, Thorn and even Flora.

Spense slammed his hand into the earth, reaching for the stratified layers of rock and clay beneath. He pulled his hand up, as if yanking on a lever. A ripple of dirt and stones knocked Tun from his feet. His goblin companions went down, too, along with the Telridgians.

Blast it all.

In a quick scramble, Spense launched himself onto the goblin soldier, whipping his own hawthorn blade free, and angled it towards Tun's chest. A reversal of their encounter back in Telridge. How many days ago had it been?

Tun's deputies were quick to recover, already tangling again with Gerry and Xendra. They were going to find out in a very real way what it meant to go up against fully-trained Telridge Knights.

"Call them off!" Spense screamed.

Tun bared his teeth.

The road filled with a whoosh of chilled wind. A slender faerie somersaulted into the fray, wielding blades in a blur of silver and blue.

Sparks flew from Telridgian and Winter swords as they clashed. And elemental—air—magic swirled in gusts, keeping the Telridgians off-balance.

"Stop!" Spense bellowed, his voice terror-filled and guttural, praying someone—anyone—would hear.

They did.

They froze.

Every single one of them. Goblins. Humans.

Faeries. Horses?

He blinked slowly, and swiveled his head, taking in the mid-battle montage. Arms, legs all in a frozen rictus. Spense looked at their faces. At their widening eyes and open mouths. He watched as recognition dawned.

Thorn was the first to recover, lifting his blade and skipping swiftly away from their attackers.

"What did you do?" He breathed.

"I…don't know."

The humans were beginning to break free, their movements slow and sluggish. The Winter denizens remained stiff. Stuck.

"Can you release them?" Thorn asked.

"I…maybe." Spense cocked his head, examining the over-eager scouts. He caught sight of their leaders at the edge of the forest, whose arms were raised, and mouths were open, as if they were about to issue a delayed command. "Misty? Frost? What…"

Misty's eyes grew impossibly wider. Her mouth moved into something that might've aimed toward a smile, but with the effort it required looked more like a grimace. Spense closed his eyes and shook his head. Relief loosened his own stance. And with it, his hold on the magic.

"Stand down." Misty coughed. She took her first unrestrained breath and repeated the command.

Tun and his goblin soldiers scurried away from the Telridgians, some holding their sides or heads, some limping. Not one walked away uninjured. Frost's blade-wielding servant returned to his side at a signal from his lord.

The Telridgians maintained guarded positions.

"I should've known it was you." Misty took a step forward. She spread her arms wide and performed a bow. "Welcome to the Winter lands."

"Nice receiving party," Dirk mumbled.

"Apologies, lord prince." Misty straightened and slid her blade into its sheath. "Mustn't deprive loyal soldiers of their fun."

"So, your approach is to attack first and ask questions later."

"We all seem to be in one piece." Misty shrugged. "For the most part."

Dirk scoffed but nodded to his companions. Misty winked in Lady Xendra's direction as the Knight found homes for her long sword and dagger. She shook her head. A slight smirk appeared on her face.

Spense glanced at his friends. They were in much better shape than the Winter scouts. Dirk met his gaze. A scowl formed on his brother's face which drained away to alarm as he rushed over and grabbed Spense around the shoulders.

"Are you all right? What happened?" Dirk asked.

"I'm fine, just a little dusty. That's all." Spense brushed his hands on his clothes. They came up wet.

"Spense, you're bleeding."

"What…no, I'm not…" Spense's stomach clenched and sank. He collapsed to the forest floor.

A clamor rose up around him, as Thorn and the Telridgians surged forward surrounding him. But he held up a hand.

"It's not my blood," he said miserably. He couldn't hold back the crack in his voice.

He opened his pocket and removed broken shards of the glass vials he'd stolen from Lady Radiant. The

341

spilled blood leaked through his tunic and waistcoat, making a dark stain on his belly. It might as well have been his own, though. The ache in his chest was real enough.

"We've lost the blood of the Heir."

Chapter 70

Dewy ate when necessary. She slept a little when exhaustion consumed her and she had no choice. She spent her waking hours in an in-between place where senses took over and she reserved her focus for one thing only. Locating the blood of the Heir. Tracking its musical water through forests and mountains. Its beat kept time with the falling snowflakes in the Winter lands. And its melody progressed, making its way toward The Silver Horn.

Voices broke through her reverie.

"I know how important this is, Lumine. And why you shouldn't be so reckless. Give the girl a rest."

Lumine grumbled something incomprehensible.

Dewy opened her eyes and shifted her gaze. Gentle hands held hers. Warm eyes sought hers as her vision cleared and returned to the present reality of the hall. The music of the blood faded.

"Siskin, bring another blanket. She's chilled through."

Cinna waved to her great-grandson, who darted off to some unknown corner and returned just as quickly. He tucked a shawl of soft wool around her shoulders.

"Thank you, Siskin," she said.

"Of course, Lady Dew Drop."

Cinna chafed her hands, bringing warmth to them. "Really, Lumine, are you so blindly desperate you didn't notice how pale the girl's become? You should know you can't maintain this level of magic for hours like this."

Lumine gritted his teeth but had no rebuttal to Cinna's admonishment as he paced in front of a well-tended fire. Tiny droplets of sweat glistened on his forehead. Dewy had never known Lumine to be anything but cool, as if he carried the winter wind with him.

"It's a good thing I was notified, or who knows what state the lass would be in!"

Dewy considered those words. Lumine had left strict instructions they not be disturbed, except for the most minimal of respites. She wondered who'd gone against the king to summon Cinna, perhaps the only member of the kingdom with the authority to credibly challenge him. From the pairs of eyes peering through the large oak doors, she guessed it was a group effort.

"Here. Drink this."

A steaming mug was placed in her hands. It smelled of mulling spices and heated fruit. Dewy sipped, letting the hot wine warm her throat and belly. She took a deep breath, her lungs filling and deflating completely. Her chest ached—in a good way—and her mind cleared.

"There now, there's a little color. Do you think you can walk?"

Dewy frowned. "Of course."

But as she unwound her legs, she realized they'd become numb. The sensation of placing her weight on them was sharp. Agonizing. Siskin supported her, lifting her before she crumpled to the stone floor.

"Oof. Sorry. I-I didn't realize."

"You've got nothing to be sorry for. As to others…" Cinna turned her pointed gaze to Lumine.

"I wasn't aware she'd weakened so much," Lumine said. He opened his hands wide in supplication. "I shall endeavor to pay closer attention in the future. Does that satisfy you?"

Cinna pushed herself to her feet and put her hands on her hips. "Your attentions are what got her to this point."

Dewy glanced between the king and the wise woman. What else could she do? She'd been training with Misty for weeks, extending her endurance and honing new muscles. She'd capitulated to the Winter faerie diet and found new reserves of strength. And she'd let Lumine become her teacher and guide.

But it wasn't adequate. The magic she needed danced just beyond her grasp, her abilities.

"Please," Dewy said before their bickering escalated further. "I'm fine. Truly. I will try harder."

At this point, she wasn't doing anything she wasn't motivated to. King Lumine wasn't pushing her any harder than she was pushing herself. A stroll about the room and maybe something to eat, she'd be ready to go back in. This Heir wouldn't miraculously appear on their own, and if they were traveling, she wanted to keep a close watch on those movements.

****

It took a good hour of eating, walking, and in the end, outright cajoling before Cinna gave her leave to seek out the blood of the Heir again. And only with strict time limits on how long Dewy tracked. It was as if she and Lumine had become willful children in the face of their grumpy old grandmother, begging for just a little more play time.

She and Lumine. A team allied against Cinna, the wise woman who tutted her disapproval, no matter how many frosty eye rolls King Lumine directed her way.

"Fine, fine." Cinna held up her hands. "If you must return to this quest, then you must. I won't stand in your way."

Never mind that's all she'd been doing since her arrival. If it was like this whenever Cinna was nearby, no wonder Lumine preferred her to stay out in her cabin in the woods.

"But do an old woman a courtesy and listen carefully."

Lumine folded his hands in front of him and raised one eyebrow. Dewy waited. Quietly.

"You're strong, Lumine. Lady Dew Drop is stronger. Imagine what you could be together."

Lumine pressed his lips together. "Is it not enough that I admit the Summer Princess bests me in magical depths?"

"Don't pretend at humility, Lumine. It's not in your nature. You've tried everything else. This may be the only thing that will strengthen her enough to do this."

Lumine dropped his head. "I don't know that I can do that. I don't know that it's possible."

"You have a short memory. Think."

"The ice lock," Dewy said.

She remembered the flood of magic that coursed through her when she and Spense had joined their elemental gifts of water and fire. Together they had broken—melted—Lumine's ice lock.

"Ah. Smart girl." Cinna tapped her temple.

"Perhaps they overcame my lock because they were joined, but even if that were so, isn't it likely the result of the spell the human mage had cast upon her?"

Cinna folded her arms over her chest. "Girl, did the mage compel you to join with him? To use your magic together?"

"Not hardly." Dewy shook her head. "If anything, it was the other way around."

"You see?" Cinna turned back to Lumine. "Not the Claiming."

"But they were bonded in other ways as well. We are not. I have never—in all my long life—performed such a magical union. Why do you think it would work here?"

"How does any magic work—with intention—and you've got plenty of motivation, I'd say."

Dewy glanced at Lumine. He wore a contemplative frown, what she'd come to think of as his scheming face. The face he wore when he was about to suggest something terrible, an offense he justified with need.

"What would we have to do?" Dewy asked.

"I suppose whatever would signify to you the joining of magic—the intention of working together, and in our miserly king's case, the giving over of his power."

"That's not a small thing."

She leaned back. Her gaze was drawn to Lumine. His hands began to shake, and he tucked them away inside his sleeves. Moisture beaded up along his hairline.

"No, it's not. But consider what the Heir means. Is there anything you wouldn't sacrifice, dear King? Think of all you've done already." Cinna chided.

Lumine stood straighter, pulling himself to his tallest height.

He took deliberate steps toward Dewy. His face was washed in gray, the aloof iciness drained away.

"You better mean it." Cinna emphasized her point with the tapping of her walking stick.

The king stretched out his hand. His initial tremors stilled. "Lady Dew Drop? Are you ready to seek again?"

For all the time she'd spent in Winter, Dewy had never touched Lumine. She wondered who did. He always commanded the room, but never shared small intimacies, not even with his niece and nephew.

Now, his long, pale fingers were offered toward her in invitation. Openly and without reservation. No matter the cost. No matter the humbling it required.

She need only take a step. To accept this offering.

Dewy extended her hand, slid it into Lumine's. He wrapped his fingers around hers and exhaled fully.

She felt the strength in his sinew and bone, encased in skin the texture of aged parchment. From his hand came the flow of sparking, icy energy, so very different from Spense's earth and heat. Dewy closed her eyes and drew it in, while reaching out with her senses, out into the world, seeking, searching for that musical chord that resonated with Lumine's own blood.

And she heard it, so much more vivid and vibrant than before. A symphonic chorus of vitality. The Heir's blood harmonized with Lumine's, a call and response. But there was something else. Another line of melody. And Dewy felt that pull of music. It came from a completely different direction.

How could that be? Two lines? One in Winter, and

still coming closer. The other…much farther away. She chased it down, a hound scampering after a hare. Bounding through forests and mountains to a city. And a human castle. A humming deep in the heart of the keep.

"Something's happened," Dewy whispered. "The blood…has split."

"What do you mean?" Lumine's voice was equally quiet. A susurration of breath, as he continued to pour power into her.

"There are two strains contained in two places."

She tried to explain, but her explanation seemed weak. What would cause that? A schism of melodies.

"Is it possible that your grandchild has a child of their own?"

Dewy opened her eyes, and looked at Lumine, read his expression. Thoughtful, wondering.

"Yes, it's very possible. Maybe even likely. But then…who is headed our way? My grandchild and Heir or great-grand-child?"

"I don't know, but I think we shall soon find out."

Chapter 71

"You've lost the blood of the who, now?" Misty tilted her head and narrowed her ice-blue eyes.

Spense waved at his soaked tunic. "This is the result of Tun's exuberant greeting. The vial was destroyed when he smashed me into the ground."

He nearly choked on the explanation, the sad evidence of what had been lost. After months and months of searching for any clue, this small vial of blood was the only thing he had to show for it, nothing more than a darkening stain on his travel-worn clothes.

"But how did you come by it in the first place?" Misty approached him slowly, staring at his damp midsection.

"Uh…"

Thorn stepped forward. "We had guidance from the Oracles. They gave us knowledge to acquire it."

Spense raised his eyebrows. Thorn was really good at this type of thing. It'd be disconcerting if he wasn't on their side.

"We thought that the blood would help King Lumine track down the Heir, even if we can't tell him who that is, yet," Dirk said.

"You're here…to help the Winter faeries?" Frost asked. He'd been conspicuously silent up until this point, lingering on the edges of his own group, far from the Telridgians and Thorn, where the snow was clean and white, not streaked with mud and blood. "But you hate us."

Dirk eyed him squarely. "Doesn't mean you don't need the help."

Frost's eyes widened. His nod to Dirk was short and terse. As much of a thanks as the icy Fae could probably muster. Gratitude wasn't really Frost's style.

"Too bad you let your scouts and servants go unchecked." Dirk gestured at Spense's soaked clothing. "Or we might have a little more to offer."

Frost clamped his jaw tight and lifted his chin. He didn't speak, not to respond in kind to Dirk's insult, not to defend himself, and not to offer regret. The adversarial commanders stared at each other in frozen stalemate, while the rise of frustration, like ice-cold spears, burned through Spense.

Misty whistled. "Hoo, well, in that case, I think some apologies might be in order. This is awkward. Lumine's not going to like it at all." She shook her blue-haired head and planted her fists on her hips.

Her goblin soldiers scowled sheepishly in Misty's direction. Spense guessed what they were feeling extended beyond awkward. If they were smart, they'd feel fear. Dirk and Frost shifted their gazes to her, their deadlock broken for the moment.

Spense pushed himself to his feet. The feelings surging through him were not as easy to shake off. One thing he was sure of, everyone here dreaded a meeting with the Winter King.

****

Before long, The Silver Horn loomed before them. A crafted architectural wonder, blending in and jutting out from the cliff side, deep in mountainous forests. His

Telridgian companions were wide-eyed and open-mouthed, no doubt marveling at the magnificent presence of the Winter Palace, Lumine's seat of power, the center of the kingdom. It was towering and glorious, a cornucopia sparkling with icy majesty.

Spense hated it.

He saw it for what it was, a prison where his heart was kept behind frozen walls of ice-encrusted stone.

"Shall we?" Misty asked. She led the way through the snow to the grand entryway.

The patrol guards bowed and hastily opened the doors. A quite different welcome than the last time Spense had arrived, bound and gagged, and dragged inside with no more ceremony than one would give to a rat they'd found on the grounds. As far as they were concerned, that's all he was—a human rodent. And when he'd been banished all those months ago, it had been with the same indifference.

Returning and being welcomed officially, especially after how badly things ended during the Winter visit to Telridge, felt like a small redemption, like a thing lost had been found. But none of that mattered if it meant Dewy's continued imprisonment. And without the vial—only a rust-colored stain on Spense's waistcoat—there was minimal hope for her release.

It didn't mean he wouldn't try to argue on her behalf, though. Spense straightened his spine as their faerie entourage led them through the corridors. His companions gawked at the full timbers used to form the posts and beams of The Silver Horn's inner construction. He wasn't impressed. There was only one thing worth his focus. And she was much more impressive than any architecture.

Faeries darted about as Misty walked at the head of their little procession. A few common faeries—likely servants—whispered questions, received muted instructions, and bowed before zipping off to fulfill whatever commands Misty and Frost had given.

Every clipped step brought them closer. The doors to King Lumine's great hall rose before them. They opened, as if on their own, but Spense knew that elemental air magic was strong in the Winter court, and Lumine enjoyed his theater. No doubt intended to intimidate.

"Welcome, friends. Telridgians. Thorn." Lumine's voice carried across the spacious chamber. The Fae himself lounged upon his massive timbered throne. "What a delightful entourage arriving in our lands." He hardly sounded delighted.

As they entered, everyone ducked into a bow or curtsy. Spense stepped past them and skipped the formality. His gaze sharpened to meet Lumine's, bobbed his chin—it could hardly even be called a nod—and quickly moved on. Scanning every face in the court. But the grand space was largely vacant. A few Winter servants and the king.

"Where is she?" Spense asked.

Lumine arched a single brow. He cocked his head and waved to the entrance.

He needn't have bothered. Spense knew that floral scent. It was imprinted in his mind and soul. One inhalation and he was returned to the countless moments when she'd been close enough to touch, to breathe in. He turned.

Her hair was longer. Darker. The coppery strands

held more brown. Her face had paled. Many of her freckles were faded, and there was a tightness in her features he didn't remember.

But it was Dewy.

Spense opened his mouth. Words didn't come.

His feet spoke for him, propelling him forward. Stopping just out of reach. He wanted to embrace her, enfold her in his arms and never let go. But would that be welcomed? He thought their letters made their feelings clear. And yet, standing before her, an arm's length away, he froze.

Her eyes widened, but she took no more than a step toward him. Her forehead creased and mouth parted.

It was others who did the speaking, the greeting. Thorn didn't falter, layering on the diplomatic appeal. Even Dirk figured out how to add "charming" to his princely qualities. But to Spense, it was all a blur of meaningless words, droning in the background.

All he saw was her.

All he heard was the nothing from her.

She wasn't speaking. She was barely breathing.

The girl he'd left behind all those months ago was not the faerie standing before him now. She was more. And different. It wasn't just the subtle changes in her appearance. It was as if something in the core of her had…frozen.

Spense wrenched his gaze away from Dewy. Glared at Lumine. "What have you done to her?"

Chapter 72

Dirk read Spense's expression and the king's. Neither one of them flinched.

Wicked Winter. This wasn't the opening salvo they'd been hoping for. Not as Spense bared his teeth and shot angry glares at the blasted King of Winter.

Lumine rose to his full height, his features hard. Glacial.

Maybe that's where Lord Frost learned the art of the cold stare, but in comparison to the king, Frost was a melting pile of dirty slush. This moment highlighted the difference. And that new wide-eyed, alarmed look from Frosty boy meant...

Shit.

Spense stalked toward the king. Full of every bit of righteous indignation he possessed. And Dirk knew the fire in his little brother's eyes was not of the metaphorical variety.

"What did you do to her?" Spense hurled his question at the king.

"I did nothing she did not invite herself." Lumine's ice-grey eyes flickered with cold reserve.

Spense was having none of it. He flung one hand toward Dewy, who stood as still as stone, her eyes unfocused. "This is not nothing!"

He raised his other arm and hurled a swirling orb of fire right at the king. Lumine batted it away with a blast of icy air, leaving flaming sparks to fall harmlessly to the stones beneath their feet.

Winter Court faeries and Telridgians all joined in high alert, scrambling behind solid wood posts and backing against stone walls. Spense ignored it all. He focused solely on the king.

"She took your criminal bargain and the burden of living in this frozen, forsaken wilderness."

Each phrase was punctuated with flames. Fiery reds and oranges that met Lumine's defense in a shower of sparks.

"With none but you for bitter company. None but you, you spineless, selfish, bastard king."

Faeries, humans, and goblins ducked from the flying sparks and crystallized ice shards. The weirdest and most violent game of lances ever played. It made his own little tussle with Frost look like childish tantrums. Lumine blocked the flames, beat for beat, defending, but not fighting back. As if he were letting Spense pummel him with vitriol and heat.

Dirk knew Spense was angry. He'd been frustrated for months. They were all disappointed by the confusing and hazy messages from the Oracles, discouraged by the breaking of the vials. But for Spense, it wasn't disappointment. It was a hopelessness turned into rage. And he was directing every bit of it at the king.

Who wasn't fighting back.

"Spense, stop!" Dirk lunged forward.

Gerry and Xendra stayed right beside him.

But with a wave of his hand and barely a glance toward them, Spense caused the flagstones at their feet to erupt. The Knights stumbled and fell. A branch whipped out from a towering evergreen and knocked Dirk on his back.

He rolled to his stomach, winded.

The faeries and goblins around them received similar treatment as they each in turn, tried to reach Lumine and protect their king. Spense blocked Frost's air magic with his roaring, swirling flames, turned the magical gusts into food for the fire. And he stalked ever closer to the king, who remained a cold, solid rock, who did not break against Spense's onslaught.

But neither did he shift to the offensive. Not once.

Dirk's chest pounded. He gasped for the air knocked from him and his heart thudded erratically, aching as Spense took each slow, deliberate step. What would happen to his brother when Lumine grew tired of this display? When he released whatever held him back?

Was there no one who could stand between them?

A shadow with long, coppery hair blew past him.

She darted in between faeries and goblins, too fast for his dull human eyes to track. One moment at the entrance to Lumine's great hall, the next beside Lady Mist. And the following, in between his brother and the king, a blade of sharp, honed hawthorn held lightly in her hand, and a fierce blaze in her expression, burning through the vacant haze.

"Wait," Dewy said. Her voice was barely more than a breath.

Spense stopped.

A curling flame simmered in his palm, but he did not release it. As if her one small word could command him. Perhaps it commanded them all—faeries, humans, and goblins all froze in a bated tableau.

She held a placating hand up to King Lumine. "Listen."

Lumine raised his chin and slowly tilted his head, leaning in, as if to a familiar and favorite song.

When his eyes widened, Dewy nodded.

She stretched her hand towards Spense. He lifted his in response, stretching toward her. Just as their fingers brushed, she slashed that hawthorn knife crosswise in front of her, where his little brother stood. Who had dropped his defenses and extinguished his fire because the girl he loved—who stood in front of him, unflinching and eerily cool—told him to wait.

Dirk roared. The sound ripped from his throat, feral and raw, as his brother's blood sprayed across the cold flagstones.

Chapter 73

Spense knew that wild light in Dewy's eyes. It was the same one she'd worn when she commanded the waters of the River Selden and brought countless attacking faeries to an abrupt and choking halt. It commanded him now, cooling the fires he'd conjured and dampening his rage at Lumine.

Replacing it with pain. His.

Spense clutched his forearm. He dropped to the hard stone floor, buckled and warped from his own magical efforts. The sting of the cut was followed by the flow of his blood, leaking through his fingers.

"Do you see, now? Do you hear it?" Dewy whispered to the king.

Lumine stumbled forward. "It's you." He fell to his knees and grabbed Spense by the shoulders. "How can it be you?"

Spense bowed over his arm, pulling it close to his body. The sudden gush of blood, the sharp heat from the unexpected wound from Dewy—who was not the Dewy he knew—and Lumine's stunned, tear-laced question—it was too much.

How can what be me?

There was a scramble of feet and fingers. Gentle. Holding him. Lifting his bleeding arm. Whispered words. His blood slowed to a trickle.

But his vision blurred around the edges. Moss

green eyes before him. A lavender and sunshine scent, accompanied by pine and new snow. The strong fingers of…the king?

His instinct was to pull back, shy away. Dewy and Lumine—the unfathomable pair of them—were instruments of violence. But the cool, soothing healing called to him, and he leaned in, keening.

Lumine wrapped a torn, blue cloth around Spense's arm. It was the same midnight fabric as his robes.

"How is this possible?" Lumine whispered. "Why didn't I sense it before? Have I been so blind?"

"Spense." Dewy settled before him, in a prayerful kneel, ignoring Lumine's questions. "Are you hearing me?"

He closed his eyes. Nodded weakly. Her voice was full of sunlight and warmth, lilting and reassuring, the timbre he'd come to associate with the surety of home, even while his arm still pulsed from her wound.

"I hear it…it sings," Lumine said.

"Yes," Dewy said. "The same melody line. But with a variation."

"What's the other? It's so faint."

Spense tried to re-order their words, but the meaning was elusive. What melody? He heard nothing.

There were more bodies closing in around him. He heard their footsteps, felt the closeness of breaths and heartbeats. Telridgians. Winter faeries. Goblins. Even Thorn. Echoing the same questions.

"What do you mean, it's him?"

"What music? I don't hear anything."

"How is that possible?"

Dewy's clear voice cut through them all. Her thin fingers were on his chin, nudging him to look at her. He opened his eyes. The rest of the room fell away, along with their anxious, questioning whispers. There was just Dewy, intent upon him, the same and not the same. Trusted. Dangerous.

"Who were your grandparents? Can you tell us?"

Spense shook his head. "You know this already. I never knew my grandmother. And I've told you about Grandfather Clove."

"Did you say...Clove?" Lumine pushed back, sinking into his heels on the broken flagstone.

More hushed words. Frenetic. Excited. Coming from the Winter folk.

"Your mum, Spense, did she ever speak of her mother?"

"No. She never knew her. Grandfather didn't want to talk about her."

Dewy closed her eyes. He knew that face, the expression she wore when she leaned into her magic, reached out with her senses. "Oh...I see now. But why is your mother's blood all over the tunic in your satchel?"

"My mother's? No. This is the blood of the Heir. We acquired a vial of it, but it...broke." Spense's voice choked on the last word, the failure too painful to confess.

Dewy smiled, soft and kind. Her eyes grew bright. And her fingers slid from his chin to cup his cheek. "They are the same."

Spense's mouth parted. All the air left his chest in heaving, choking spasms.

The voices around him grew to a crescendo.

But he neither heard nor understood what they were saying. He just saw Dewy over and over. Before him now, fierce and sure in her magic. She wasn't frozen like he'd first thought but chiseled and re-formed. That was the Dewy whose coppery hair lifted in a current of heated air when her hand drew a perfect, single arc with the hawthorn blade. Revealing in that crescent of already clotting blood the impossible truth.

Spense, the unimportant, forgettable, bastard-born mage from Telridge, was a direct descendent of the Winter King.

Chapter 74

Dewy met Spense's gaze. His eyes grew wide with understanding.

The truth, so simple. So very heavy, the crush of the burden she laid upon him.

It changed...everything. Shifted the world, re-oriented his place in it, and so many others along with him. The air swirled over her as so many voices whispered in awe, or joy, or disbelief.

"If this is true...then you've found the Heir, Dewy." Spense choked on a dry laugh. "You're free."

Dewy turned her eyes toward Lumine. He nodded, acknowledging what she'd done, what she'd revealed. With the simple gesture, his tear-filled acceptance of the unimaginable truth, her bargain was fulfilled.

Her shoulders lifted, as if a heavy pack had been removed. One she didn't consciously know she'd been carrying. Her arms hung loose by her side, her fingers tingled, even as she raised her hand and stroked Spense's wondering face.

"I'm free." Dewy sobbed.

"You can go home now."

He reached up with his unbound arm to cup her face, thumb away the tears that flowed freely. She could leave Winter. She could return to Summer. But that isn't what he said.

Spense said home. And *home* was crouched on the

cold stone floor in front of her, brushing away her tears with one hand because she'd injured his other arm, and smiling through his own bewilderment and pain.

No bonds held her, but her heart and mind had been connected to this place, this purpose, for months. The release was dizzying. And she dipped her head toward Spense, finding security in his shoulder, his presence a steadying force, even while the world unraveled and spun.

Because…he was Winter.

She was Summer.

Two lands. Two people. Forever separated by an ancient treaty, the leftover fragments of long-ago war.

Her tears redoubled. Dewy could return to Summer. She could freely journey from the highest mountain in The Peaks to the most remote of the balmy Brecken Isles. She could embrace her aunt again. She could become the queen she was meant to be.

But with this new clear white truth, blinding and cruel, she could never be home.

Chapter 75

Spense clung tight to Dewy as he raised his eyes to the whispering, wide-eyed crowd. Locked eyes with every person of every race. Friend and adversary, royal and common, they all wore the same stunned expressions.

His gaze stopped on his brother, who held onto Flora as if she were the only thing tethering him to the earth. Dirk's skin was blotchy and pink. He worked his throat but didn't speak. And his eyes filled with water. Because of this revelation or because Spense had unceremoniously batted his older brother down during the fray with his magic.

His magic. So subtle and quiet in Telridge. Now, it screamed. His blood—and what could be sensed in it—revealed his ancestry. Crouching in the great halls of The Silver Horn, breathing in the wintry, charged energy of this place, revealed so much more.

Hadn't he been growing stronger the longer he was in the faerie lands? The mountain trekking took no more breath than a casual stroll through the gardens. And his magic had surged. He'd lost control of it—of himself—more than once on this journey. It wasn't just his heightened emotions.

Spense was waking and rising, opening his eyes and his senses, at the very moment when a sea of faeries and goblins bowed before him. Ducking heads, closing eyes. It wasn't a refusal of the truth.

It was in deference. To him.

"Prince Spense," Misty said. She lowered to her knees, humbling herself before him. There was no hint of her playful, mischievous taunting, only solemn courtesy to her lord. "We are so happy you've come home."

Misty's brother, the perennially arrogant Lord Frost, stumbled to the ground beside her. He met Spense's gaze and dipped his chin. His actions matched his words, clipped and terse. "We are here to serve you in any way you require."

Spense glanced from one royal to the next. He met Lumine's gaze. The king—his great-grandfather—nodded encouragingly, his cool features thawing, ice breaking.

But there was a member of their newfound family conspicuously absent.

"I…"

"Yes?" Misty blinked, her crystalline eyes sparking.

"Is there a way to contact my mum? It seems she's the one you really need to meet."

Lumine lifted his head. He smiled. It wasn't an expression Spense had ever seen on the Winter King's face, at least not like this. This was joy. Clear and simple, like the first rays of sunlight on new snow.

"Yes, of course. Nothing would please me more." Lumine rose to his feet, offering a hand to Spense. "Let me show you how."

He grasped the king's hand and rose, pulling Dewy along with him. The dangerous pair, now a trio, wondrous and strange. As they took their first steps together, Dirk lunged forward.

Spense shook his head. "It's all right."

He turned from his stricken, speechless brother and exited through the great oak doors, King Lumine and Lady Dewy beside him.

They left a hall full of gawking courtiers and staff, human and faerie-kind behind them.

Chapter 76

Master Spense walked tall—regal, even—as he departed with the king. Flora released a shaky breath. Her head spun. The one person in their party she'd always identified as normal—at least, closer to normal, certainly closer to her than any other—had just disappeared. As if a favorite meadow flower, overlooked by the court gardeners, dismissed as nothing more than background for the extravagant floral arrangements filling the castle, was now set aside as a prize specimen.

But also, her friend was leaving.

Flora squeezed Dirk's hand. His grasp tightened. Hers wasn't the only shaky breath.

Sir Gervais and Lady Xendra flanked Dirk—their prince and commander—on his other side.

"What does this mean?" Gerry asked. Of course, it was Gerry. He wasn't inclined to keep thoughts in his head on an ordinary day, and something this big yielded too many questions. "What do we do now?"

Dirk's eyes shuttered. He shook his head. Flora didn't have any answers either.

"My lords and ladies?" One of the Winter faeries approached. He was lean and, like so many faeries who dwelled in these cold mountains, had equally cool features. But unlike some of his counterparts, his face was open, inviting. "I wonder if you'd like to take respite in private quarters?"

Flora glanced at Dirk. His head twitched in the smallest of nods.

"Yes, thank you." Flora paused. "I'm sorry, but I don't know your name."

The faerie smiled. It felt genuine, if subdued. "My name is Siskin. I'm a court attendant."

"Thank you, Siskin. That would be most appreciated. This has all been—" Flora searched for the words to capture all that had happened, was still happening.

"It's quite a lot for all of us." Siskin bowed his head.

Flora couldn't begin to imagine. After so long, how would the Winter faeries receive their lost Heir? Heirs, it turned out.

She found her thoughts returning to Rosehip in the Summer lands and her niece Petal in Telridge as their party sedately followed Siskin out of the great hall and through the corridors of The Silver Horn. What would Rook think when she told him that she'd embraced and cried with the mother of his child? Would he welcome the news or had resentment grown up in the place where affection had once bloomed? Would any of the Winter folk have similar feelings? She guessed that Lord Frost couldn't be exactly pleased, not after the things he'd said during his visit to Telridge.

While her thoughts wandered through questions too complex for her tired mind, they drifted to a suite of rooms not so different from the quarters they'd occupied in the Summer lands. The collection of adjoining chambers had timbered walls, actual ceilings, and a large common hearth, but despite those obvious differences, were equally as comfortable and inviting.

Siskin gestured to a serving tray with cups, a pitcher, and what looked like a fresh pot of tea.

Gerry and Xendra found chairs near the hearth. Dirk slumped in a low couch, as if his overworked brain and heart had no reserves left for his body. Flora kept an eye on him while she thanked Siskin for his help and assured him they had everything they needed.

At least physically. There wasn't much to be done about the astonishment and grief they all seemed to be cycling through.

Flora found her way to Dirk. She waved feebly at the pitcher and cups. "Can I get you anything, my lord?"

Dirk lifted his gaze to hers. "Just…stay. Please." They were the first words he had uttered. His voice was raw, cracked.

Flora settled on the fur-covered lounge next to him. He held out his hand to her. It was rough and calloused from hours of training, riding, and battle. The shock hadn't left his eyes. There were no calluses to protect against this type of blow. She hesitated for no more than a moment before slipping her hand into his. Whatever loss she was feeling by the abrupt transformation of her friend, Dirk's own reaction would necessarily be that much greater. Spense was Dirk's brother and in the space of a few moments, everything about their relationship changed.

Flora leaned back. Of course, she'd stay with Dirk. They'd anchor each other in this world that had just tipped over sideways. It was the smallest and simplest thing she could do. But maybe, the most necessary.

"Always, my lord."

Chapter 77

Spense tracked the crows as they left the rookery, a squawking flurry of message bearers. The very birds he'd ducked to avoid so many months ago when he'd been thrown out of Winter. He loosed a hard breath. They might've left him terrified and furious, but those black birds had done good work that day, delivering missives to the armies of Winter to stand down, to retreat. That murder of birds—incongruously with their name—had saved Telridge.

They were headed there again.

He could only imagine how his father—and mother—would react when they received the crows today, with an equally important, but very different message. He watched until the birds were long gone, not even swirling black specks on the snowy horizon. He could almost imagine they'd never existed. And the message they were bearing wasn't real.

"You're worried," Dewy said.

"That obvious?"

"Your chin. Gives you away every time."

Spense chuckled. "The Ferrous Frown. Of course. Didn't think you'd remember that."

"I remember everything."

Spense turned from the window and gazed at Dewy. They were blessedly alone. Lumine took his leave, after demonstrating how the royal family was able to send messages and commands. The next steps were important, and the king seemed to understand that Spense might need a moment. He knew a few shuffling attendants waited at the base of the rookery stairs, though.

They were the first subtle gestures, of what would likely be many more to come. Being swept into the family meant learning the secret to an exclusive messaging system and gaining a new set of permanent companions. For protection, apparently. More security would inevitably mean a loss of privacy. He'd seen what it was like in Telridge and wondered if this would be his last unattended moment with a member of a rival court.

He'd have to thank Lumine—his great-grandfather—for allowing Dewy to stay. Idly he rubbed at his rapidly healing arm. Whatever combined magic Dewy and Lumine had used was working, but it seriously itched.

"I suppose I should apologize about that." Dewy gestured at his arm as she crossed the rookery tower to stand by him.

Spense unwound the dark blue cloth that served as a bandage. It was now unnecessary. He examined the remnants of the wound. There was a pink line across his forearm, as if he'd been scratched by an innocently reaching thorn bush, not cut with a blade.

Spense held up his arm. "It seems there's no need."

He met her gaze, scanned her face, again noticing how her skin and freckles had paled over the last few months. Her darker hair was pulled into a loose plait, kept efficiently out of her face. There was a strength in the way she held herself that was new, too. Her bearing was steady, her shoulders back, her stance planted, firmly rooted in her honed muscles that her snug leather leggings displayed. She'd always been strong, but some of the willowy flexibility was gone.

"Your magic did this?" Spense asked. "I didn't know you had that ability."

"I've been...developing since I've been here."

"I noticed." He dropped his arm and released a stilted chuckle. "You look different."

"I was just thinking the same about you." Dewy traced his jaw with her fingers. She had to reach up to do so. "How am I different?"

He leaned into her touch, savoring those thin, strong fingers. There were weeks, so many months ago, when Spense was the only person Dewy could share touch with. Now, when she was free—in every imaginable way—he understood the gift for it was.

But he hadn't answered her question. "Stronger, I guess? I mean, you're wearing leather."

"Oh. That." Dewy dropped her hand and turned away. "I've come to some realizations."

Spense darted around her before she wandered too far. "Like what? Tell me."

She shrugged. "I've assumed quite a lot of things about the world that were incorrect and unfair. About faeries and humans." She waved toward him. "Oh, but I guess you're not all that human, after all." Her laugh was dry, humorless.

"Does it matter to you? Who I am?" It was a lot to take in. He was having plenty of trouble with it himself.

"It never mattered to me before. Why would it now?"

Her answer was simple and automatic. Too easy.

But Spense wanted to believe her. Desperately. He stepped forward and cupped her face, searching her green eyes, the color of early spring. They were filled with challenge and bravado. He wanted to revel in that confidence. Believe the words they'd shared were still true, even if written by more naïve hands.

Everything he'd worked toward for so many months led to this point. This reunion. Even if it wasn't what he thought it would be.

He didn't care.

Spense leaned down and brushed his lips across hers, remembering the familiar curve and bow of her mouth, unchanged, despite so many other shifts for them both. He let his hands go loose, allowing her space, and wondering if she would withdraw.

She didn't.

Instead, Dewy grabbed his collar, drew him close, and pressed her soft lips to his. Firm and eager. It was a kiss of longing stored up over months. Defiant. Pushing back the truth.

But Spense couldn't keep their new impossibility from intruding and pulled away. His breaths were short and quick.

"It does matter, Dewy." He tipped his head until their foreheads touched. "You know it does."

Silent tears coursed down her cheeks in thin rivulets. "We'll find a way."

"I hope so."

He wanted to believe it. But his own eyes betrayed him, stinging with the same hot tears.

Chapter 78

Since that first swipe of a hawthorn blade and the arcing stream of his brother's blood, Flora had been by his side. Every revelation and astonished discovery that came after, she remained.

He'd asked her to stay. She did.

Dirk reeled from exhaustion. His eyes were heavy, and a weight had taken up residence on his chest. He felt like an idiot for missing so many signs: Spense's magic growing stronger in faerie lands, and his weird ability to command Winter Fae. Flora let him curse and pace until he collapsed. Without a word of judgement.

She was there now in the more than comfortable quarters King Lumine's staff had provided, along with Gerry and Xendra, ever loyal, but wary and watchful.

It was Flora he clung to when his brother knocked on the heavy oak door to their chambers and made his appearance. Lady Dew Drop accompanied him. Dirk narrowed his eyes at the Fae. His brother's arm was unwrapped, a faint, small scar the only evidence of the earlier violence, almost as if it had never happened. For his part, Spense seemed perfectly at ease with his feral beloved. Dirk couldn't say he felt the same.

A quick squeeze from Flora and Dirk redirected his attention.

"What news, brother?" He managed a basic greeting, and an inclination of his head as the pair approached.

Spense lifted his chin in acknowledgement of the terse, simple words. "I wanted to inform you that we've contacted my mother."

Such formal language, as if Spense had already taken on the mantle of faerie nobility and the icy veneer that came with it.

Dirk squared his jaw, took deep breaths through his nose, trying to consciously relax.

But then their gazes connected, and the ice broke. Spense took one step, then another. He released Dewy's hand.

She was still reaching out when Dirk strode forward and grabbed Spense's shoulders. "You're never short of surprises, are you?"

Spense lifted the corner of his mouth in an irreverent, pathetic grin. "I've got to keep you guessing."

Dirk released a choking bark of a laugh. The tension he'd been carrying—like a breath held too long underwater—rolled off, as he enfolded Spense in a back-breaking embrace. They wept, chuckling as only brothers did.

"What am I supposed to make of all this…now that you're *you*?"

Spense sighed as he released Dirk. He returned to Dewy and again slid his hand into hers, offering her a quick, almost shy glance. "I'm not sure yet. We've a lot to work out."

Likewise, Dirk returned to Flora's side. "Whatever you need…you know I'm there for you."

Spense's throat worked. "You always have been."

"Maybe not always. But I'm here now."

"Thank you."

"What happens next?" Flora asked.

"I'll wait for word from my mum, but you..." Spense glanced at his Telridgian friends. "You don't have to stay. Our mission is completed. I'm sure you'll want to be headed home soon." His voice caught on his words.

Dirk lifted his chin. "I'll stay with you."

"I will, too," Flora said.

"We all will," Gerry followed.

"Of course, we will." Xendra took a step forward. "We've come this far with you. We'll wait."

Spense ducked his head, while his cheeks flushed pink. "Again, thank you," he whispered.

"No thanks needed. You are my brother. No title will ever change that."

Chapter 79

"You called for me, Lord Ferrous?"

"You saw the crows?"

Cait bobbed her head in a quick nod. She drew in her breath and held it.

Ferrous had no intention of making her wait long. "Come in. Sit, please."

She made her way to a cushioned chair and perched on the edge. She was buzzing with impatient energy, but too polite to do more than look intently at the scroll he held in his hands.

He lifted the letter. "It's from Spense."

"Truly?"

"Yes. He's in Winter. He says..." Ferrous couldn't finish. It was too much. He sat down hard and offered her the rolled parchment with a shaking hand.

It was his turn to hold his breath while Cait read. Her eyes grew wider as she scanned the words. She shook her head—her brows lifted as she re-read the lines. He'd done the same.

When she finished, her hands slowly lowered, curling the scroll in her fingers. "How can this be?"

"You've always known you were part faerie."

"I didn't realize you knew."

He shrugged. "You might remember that I've seen you without your head scarf. I saw the scars and drew my own conclusions."

"Why didn't you say anything?"

"You've done so much to hide it—I saw no need to bring it up."

"But you hate faeries."

"Not all faeries. I've spent much of my life angry with the Fae, King Lumine in particular. But his people aren't to blame. You're not to blame. You never have been."

Cait clutched the letter in her hands. They trembled.

This news—it was shocking and yet, not surprising. He'd always known she was magical. He knew of her murky, mysterious past. Sweet Spring, he'd tasted the results of her elemental magic in every dish she prepared.

"Will you go? To be with our son? And meet your grandfather?"

"I feel, perhaps, that I should, but..." Cait lifted her gaze to his.

He reached out and took her hand. Small, warm, and strong. "Whatever you decide, you will always have a place here in Telridge."

Chapter 80

Dewy leaned back on the downy pillows of her bed. Spense sat across the room from her, perched on the bench of the hearth. The space itself was small, but more than comfortable. All this time, he'd been picturing her in a dank, dungeon prison. Instead, this was downright cozy. Except perhaps for the two attendants who hovered in the expansive hallway outside, though she reported that this was a new addition.

He'd been given quarters befitting his station, but Dewy's room had already become his favorite place in The Silver Horn, with piles of books and half-full teacups, placed haphazardly on tables and shelves, and the lingering floral essence of Dewy in every surface.

"What is it?" She tilted her head, causing waves of coppery hair to fall across her strong shoulders. The wiry muscle was new, too.

"You know I researched for months. I dragged a team to The Oracles, if you can believe it, stole from Lady Radiant, and made my way here, thinking I'd failed you yet again. But you never needed my help. You found the Heir"—he waved at himself—"all on your own."

Dewy scrambled off her quilt-covered bed and sat beside him in front of the fire. She took one of his hands in hers. "It means quite a lot to me that you were trying, though, that you came here. For me."

"Even if it turned out to be unnecessary."

"Let's just say we met in the middle."

His lips curved, and he leaned toward her, quite content to meet her in the proverbial middle again and again. But a brisk tapping on Dewy's door interrupted whatever plans he might've had.

"Wicked Winter," Spense cursed.

Dewy cocked her head, listening, and grinned. "Quite right. And a little Summer, too."

"My Lady Dew Drop? Prince Spense?"

"Yes, Thorn, do come in."

The ambassador-steward-spy slid Dewy's door open and ducked his head around the oak. "Sorry to interrupt."

Spense bit back a response, clamping his teeth tight. These moments were limited, he knew. And would end all too soon. Every knock, every interruption felt like a theft.

Dewy glanced at him. Her eyes sparked and she gave his hand a squeeze. "What is it, Thorn?"

But it wasn't Thorn who responded. Misty pushed her way past him, swinging the heavy door open wide. "Your canoodling will have to wait. We've received news."

****

Spense all but burst into the Telridgian quarters, an entourage of attendants and members of both faerie courts following in his wake. "We've received correspondence from Telridge. My mu—" At a sharp look from Thorn, Spense checked himself. "I mean the Lady Cait, will journey here, soon."

"That was quick." Dirk pushed himself from a seat

381

at a generous oak table. A scowl shadowed his face.

Misty nodded. "I believe she appreciates the urgency for the Winter lands and for that we are most grateful."

No one could ever accuse his mother of shirking her responsibilities or neglecting her duties. Of course, she was on her way. And she'd said she wanted to see Spense. He wanted to see her, too. Desperately.

"We're already preparing an escort to meet her," Misty said, gesturing to the Winter faeries around her.

Dirk's gaze roamed over the faeries and focused back on Spense. "You're not going?"

"I...no." He shook his head. "We've decided it would be better if I remain here." He shot a quick look over to Misty.

In truth, it was others who decided, but the command came from King Lumine, and Spense felt the weight of it, the authority as a physical binding.

"She should be greeted by familiar faces."

Spense took a breath and lowered his eyes. "I know, but..."

"I can go."

Spense lifted his head, met his brother's earnest gaze.

"In your stead."

"We all can." Flora laid a hand on Dirk's arm, a quiet offer. Dirk returned the gesture and covered Flora's hand with his own. Spense had watched them over the course of this journey form into a pair, a partnership. The idea of parting from his older brother, just when they finally seemed to become friends and equals brought an ache to his chest. But knowing that Flora would be there, to read and understand Dirk's thoughts lessened that sadness. Assuming Dirk was aware enough to recognize the gift he had in front of him. Restricted by nothing but his own pride and adherence to tradition.

Misty glanced amongst them. "Certainly. If that is what you wish."

"If that settles it, we'll prepare right away." Dirk cast his gaze from Spense and received nods of confirmation from Lady Xendra and Sir Gervais.

"Thank you," Spense whispered. "All of you. For everything." He worked his throat, but his mouth had gone dry and empty. He embraced each of his friends in turn, clapping his brother fiercely on the back and squeezing tight. When he got to Flora, he murmured in her ear. "I'm trusting you to look after him now."

"I will, my lord." She ducked a small bow.

Spense blinked as he pulled away but didn't correct her. He was a lord, now, and according to the customs of honor—both human and faerie—was due the courtesy.

He turned from the room and the remaining party of Telridgians, no longer one of them. He'd become something other. Spense lowered his shoulders, but lifted his chin as he walked away, bearing the mantle laid upon him, recognizing the weight he now carried.

He'd never realized how that weight could act as a barrier forever after, setting him apart.

Chapter 81

Dirk spent most of the night checking provisions, tending to the horses, getting clearance and assistance to send his own messages. All necessary tasks.

In truth, he was hiding from his own racing thoughts, and from the pitying looks of his friends.

Dirk cursed his cowardice as he made his way back to quarters and found Flora in conversation with Thorn, while buckling down the flaps of a satchel. She set the bag out in the corridor and spotted him immediately. It looked like her packing was near-complete. They'd be on their way soon enough. First to meet Lady Cait. Then, back to Telridge. And their lives.

"Where have you been, my lord? I—we—were concerned."

He waved down the long, timbered hallway. "Looking after the horses."

She tilted her head, reached forward, and removed an errant piece of straw from his tunic. "Did you sleep there?"

Dirk lifted one shoulder. He'd laid down in Lightning Storm's well-appointed stall. He'd closed his eyes. There was no sleep to be found.

Thorn stepped forward. "I came to offer my farewells to all of you. Since Lord Spense will remain here to await his mother, the Lady Dew Drop has elected to stay with him."

"Dewy is staying? I would think she'd be eager to get home," Flora said.

"She said she'd like to stay until Lady Cait arrives," Thorn explained. "Radiant has been notified."

Dirk frowned. "I can't imagine she's too pleased at the delay."

Thorn nodded sagely. "She's an aunt missing her niece, and regent of a land missing its future queen. But I think Radiant understands what it means for Spense and Dewy to have a little time together."

"Before they become the rulers of the faerie world?" He couldn't keep the bite from his words. He'd known that his little brother was meant for great things. It took him a while, but he'd known.

He assumed that they'd be by each other's sides when that happened, though. Isn't that how all the stories went? The knight and the mage, adventuring together? The future king and his wise councilor? That vision was crumbling, that possible future lost. Nowhere in those stories and legends did the brave knight and his closest friend part so that one of them could become the Heir Apparent of an adversarial kingdom.

"Something like that, yes." Thorn locked eyes with him, and his expression softened as if he could read every painful thought, and the vacancy that remained. "Be well, Lord Dirk. Lady Flora."

"You also," Dirk murmured, dipping his chin in a small bow.

"Thank you, Thorn, but you know I'm not a lady." Flora placed a small kiss on the steward's cheek.

Dirk chuckled. He hadn't noticed Thorn's gaff. It sounded so natural.

"We'll see about that." Thorn winked as he turned to leave.

When Thorn was well past them, Flora frowned up at Dirk. He met her open gaze, read every question in her eyes.

"I'm sorry that you worried." Dirk shook his head.

"It's all right. Really. We all understand if you needed to be by yourself for a while."

And there it was. The kindness and grace he could hardly bear. But retreating had been the wrong choice. This was where he needed to be. With his friends. With Flora. To face whatever came next, however hard it was to endure.

"Do you—are you better now?"

He leaned against the open doorway, unpacking the layers and possible meanings in that question. "Yes, and no."

He longed for the predictability of Telridge, understood responsibilities and expectations. This time on the road had delivered too many shocks and surprises. Overwhelming and perplexing.

But it was also a cleansing for him. It cleared away the nonsense, sharpened his priorities and opened his perspective. Maybe there was something to all that Oracles business after all. That was part of what he'd come to understand lying in Storm's stall, hiding out from the world, from his friends.

"That's quizzical and mysterious." Flora raised an eyebrow. The corner of her mouth lifted.

She was teasing him. Again. As only she could. It was how they were together. The veneer that protected them from saying anything real. He wondered if she'd be this way if she knew the tangled nature of his thoughts. He released a dry laugh. Of course, she did. It was likely why she teased.

He didn't want to pretend anymore. If the last day had taught him anything, it was that hiding the truth caused nothing but strife. "I think you know me better than that. I doubt anyone would ever call me mysterious."

"I think…you have your secrets."

"Perhaps. But they're not so secret to you, are they? You always see through me."

Flora slowed her bustling actions. She bit her lip and turned her eyes from him. "There's no possible answer I could give to that, my lord."

She forced a chuckle. But it lacked mirth. She couldn't muster that slight teasing anymore.

Dirk reached out, before he even knew what he was doing. He couldn't let her turn away, pretend that it was all a jest.

"There's only one answer I would ever ask of you, Flora. Your true and honest one." Dirk stretched his hand out but stopped himself and pulled in before he could wrap his fingers around her arm. "Please."

She lifted her eyes, those soft brown eyes that saw so much. "I see…"

"What?" Dirk whispered. He took a slow step toward her. Waiting. Searching.

He'd asked her to stay—when he could barely form words—and she had.

But at the first moment he could, he ran.

He didn't stay.

He fled into responsibility, into his duties. It was all bullshit.

She knew it. She had to know it. But here she was,

when he finally hauled his ass back to his team.

He didn't flinch when she placed her small, work-calloused hands on either side of his face. Or when she raised herself on her toes and brushed her lips against his, a featherweight whisper of a kiss. A breath of air.

It was the answer and the question to everything he'd been asking.

And like so many times before, it was as if she understood what he couldn't say, when he was all out of words. And she spoke to him in a language he knew.

Before he could form a response, footsteps scuffled and voices carried along the corridor. Flora pulled back. She smiled. Placed her hand on his chest, right over his heart.

"Let that be your answer."

She grabbed the satchel and retreated down the corridor.

"Was that Flora?" Xendra trotted up, along with her permanent sidekick, Gerry.

"Uh, yeah...she, umm..." Dirk waved generally down the hall in the direction Flora had gone. "She's packing."

"Oh, good. That's good, right?" Gerry asked.

"Yeah. It's good."

"So, we're leaving soon?"

Dirk nodded.

"It'll be great to get back. Weird that Cait won't be cooking at the castle anymore, though, right?"

"Sure. Right, that'll be weird." Dirk didn't have any worries about Cait. As Telridge's Head Cook, he'd witnessed her rule over her kitchen, and had no doubt she could handle the mantle of sovereignty.

But too much of this situation felt sideways and

upside down. It was hard to focus on just one part.

He flexed his tingling fingers. Whatever muddled state his thoughts were in, his body reacted to the only thing that made sense, straining to return to the comfort and understanding of a certain stable maid. She saw him, all of him, and still had faith. She cared for him, the man, not just the prince.

Maybe someday he'd be worthy of that faith and the young woman who outranked him in every possible measure, every way but title.

Chapter 82

In the space of little more than a day, it felt as if all seasons happened at once. Dewy wanted to slow time, linger in each fateful moment. She needed space to properly react and understand every new thing, the twists in every relationship.

But she knew of no magic that could halt the seasons and wait for her to feel ready for every change, each turning of new growth and inevitable regeneration.

She heard the slight increase in heartbeats around her, throughout The Silver Horn, the forced shushing of blood, and knew she wasn't alone. Most especially, she tuned herself to the melody of Spense's lifeblood, the singing in his veins.

And she remained with him, her arm tucked into the crook of his elbow, or fingers intertwined with his, both waking and in the few hours of sleep stolen from a mostly anxious night. It was her natural place, even if it was fleeting. Even if she'd soon know the pangs of separation yet again.

For these past many months, it was as if they'd been together, she by his side, and he with her, looking over her shoulder, encouraging her when she was spent and exhausted.

As she was now. As they all were.

When the earth turned and the morning rose, the Telridgians made their departure. Most of the Winter

Fae, along with a healthy crowd of common faeries and goblins, all gathered near the great gates of the Horn to see them off. It was to be the first goodbye, but not the last.

Dewy's heart squeezed as the brothers Ferrous grasped arms.

Dirk, the prince she'd once thought a brute, closed his eyes. "I will miss you, brother." He could barely form the whispered words.

Spense's eyes softened. His smile wavered. "And I, you."

More final goodbyes followed. There were kisses on cheeks, hearty pats on the back. And details discussed that meant the breaking up of a family, even while a new family was formed. Her chest hollowed, leaving her short of breath.

To Dirk, Flora, and the Knights she'd barely said hello. Already she bid them farewell. She knew that Spense, too, yearned for more time. They all did. There was much left unsaid, unresolved.

But in truth, she doubted the brothers could have managed anything drawn out. Their goodbye was no less heartfelt for its brevity or for the great collection of souls witnessing it. The wise woman Cinna—Dewy's teacher and friend—laid a blessing on the traveling party. King Lumine shared his own words of thanks and encouragement.

And Dewy leaned her head against Spense's shoulder as the group filed through the ice-encrusted forest, human, faerie, and goblin, along with their equine companions. A light snow fell, covering over and filling the footsteps they left behind.

Many of those gathered quickly returned inside to

the warmth and security of The Silver Horn. Dewy and Spense lingered in the whispering snow, long after the jangling of horses' reins and marching feet had grown quiet. They were the last to turn in.

Over the next few days, Dewy knew she would repeat this scene again and again. But until then, she would savor every precious, stolen moment she could with Spense.

Before the strictures of this world, and these fractured kingdoms, again tore them apart.

Epilogue

"You've received correspondence, Lord Spense. Again."

Spense took the letter from Siskin and thanked him. In the past few weeks, he'd come to know more of the spindly attendant. It turned out he'd become close with Dewy during her time in Winter. And was a relation of Cinna, who would surely berate him for arriving late if he took time to read the letter now.

Spense smiled, pressed his lips to the seal, crested with the mark of Summer royalty, and opened the letter. A letter from Dewy was worth a scolding from Cinna, his new self-proclaimed tutor in all things magical and historical.

He settled into one of the several cushioned chairs in his study and scanned her words, imagining just how Dewy would form her lips and which lines would get special emphasis. He heard her teasing, lilting voice. With every turn of phrase through to her simple, informal signature, his heart lifted and ached. He cherished her words. He craved to hear them in person.

When his mother arrived, it was a comfort to him and a balm to all, the first crackles of a spring thaw, soothing the Winter lands and its people, leaving room for joy again, safe spaces for hopeful smiles, tearful grins.

Already preparations were underway for the

ceremonial event that would anoint Cait as the declared Heir of Winter. He sensed the charged magics from the land as if the forest and mountains knew of the coming changes and rejoiced. Reports of the feral margins already lessened, delivered to him by Misty, of course.

Spense wouldn't begrudge the people—now, his people—the peace and stability they craved.

But his own heart wouldn't settle, as long as he was forced—by ancient treaty—to live this life without Dewy.

They'd shared their bitter farewells. Dewy and Thorn returned to the Summer lands. No doubt, Lady Radiant and her court rejoiced, just as there'd been celebration in Winter. It was a cold comfort knowing that Dewy was free in her own lands. But whatever solace it gave him, it was always tempered with the pangs of her absence.

Since her departure, his tears had dried. In their place, icy determination pulsed through his veins. Growing stronger with every letter exchanged, perfumed reminders of renewed love. Fragile hope sprouted, as brittle and delicate as a snowflake.

It was a timeworn treaty made between faeries and humans, and sealed with powerful magic that kept the Winter and Summer faeries from reuniting their torn lands.

But treaties could be broken.

And magic—no matter how powerful—could be overcome.

Acknowledgements

There are so many people who are a part of making a book, and with a sequel, it feels like I have even more people to thank.

Let's start with all of you lovely readers—so many delightful fans who have named yourselves The Fae Council. You are the best!

Of course, without my editor Claudia Fallon, Rhonda Penders, RJ Morris, and everyone at the Wild Rose Press, we wouldn't have a book, let alone a series. Thank you for believing in Fractured Kingdoms and for bringing this world to the printed page. Jennifer Greef, you have done it again. Thank you for the beautiful cover and for sneaking in those little details that make it so special.

To Lizz Nagle and Alisha West at Victress Literary, you have created a community of writers and friends. Shan would be so proud. Extra hugs to the OMN crowd—thank you all for pushing me and encouraging me and knowing which I needed. Steph and Josh, you both ask me all the hard questions, cheer for your favorite characters, and celebrate with me when it all works. And Roots, your beta read comments both push me and make me laugh. Thank you, all.

Thank you, Mary, Adria, and Shelly, for your professional advice and support. To my author and artist friends from so many communities, your support, helpful critiques, and encouragement mean so much. There are dozens and dozens of you all over the world in The Glen Workshop and the L'Engle Writing Retreats, SCBWI, PNWA, AbsoluteWrite, and MomsWritersClub. I wish I could thank each of you by name but know I wouldn't be here without all of you. You gave me permission and you helped me find my voice. Dear ones. Tesser well.

Special thanks to the bookstores and libraries and school districts who put the first Fractured Kingdoms book on your shelves. I'm so honored. To the students and staff in Peninsula S.D., the dancers from Haley Prendergast, and so many friends across the Pacific Northwest, your enthusiasm and support are unbelievable. Thank you, thank you!

To Mom, Dad, Jeff, and my great big family, near and far, those who've been fans from the time I could hold a pencil, and those who've joined along the way. Thank you—all of you—for your endless support.

Molly. Dots. You've been my writing champion from the beginning. Your excitement and encouragement and complete willingness to geek out with me are the biggest gifts, and I am so grateful.

To Jamison, Scott, and Paige, you've been on this journey with me every day. Thank you for the wonder you bring to our home, and for believing in magic. And gnomes. And dragons.

And, as always, thank you God for giving us words.

A word about the author...

J.A. Nielsen is the author of the YA Fantasy series, Fractured Kingdoms, and winner of the 2020 Pacific Northwest Writers Association Literary Contest for Young Adult literature. She has spent most of her professional life in education as a therapist, teacher, librarian, and administrator.

When not writing, she is most likely playing with her family in the forest, on the water, or in the mountains of the Pacific Northwest.

****

https://janielsenauthor.com/

****

If you enjoyed this story, leaving a review at your favorite book retailer or reader website would be much appreciated. Thank you!

Thank you for purchasing
this publication of The Wild Rose Press, Inc.

For questions or more information
contact us at
info@thewildrosepress.com.

The Wild Rose Press, Inc.
www.thewildrosepress.com